MW01109441

THE REAL LIFE DIARY
OF A BOOMTOWN GIRL

THE
REAL LIFE DIARY
OF A
BOOMTOWN GIRL

A Novel by

DAVID BRESKIN

VIKING

VIKING
Published by the Penguin Group
Viking Penguin, a division of Penguin Books USA Inc.,
40 West 23rd Street, New York, New York 10010, U.S.A.
Penguin Books Ltd, 27 Wrights Lane, London W8 5TZ, England
Penguin Books Australia Ltd, Ringwood, Victoria, Australia
Penguin Books Canada Ltd, 2801 John Street,
Markham, Ontario, Canada L3R 1B4
Penguin Books (N.Z.) Ltd, 182-190 Wairau Road,
Auckland 10, New Zealand

Penguin Books Ltd, Registered Offices:
Harmondsworth, Middlesex, England

First published in 1989 by Viking Penguin,
a division of Penguin Books USA Inc.

10 9 8 7 6 5 4 3 2 1

Grateful acknowledgment is made for permission to use excerpts from the
following copyrighted works:

"Rocket Man (I Think It's Going to be a Long Long Time)" by Elton John
and Bernie Taupin. Copyright © 1972 Dick James Music Limited. All rights
for the United States and Canada controlled by Dick James Music, Inc. International copyright secured. All rights reserved. Used by permission.
"Saturday Night's Alright (For Fighting)" by Elton John and Bernie Taupin.
Copyright © 1973 Dick James Music Limited. All rights for the United States
and Canada controlled by Dick James Music, Inc. International copyright
secured. All rights reserved. Used by permission.

LIBRARY OF CONGRESS CATALOGING IN PUBLICATION DATA
Breskin, David.
   The Real Life Diary of a Boomtown Girl: a novel / by David Breskin.
      p.   cm.
   ISBN 0–670–82828–9
   I. Title.
PS3552.R3878B6   1989   88–40654
813'.54—dc20

Printed in the United States of America
Set in Garamond No. 3

For
Barbara & Don
and
Hattie & Al

The author wishes to thank these good souls for seeing this book through—Nan Graham, Kathryn Harrison, Bill Biederman, Mark Rowland, Randi Semler, Joleen Grussing, and Kathy Robbins.

THE REAL LIFE DIARY
OF A BOOMTOWN GIRL

SWING

What I remember about growing up is mostly the wind. It was always pushing you one way or another, even in summer. The wind is like someone else poking you in the ribs, a distraction from being by yourself, just totally. And there were no trees out by where we had the trailer house, it was a 1964 New Moon, so the sun was really sun and nothing stopped the blowing.

When Mom would go off to town, or maybe out with dad to service wells—he was in the oil field service business—they'd go off on their snowmobiles and she'd say, "Randi, don't let the house blow down and don't let you and Betsy get blown away." Well, the roof would rumble in the wind, since it was only one piece, but we had the old truck tires on top to keep it down. In your high wind areas, everybody with a trailer puts something on the roof. Stones do a better job but they're harder to get up there + there are more tires around here anyway.

Anyway the T.V. would always go fuzzy and all squiggly during the best programs—we only had two stations to begin with—but we never did get blown away. And at bedtime, I'd tuck Betsy in like I was Mom, and we'd listen to it blow through the fence and up against the siding. We made up stories, about how it was going to carry us off to the North Pole, or Canada at least. And we made up a contest about the door banging. Because even if you hinged it the screen door would come loose and bang. The contest would be about how many times it would bang in a minute, and so one of us guessed and the other timed, just to make sure it was fair. And then we'd switch. I think the record was it banged like 18 times in a minute. I know that seems impossible.

And when Mom and dad came back from the wells sometimes it would be after midnight. We'd wake up when we heard the snowmobiles. When it was coldest the cold made them sound like chainsaws in the snow, and we'd put on our mukluks and run to the door, and wait for them to come in. Dad would have icicles falling from his mustache and we had the Beatles by then so we'd shout "Daddy is the walrus Daddy is the walrus is the walrus is the walrus," whatever that was supposed to mean. We didn't exactly know.

Things were slow and easy back then, and not just cause we were kids. When they weren't working the wells they'd take me and Betsy out to the reservoir and set about turning us into waterski champs. Westhope Reservoir. They bought a ski boat with twin 'Rudes with all their money. We competed, starting at 10 years old and at 8. Betsy was graceful and she could slalom real good. I was stronger, so I went in for the tricks—little skis, disks, jumps, fancy rope stuff, barefoot even once or twice. We'd go out to Westhope on the weekend, have red hot dogs B.B.Q. and ski, ski, ski.

I remember the water rushing through my legs when I'd start—it would always swoosh and tingle. That's why I never wanted to do flying dock starts, which they didn't understand. Sometimes I'd pretend I was having trouble with the line or couldn't get my tips up—that was the best. I just loved how it felt being dragged. Mom would yell from her spotter's seat at the back of the boat, "God darn it Ran-di, you're wasting time and fuel, get your God darn tips up!" Mom was real serious about it. She would never go in the water herself but she took lots of pictures of us skiing and glued them to the fridge door in the kitchen, so we could never take them down. Reminders of future glory, she thought.

What dad did mostly is drive the boat. It was so powerful he could make it around the reservoir in 6 minutes. He knew all the angles. He could slide through the corners. He could turn back on himself and jump his own wake. He could dump even the best skiers. He was the best operator out there and everyone from town was always asking for rides on account of that.

One summer we made this little jump out of fiberglass and wood and I loved going over it. It gave me that funny stomach feeling like on a swing, only more like when a plane hits an air pocket. And when you'd come down, the splash would send water everywhere. For a second you couldn't see anything—everything was completely water—cause you'd have to crouch low when you hit. I remember before I jumped the first time dad told me, "Use your knees like the shock absorbers on the Yamahas." I didn't really know what shock absorbers were, I mean how they worked mechanically, but it sounded real slick—shock absorbers—just the way it sounded and those snowmobiles were pretty nice machines so I didn't mind being compared.

We'd get worn out, Betsy and me, in and out of the water all day, feet all wrinkly purple and cheeks pink like Mom's toenail polish. Mom wanted us to be #1 in Wyoming but she knew the vacation people over at Jackson Hole had always been the best, with their money and time and all, and that got her pissed. So we worked hard at it. Betsy got up to #9 in Rocky Mountain Juniors. After we'd finish for the day, we'd eat hot dogs and Ruffles and Kool-Aid on the rocks. Then we'd be told to go play with the other kids and their families so Mom and dad could go out in the boat alone. We'd take in the rope and put on our Bruce Ski Sisters windbreakers. They were orange, day-glo. Then we'd watch them go off.

They'd cruise around the lake and the sky would get big and that summer black-and-blue color like the bruise I had between my knees on account of the tow rope on my no-hands tricks. After a while we couldn't see them—just the boat bobbing out in the middle of the reservoir, with the little green light and the little red light, and little lights above them too, which were all the stars we learned about in school which the teacher said we should feel lucky about because people in the East and the cities couldn't see them. Mom and dad always brought a bottle with and they said they liked to drink and drift, just drink and drift. And I asked Mom once why we couldn't see her and dad out there and she said, "That's because we like to lie down on the bench seat together and look on up at the stars." But whenever their heads would disappear from what we could see from the rocks, I would always turn to Betsy and giggle a little. I was older.

3

SWING

Last night he came to get me again in my sleep. He was dressed like a cowboy, but he wasn't a cowboy. It was more like he was dressed up in a cowboy costume. And I was just laying there sleeping when he came in the front door, which should of been locked. I'm sure I locked it. But it wasn't. So he comes in and looks around downstairs—it's like he's looking for something, the way you look for keys or matches, like it was something he lost. I don't know why I could see him since my door was closed—but I could, in my head. That's the way a lot of my dreams are. And then he didn't find what he was looking for and so he came up the stairs and opened my door, and he walks into the room like it was his room. As soon as I open my eyes the first thing I see—because I'm sleeping on my side so I'm looking sideways and down cause I like laying right at the edge of the pillow and the edge of the bed—so the first thing I see is his boots, his black boots, coming up through the green shag carpet. And then I see his hand reaching down to brush off these little fuzzballs that had come off the carpet onto his boots, and he says, "Damn." And as soon as he said that, I woke up. I was sort of scared. But I don't know why really, because he might of been coming up to my room just to say hello, or drop something off, or to see how I was doing. I mean, any of the normal things your dad would do.

SWING

The reason I'm doing this is cause there's nothing else to keep me from going crazy hauling coal. I mean, when music was allowed everybody had radios and everybody listened to KOAL, and that was pretty cool, even if it does play the same songs over and over. But then they decided that we couldn't have radios in the trucks, so some of us smuggled in those new tiny little tape players that

4

have headphones. But they caught on and stopped us. They made it a suspension if you got caught.

So we had to settle for reading, which was okay with me—but a lot of the guys were bummed that don't like to. Long romantic paperback stories could get you through a week probably better than anything, except getting interrupted was bad. So mostly I just ended up reading People or Time or one of Spike's Penthouses.

But pretty soon they decided that we couldn't have reading in the trucks either, cause there were still too many little accidents going on and mistakes being made. Nothing major, but still. Of course everybody knows what's really causing all the screw-ups. The company isn't so dumb that they don't know. But it's a lot harder for them to stop all the candy and the crank and the weed and stuff, so they took everything else away instead. Which figures. So now all us haulers are left with nothing to do but haul. And it makes the deadtime—like being loaded or waiting to dump or waiting on a blast + breaks and downtime—it makes it really dead.

So all I got to do is sit in my truck and think about Spike, who is my sexy supergreat old man who works for Antelope Exploration and is going to be making beaucoup bucks pretty soon and is going to be marrying me pretty soon. And thinking about all of it sort of drives me crazy, so I have to have something else to do. Sam suggested it actually. She said, "You're always telling stupid stories about stuff. Why don't you write them down to keep from going stir." See, they kept Sam on blasting when they broke up the Boom-Boom Girls. They bumped me up to hauling, but she's still down in the pit. She doesn't have to worry about falling asleep down there. But in the haul trucks, forget it.

All these rules came down in the middle of last rotation, when I was on days, and on days I spend half the shift trying to wake up. And without tunes or reading, it was getting impossible not to fall back asleep. So when swing came around, doing nothing was getting on my nerves so much I just started this. I had one once before, about 6 years ago, but I had to stop because Betsy stole it from me one day when she was supermad at me. I forgot what it was we were fighting about. But she stole it and hid it for like two weeks. It was the worst—because I was sure she was reading the whole thing in secret. She finally gave it back and swore that she didn't look at it. She showed me how the lock was still locked. She never had the key. But after she gave it back I just didn't feel the same about it. So I stopped.

The good thing about it now is they can't see it cause it's down on the seat. So nobody knows I'm doing anything. I mean, some people are still sneaking in tape players but the bad thing there is if they call you on your radio and you don't answer, then they know right away you got headphones on. And I can't afford to get suspended. So first I've got to catch up on how everything got to right now + say other things I'm thinking. Okay.

Okay, to begin with Mom is from Lead, South Dakota, and all her folks are from there too. There and Deadwood, which is really like a twin-cities thing, since all the gold runs under those hills and doesn't know where one town starts and the other stops and it's the gold that's the reason for the towns anyway. Lead is where Homestake is, they about own that town all the way to a mile underneath. I think they're down to 8,000 feet now. Grandma Hattie used to run a dress shop in town, for the unfancy ladies, just the regular wives and all, and Grandpa Al was a surveyor for Homestake. They're both passed away on account of the Big C. I remember them sick and in bed. Mom's an only.

Dad's from Sundance which is almost the Black Hills on the Wyoming side. You cross the border on the innerstate but it's the same country really. I never really knew anything about dad's family except that Mom said we weren't supposed to talk about them. That was pretty easy to do, since I never knew anything to talk about anyway. I think they're from up near Ashland, Montana. Because one time we were driving up there, all four of us, just down this snakey dirt road in this valley, and dad was talking about it like he owned the place. It was just miles and miles from no-where. I think he worked for some ranchers there when he quit high school.

The deal on Mom and dad turning into Mom and dad is that they met at Devil's Tower. It was 1959 or 1960, around then. They weren't actually at the Tower yet, but below it on the road where there's the prarie dog town on the grassland and you can pull over and watch prarie dogs pop out of their little holes and take pictures.

6

You can walk out there too, but there are rattlers so the rangers are not responsible if you do.

The way Mom tells it is always the same. I think me and Betsy have heard it about 100 ×, because she tells about everyone she meets. She always goes—

"My best girlfriend Helen and I had pulled off to take pictures before we went up to the Tower. And we're waiting and waiting for a prarie dog to pop up, or a family to run around, or just something, cause nothing was happening. It was super hot and sunny. And a bunch of other people were there too, waiting. So some guys, hot-shot type guys, high schoolers, start picking up rocks by the roadside and throwing them out at the town, to see if they can get something happening out there. It looks like they're trying to throw them right down one of the holes, contesting each other—like who can get closer? Like they would of conked one of the dogs right on the head if he was coming out to take a look around. Me and Helen were watching, and a few other folks. We had our cameras ready but there was nothing to shoot.

"Then this guy, this real tall guy with blond hair and gorgeous brown eyes, jumps out of his pickup, I'll always remember it was a Ford, a green Ford, and he starts yelling at these kids. He's yelling, 'What in the hell you doing? You so stupid you don't even know better?' The kids look at him, and then keep doing it, keep throwing the rocks. So dad says, 'How would you like it if the prarie dogs came to your town and started throwing rocks at your houses to get you to come out just so they could see you, but you were inside watching T.V. or sleeping, eating lunch. Would you much like that, you little turkeys?'

"Everybody started laughing, just the thought of it. The high school guys looked really confused, like maybe everybody is laughing at them. One of them, he had a mohawk, picks up another rock, and guess who says"—at this point of the story, Mom always goes and guess who says—'You throw that rock out there, your friends'll have to scrape you off the road.' And the kid just dropped the rock and they all got in their car and drove on up to the Tower. And after that, everybody was looking at this guy, everyone was his friend.

"And he walks over to me and Helen and says, 'God that makes me mad.' We tell him 'Thanks' and all. Then he says, 'Soon as we get a little cloud cover, the dogs'll pop out. Don't worry, dogs'll show.' It was true. And when my camera jammed up on me, he fixed it. Well, me and him just picked up right from there."

Then Mom looks at you like it's the most logical thing in the world. You know, that after this little prarie dog town incident it's completely obvious that they would get married, just that it was a matter of time. Sometimes Mom goes on about one thing or another, like what he was wearing—sometimes it's a white Sundance Feed cap and sometimes Ashland Oil—and the way he intimidated those kids without even laying a hand on them—because he wasn't really much older than they were. But basically it's the same story every time, when she's telling anyone about her and dad, how it started. They were married in six months about, in Deadwood.

SWING

First we lived in Sundance, then after Betsy, Midwest. Then we got the trailer near Spotted Horse, which is where I start remembering things. Spotted Horse wasn't a town so much as a spot on the road near the tracks, an old post office trailer and the rest of nothing much. I'd ask Mom why do we live out here and she'd say, "Cause we like living in the superboonies." She always called it the superboonies. Sundance or Gillette was the boonies and where we were was the superboonies.

It's true we liked it. Most of the other people out there were ranchers and we weren't ranchers, but we had room to run like ranch kids. Even though we lived in a trailer, it was a double-wide and that gives you room to run around when you're little. But I always heard Mom saying to dad, "Peter, the carpet." She'd go, "Oh Peter, the carpet!" I guess we were hard on it.

When we weren't skiing, we'd take these long drives on the weekends. We'd go visit Grandma Hattie and we'd drive on out to the Badlands the next day, getting up at about 4:00 in the morning, so we could get there when it was the most beautiful

8

with colors. I remember standing at this scenic lookout just about forever and dad finally said, "Isn't it weird? Isn't it about the weirdest?"

Betsy and I always remembered that. Sometimes we laughed about it. Later when we were in school it was like a secret code. Something would happen in gym class with a boy, or some teacher would give you the devil's eye, and we'd meet in the hall and say "Isn't it about the weirdest?" and crack up. We always thought it was pretty weird to think that a bunch of rocks were the weirdest, cause they hardly are.

If we didn't go drive around the Badlands we'd go to some cave or someplace where the magnetic forces were supposed to be all crazy, or we'd go to Rushmore like everybody else. I remember when Bedrock City first opened down in Custer. It's this Flint-stones theme-park campground and stuff. I always wanted to go there, but they never would take us—we always had to go to a hot springs or Wind Cave or something natural like that. Betsy and me used to ask them so much if we could go there and Mom and dad started saying that we would NEVER go there cause of the way we were carrying on.

That's when I learned the word *Attitude*. Mom kept saying to dad, "Where did this attitude come from?" She'd say real loud to Betsy, "What's this attitude young lady?" I finally looked it up. The next time she got mad and said, "Watch your attitude young lady," I said back, "Watch your attitude Mom." She got dad from out back and he came in steaming and used his belt on my butt. Mom was so angry she went into the bathroom and threw all Betsy and my Flintstones vitamins down the toilet and said she'd never get them for us again, that we'd have to take Chocks forever. That night we cried so hard in our room. It was like everybody in the house stopped breathing.

But other than not going to Bedrock City, we had a lot of fun— at least when school was out. We'd get bumper stickers from every place we went to and when we ran out of bumper room dad let us put them up on our shower door—I think the first one was Western Woodcarvings. It's this place where they have little scenes of old-fashioned towns with carvings of little people and animals and they talk from speakers you can't see.

My favorite part of those trips was coming back after a long day and ice cream which we got with dinner on Sunday night, every Sunday night. Me and Betsy would be tired of looking at everything so we'd lie down in the back seat. She'd put her legs up on one window and I'd put my legs up on the other window, and we'd lie there on our backs with our heads going different directions, sort of overlapping so that we were ear-to-ear. Sometimes we'd make our ears touch so we could listen to each other's thoughts. A lot of times we did actually say the right thoughts the other one was thinking. It's true.

We'd lie back there and we'd stare up at the ceiling of the car and watch the other car headlights make shapes that changed as we drove by them. We'd try to guess which road we were on by the way the pavement sounded—cause we knew a lot of the roads— and that way we could figure out how close to home we were. We'd listen in to Mom and dad talking up in the front seat, especially if they thought we were asleep. One time they were talking about something really good but then Betsy started giggling, so they just turned on the radio. I was so P.O.'d at Betsy I gave her a green crippler right then on her arm and she yelled, and because of that we didn't get T.V. that week.

But most of the time we would go to sleep, which was better than listening anyway. We got so good at the ear-to-ear position that we could ride through all those super windy Black Hills roads and not even wake up. If dad was driving fast, I'd call "Special" to Betsy. I was the only one that could call it. "Special" was when she put her hair under my head, and I put my hair under her head, and then we both put our heads back down. She had this long blond hair and I had this long black hair. We figured it helped keep us both from sliding off the seat in case we went around a curve fast. It felt good to fall asleep like that, listening to the different sounds of cars going by you until you don't hear anything anymore.

I still like to do that. Not the same back seat thing, but when it's real late and I'm coming back from somewhere a long way away with Spike, I like to lie down in front and put my head in his lap and just listen. I like feeling his forearms going back and forth on my face while he's steering. He rests them on me. I love falling asleep that way—just listening to road sounds and thinking about us getting married.

It's nice to think about cause that's all I can do about it right at the moment—since we don't have a date yet and it's still this big secret. So it's nice to drift off like that and dream about stuff. It turns it from this boring ride that you've done a million times into something that goes by in no time at all. Then as soon as I know it, the blinker sound is waking me up. And I don't mind it when that happens, because it means Spike is turning off the highway and that means we're near home anyway and it's almost time to wake up and go to bed.

SWING

Boy, I had a wild one last night. I was at the Frontier Museum all alone, looking at this old stuff, mostly rifles and corsets and wagon wheels and about 10,000 arrowheads. And I was remembering what Grandma told me when she took me there. I was noticing the rust on the belt buckles, cause she told me, "Always look at the rust, that's the pateena, that's how you can tell how old something is." Then I was looking at this painting of these pioneer guys standing by a cabin that had grass growing on the roof when 3 of the guys came out of it. I mean, they just kept getting bigger and bigger and so they naturally just came out of the picture, because sooner or later they'd have to be 3 dimensions. But when they came down from the picture they were just little kids in overalls with blond hair and two of them had toy guns. They were toy guns but when they shot them through the ceiling the bullets were real. So one of them goes to me, "Lady are you coming with us, or are we going to have to make trouble?" And I said, "No, no trouble, I'm coming with." But then these guys go up to the old lady at the desk and they make her give them all the money in her till, and then they make her take off her glasses. But she doesn't want to, so these guys start yelling in these totally adult voices, "Take them off lady! Take them off!" So she does, and one guy throws them up and another guy shoots them right out of the air and of course they disintegrated. And then one of them goes, "Let's get out of here." And another one has this little wagon that says RED FLYER and he tells me "Get in" and so I do. I mean, I wanted to get out of there. I thought the police would be coming + that old woman was giving me the creeps—she was just holding out her hands to me, sort of mumbling. So this little pioneer guy kicks the door open and pulls me outside where it's pitch dark. He starts pulling me through the parking lot and down onto 14-16. I don't know where his two friends went. I'm yelling, "Go faster, go faster" and he's pulling me, but then his hat flies off, and when he lets go of the wagon handle for a second to reach for it, I keep going without him. And it feels like I'm starting to go faster and faster, because the handle is starting to make faster scraping noises on the pavement, faster noises. I'm going downhill right into town. I can't see anything, but I know town is there cause I've driven it a million times, and I start getting scared about crashing. So I try to pull the handle up from the ground to steer with. But just as I reach for it, it hits an uneven spot in the road—like a concrete section a few inches out of whack—and the handle flies right back through me, like goes right through my stomach, and right then I wake up, right when it hurts.

GRAVES

Coming in to work tonight, I followed this horse trailer for about 30 miles. I could just see a tail sticking out, flying around in my headlights like one of those brushes at the car wash. It reminded me of how much I always wanted one. I used to beg Mom for a horse. And she would go ask dad for me. This was during junior high.

Every time I'd watch Mr. Ed, which was on after school, I'd be all crazy about it by the time they came home from the wells. Of course I knew my horse wouldn't talk, but I would be able to talk to him and he'd understand the same way. I was never very good about being quiet about it. I remember calling her "Mommy," which is what I always called her when I needed something bad. I'd go, "Mommy, can I please get a horse? It could count for my next 5 birthdays + Christmas gifts too. It could even count for my next 10 birthdays."

Mom would always say, "I'll talk to your father." And that would be it. Then in a few days I'd figure enough time had passed, and I'd wait until I had cleared the table at dinner and done the pots and turned the dishwasher on to bring it up again. I thought if she saw me drying the pots at the same time she heard the dishwasher going that it would help—that it would make her think that I deserved a horse more. I tried it a couple times. But she'd always say, "Your father says we can't afford a horse."

One time I said back, "But half my friends have horses." She said, "Well they have land." I said, "So big deal! We're not poorer, we're not." She walked up to me and took hold of my wrists real tight and made her eyes go real small. She said, "You have the motorboat. Do your other friends have a motorboat? Do your other friends have brand-new snowmobiles?" She was shaking me by the wrists. She goes, "Listen young lady, you can't have a motorboat and a horse too." And then she let me go. I had her white finger marks on my wrists.

But I never thought a motorboat was in the same category as a horse. It didn't seem fair to compare them that way + the boat wasn't even mine really. I stopped asking anyway, because I knew I would never win. So I just pretended for a while that Tar Steps was my horse.

She was my rabbit. I named her that because right when I got her we took her out with us servicing wells and while I was reading meters for dad she got off the rope and ran through a little spill by the treater tank. It was easy to catch her though, because her feet were so sticky. The thing is, I knew 7th grade was too old to have a rabbit, even though I still loved her a lot. So I just changed Tar Steps into a horse. I'd take her out back behind the trailer to the tool shed, where I imagined keeping my horse, and I talked to her, pretending she was my horse.

One time Betsy saw me back there with some sugar cubes that I took out of a box on the highest cabinet of the kitchen—she heard me telling Tar Steps to eat them so she would win the Kentucky Derby and Tar Steps saying things back to me in my horse voice. She came up and said, "Isn't it about the weirdest?" I was so embarrassed. God, it was horrible. I begged her, "Please Please PLEASE don't tell anyone at school." She went, "I don't know." She was smiling. I yelled at her, "Don't. Don't Betsy. Just don't. Okay?"

After that, I stopped pretending about Tar Steps. I decided I was never going to pretend about anything. I decided I was too old for that. Also, I did two weeks of setting the table and garbage-taking-out for Betsy to make sure it stayed a secret.

GRAVES

I don't feel like this tonight. I feel like getting out of here is all. Second shift after turnaround is always the worst, because during the first one your body's easy to fool, but on the second your body knows it's being forced to stay up working all night. I'm just going to staple this in cause it says what I was going to say anyway, about what happened to town. Spike saw this ad in the back of the Quad Cities paper about where to get jobs, and he sent away his money— it was like $18.95—out to some P.O. box in Eureka, California and they sent him back this little xeroxed booklet, and after he read it he decided to come out here. So he came to town with it, and he always kept it, even after he didn't need it anymore and knew a lot of it was B.S. And so later, I always kept it—like fate— what brought him and me together. I just always kept it in my glove compartment. I know it's dumb.

CONFIDENTIAL REPORT
ON EMPLOYMENT OPPORTUNITIES
IN AMERICA

A RECESSION IN AMERICA IS CAUSING HARD TIMES FOR MANY, AND A DIFFICULT TIME FOR A MULTITUDE OF PEOPLE. AS AMERICA CHANGES ITS PERSPECTIVES THE WORKERS MUST ALSO CHANGE TO KEEP UP WITH THE COUNTRY.

AS AMERICANS LEFT THE HORSE AND BUGGY DAYS AND ENTERED INTO THE MECHANICAL AGE THE NEED FOR PEOPLE TO MANUFACTURE BUGGY WHIPS DECREASED WHILE THE NUMBER OF PEOPLE NEEDED TO MANUFACTURE AUTOMOBILES INCREASED.

TODAY WE SEE AN EVER EXPANDING NEED FOR ENERGY, AND A NEED FOR MORE PEOPLE TO WORK IN ENERGY RELATED FIELDS. BECAUSE THIS IS A NEW FIELD, MOST JOBS ARE AVAILABLE WITH NO PREVIOUS EXPERIENCE NECESSARY. ALL YOU WILL

NEED IS A WILLINGNESS TO LEARN AND A DESIRE FOR A SUPER INCOME.

THIS REPORT WILL TELL YOU ABOUT SOME OF THE SUPER JOBS NEEDING YOU RIGHT NOW, TODAY. THERE ARE JOBS AVAILABLE BY THE THOUSANDS. THESE AREAS ARE THE NEW FRONTIER.

GILLETTE, WYOMING

BOOMTOWN, USA. WHEN YOU FIRST DRIVE INTO TOWN YOU WILL BE IMPRESSED WITH THE GREAT ACTIVITY HERE. MOBILE HOME PARKS ALL OVER. IT LOOKS LIKE A TOWN WITH EVERYTHING NEW; NEW CONSTRUCTION, NEW MOBILE HOMES, NEW STORES, NEW STREETS, NEW EVERYTHING.

I'M SURE YOU HAVE SEEN ON T.V. OR THE MOVIES WHAT A GOLD RUSH TOWN OF THE OLD WEST LOOKED LIKE, THAT IS WHAT THIS TOWN WILL REMIND YOU OF. LONG BEFORE YOU GET INTO TOWN YOU WILL SEE THE OIL WELLS IN PRODUCTION, THE OIL DRILLING RIGS EVERYWHERE, OIL FIELD STORAGE TANKS, FULL OF LIQUID GOLD, DOTTING THE HILLSIDES.

NOT AS EVIDENT IS THE GREAT ACTIVITY IN URANIUM-235 THAT HAS RECENTLY STARTED, BUT THEY ARE OUT THERE IN THE HILLS AND PRAIRIES DRILLING AWAY LOOKING FOR THE FUEL FOR THE NATIONS AND THE WORLDS NUCLEAR REACTORS. THEIR JOB HAS JUST BEGUN!

IF YOU ARRIVE FROM THE EAST, JUST OUTSIDE OF TOWN THERE IS A HUGE POWER PLANT AND COAL MINE, AND IF YOU AREN'T FAMILIAR WITH WHAT A NEW STRIP MINING OPERATION LOOKS LIKE TAKE A GOOD LOOK. THOSE HUGE SILOS, CALLED TIPPLES, ARE HOW THEY LOAD TRAINS WITH COAL. THE TRAIN WITH FIVE ENGINES IN

FRONT SLOWLY DRIVES THROUGH THE BASE OF
THOSE SILOS AND AN OPERATOR, WHO TAKES A
SUPER WAGE, PUSHES BUTTONS AND LOADS THE
WHOLE TRAIN IN JUST A FEW MINUTES. THEN OFF
TO THE EAST GOES ANOTHER TRAIN LOAD OF
ENERGY.

CAMPBELL COUNTY, WYOMING, THE COUNTY
GILLETTE IS LOCATED IN, IS DESCRIBED AS THE
RICHEST COUNTY IN THESE UNTIED STATES.
TAXES ON HOMES AND MOBILE HOMES ARE
EXTREMELY LOW, LIKE $30/YEAR ON A $20,000
MOBILE HOME. YET THERE IS SO MUCH ACTIVITY
IN MINING AND OIL THAT THE NEED TO TAX
PEOPLE WILL REMAIN LOW. THE POLICE FORCE IN
GILLETTE EVEN PROCLAIMS "ENERGY CAPITAL OF
THE NATION" ON THE DOORS OF THEIR CARS.

JOBS

WHEN A PERSON ARRIVES THE MOST PRESSING
THING TO DO SEEMS TO BE TO GET SOME INCOME
FLOWING IN, WHICH MEANS YOU TAKE THE MOST
AVAILABLE JOB FIRST. THE $15/HOUR JOBS HAVE
QUITE A BIT OF COMPETITION FOR THEM, SO IT
MAY TAKE A FEW SHORT WEEKS TO ADVANCE
YOURSELF TO THAT LEVEL. TAKE A LOWER PAYING
JOB, PUT IN YOUR APPLICATIONS FOR THE BETTER
PAYING JOBS, AND BE PREPARED TO WAIT A LITTLE
WHILE. OF PRIMARY IMPORTANCE IS NOT TO GET
DOWN IN THE DUMPS, IT IS GOING TO HAPPEN.

BEFORE YOU THINK THAT BY LOWER PAYING
JOBS I MEAN MINIMUM WAGE, FORGET THAT. A
LOWER PAYING JOB IN THIS AREA PAYS $400/WEEK.
SURE BEATS UNEMPLOYMENT COMPENSATION
THOUGH. HERE'S THE WORK:

ROUSTABOUT—$5/HOUR TO START—NO EXPE-
RIENCE. ROUSTABOUT IS OIL FIELD LABOR, WORK

ON PIPELINES, SET UP PUMPJACKS, SHOVEL WORK OR OTHER MANUAL LABOR IN OIL FIELD CONSTRUCTION. EXPECT 12 HOUR DAYS FOR AS MANY DAYS A WEEK AS YOU CARE TO WORK, TIME AND A HALF FOR OVERTIME.

FLAGGER—$7/HOUR TO START—NO EXPERIENCE. 60 HOUR WEEKS AT $490/WEEK. WYOMING SEEMS TO BE BUILDING HIGHWAYS EVERY PLACE. HUGO CONSTRUCTION WAS HIRING WOMEN AT $7/HOUR WHEN I WAS OUT THERE. WOMEN— UNDER EQUAL EMPLOYMENT OPPORTUNITY YOU ARE IN DEMAND AS MUCH OR MORE THAN MEN. THERE IS ALSO A SHORTAGE OF WOMEN THROUGHOUT THE AREA SO IF YOU WISH TO WORK IN RESTAURANTS YOU CAN PICK AND CHOOSE WHERE YOU WISH TO WORK AND WHEN. TIPS ARE GREAT.

SILO BUILDERS—$8/HOUR TO START—60 HOUR WEEKS. WHEN A SILO IS GOING UP EVEN MORE HOURS BECAUSE IT IS SLIP FORMED AND CONSTRUCTION CAN'T STOP FOR EVEN A MINUTE. A SILO HERE ISN'T FOR PUTTING GRAIN IN, IT IS FOR COAL.

CARPENTERS—$13.10/HOUR—NON-UNION, JUST SHOW UP ON A MINE BUILDING SITE WITH A TOOL BELT WITH THE USUAL TOOLS OF THE TRADE. THE JOB CONSISTS OF BUILDING SHEDS FOR COVERING CONSTRUCTION EQUIPMENT, AND ROUGH FRAMING, NOTHING THAT REQUIRES MORE THAN COMMON SENSE TO BUILD AND A WILLINGNESS TO WORK.

FLOOR HANDS—$6.50/HOUR—WORKS ON URANIUM DRILLING RIGS. WORKS UP TO 16 HOURS A DAY, BUT NOT A VERY TOUGH JOB. SOME PEOPLE REPORT IT VERY BORING, NOTHING TO DO BUT WATCH THE DRILL GO ROUND AND ROUND. A GOOD JOB TO START WITH UNTIL YOU GET INTO

PHYSICAL CONDITION FOR MORE SERIOUS WORK LATER.

MINE TRUCK OPERATOR—$12/HOUR—60 TO 72 HOUR WEEKS, PLUS HEALTH, LIFE AND DENTAL. THIS IS JUST ONE OF THE SUPER JOBS IN A STRIP COAL MINE. WORKING FOR A COAL COMPANY IS THE JOB ALMOST EVERYONE SHOOTS FOR. I FOUND A MAN AND WIFE TEAM THERE MAKING $22/HOUR BETWEEN THEM. ANYBODY CAN GET HEALTHY QUICK AT THAT PAY. AND REMEMBER THERE ARE NO UNIONS TO TIE YOU DOWN.

GETTING HIRED AT AN OPERATING MINE IS FAIRLY TOUGH AT PRESENT TIME, BUT, SOON THERE ARE 17 MORE MINES SCHEDULED TO OPEN. YOU MUST BE OUT THERE AND HAVE YOUR APPLICATION ON FILE WHEN THEY START HIRING. NO EXPERIENCE NECESSARY BUT YOU MUST BE READY TO WORK WHEN THEY CALL.

EACH MINE SEEMS TO HAVE A NAME LIKE "BUCKSKIN," "RAWHIDE," "BLACK THUNDER," ETC. THE COMPANIES THAT ARE OPERATING THEM ARE AMAX, ARCO, CARTER, KELLER, KERR-McGEE, MOBIL, PHILLIPS, SHELL, ETC., ALL BIG COMPANIES AND THEY WILL TREAT YOU RIGHT.

BURLINGTON NORTHERN RAILROAD—WITH ALL THESE MINES OPENING UP THERE ARE MILES OF TRACK TO BE LAID AND HUNDREDS OF TRAIN CREWS TO BE HIRED. I UNDERSTAND THAT THE RAILROAD WILL HAVE A COAL TRAIN LEAVING GILLETTE, FULL, EVERY 12 MINUTES, 24 HOURS A DAY AROUND THE CLOCK. PUT IN YOUR APPLICATION AT BURLINGTON'S OFFICE DOWNTOWN.

GIVE NOTICE WITH AN EMPLOYER WHEN YOU SWITCH JOBS IN GILLETTE? IT IS ALMOST UNHEARD OF. TAKE THE FIRST JOB OFFERED AND WHEN SOMEONE WANTS YOU FOR A BETTER JOB THAN

YOU'RE IN, JUST DON'T GO TO WORK THE NEXT DAY AT YOUR OLD JOB. EVERYONE THERE DOES IT THAT WAY AND YOU SHOULD TOO. THERE'S NO TRICK TO IT . . . REMEMBER THIS IS A "BOOM TOWN."

A WORD OF CAUTION

SINCE THIS IS A BOOM TOWN ONE OF THE REASONS THERE ARE SO MANY JOBS HERE IS BECAUSE NOTHING HAS CAUGHT UP WITH THE DEMAND. VERY LITTLE GROWS IN THE AREA, SO EVERYTHING MUST BE TRUCKED IN. FOOD IS HIGHER THAN BACK EAST, HOUSING IS SCARCE, MONEY IS EVERYWHERE BUT THERE ISN'T MUCH TO SPEND IT ON. THERE ISN'T MUCH COMPETITION FOR CUSTOMERS BECAUSE STORES KNOW THAT IF YOU DON'T BUY IT HERE THEN YOU CAN'T BUY IT FOR ANOTHER 150 MILES. THERE ARE MEN WHO DRIVE UP TO 200 MILES TO WORK EACH WEEK, SPEND 5 NIGHTS IN A MOTEL AND DRIVE HOME ON THE WEEKEND.

PROBABLY THE WORST THING TO DO WOULD BE TO LOAD UP A TRUCK WITH YOUR FURNITURE, THE WIFE AND CHILDREN AND MOVE TO WYOMING. WHEN YOU GET THERE YOU WILL PROBABLY FIND ALL THE MOTEL SPACES ALREADY RENTED FOR WEEKS IN ADVANCE.

THERE IS A WAY TO DO IT THOUGH

DO THIS AND YOU CAN MAKE IT. COME OUT BY YOURSELF, DON'T BRING MUCH WITH YOU, ONE OR TWO SUITCASES SHOULD DO IT. MOVE INTO A BUNKHOUSE FOR $25/WEEK, OR THE OLD BUFFALO HOTEL FOR $60/WEEK PLUS MEALS. GO TO WORK, SAVE YOUR MONEY, GET THAT JOB PAYING $1,000/ WEEK, THEN SEND FOR YOUR FAMILY.

OR, PULL A SELF-CONTAINED CAMPER OUT, LIVE

IN IT YOURSELF AND MAKE SOME EXTRA CASH BY
RENTING OUT YOUR SPARE BEDS!!

<u>I'LL SEE YOU IN WYOMING.</u>

GRAVES

We all pretty much grew up right along with town. Things were
great right after that Arab oil boycott, everybody had work. There
was usually too much of it. Sometimes Mom and dad worked 20
hours straight, and me and Betsy would go out with them, logging
and stuff, helping out, getting dirty. But there was so much money
out there that the bigs finally came in. Dad used to call all those
big companies "The Heavy Hitters." I remember him standing in
our driveway, telling the guy he was selling our truck to something
like, "The economics just aren't there for us now the heavy hitters
are in." It all seemed pretty mysterious to me.

So Mom went to work for Westwind Airlines, which was just a
single-engine Cessna in the very beginning. She had to get up early
and go out in the morning and chase the antelope off the dirt
runway so the commuter flight could leave for Casper. She'd drive
down the runway honking her horn and flipping her lights on and
off and the pronghorn would scatter up toward the butte. She liked
the driving fast part of it, and she let me do it a few times once I
got my learner's permit. I'd hang around at the airport Saturdays,
and sometimes after school. I liked looking at all these new people
coming into town—they all had briefcases and cigarettes and sun-
glasses—but also because my first major crush was the Westwind
pilot.

He had dark hair, dark eyes and dark skin. I guess he was pretty
much of a raccoon but I thought he was cute at the time. He had
plans for the Navy, but since the end of Vietnam he figured it
would be so long until the next war that he just decided to go
commercial. I thought it was real romantic, him flying that plane
over the mountains. Mom said he was too old for a 16-year-old
girl from the superboonies, and she wouldn't let me go out with

him. I told her I wasn't from the superboonies anymore—since we had moved to town when Betsy started freshman year and I started junior, because the driving back and forth from Spotted Horse was driving everyone mad, especially in winter. But she still wouldn't let me date him.

I believe Hunter, that was him, wanted to go out with me too. And I was ready to lose it with him. I swear I was. I thought it would be a good idea, as opposed to one of the jerks in school, and Betsy agreed with me, not that she knew anything. I remember when Westwind got its first Twin Otter, he took me up in it. And we were over the Big Horns in great weather, and I thought maybe he would flip on the autopilot like in the movies and draw the curtain and I was just going to jump on him, right on his seat, if he didn't jump on me first. I guess Otters don't have autopilots though and it never came up.

Once Mom started with the airline, dad sold all our service contracts to the heavy hitters and hired on with Burlington Northern—welding ribbon rail out to new mines and stuff like that. But he quit real quick and went to work for McMahon Construction, which is out of Salt Lake City, and he got to be a big-shot with them mighty fast. I guess he had to go down to Salt Lake a bunch and the jobs kept getting bigger and more complicated. Mom didn't like him having to be with all these out-of-town people all the time. I remember one time at dinner she called him "Mr. Big Man On Campus" and me and Betsy had to get her to explain that to us later. That always stuck in my head. But Mom switched jobs too. After Westwind, Mom went to work for Amax, doing payroll at their office in town, and dad, I guess he got to be an even bigger shot. We all grew up and out is the thing.

Now we got a K-Mart, two Kwik-Marts, a Colonel Sanders, a Wendy's, a Ramada, a Quality, a Best Western, about a dozen booze-bins with drive-up windows, a Macs, a Holiday Inn of course which is one of those Holidomes with the pool inside and all, a couple 7/11s, more bars than's worth counting, a bunch of softball fields for summertime, High Plains Honda and Cut-Across Kawasaki, a new hospital across the street from the Long John Silver's, Pizza Hut, Econo Lodge and Taco John's, + we got subdivisions up the ubangy and all the people that comes with them. I remember once I went to the Super 8 motel when dad was building it and he let me go up on the roof with him. He pointed to the old part of town and said, "A few years ago you might find yourself stepping in a serious pile of horsecrap right outside the Paramount Theater." Now of course you're more likely to be run over by some tanked guy in his 4×4 late for his shift. But the thing is, it gossips just like the cowtown it was when I was little.

Mom says it was really just a sneezetown, you know, where ranchers took cattle to the railroad and bought supplies and sat around Bobbie Sue's shooting the shit, drinking coffee and eating her pies. She says it was slow even for Wyoming, which is pretty slow. You know what a sneezetown is—if you sneezed you missed it driving through—that's what Mom called them on our drives back then. I remember Betsy made up one for towns smaller than Mom's. She called them blinktowns—like Shoshoni and Story. And so I had to come up with one better than that. So I called the smallest ones tit-towns, like Spotted Horse and Ten Sleep, which were towns so small you could keep your eyes open and look right at them and still not see them. The reason I called them tit-towns was to tease Betsy, about hers.

GRAVES

Once we moved to town everything started going much faster for me and Betsy too, like smoking doobies in the car on the way to school and things like that. We both got jobs at the Holidome. Betsy worked in the gift shop selling candy and postcards and little statues of animals made out of coal, and I waited tables. First I waited in the Cafe Kauai ("A Touch of the Tropics Amid the Fast-Paced World of Energy"—yeah right!) but then I got them to switch me to Jesse's bar and disco, after a lot of big tips from guys made it obvious. With makeup I looked older than 17, and me and Samantha—she gets called Amazon Sam she's so tall and big-boned, she's got this wild red hair with bangs and braids and all and she's a real looker—anyway, me and Sam we were a good team, which the management people liked.

The Holiday is THE class bar in town, not many fights and a pretty good class of people. It doesn't have as much of what townies call your scum and riffraff as Wilby's or the Terminal or even Ranchers—the bar not the bank. I mean, at the Terminal it's not if there's going to be a fight it's when. Jesse's and the Roaring '20s get the best bands too. They come in every two weeks. It might be rock or disco or Las Vegas, just depending.

The stuff me and Sam did to some of those guys in the bands after their shows, or let them do to us, or together with them in their rooms, was really unbelievable. The desk clerk always made their rooms in the corner up on the third floor, facing the back parking lot—which was just a bunch of semis sleeping—so we could party hearty without getting anybody angry. The guys in the bands were usually pretty tired and discouraged, cause there's not much audience reaction here on account of the drink being so heavy all around—which comes from the work is how I explained it to them. People here don't care what they play as long as they play loud. So we'd try to cheer them up.

Sam and me were a team. We'd clear the drinks fast after the last set and wipe up the tables. We'd tease some customers, mostly out-of-towners because we didn't want anyone to get an attitude on us that lives here. Some of the same people you see night after night, and you see who they're with. It can be funny. So after we finished work we'd go up to the rooms and sometimes we were even there first—if the band was hanging around the bar having a last one. We could get in because we had a passkey that Dean gave us on the sly.

Dean was one of the maids—he was this guy, this funny guy that came out all the way from Tennessee and couldn't get on with the railroad, so he ended up cleaning rooms to make ends meet for the time being. He was a scream. Just this short little Southern boy with the accent and the muscles and you'd see him moping around the halls in the afternoon with his cart and his sheets and his little purple antiseptic sprays and he'd be wearing his "#1 in People Pleasin'" Holiday Inn name tag. One day I felt so bad for him and also I realized how cute he was that I followed him into the maid's closet where he was getting his soap refills and started making out with him and ended up giving him a real fast blowjob.

It was pretty stupid, but it was cool. After he came he went, "Randi, y'all are #1 in people pleasin'." We laughed so hard. It was good he said something right then cause I didn't know what in the hell to say. It was after that that he gave me the passkey. Then sometimes he'd come down to the bar and say, "Y'all fixin' to do some people pleasin' ta-night?" I think he was a little jealous of the guys in the bands.

Some nights if we were in the mood, me and Amazon Sam put on big production numbers when they'd come upstairs. One time we went into the closets of Posse, this real kick-ass band, and put on a bunch of their stage clothes, and a couple times with these really good guys from The Predators we pretended we were expensive call girls from Beverly Hills. But we never got paid. I mean, we probably could of if we wanted to, since it's about 6-to-1 single guys to girls around here—so you don't exactly have to be Xavier Hollander to get action. The police chief got in trouble cause he told some guy at the Daily Call that the reason we don't have a prostitute problem like down in Rock Springs is because the girls in Gillette are so dumb that they give it away for free. So the guy went and put that in his column. Can you believe that? Chief Dyckman, what a pantywaste.

Besides, usually it was a lot of fun. Sometimes not so much if the guys in the band started thinking that we were theirs or something, but that didn't happen much. We tried to make sure that didn't happen. And if any of them started to get attitudes on or the littlest bit rough, which happened once or twice with some of the older guys, we would just split right away. We had good rules about it so it would never get bad. Like if there was a husband-and-wife team or boyfriend-girlfriend in the group, then you just didn't handle that merchandise. Because it wasn't worth it, the trouble.

I mean, the whole thing was for it to take us somewhere else anyway. Like we were on the road with them. Or like we were in the band. Also, we didn't want the bands to think that there was nothing good about this place. So we were like their little welcoming committee. We'd bring drinks up from the bar. I'd always have a vodka sour and Sam would have a Tom Collins and then we'd both have screwdrivers. And we'd always joke about the

screwdrivers in front of the guys—just how we said the word. We'd
have doobies with us all the time and if I got really cracked I'd
feel like I had the whole world inside of me and it felt good.

It wasn't bad. I don't think it was bad even though I'm not that
way now. I think now I'm a lot more conservative. Or maybe I'm
still the same way, only it's with only one person.

GRAVES

Some girls think it's stupid to screw around with a lot of guys. But
most of them—it's just because they're scared + they don't have
any experience. It's not because they <u>know</u>. I think the only one
I know that's got a right to say that is Annie, and that's only because
of what happened to her made her paranoid, which I can't blame
her for.

Annie's the real attention-getter around here. She's thin and
damn near always tan, which is a trick in Wyoming + she's got
eyebrows and skin like Brooke Shields. Only she's older, like 21,
and she's got this beautiful long blond curly hair and these super-
blue eyes—which look so cool when she's tan. And sometimes she
goes crazy on Ladies' Night at Roaring '20s—which is really Men's
Night, right, cause all the women get drunk cheap and don't act
much like ladies. Anyway, sometimes Annie will do a headstand
on her table. And whoever she's dating just has to sit there and
watch along with everybody else. She likes to see how long she
can hold it and take a sip of someone's drink with a straw at the
same time. It seems impossible, but it's not. One time she even
got 86'd, because she was carrying on for so long that everybody
stopped dancing and buying. The bouncers have walkie-talkies
there, and they all circled around her at the same time and carried
her out still half upside down. A white t-shirt, short short blue
jean shorts and sandals is all she had on.

Anyway, Annie used to work laying track for Burlington Northern. Some people say that B.N. hires women just so the foremen
can fuck them. Because the track crews always end up a long way
from town, and camp is wherever the bunk cars are—on some

siding a long way from no place—so that sort of figures. Because the girls don't work that much on roadbed. Big O, who's this B.N. foreman from Seattle, he's 23 and he's got this Fu Man Chu mustache—he had a crew working south of Sundance last summer—and when you ask him about girls on his crew, he always laughs and goes, "I always keep one hanging upside down in my room for a spittoon." But he's just joking. He's a good guy.

So one night last fall Big O and me had pizza and Heinies at the Pronghorn watching big-screen football, and he told me—and he was being serious this time—that after mess one night Annie took 5 guys on her top bunk in the sleeper and then 4 after that out by the siding. And supposedly some of the guys she did it with were M.W.C.—Mexicans Without Cards—which is really what nobody could believe. Of course the story got around the camp. So the next day her gang boss had her setting spikes in the morning and drilling them in in the afternoon, as kind of a joke. And supposedly, nobody talked to her that day. Not even the other girl on her gang.

Big O said that after dinner the next night Annie got chased down the tracks by 5 crew who were fucked up to the max, and that they had a jar of vaseline and they were scaring the shit out of her. I asked him were they M.W.C.? And he said, "No, they were all just N.A.M. But she ran a mile down the spur, hitched back to town and never came back to work. I made sure the railroad sent her her back pay." (N.A.M. means "Normal American Man" or "Men" by the way—which was like a joke that Krysten Thompson, one of the bartenders at the Antler, started using last year just talking with other girls, but then the guys picked up on it and started to use it too so the joke sort of changed.) I told O, "All everybody knew was that Annie was working track crew one day and the next day she wasn't." And he goes, "That's why."

Word is that some of the guys around town and her stepdad in Arizona support her now. She paints windows of storefronts for fun sometimes, nature themes like rainbows or maybe psychedelic if it's a record store. Last summer she blew everybody on the Merchants' softball team so she's got a lot of contacts for business. At least that's what people say. Also she's got some kind of kidney failure and a strapped-on little bag of blood-cleaning stuff going into her guts that she won't let anybody see. Most of the guys that know her think it's a big turn-on or something, but Annie stays away from the beef now. She can't take it.

GRAVES

Sitting here, 4:53 a.m., watching the water truck spray down the haul road, sitting down in the pit, waiting to get dumped on, klieg lights just about burning through my safety shades, sitting here it seems to me like school was forever ago. But it was hardly more than a year ago I was sitting there in Bio dying to get out. I mean, what was I going to use all that stuff for out here?

It was worse for the boys, because none of them even wanted office jobs, where you'd figure some girls might end up in an office. So they'd be sitting there studying, let's say how frogs excrete stuff for example, and their buddies would be out in the oil patch pulling in beaucoup bucks and being out all hours and drinking while these guys were still doing homework about shit. Friday afternoon there'd be a parking lot party after school if the weather was decent and you know these guys would come off the rigs and cruise by in their new pickups and they'd have a keg in back and they'd be sort of recruiting guys out. I mean a lot of them used to be guys' classmates. So the dork standing there in the lot with his books in his saddle bags feels like a total wimp.

I remember when Clint Cooper came by one Friday in his new longbed Bronc. He was sitting in back, almost laying down, drinking Jack out of a beer mug. And all the girls came up and some guys too, and so he says to Troy—who was an old friend of his that stayed in school for senior year—"Hey Troy, which would you rather do? Sit in there studying the frigging Constitution or come on out and drill!" So Troy went over and threw his Civics book in the dumpster by the loading dock and drove off with them. I think he did it to show the girls more than Clint. Coach Olfson was pissed! That's why our football team always sucks the big one. Best boys always quit for the oil patch.

It's not that I didn't like learning stuff in school, because I did. Weather was interesting, and History except I could never remember dates. I liked writing stories, but teachers said it wasn't as much for me as I was for it. The best one I did was one I made up out of one of those math story problems. I remember the first part exactly. It went, "Mr. Smith lived in one town and had to drive 50 miles to work in another town." The deal was, was it better for him to drive that far if the cost of gas was X or something and his mileage was Y, or to move to the 2nd town where the apartment rent was Z dollars more? So I just took that situation and made up a story about Mr. Smith. Mrs. Grant said she thought I was onto something, so I did a few more the same way but they were never as good as the one about Mr. Smith. Maybe the problems weren't as good.

Basically I was smart but I hated the tests and the dress code and all the normal B.S., teachers treating you like you're 12 years old. When it got the most boring, I'd sit there and watch the snow blow outside the window and totally space and they'd always call on me, especially if I was high. I'd look at them and not know what to say and all I could think of is what they must look like screwing. Sometimes I'd be giving an answer—you know, "Rugby, North Dakota is the geographical center of North America" or like "Gatsby wanted to believe in the American dream," or whatever stupid thing that the subject was—and I'd just start laughing at the thought of Mrs. Tressel on her hands and knees.

There were plenty of times I thought of splitting early. I had plenty of day job offers. But Mom wasn't about to let either me or Betsy take off from school. She wanted us to go to college big-time. I don't think dad cared that much about it. Mom's the one that kept us in school. One reason was because she was trying to turn us into these star dancers. See, we had both given up on waterskiing and she was real disappointed about that. We still did it, but we didn't compete—because we liked snow skiing a lot better.

So I guess she thought we needed a new thing to do. I liked the dancing part of it but the Mom part was UGH. I had this yellow spangled costume. Sometimes I danced during my whole lunch period at school. Then Mom entered me in the Junior Miss Pageant for Wyoming and I came in 5th. But I won the prize for best interpretive dance to a contemporary piece of music—which I used "At Seventeen" by Janis Ian for—cause it's real sensitive to things, especially things the boys don't listen to or know about, that kind of folk music.

I didn't really know why I was trying for Junior Miss but I didn't mind showing off, which is all it really is. Mom said it would be a good experience for me. We were in town once picking out a swimsuit which would be like the one in the contest—so I could start getting tan and wouldn't have lines in the wrong places—and we just couldn't find one that fit me right and after about 7 suits with Mom pinching and poking like she was trying to make me petite or something, I just started crying.

Then Mom said, "When you finish with this whole thing you will come out on the other side with something that no one can ever take from you." That's all, like she thought I knew what it was I'd have, like it was obvious. After a while I said, "What?" And she just goes, "Poise."

Great, so I'll be poised. Big deal, right? The real reason I think she had me doing Junior Miss was because there's money in that kind of exposure + a college scholarship if you win. I think that was Mom's alterior motive. If I got a scholarship then I'd about have to go to college. But she didn't want Betsy to feel like she was favoring me, so she got her entered in a dance contest in Laramie and she won 3rd prize for a real rev-up to "Takin' Care of Business," which was real good for her class.

Dancing was about the only good part of school. Since we never had boys around—there aren't any boys out here who would dare do Creative Dance—we had to pretend taking the guy's part in duet dances sometimes. It was funny to lift Betsy. I remember when I started getting different muscles than I had from water-skiing. I wasn't sure how much I liked that. But we rehearsed every day anyway.

And then one day at lunch before this Casper talent contest thing Betsy comes up to me all hysterical cause she—Virgin Betsy I called her since she didn't spread herself around so much as other girls—cause Virgin Betsy comes up to me and says she's pregnant, by God-damn Neil who I can't stand to begin with. She says, "Mom

30

and dad can't know about this, they can't." I told her they wouldn't find out, and she just kept saying about how they can't know, especially dad, because it would be all over if he knew. Then she said she couldn't wait till after the talent show cause the thought of dancing with a fetus was enough to make her vomit, just the thought.

So we decided to get it taken care of, without messing with school counselors—who always rat on you—but with all sorts of tears. By me, not Betsy. I drove her to Rapid City to have it done, and waited for her. The waiting room had these big wide colored stripes on the wall. I just remember sitting there reading this copy of Glamour and trying not to cry.

When we drove back, I was being Mrs. Big Sister about it—real calm and helpful—right up until we stopped at the Dairy Queen in Spearfish for dinner. And then I just started bawling about it. I don't know why. I really got hysterical for a second—just thinking about her being able to have a baby already and picturing what it must of looked like, even though I kept trying to get that out of my mind. Betsy was okay though, she was better than me. She didn't cry. She told me, "It wasn't so bad as they say." So I said, "What does it feel like?" And she just said, "Sort of deep and sort of cold."

When we got back in the car, Betsy cranked the tunes and we shared a doobie. She was sure we were going to be stopped by the state trooper for speeding and then Mom and dad might find out where we were and come on with the questions. So I drove so slow it was funny. I drove about 45. She kept telling me to go slower. We kept laughing when the trucks zoomed by us and shot us looks in their mirrors. The whole thing was like slow-motion. Which was great cause we didn't really want to get home anyway. By the end of the ride she promised she was going to break up with Neil and we were superclose. You should of seen us dance in that talent show. First place.

DAYS

Soon as school was over I was trying to get enough money to move out of home, so I was working for dad at McMahon + working Jesse's at night like usual. After a while I got enough to move in with Sam. She was renting a trailer out in Outer Limits. It was a single-wide and I slept on the sofa but it was good to be on my own. Because it was hard enough working for dad without having to go home with him—Jesus it was like we were married or something, seeing each other all the time. And I was sick of hearing him and Mom go at it through my bedroom wall. That little prefab wall was about ready for my fist. Whether they were making nice or making mean, I didn't want to hear them anyway.

One night, after I came back from work it was about 3:00 and dad had just got in, probably from the Outlaw Inn. I heard Mom say, "Damn it Peter, ever since you took up with those construction people you've been acting like such a big-shot." He just goes, "Well, excuuuuse me"—like he's Steve Martin or something. Then no one said anything for a while.

And then Mom goes on, "Spending all your time down there building Wright, spending all that time with those out-of-town people, you think you're too good for us." I could hear Mom had those real Mom-tears in her voice and dad shoots back, "Well, if Amax gave you anything more than shit work you'd be happy for me." And it went on from there, like a lot of nights. A lot of nights, they'd be fighting and screwing and screwing and fighting. It got to the point with the sounds from in there that I couldn't tell which was which.

Dad was building Rustler Steakhouse and also some of Wright

for ARCO. Wright's not going to have stores on a street or any-thing—everything faces inside this mall. There's the library, the P.O., Kountry Kuts beauty shop, Jordan's food mart, a fast and a slow restaurant, and a True Value. We were building the True Value.

I learned a lot on that job—some brick work, a little carpentry, but most of it was concrete. That's what I liked best, concrete flooring. We were so careful on that floor. I remember standing by the mixer afterward wondering was it going to be okay?—when I thought that it wouldn't be flat because the earth isn't flat. It's supposed to be <u>perfectly</u> flat. But how could anything be perfectly flat? There would be a weensy curve to everything. The guys just laughed at me and thought I was joking. So I went along like I was.

I didn't mind working construction. McMahon was a good outfit and they were in the money so they had a softball team and picnics and all, beer busts every Saturday after work on the company. But I didn't really like working for dad. It was like he was harder on me than anybody cause he didn't want them to think that I got the job cause I was kin + I'm a girl. I got used to that. Also, some of the guys got on him after a while and told him to ease up. When we were working on the new hospital, we were pouring the ramp to the helipad for the medi-choppers to use and it started raining, and dad got all jinked out that it wouldn't cure right. So he yelled at me about my leveling. Then I overheard Bobby Douglas tell him, "Ease up Peter. She does better leveling than anybody." And he meant it. The guys accepted me pretty good.

But dad kept hassling me, like even over my clothes. It got so every day I came to work not wearing a bra he threatened to fire me. He said I was distracting the guys. Bull. A bra wouldn't have anything to do with me distracting them or not. I knew how to if I wanted to and most of the time I didn't. The real deal was he was looking hard at this Shari girl who's 23 and from Denver and works for McMahon, and he doesn't want anyone else looking good around the job except her. It seemed like something funny was up with her. Cause from what I could see, all she did was carry around his clipboard.

So after he warned me this one time, I came back to work the next day with a t-shirt on and a work shirt over that but no bra.

The day got killing hot and we were in the sun so I took off the work shirt and he fired me. Right there and then. Then I really knew something was up. I just threw my level into the cement for him to fish out.

I remember driving back from Wright. I was so angry. I remember noticing this sign out by some huge ranch out there, it's got a picture of this big steer on it and says—

Van Horne Herefords
More Size More Pounds More Profit
The Proud Breed . . . with the white face

And that picture just reminded me of dad right then, I don't know why. Probably cause he's getting so pasty-faced and fat in his old age. Like he's such a cow. Like he's so full of shit. By a half-hour later I was near town and I was laughing about it—the bull head being this portrait of dad—but I was still pissed at him. I was feeling better though, because I had decided by then that I was going to quit the Holiday too and go to work in the oil patch for better bucks and a killer tan. Like fuck him.

DAYS

Sometimes I'm just about ready to give up. But I don't give up. Sometimes I'm just about ready to quit, but I don't quit either, because quitting means giving up and giving up means quitting and everyone accusing you of everything, including being a girl. And you accuse yourself when you do that of being a girl and worse things too. It's just that sometimes there's just too much stuff to hide out from. It's like I can't work it away or sleep it away. Or smoke it away or screw it away. It's just there no matter what I do and that's the scariest thing. It's like a thing, like The Thing That Wouldn't Leave. Like some bad monster, only it's inside me and I can't get it out. Sometimes when everybody else is around I can hide from it in the middle of them. Because everybody's voices are loud enough to drown it out, to drown out what it feels like. But then when I'm back by myself it gets so loud—it's like the thing has its own voice—and I want to turn it off, but there's no volume control and no OFF button. Sometimes I want to rip my own socket out of the wall and turn myself off for good.

DAYS

The last job I had before this one was roustabout. I remember my first day like yesterday. I got the job from some guys that knew me from dad's old company. They knew me back when I was a little girl and when I walked into their office they couldn't believe how much I changed. They knew I could work just looking at me + I ain't going to wimp out on them when things get tough because dad never did. (Say what you want about the Bruces, one thing we got in our genes is the anti-wimp chromosome.)

Driving out to the rig, I remember how happy I felt—no more balancing margaritas on high heels for sleazoid businessmen and no more answering dad. I was just looking out at the cows and the pronghorn and the sage and counting the hills, because the guys in the office told me the rig road was off to the right after the 4th titty hill past the Rawhide Creek bridge. (That's what a lot of the guys call them, those grassy pointy hills with those red scoria rock tops like nipples.)

So I counted the hills and turned off, scoping out all the little plants I used to know about—brown-eyed susan, shark's breath, pussy toes, littleflower bluelips, nice flowers. But then I see this sign—

THIS IS A RANCH ROAD NOT A RIG ROAD
SURVIVORS WILL BE PROSECUTED

—so I had to back all the way out, just swearing at these damn ranchers, you know turning into millionaires with their mineral rights and they still got an attitude on progress. I turned in another

35

half-mile down, and as soon as I saw the American flag on the top of the derrick I knew it was the right road. I drove up to the rig— waste water pouring into the mud crater, drill whining, and the pumps punching it out and then the vibration up on the platform— and figured, all right girl, SUMMER! It seriously beat McMahon, sitting around town pouring the Rustler parking lot.

I learned a lot out there, about drilling and the seismograph and how far down they go with these diamond bits. Also, what's dangerous and what's not. You had better know that. Gary Sloan, it was his rig, told me certain kinds of gas could mean an explosion and went, "I don't want to see you running around like that poor colored comedian on fire." If you work long enough out there, you'll see a lost finger or a joint or something. Second week I was out there Ronnie Lester's index above the top joint got mashed into pancake batter and they drove him howling back to the hospital in town. Everybody out there says you haven't done an honest year in the patch unless you've at least <u>almost</u> lost a finger or a toe or your mind.

When I think of last summer, I remember a line from a song in this movie Mom used to watch every time it was on T.V. She always made me watch it with her. It went on about how diamonds are a girl's best friend. So for some stupid reason I had that stuck in my head—you know the way that happens—and every time at the rig they were talking about the bit or the drill collar I would have that little melody up in my head and end up singing to myself, "Diamonds Are a Boy's Best Friend." Sometimes I would even whistle it, over and over, until one time Terry Teagle, this roughneck, said "All right Randi we're all ready for the rest of that God-damn song" and after that I only whistled it to <u>myself</u>.

But I liked working with the crew. They showed me everything I needed that I didn't already know. None of them was prejudiced about me. We liked hanging out, hitting the bars. One time we all went down to the laundry and threw our shit into the "Greasers Only" machines and just got wasted watching it go around and round. But usually we didn't even wash work clothes—you just wear them till they're disgusting and then throw them out and buy new ones. Nigger Rich is what everyone calls oil field trash and I was O.F.T. for the summer. I guess people think junking hopeless

36

clothes is being Nigger Rich. We didn't care. We all got bumper stickers that said—

DON'T TELL MY FOLKS I WORK IN THE OIL PATCH!
THEY STILL THINK I'M A PIANO PLAYER IN A WHOREHOUSE

People always say Gillette is not the place to sit on your butt and watch the grass grow—cause by the time you're done watching it someone will have run it over. And I felt that way more out there drilling with those guys than I ever did anyplace else. Because when you're out there, you think everybody else is doing a little less than you are. You know at night the lights on the derrick all the way up to the crown block make it look like a launching pad for a rocket, and sometimes it feels like you're going about that fast.

Not that you don't have any help. There's a lot of crank out there and greenies too. Say you're doing 16 on, 8 off for a couple days straight. Well, you need something. Sloan gave them out himself—it wasn't like it was behind anybody's back. I even saw a guy who was into mainlining crank right on the platform. Because it's mostly monotonous but then it's dangerous for a fast second and then it goes back to being monotonous again. I pulled double-shifts, all-nights, back-to-backs, winch work, tank treater work, bringing up pipe, mud pumping, sending pipe back down. You hustle your butt off. If the night gets real cold you might hear a coyote to make up for it, and if the sun's too hot there's beer in the work trailer for everybody. But still you need fuel. Everybody knows it. It's no problem, except I didn't like it when Sloan got too snowed, cause then it got weird. He got weird.

That was my only problem, loose hands on the job. It's one thing to cop a little touch if we're all working together and I admit there was times rigging wires or pushing pipe that I did my share of it myself. Mostly it was just having fun and screwing around, being friendly. Like baseball guys pat each other's butts all the time. I never asked for nothing more than that, but one night last fall I got it.

I was on the other side of the truck to see about the hydrotarder clutch and just like that there's a hand in my pants. I turn and see it's Sloan, old friend of dad's and your basic good old boy. But he's pretty much the dispenser of my pay and now he thinks he's going to explore a hole that ain't his to drill + I don't even want to tell him how pissed he'll be to find out after all that work, it's dry. See, Sloan thought I had the hots for him, but it was just being friendly is all.

I said, "Damn it Sloan that ain't funny! That ain't shit! What the fuck are you doing?" He pulls his hand out from the back of my jeans and then he pulls back and gives me a little-boy "I'm sorry" look and gives me this real teddy-bear hug, real friendly. I remember thinking, It's over. He caught himself and that's it, we'll forget it. So I was breathing easy for a second. But then just like that he pulled me down to the ground. And the ground was all criss-crossed with tire tracks that don't lead anywhere, I remember feeling the ridges of them on my back in the dried mud. He's holding me down and says, "Randi do you know how long I've wanted to give it to you?" I say, "No, let me go." He's fucking laughing. Then he said something about his oil or something, I don't know, something weird, he was really wired, and I just said, "You're sick, man. Let me go."

I mean, what was I going to do, right? Screaming's not going to do any good over the noise of the winch pulling pipe and Terry and Red out by the treater shack and no ranch within miles to run to. What a fucking joke. All I know is I refuse, absolutely refuse, any sort of rape. But I didn't dare hit him, cause then maybe I really would of gotten it. So I looked him right in the eye like I was his friend and went "No way, no way Sloan. Just calm down, man, come on." And he seemed to go along with me a little. But he was still looking like an animal, real scary and hurting my back. He said something like, "I won't force myself on you baby but you can help out old Gary with your pants on too you know." So I guess we had just struck a bargain.

I remember the crank was turning my heart so fast I was spinning. I remember he held my shoulders down real hard while he stood up, and I told him to loosen up, but he wouldn't. When he dropped trou the clink of his belt buckle was like this ugly little explosion, and the sight of his rig was so God-damn, like, almost industrial I almost got sick to my stomach and I still do thinking about it. But I took it anyway cause it was the only way out. My mind was going so many ways—like what if Red came around to this side of the truck to check for a pressure violation or what if Terry needed the expansion pump from his truck, and what if they thought I <u>wanted</u> to do this. Because I really liked those guys.

Sloan was trying to talk all this sexy bullshit to me but at least the machinery was loud enough to cover that up, and I <u>tried</u> to space-out pretending it was a Good Humor X-15—you know, like thinking how much I used to love those when I was little—so it wasn't so impossible. And I was trying to do it quick but it was like he was holding back. God, the temptation to chomp down was so big. I should of really done it, but I didn't. So I was doing it, and it kept going on, and it seemed like it was going to end real soon, but then all of a sudden there were these headlights in my face. I thought, Shit it's crew from Davis #13 going past us on the rig road. It felt like their lights were on me forever, even though it was probably just a second, cause the road curves around. But it was like they flashed their brights on and then off again.

So of course Sloan needed more time then—cause it screwed up his concentration or something—so I had to keep going and going and then finally he finished and I gagged and tried to spit it out cause it was worse than the oil and the mud and the gearshift lube fluid and everything else that they ever invented. And I remember not saying a word to any of them for the rest of the night and I changed back into my street clothes in the work trailer and didn't say anything all the way home.

Terry dropped me at Sam's. He was nice. He knew something was wrong, but he was nice enough not to pry about it. I remember I shivered when I stepped out of the truck, like you do when you've taken some awful-tasting medicine. So I went into the trailer, it was early morning and Sam was sleeping. I wanted to throw things, really, just throw things, but she used to get off late at Jesse's and I always tried to be quiet for her. So I took off my boots at the door and got some lighter fluid from below the sink and went out behind the trailer and threw my work clothes down on the dirt and lit them and watched them burn.

DAYS

I liked the oil patch okay while it lasted. I liked working outside,
way out of town, specially in summer. But you burn out fast out
there + when it starts getting cold a lot of the good goes out of
it. Not that I quit because of the cold. It wasn't hardly winter yet.
I worked out there for a few more months after it happened. I
tried to forget about it and it got so I didn't think about it. I got
put on another rig, same company though. Eventually I just told
the guys I was tired of it + I didn't like the cold. I got a better
job is the thing.

What happened was I was at Roaring '20s on Ladies' Night,
getting shitfaced with Spike and the crowd—Joleen, Darryl and
Mike, Reggie, Annie was there, Sam of course—and Spike went
to take a leak. He always says you don't buy beer you rent it. So
he's off paying the rent and this guy comes over and asks me to
dance. I said "Cool." Because you never know what it might lead to.
Not that I really wanted to dance, cause Power Tools was playing
that night and they're pretty metal and I don't really like dancing to
metal. No one does really. You more just move around and yell
over the music, unless it's a slow song you can slow dance to.

So I got out there on the floor with this guy, he's an older guy,
maybe 25, 26 about, and he seemed a little loose too. I'd seen him
around. And he says, "You're Randi right?" Right. We dance some,
and I'm trying to figure him. And then he shouts something about
being over to the Amax office the other day talking about some
leasing thing and he ran into my Mom, who I guess told him I
wasn't having the peachiest time in the oil patch. Because I told
Mom that, but not all the reasons why. I couldn't hear everything
he was saying. But I did hear him say something about coming out
to work at someone's ranch. I shouted, "Hey, fuck that!" but
friendly, in a friendly way. I mean, there's no pay in ranchwork +
I'm not a shitkicking cowgirl. And if I was a shitkicker I wouldn't
be at the '20s, I'd be at the Antler or Hole-in-the-Wall, and hell,
if he was a shitkicker he would be too! Not that you can always
tell—cause now you see a guy running around town in tennis shoes

you figure he's a rancher and you see a guy in cowboy boots you figure he's a miner.

Anyway, this guy says, "No no no Randi, not ranch, branch. Split Branch." So I thought, Shit yeah! but I don't say nothing right off cause I wanted to know what his alterior motives were before I played my hand. He goes, "And your friend Samantha, your Mom told me about her, that's her over there right?" I say, "Who does it look like?" He goes, "Well she can come down too if she wants. If you guys pass a few tests you can start training in a week, and not in the office either." Well, I figure Split Branch ain't that pretty a mine and he's just wanting a little better scenery around there + I figure everyone knows what Mr. Peanut President said down in Denver last month about the Equal Opportunity thing in energy—because it was in the Daily Call. So now I got it totally figured why he's chasing tail at Roaring '20s. So I tell him, "Sure, I'll show up Monday with Samantha." I wasn't going to argue with the money and security of a mine job. No way. Then we both sort of stood there moving around, just sort of grinning at each other. I mean we were both faced.

Well, as all this was going on I saw Spike had come back from the head and was looking around for me. So I was trying to keep the guy in between us so Spike couldn't see me dancing with him, which wasn't easy, cause there weren't many people dancing— because like I say, no one much likes dancing to metal. So then I saw Spike saw me and when he did I shot him a "Hold on" look, but I could tell he was pissed about it.

So after Mr. Equal Op left I went right over to Spike and Sam and called a huddle. And a few friends got up from their table and joined. It's like a football huddle, only everyone puts their arms around each other—we do it when something big comes up or there's going to be a fight and we have to figure out what to do or if we got to decide to stay or go to a different bar. So we huddled up, and I said, "You guys will not fucking believe this—some guy from Keller Coal, that guy I was dancing with" and Joleen goes, "I wouldn't call that dancing Randi" and everybody laughs, and I said, "Shut up Jogi, listen to this, that guy just got me and Sam into SPLIT GOD-DAMN BRANCH!!!" And everyone went crazy, except Darryl who had about 10 applications circular-filed at mine offices around town. I remember hugging Sam and Spike and Spike hugging Sam, and Reggie, who runs the shovel down at Black Thunder, ordering a round on him and then we really started partying hard. It was the happiest night.

Then I remember me and Spike making out at the table, just kissing for the longest time. I remember a lot of music, screwdrivers for half-price that other people were paying for, fingers in my hair. Spike has the most beautiful pair of hands. Thinking about them any time of day is liable to set me off. They're strong and soft too cause he works out so much with the gloves and sometimes I hold the heavy bag for him when he works out in his basement. Then Power Tools started playing "Stairway To Heaven" and a lot of people danced, cause it was about 4:00 and they always play it for their last song.

Spike was holding me real tight. I was teasing him in his back pockets, and he was squeezing me back in mine. I could feel he was thinking about something, and I said "What?" And he came on about how seeing that man dancing with me when he came back from the head made him think. Especially before I came over and told everybody what was what. So I said, "What did it make you think?" And then he pulled my hair back and whispered up close to my ear—he asked me if maybe I wanted to get engaged, just privately, without telling anybody.

DAYS

That's how I got set up at Split Branch and set with Spike all in one night and here I am driving Wabco belly-dump #2022. That's the way it goes here—nothing happens nothing happens nothing happens and then all of a sudden everything happens in about a second. I've been engaged to Spike and stripping coal a little over 7 months. Mostly it's been cool.

I've progressed pretty far in hauling already, which is Level 5 out of 9 levels. But the company didn't hire me and Sam to haul, they hired us to be two of the three girls on the first all-woman blasting team in the country. That turned out to be pretty much the point. They got a lot of good publicity out of it too. Media Relations down at company headquarters in Texas arranged all these photos for us, and we did a local story for the Daily Call, a story for the Rocky Mountain News, and one for U.P.I. service that supposedly went all over the world. It was good for the company to get the publicity.

I remember when we were doing the Rocky Mountain interview, they flew this little nerdy guy up special all the way from Denver for it. And he shows up with a tie and sports jacket on and leather shoes. Like what was he expecting? So at the office they gave him cloppers to put over his shoes—it's fedreg, cause you're supposed to have steel-toed boots—and his hard hat and his safety shades, and drove him out into the pit. And it's about zero out and the wind is blowing his notebook pages all over and he's following us around on top of about a zillion tons of coal, while we're packing powder and rigging for a blast, and he's asking questions which half the time we can't hear. We showed him about the ammonium nitrate and the mixtures with fuel oil, and we drilled a few holes for him with our new Robbins RR11-E, which is a real mother, and he was in the truck with us when we blasted. When he felt the charge and saw the coal come down, none of us said nothing cause we were waiting for him to ask us something. But then he just said in this dorky voice, "Hey, that's impressive!" Well, it is, sure.

But this guy, he kept tripping over coal chunks when he tried walking and taking notes at the same time and every time he tripped one of his cloppers would come off his shoe and he'd have to kneel down and put it on again. By the end of his tour, he was asking us dust-parts-per-million questions and environment-type questions and both the knees of his little blue pants were black. Me and Sam laughed so hard when he left. We kept thinking about him walking into his little suburban house outside Denver that night and his mousy little wife coming to the door and going, "Honey, where have you been!"

The company liked the story, it was in the Sunday edition. There was a big color picture of us loading a hole and one with

Sam's finger on the trigger. Except they didn't like one thing about it. The Media Relations guy called up from Houston and told us it was all great and stuff, except that I was quoted in the wrong way. He said that I shouldn't call it a strip mine, that I should call it an open pit mine instead, like in the B.B.Q. sauce. Well EXCUUUSE ME!!!

The name everybody called us, I think the company started it, is "The Boom-Boom Girls." It was me and Sam and Melody, who is the senior girl, 24, and had the blasting experience already when we started. We took a lot of pride in it, and we were better than some of the regular crews you see around at Rawhide and Eagle Butte and Clovis Point and just about any mine you walk into. We didn't take shit from anybody, except maybe our boss. We knew what we were doing. After the first article, the local one, Jim Ruhman in maintenance saw us coming off shift, and hollered out, "Hey, how are the P.R. Girls?" I hollered back, "P.R. don't make the coal come down, asshole!" After that, no problems.

Blasting is not as dull as the other jobs. You can see what you've done, you can see your accomplishment, and you're not cooped up all day in the machinery. When you're hauling spoils or coal, it hardly seems like you're making a dent. It's so little-by-little and it takes forever. Blasting, you make a big dent. It's like a little thrill, after doing all the drilling and filling, to call in the warning sequence, and then BAM—the impact going right through your feet all the way to your ears—and then dust everywhere for a while like a cloud just minding its own business, in no rush to leave. And then the coal will come down, just clean and loose and it almost looks soft, a nice collapse. We did that—I did that—is what you think.

The only problem with being a Boom-Boom Girl was having Bob Zorn for the boom-boom boss. Now he is a prejudiced guy anyway, you should hear him go on about fat people, not to mention your red and your black. But the problem was that when we went to another mine to watch a blast or go through some new mixing techniques, whatever it might be, he tried to make it look to the men at the other mine that he was sleeping with us or that one of us was in love with him. That's what he made it look like. It might just be him making a little joke that you could take two

44

ways or something like that. I mean, what are we going to say, in the middle of Black Thunder or Belle Ayr with him winking at them while he's talking feed tubes and drill holes. I mean, come on! One time, he took us up to Colstrip, Montana to see a new blasting technique they're doing and first he said we couldn't go unless me or Sam stayed in his motel room with him overnight. Little smart remarks like that. And then he says to us that neither of us is going to heaven—because we haven't been baptized. He really said that one time.

Even with him crawling around, The Boom-Boom Girls was about the best thing about the mine. Zorn's more like a garter than a rattler anyway (which by the way we saw one up at staging yesterday, dozing under a scraper, and when T.J. got on the scraper and drove off, the thing did not even <u>move</u> one inch, now that is cool). But we weren't known as Boom-Boom Girls at the mine— just outside it. Well, maybe some of the office people called us that, but down in the pit everybody called us "The Charged Holes." Me and Sam thought it was a scream, but it got Melody riled up when she heard it, cause except for the company she keeps at work (us!), her repute is not in dispute. Not at all. When we're punchy enough from work, Sam and me call her "The Plugged Hole," but never ever to her face. She's so nice you could cry.

SWING

I had a dream about this girl band, backstage at a concert in Denver. The lead singer had a chain on that said "Raven" and everybody in it was real good-looking, like a whole group of Pat Benatars. Not necessarily looking like her, but on that level of looks. And Sam was the bass player. She was the only one I knew. And I joked to her that the band should get new outfits, silver jumpsuits with monster platform shoes. No one laughed though. Then this person on the dressing room phone came and got me and put me on. The operator said it was an "Emergency Breakthrough" call. She went, "I have a party of Dad Bruce that needs to talk to the party of Randi Bruce, are you that party?" I go, "Yeah." She goes, "Hold the line while I get authorization supervisation" or something like that. Then dad comes on and says, "Hey Randi Candy, how are you doing?" I tell him, "Fine, what's wrong?" He says, real calm, "How's our Samantha?" I say, "She's fine, dad what's wrong?" He just tells me he's at the Pronghorn watching Monday Night Football with some of his boys, and he's asking me who he should bet on, the Redskins or the Bears. How do I know? I can't believe he called an "Emergency Breakthrough" call to ask me something like that. Something so stupid. I just hung up. I expected he was calling about Mom and that there was something horribly drastically wrong at home. And in a weird way, I was a little disappointed that nothing was wrong. Almost like I was sad about it. But then Sam came over and showed me a headline in the paper. It said, "Devils Skate Against Penguins in Salt Lake" and everybody laughed. But I was still let down from the call.

SWING

Living with Sam is the greatest + having the same job again like we did at Jesse's makes things pretty easy. I mean, since I've got Spike and she doesn't have a steady, sometimes things are a little funny but never bad. She's the only one I told about the engagement. I had to tell someone.

People think that just because Sam's beautiful everything is easy for her but that's not true. Sometimes it's harder, cause even dogs get sniffed at in this town on account of all the boomers, and with her looking like she does it just never stops. Mostly she likes the attention and I'm not too jealous because I get enough. There's been one or two of the guys she's had that I really liked, but she said she wasn't happy enough about them to stay with them. I don't think they were rich enough for her is the thing. That's one way we're different.

I remember the first time I met Sam was a couple of summers ago. I was hanging outside the Rusty Nail waiting for some friends, we all had fake I.D.s and we were going to try to get in. Then I saw this girl lying on the hood of this pickup a few spaces away. She was lying on her stomach and she had on a purple halter-top and jeans and boots and she was reading a magazine that she had laying up against the windshield. She was just lying there, resting on her elbows and cracking her gum, and every couple of minutes she'd turn a page, and she kept clicking the heels of her boots together up in the air. I think she felt me staring cause she looked up and looked right at me. Didn't say nothing though, and just went back to turning pages. I guess I kept looking, cause she looked up again and just said real sarcastic, "Am I illegal or something?" I knew we'd get on right there.

So I walked over and said hey. Turns out she'd come down from Butte just for the summer. I asked why, and she said, "Looking for boys driving around in their Corvettes." She was the same age as me, 16. I said, "Aren't there any boys in Corvettes in Butte?" She looked at me like I was crazy. She said, "You ever been to Butte?" I said I was through there last summer, driving from Yel-

47

lowstone to Glacier with my Mom and dad and my sister. She said, "Well then, you know."

So then she asked me, "How did you like Butte as a whole?" I said it was okay. But then she said again, "How did you like Butte as a whole?" I told her, fine, like I said. So she starts going, "How did you like Butte as a hole. How did you like Butte as a HOLE?" Finally I got it. But she made me feel kind of stupid for a second. She said Bell Diamond was the deepest copper pit in the world, and I went, "I know that, you know. We took the tour." I guess Anaconda had stopped mining it so it was just a hole now. She said, "It's the pits, really." We started laughing.

Anyway her brother got laid off up there, and so he came down here for work and she was staying with him in a little apartment in the old part of town. She said, "This is his truck I'm laying on and this is his Playboy I'm reading." Her brother was inside, drinking with his buddies, and he had told her it would be just a few minutes and then he'd be out. But it was already an hour later. She was babysitting his truck for him—cause the passenger door lock was broken and he was afraid of it getting stolen, cause this was a lot where that could happen pretty easy. I remember I asked her, "You mind babysitting his truck?" And she said, "It's better than everyone babysitting me, back home."

When my friends showed up I told them to go on in cause I wanted to stay outside with Sam. And we sat up on the hood and watched the sun go down behind the Rusty Nail and she showed me funny things in the Playboy, like one of the centerfold's turn-ons was Willie Nelson—I remember we both said "Gross" at the same time—and we just sat out there and talked until it was dark and the mosquitos attacked us because of course we were under the one light in the parking lot. So we went inside the truck and rolled up the windows and waited for her brother. She turned on the radio loud, but after awhile I told her it was probably draining the battery so she turned it off.

She looked at me like she was glad I told her, but she was starting to get pissed at her brother. She just started swearing at him. Then she took his rifle off the rack behind us, and I said, "Hey what are you doing?" She put the rifle on our laps, and cocked it open, and fished out this little orange thing from the chamber. It didn't look like any kind of shell I'd ever seen. She said, "He always keeps one in here for emergencies." She unscrewed the top and put some stuff on her finger and then I knew what it was. I couldn't believe it. She put some more on her finger and put it under my nose and told me to breathe in real fast. I remember my nose going numb. It smelled like the dentist. I didn't really get it. That was the first time I did candy. Then she put the top back on the vial and put it back in the chamber and put the rifle back in the rack and said, "What he don't know can't hurt us."

Later when we were still waiting for him to come out, I got her phone number at work because she didn't have a phone at home. That summer she was part-timing at Hair Affair beauty shop. I asked her, "Why really did you come here for the summer?" And Sam looked at me and looked kind of aggravated, like it was something she already told me + it was obvious plain as day. She said, "I came down here to find rich men and money, that's what my grandma said was here." Then she started saying that her grandmother says the single men outnumber the women by like 10 to 1. I said, "No way it's that much." She said she thought it was true. I remember I told her that I lived here all year and no way is that true.

I remember thinking, How could she be so advanced if she was from Montana and I was still just hoping Hunter the Westwind pilot would smile at me when I drove out on the tarmac with Mom? I mean, really. We hung around most of that summer but then Sam had to go back to Butte for junior year. We kept up though, since Mom let me have one phone call a month for free + we sent each other Jackalope postcards. We made up a law that said the only kind of postcards we could send were Jackalope ones, and the rule was, the worse the better.

But in the middle of that year Sam dropped out of school and in spring her grandmother let her come back to Gillette and stay. She stayed with me at home for a few months—cause her brother didn't have room—and everybody liked her. Mom because she was so funny, and dad cause she was so pretty and tough and flirted with him, and Betsy cause it was like having an older sister that wasn't ever going to act like an older sister. And I think she liked living with us cause me and Betsy were like the sisters she never had—she just has all these brothers—and + her Mom had died in an accident when she was little, so. But she went back to live with her brother when he moved into his new condo, and she stayed with him up until she got her trailer in Outer Limits. Now it's our trailer.

It's a yellow Fiesta, about a 1975, so it's not too beat up. It's home-sweet-home for us so you better not complain about it if you want to be our friend. Not that there aren't things to bitch about, like the vomit green carpet or the shower that sort of drips out onto you so that if you don't move around when you're under it you could practically stay dry. We like to boogie around in there just the same, singing and hollering. Today before we drove out to work, Sam was in there singing "What A Fool Believes" by the Doobies. That's what she always sings when she's scheming about rich men, which I never really did much and hardly have to now cause I already got mine.

SWING

Spike is from Quad Cities, which sounds like something out of the Wizard of Oz but he tells me that's hardly right. The thing is, if you want to be oil & gas, you got to go where the oil & gas is. So he did. Came out a few years ago and now he's worked himself up to crew chief at Antelope Exploration. He says everything at home was as slow as the Mississippi, which I figure is slow. I've never seen it, but he hasn't exactly threatened to show me home, the way a lot of boys do. I've told him I'd like to take a driving trip back there to see where he comes from and meet his folks before we get married + I've never been east of the Badlands. But he always says, "It's just corn." And then I always say, "Well what's wrong with corn?" And it always stops right there. I don't think he wants me to meet his folks.

Spike says that was a whole nother planet back there, and when he left it he left it to leave it not to go back. He left on July 4th, 1976. He always makes such a big deal about leaving on the bicentennial day. He's told that story to everyone. He says, "Everybody was sitting around celebrating on their butts, and I was going somewhere." He drove straight out, with the little xeroxed employment booklet tucked up in the sun visor, got here and hooked on with Antelope right away. He hasn't gone back once in three years. Sometimes I think he doesn't even like to drive in that direction, even if it's only to Rapid for a concert.

I think there must be a lot of old girlfriends from Rock Island High back in the Quad Cities who'd be ready to scratch my eyes out or something like that, if he came back and showed me around. One night we were doing hash and Quervo, this picture came into my head like a dream of all these girls popping out of their hall lockers and hitting me over the head with cornstalks. Spike got hysterical laughing, and then I did too and we both ended up on the floor.

He always teases me about that now. Like once he rigged up my locker at work with an ear of corn tied to a broom handle so it fell out at me when I opened it—which was funny—but it's like he uses it to cover up that there's really something back there. He always says, "There's nothing back there." And that means including his parents, who he doesn't ever talk about and I don't think hardly talks to, and his little brother who goes to college in St. Louis. His brother sent him this program from a St. Louis Cardinals game he went to—which I thought was pretty nice—but Spike used it to balance the leg of his lopsidy kitchen table.

I love Spike alot even though he can be like that. When I tell Sam about this or that, she just goes, "Is he good to you?" And I have to say "Yes" cause he is, but he gets in screwy situations with his crew and some of these people who he calls friends. One of them is a developer guy that's building Grandview Hills for the really rich people, and Spike says this guy is cutting him in on some stuff but I can't figure why the guy would do that. I asked Spike once, and he told me, "I'm an investor" like he was telling me "Mind your own business, woman." Okay, so I do about that stuff.

He is good to me is the thing. I told Mom how serious we were—without saying anything about our secret—driving back to the house a few weeks ago. She drove into the garage and we just sat in there in the car talking for the longest time. She was treating me like an adult. At the end she said, "Would you still love Spike if he didn't have a great car and wasn't ever going to own a great house or ever be something in oil & gas?" I said, "Yes, course." She said, "Well then" and got out of the car, and I did too, and she gave me a big hug and I drove home. I think I might have been lying.

Only because if he wasn't going to have all those things he'd be a different guy and not necessarily a guy I would like, maybe like but not love. Not because of the things exactly but because he would be like a lot of other guys who are just wanna-be's. When I first saw him at Jesse's he didn't even look like a wanna-be. Me and Sam both liked his looks—I mean who wouldn't, unless you don't like supertall, dark and handsome—but he sat at my station and the rest is the rest. I keep wanting to set a date, so I can tell everybody, which I'm dying to, but Sam says just to be patient (it's been 8 months!!) and not to even ask him about it. She says "It'll spook him." Like what is he, a horse or something?

SWING

Hey, you, get off of my cloud! Hey, you, get out of my mine! I'm feeling so stupid today, just the things going through my head. 1 2 3 4 5 6 7 8 9. Give me a niner. Roger you got a niner. 10-count till blast. 9 8 7 6 5 4 3 2 1. Boom!

I cut on the radio and ask Blaine, who's blasting, in my most sexiest Pet-of-the-Year voice, "Oh, Blaine baby, was it good for you?" He comes on, "Damn, Randi! I really got my rocks off." Ha! But that's old. That's an old joke around here. The mine is alive, with the sound of blasting, dee de de dee, my truck is alive, with the sound of sniffling. Oh my, oh my gosh! What would Mom say? She'd say never take candy from a stranger. Mr. Stranger

Danger, no way. She'd say cross-on-the-green-not-in-between and watch out for Mr. Stranger Danger on Halloween. She'd say buckle up for safety.

I can see the tour bus up on the rim taking all the visitors around. They got their little hard hats on, they must feel real cool. They're showing them the one-and-only Split Branch Wildlife Enhancement Feature. Ta-da. The tour guide is going, "Our Wildlife Enhancement Feature shows you the success of our land reclamation success"—she's saying something like that. Well, boys and girls, the truth is the Wildlife Enhancement Feature is just some big rocks and a dead tree branch stuck in the ground which eagles are supposed to like. I guess it's supposed to enhance their wild lives. Ha!

"And the answer is: All the grass and rocks and topsoil and soil on top of the coal in a coal mine." Mary, in third fucking place, the question please? "What is overburden?" "That's right, what is overburden, or what is spoils?" Woooo! Hot damn! Fifty bonus points. Alright Mary quite untrary. I'm hauling spoils today and I feel spoiled. It's what you look out at on all those scenic turnoffs on the highway—spoils. Course we're going to put it all back when we're done. Done STRIPPING. Bah bah bum, da dum dum, Noxzema medicated afterstrip. Hey, you, get off of my cloud! Hey, you, get out of my mine! Never take candy from strangers—cause it will always I don't know. I mean, the moral of the story is, uh—

SWING

Today Mom called up about at 11:00 and said she wanted to meet me for lunch. I said okay, but it had to be early cause I had to go over to Spike's house before work to help him train for the Tough Guy Contest. Mom sounded like she was hot and about to boil over, only she was keeping the lid on until she saw me. I said, "Did I do something?" Because a whole week had gone by without her calling. So I thought maybe I did something. She just said "No" and that she'd meet me at Wendy's in an hour.

I went over there and sat and waited. The air-conditioning was hyper-ventilating like normal. Sam and me made up levels of Wyoming air-conditioning when we were working the Holidome. Hyper-ventilating is just plain cold, that's level 1. Knee-knocking is level 2, pretty uncomfortable, like at Skyline movies. Level 3 is Freeze-dried, like at Sunset Supermarket. Level 4 is Suspended-animation, which is where your teeth start hurting like at city hall. But we needed a level above Suspended-animation. So Betsy gave us the name for level 5, which she had just learned in advanced Bio. Level 5 is Kryogenic. That's like for those tour buses going to Rushmore and Yellowstone, where the senior citizens come off all stiff and blue.

So anyway, I just sat there staring out through all those plastic bead chains in all those colors, watching the traffic go by on 14-16. It's real old-fashioned, waiting for Mom, looking at all these old pictures of town they have up on the walls, that they blew up from 1910. All the fast-food places have old pictures of town on the walls. People getting bucked off horses and a lot of dust swirling around, that sort of thing. The sign out front under the main sign, in those black stick-up letters like the movie theaters have, says

WE'VE GOT
THE BEST
SINGLES
IN TOWN

It's said that for the longest time. They ought to change it. It's getting on people's nerves—like married or engaged people.

Finally Mom drives into the lot in our Honda Accord (which we always take a lot of shit for, since having a foreign car makes us real liberals out here) and she waves to me. I could tell standing in line to order she didn't look so good. "Double burger with lettuce tomato and onion—I got bad news," she goes, "terrible news today Randi—small order fries and a medium frosty—I should have known it all along but I didn't want to believe it." I ordered a shake, onion rings and a single with everything and asked her if she was talking about dad. She just goes, "Yes, to stay," and asks me if I got two pennies.

Mom's holding the tray and she nods her head in the direction of the window, like let's go sit over there. I went and got the salt and napkins and all, thinking, Oh shit, and went back and stared at all those old laminated ads on the table so I didn't have to look at her. Mom said this morning she called the Rec Center to schedule a racquetball time for her and dad later in the day. And the lady says, "Barbara, are you sure? Because Peter already played this morning." So Mom said, "That can't be. It must be a mistake. Wait, who do you have him down playing with?" I wonder what made her ask that.

Then the woman told her, "I have him down here playing with you, Barb." Jesus! So Mom goes and calls a friend who was at the center then and she said yes, she did see Peter there, playing this morning, on #4 court, with some girl. And when Mom asked what the girl looked like, her friend says, "Real young. Jet-black hair. Dark eyes. And *quite* a figure." Nice, huh? Like she had to put that in there about the figure. Some friend. So Mom calls dad right away at McMahon and I guess he decided right then the percentages weren't in pretending anymore. Mom told him to come home right away and he said "Fine" but Mom said when he came home he came home with the person who is "some girl"—who of course I know is Shari. And Mom says she just walked in like she owned the place. Mom said she told Shari to leave but dad said, "She's part of this whole thing, she should be here. Shari, stay." Like this bitch was a dog or something.

When Mom said all this stuff her eyes got so sad feathery and wet, and then I heard all the details about arguments and Shari splitting—in dad's car, can you believe it?—and Mom trying to kick and scratch dad and her frosty all of a sudden gave her the chills and she couldn't talk anymore. We just looked at each other.

I can't stand Shari, that scheming mouse, what does she care for anybody's happy home? I had suspicions, but no way could I have told Mom, no way. So Mom sat there not talking for a while. I pointed to her top lip cause she had a little chocolate mustache from the frosty, and she got mad at me—like how could I care about that now?—but I knew she'd want to know. She wiped it off with her napkin as soon as a little time went by so it wasn't like she did it because I told her to. I was really thinking about how

Betsy is going to take all this, still living at home. I was thinking about maybe her staying with me at Sam's. Because even on our floor would be better than moving in with Neil and his stupid friends, which I'm sure she's going do anyway next year when she finishes school, if they're still together.

I couldn't tell Mom she'd be better off without dad, even though it's true and I wanted to. So I told her it'll work out if they both try to make it work out and Mom had a mouth full of french fries and tried to say "I have not yet begun to fight" at the same time and gagged a little. It was kind of funny—we laughed right then thinking, God, men—while she cried on her fries, which I told her was the hard way to salt them.

I told her I had to leave to go pick up Spike cause I didn't want to make him wait. Mom goes, "Go ahead, don't wait on my account," real sorry for herself. She said she was going to sit there a little while cause she didn't feel like going home yet. When I walked out the door I could see her sitting there, lighting a cigarette. And then when I drove around the other side to go out the exit I looked through the window and saw Mom, standing in line again, searching through her purse for change for coffee. I keep remembering seeing her right then, through the glass in the restaurant light. Just the way she looked.

DAYS

I flipped shifts with Jay so I could go to the Tough Guy tonight. If I missed it I think Spike would just about kill me. Company is pretty good about letting us flip shifts, except you can't do it if it means you have to work a sweet 16, your shift and somebody else's straight through. Not that they'd care really. It's some fedreg thing. So here I am hauling day shift. Piece of rock, like we say.

I remember we both saw the sign about a month ago in the window of the Buffalo Hotel. It says:

BIKERS BRAWLERS BOUNCERS RANCHERS MINERS ROUGHNECKS
SO YOU THINK YOU'RE TOUGH?
Second Bi-Annual Tough Guy Contest
Big Prize Money
Country Fairgrounds August 23rd 8:00 p.m.

And it gives the number to call and all of that. I've memorized it cause Spike's got one taped up on his bedroom mirror, to psych himself up. We went to the first one last spring and it was a blast, except it drove Spike crazy cause he thought he could beat everybody, including the two pro boxers that fight at the end. It goes from town to town. So I challenged him. I said, "Next time it comes around, why don't you put your balls where your mouth is?" He said, "Don't worry."

Yesterday was his last workout. As soon as I got to his place I could hear the "umph umph umph" of the heavy bag downstairs. I walked down and held the bag for him, giving him a little resistance. I told him what's up with me and ran him down on the latest on Mom and dad. He just grunted. Then I held the jab-pad and moved around for his jabbing exercises. He doesn't even have to tell me what to do now, cause I know the routine by heart. I'm used to his squeaky shoes too—that's Spike's sound, you know how everyone has their own special sound—and his sneakers on that concrete basement floor is his. And the rosin is like his smell, like his cologne.

Then after the jabbing he did his lifting, and while he did that I worked on his robe for the fight. I designed it myself. It's got his name in all capital letters on the back over two lines of silver thread that look like rails. It's all done except a little of the K and all of the E. I can't wait till 3:00 so I can go over there and finish it and iron it, and give him a real good rubdown. It's really just a back rub, same as I usually do, but he says boxers call them rubdowns so this month we've been calling them rubdowns. He's got some pretty nice geography—it's like I've made a map of all his muscles in my mind and I know what they look like and what they feel like by heart.

But now giving him rubdowns is about driving me crazy. Because

57

this whole week he says we can't do it cause he has to save all his energy for the fight. So that's another reason I can't wait till tonight. I'm picking up his salt tablets and his bee pollen at the drugstore on the way over there + spaghetti for dinner. Only 45 more minutes. Getting psyched!

GRAVES

I sit here thinking about what happened. Just like I sat around all weekend trying to figure it out. I kept asking Sam questions, cause I thought she might be able to figure it out, but finally she got so frustrated with me she yelled, "Jesus Christ Randi, it's not like a board game you know, it's just life." After that I really needed to get wasted and I got plenty wasted, the whole rest of the weekend. I'm glad it's dark cause I don't want to see anybody around here.

What happened was I went over to Spike's, just like I said. And he seemed happy to see me, except he was nervous, which I could understand. I cooked him dinner and he was quiet. And he was quiet in the car going over to the fairgrounds, but I knew he was just nervous cause he wanted to make a big splash in front of everybody. I mean, he's always talking about how tough he is and how he knows how to box and now he's got to finally prove it. Because the results are going to be in the paper and there's no tables and chairs to use like in a bar fight + there's a $250 prize which he was counting on to buy the candygrams which he had already bought us—since he's so cocky—for afterwards. So we just drove over there. He drove, he always drives. And neither of us said much of anything.

We got to the fairgrounds and went in the old hangar-type building where they were having it and it must have been 95 degrees in there. He went off to register. There were already a couple hundred people in there—the teenyboppers, the Terminal Bar crowd, a lot of construction types and O.F.T. + some ranch families and a bunch of people from his work and my work. Sam and Annie were there, Betsy was coming, the whole Joleen and Reggie crowd.

I went over to Spike at the registration and he was telling them how he's from Rock Island—you give your age, weight, occupation, and where you're from, cause almost nobody is actually from Gillette. And then you draw who you're going to fight. He drew 4th, which meant he was fighting this guy who is a bouncer over at the 8-Ball Lounge.

We went and sat down and watched the first couple of fights. Spike didn't want to start warming up too soon and lose too much energy. He was really getting into himself. I was laughing at the card girls, ducking in and out of the ring in these red dresses, cause I knew them from high school. They were in the Paper Bag Club, that's what these guys called it. Because their bodies were great and paper bags for their ugly faces were only 10 cents. Spike laughed and I thought that was good, to make him less nervous. I mean, everything was fine.

The first fight was this Indian and this old rancher, and the rancher's wife and kids were carrying on in the front row. The rancher knocked him out, and his kids were jumping up and down and his wife got the whole thing with an Instamatic for their scrapbook. Spike just turned to me and said, "That's good. Now it's going to be a year before any Cheyenne comes to Gillette to prove anything." Which sounded funny coming from Spike, since ranchers are about one step above cows to him + I'm ⅛ Indian. But I wasn't going to say anything, not right then. Then in the second fight, some slip-form silo pourer really made this black guy look funny, funnier than he already looked since they're only about 5 in the county. Spike said real sarcastic, "He must have seen Ali on T.V. once and figured it just came natural." I guess it doesn't though. The guy really got clocked.

Then the 3rd fight started going and Spike went off to the corner to shadow box. He said, "Kiss me Randi" and I did. And then the weirdest thing happened—all these "Fight For Jesus" people came into the arena with all these posters and pamphlets and signs. And they started calling out "Jesus Loves You" and "Have You Heard The Word" and little slogans like "Save Yourself From Sin Through Him." It was like they were trying to break up the fights or something. I figured, Jesus, this is just what Spike needs now when he's trying to get his concentration. Anyway, these people—which were mostly your basic teenage fanatics with a few nerdo leaders—they didn't hush up until they started getting threats from some of the men who were trying to watch the fights. But even when they shut up, they still went around looking people in the eye trying to make them feel guilty.

By then Spike was already dancing in the ring, and two of his Antelope friends were in his corner. The bouncer had these black eyes and this real hawk nose which kind of scared me, but not Spike I'm sure. The fight was like an explosion. I was just yelling "Spike him! Spike him!"—cause that's what we called it—and I remember hoping he wouldn't get hit in the face. But I don't remember much else of it. Except the bouncer's nose started bleeding and his shorts slipped down this one time, so Sam started yelling "Nail his bun for fun Spike!! Nail him!" I don't think the Jesus people much liked her language, but what the fuck—a fight's a fight. In the 3rd round Spike really started to turn the guy into a Slinky, and so the ref stopped it before he was totally vegetablized. I was screaming. Everybody was so happy.

Spike came down all slippery with sweat and pumped up, and me and Sam and Betsy gave him big sticky hugs and his friends were strutting around congratulating him and giving him high-fives. And then we went outside in the bushes and partied out, just like we'd planned. And everyone was happy. Except Spike. I mean, he was smiling but didn't seem really happy, which I figured was just because he was tired. So then we went back in to watch some of the other fights and to goof on the Jesus Freaks. It was funny because they were practically starting a fight themselves by the beer stand. We were really going.

And then the fights ended, and some people went to Hole-in-the-Wall to party and dance, but the plan was always for Spike and me to drive back to his apartment and make our own celebration. But Spike said he wanted to drag the gut first, just up and down 14-16, to see who's out. So we started driving up 14-16, and turned around in the Ramada lot and drove back down. And he wasn't saying anything.

He was being too quiet. So I said, "What's with you?" And he goes, "Nothing." Like when you hear that, you know it's something. I said, "Come on, you can tell me. Are you pissed you didn't knock him out?" 'Cause he always said T.K.O.s are wimpy. But he just sipped his beer. Then finally he comes out of himself and says, "You know I don't want to hurt you Randi. You know Spike can hurt people and he doesn't want to."

Well, I know when he starts talking about himself like that—like he's not himself, like someone else is himself—I know when he does that that he's really got an attitude on. "So," I said. "So," he said. We just kept driving. I was starting to get that little sick feeling in my stomach. We were already on the other side of town, so we turned around again in the Long John Silver's lot and headed back down the gut. Finally he goes, "So, so I think maybe I better cut off our engagement. I don't want to be tied down anymore. But I love you."

I couldn't believe it. I think I just said, "What are you talking about?" And he goes, "Well, it's just impossible is all. Even after 20 years it doesn't work. That's why everybody gets divorced." I said, "Everybody does not get divorced." And he goes, "Well, almost everybody." He was making me want to throw up. Then he goes, "Guys need to be free. It's just natural. So it's better to do this now than after we're married."

Oh God, I couldn't believe he was doing this to me. I said, "Who said you're not free?" And he said, "Well I felt more free up there fighting that guy than I have with you for a long time." So I was just sitting there listening to this pour into my ears. It was like gravel pouring into my ears, and I looked down at his boxing gloves I was holding in my lap, and I thought, Everlast, what total bullshit! I said "Stop the car, stop it right now." And he didn't fight about it or ask why or nothing, he just pulled into the Rusty Nail lot and stopped. I opened the door, and got out, and said real sarcastic, "Don't knock yourself out, you shithead" and threw his gloves in there at him, and just walked away 1 2 3.

Then I heard the door slam behind me and heard him patch out and for a second I didn't know whether he was coming towards me—like to pick me up or run me over—or whether he was driving away from me. So I turned around real quick, and then I could see that he was driving away. I think he was glad to get rid of me so easy.

GRAVES

"Just because things like this happen doesn't mean life is a crock" is what dad said to me. Like he would know. Like he is qualified to give me advice. He probably put the idea in Spike's head for all I know. I mean—

He said he worked it out with Mom and he's not going to see Shari-the-bitch anymore and he's going to stay living at home. He said it was a good example of just things that happen, but that it shows you can work it out. Then he told me, this is all over the phone, "I'm sure Spike will reconsider." Like Spike is a God-damn judge or something. He can reconsider all he wants and it won't help him any.

That's what I told Betsy. We got stoned Sunday morning and drove up to Sheridan for no reason except I had to get out of town, and I told her about the secret "engagement" which at this point is just fucking embarrassing and she swore she wouldn't tell anyone. She asked me, "Would you take him back if he came crawling back with his teeth brushed and his hair combed?" I told her "No way!" No fucking way. There are too many other men going places in this town to hang around waiting for some dumb dry-hole puncher.

I told Betsy that Saturday night I was out with the girls and I got hit on already by some halfway okay guys. The word was out already about Spike and me, since of course he couldn't wait to tell all his friends. It figures they'd be the first to try to jump me, practically just for the fun of it. But they wouldn't call it jumping me—they would just call it "being understanding" or "being my friend" or whatever other bullshit they were saying to me. But I know damn well what they were doing. They were trying to see who could be the first one to take Spike's place in all the wild stories he probably told them about me, which I'm sure most of them weren't true.

And you sit there at the bar and listen to these guys and think about what your boyfriend might of told them and all of a sudden it's like you're not wearing any clothes. Maybe some of these guys thought I'd screw them just to get back at Spike, and they probably didn't even mind if that was the only reason. But since I knew they were thinking that, that was about the last thing I was going to let them do. Cause giving one of Spike's so-called friends any little satisfaction would be as bad as giving Spike satisfaction—it's like the transitive thing in math, only with people. And I'm not in the satisfaction business with Spike anymore.

I told some other guys about the break-up myself. Guys I had known or seen around. Usually I just said something like "I just had <u>had it</u> with him, up to here!" and then they'd buy me a drink and <u>I'd go</u> about my business getting faced. Some of them are good guys and I could tell they were interested, + there are all the guys I don't know who didn't know nothing about Spike to begin with. Except when you're on the rebound you can't let them in too fast or they think they're in charge—they think you're all whimpering inside and hurt and what you want is <u>them</u> when all you really want is <u>it</u>. That's what I told Betsy. She said <u>I</u> just probably liked all the attention again, and I said "So what?" It was just nice to know I wasn't too fat. Because I was beginning to wonder if his not wanting to Spike me anymore before the fight (God, now I can't believe we called it that!) wasn't because of him saving energy but because of my looks. Anyway.

The best thing anybody said to me so far was Saturday at the Outlaw Inn. This guy trying to pick me up. I had told him about the break-up and being sick of men with attitudes around here. He said he knew an old Gillette saying about that—which means it's probably about 3 weeks old. I said, "Shoot." So he just goes, "If you can't lick 'em, lick 'em."

GRAVES

I just want to say this because it really gets on my nerves. You sit here and you haul coal all night or all day or whatever, and you dump it in the hopper and they crush it into football size pieces and then they crush it into baseball size pieces and then they store it in the tipple and then they load it onto the trains and then driving home from work you're really exhausted and you get stopped at the Gurley Avenue crossing by what? A God-damn coal train. And there's only one underpass, all the way at the other end of town. So for like 3 years they've been promising an overpass. Well, you can't drive over a promise.

It's just that sometimes the trains can't make up their minds whether they're coming or going—they just stand there, or they just start creeping out of town one way or the other, and if it's only creeping it takes about forever to clear the crossing since most of them are a mile long—and you don't know whether to wait at the crossing or drive a couple of miles to the underpass on the west side of town and double back. This seems like an easy decision, but it's not. Because if you pull out of the line (and go through the whole forwards backwards forwards backwards three-point turn thing) and then the train pulls right through, you feel like an idiot and hate yourself for the next few hours. Because you've been beaten, and you had to go through the whole thing of turning around and wasting time driving the wrong way and back. But if the other cars start turning around and heading west for the pass, that puts pressure on you to do it also, cause if you stay there and the train does too (maybe he's got a stop order, maybe he's changing crew up at the yard in the middle of town) then you feel like a real tool.

The only real satisfaction comes when you <u>don't do</u> what the majority does and you win—like if you go to the underpass and when you double back on the other side you see the same color cars lined up through the coal cars as you drive by. Or if you see a line of cars already sitting from a ways away and you judge by the speed of the train that it makes sense to underpass and not wait, and when you get back to Gurley on the other side of the tracks you see that the train has just stopped or isn't even close to clearing—well, that's like you've <u>won</u>. (There's this one speed the trains go where it seems like if they are going that speed then they will always stop, just stop about 5 cars from clearing the crossing, which is the worst, because you can't imagine why they just can't pull a little farther up before they stop, but like Sam says, by the time there's only 5 cars left "We're old news" to the engineer.) I waited once for a good half hour at the crossing, cause I was first in line and I was sure, sure that the train was going to roll all the way out. No. You sit there thinking, no, knowing, This Is Life. Ta-da.

And the farther up in line you are means the more time you've spent waiting, so it's almost like making an investment, and the longer you wait the less you want to turn around and head for the pass, because then that's like abandoning your investment and telling everyone behind you that you made a bad decision to begin with by pulling up and waiting instead of turning off Gurley as soon as you saw the gate go down.

And when you're the very first in line, you have a special responsibility, because you set the tone. If you turn around, or worse if you have to honk and point to get someone to back up so you have some space to turn around, it's a sign to everybody else in line that the person in the pole position—who has been there the longest—has given up hope. And then the others will usually follow you the other way. It's sort of like voting. Which is why racing to beat the train is an official part of Driver's Ed around here. Which is why I'm so pissed tonight, because I didn't get there in time and when I got there I sat for about 20 minutes cause I guessed wrong. And so I sat waiting for all this coal to get the hell out of my way, just so I could come in to strip more coal, and then when I got to work they yelled at me for being late.

GRAVES

Figures I'd be on graves right after getting dumped, since it's the worst shift for partying. I feel like I'm sleeping all the time I'm not working. I mean, you can always find bars open but who wants to party after work at 7:00 a.m.? Not that I've never done it. But if I party before work it's got to be early enough so I got time to recover or if it's late I got to be real half-assed about it, which is no fun. Because you can't come to work completely wrecked or you might wreck for real. So you're sort of screwed on graves.

Not that anybody is straight all the time. Except me, of course. Ha! Graveyard is the heaviest crank shift, days mostly candy and swing is doobie delight. But I don't like crank at night though, cause it jinks me out when morning comes. Anyway, now we're all watching our intake cause the company just ran 30 off Carbon Creek on account of too many little accidents piling up. They had people in the pit for 3 months doing regular jobs that turned out to be narcs and they caught 5 dealing, 4 using and they told 21 others to either fess up and shoo or face charges. So they all fessed and ran. I guess the company couldn't keep tolerating all the accidents. Drinking off the job is what they want mostly, because that keeps everybody happy and depressed and in line. Smart people, the company. That's why they ain't out here getting a tan of coal dust over their clothes and down their throat, or dumping their mind or what's left of it into the hopper over and over. That's why the company is in an office someplace getting paper cuts.

In there if you make a mistake, it's no big deal—just change some numbers around and fix it. Out here it's the real world and you pay. Like in hauling. Tonight I could practically fall asleep cause I got the best Wabco belly dump, #2003—the overspeed autobrake is kicking in on the empty downhill run so smooth it's almost driving itself. That's dangerous, because the 120s are so big and bossy it's easy not to pay much attention to what's going on below you.

Like at Carbon Creek, a guy in a Lectra Haul just was cruising along, minding his own biz, not really watching, and he drove right over a pickup a foreman was in. Just like that. He didn't even feel anything except that maybe he had gone up on the ridge wall a little bit or run over a big coal chunk. And he didn't even know nothing until a scraper operator stopped him and got him out of the truck. And so this hauler starts climbing down from the cab and halfway down the ladder he looks behind him and he sees what he's done—that he's trashed a pickup. So he jumps down and runs back there to all the crunched up metal and then he sees the foreman's hard hat all splintered up and then he sees the rest of it, I guess part of the foreman. Nobody else was there yet. And the deal was that the pickup had cracked and flipped in a way so that the drive shaft was exposed, and it was still spinning around sharp and kind of jagged, and the hauler ran up to it and tried to do himself in by cutting his neck open. He was hysterical. But the scraper operator pulled him away. That's at least the way the story got around. All I know is when you drive into Carbon Creek that wasted pickup is up on a pedestal which is why they don't need a Safety First sign like the other mines.

Sometimes I think I know how that guy must of felt. Cause now he's got to live with it every day—where if he had done it (or if the scraper guy hadn't been there to hold him back) then everything would just be over. Sometimes I think people that drive out of town and leave their cars on the shoulder and lay down on the tracks are the lucky ones. Yeah Randi, that makes a lot of sense. God.

Oh, I'm just mad tonight. Bored. Same thing. I swear there's no one for me in this town except my truck. And I hope Spike gets run over by a train, or maybe one of his own trains of thought— that would be even better cause he so rarely thinks that a thought might just come around a corner and catch him by suprise and flatten him. Flatten him like a cartoon character. Sam is pissing me off too, saying things like "Just get on with it." It's easy for her to say. But the thought of doing anything big and dramatic just cause of Spike is about the stupidest thing I could think about + I wouldn't ever want him to think he was that important anyway. Well, he wasn't. I think I'm going to go home with T.J. this morning and do him up real good in the shower. He's always had his eye on me and maybe today is his lucky day.

GRAVES

God I am in the best mood tonight. I had T.J. eating out of the palm of my thing this morning and after was the best I slept in a week. And then me and Sam watched this great movie tonight, "Creature from the Black Lagoon." It was a riot. We made popcorn and drank a six and made up names for all the characters based on people at the mine, and of course the Creature himself was Bob, ex-Boom-Boom boss. We screamed thinking of him coming up onto one of the trucks in the middle of the night, and dragging us overboard, while we're yelling for help of course, and then taking us down, down, down into the coal lagoon. We ended up acting out our version in front of the T.V. and it was a riot except I broke the lamp using it to defend myself from the Creature who was being played by Amazon Sam and who was getting the best of it holding me down on the couch.

And then we drove to work and got stopped at the Gurley crossing. The train was just creeping along, and I was getting pissed, but then Sam said, "Watch now, the Creature's hand is going to come out of the top of one of these cars" and we went off again, thinking about a bunch of sequels. Like "Creature from the Black Spittoon" and "Creature from the Oil Patch Moon" and "Creature from the Black Man's Nose." And in the middle of laughing about that, KOAL comes on with about the best police report in months.

First off there was a disorderly conduct charge against The Brothers, our stupid little biker gang. I guess they were having a wet t-shirt party out at Westhope and it got too interesting, and so when the police got up there one of the ladies took off all her clothes and starts hugging and kissing on one of the cops, so now they have to arrest her for indecent exposure. Sam said, "They shouldn't arrest her, they should arrest all the people looking at her, like especially the cops." And then they reported 3 shoplifting incidents (I love it when they call things "incidents") in the last two days at convenience stores. The D.J. said, "Store managers all reported the widespread disappearance of male-oriented literature from their magazine racks. No suspects have been reported, but police admit the recently formed Mothers For Decency may have been responsible."

Everybody knows that anyway, cause these dried-up old busybodies (really unbusybodies!) have been warning they were going to strike soon. Sam said, "It was probably the only way they could get a look at Playgirl!" And then there were 39 D.W.I. citations for the week which was above average + there was a real good accident at the corner of Big Sky and Cut-Across—a '57 Chevy pickup and a '79 Coupe de Ville. A rancher totalled his new Cadillac.

And the last story was about Maggie Wood, who's famous for making police reports. They said Maggie fell off her bar stool at the Terminal, and immediately got up and punched the guy sitting next to her, and accused him of pushing her. So this guy, and two of his drinking buddies, knock her around a little and then pick her up and throw her out the drive-up window of the bar. So then, Hardy Tate, who's 73 years old or something, from Newcastle, drives right over her cause he didn't see her (he probably can't see period!) and she ends up with a bunch of contusions and a compound fracture of her left leg. So the scorecard at the end of this thing is—they get Maggie and this Felipe Martinez guy for disorderly conduct, and his main drinking buddy, who did most of the damage before Hardy drove up, for aggravated assault, and they held Chief-the-Barkeep for questioning. But Chief denied opening the drive-up window specifically so Maggie could be thrown out of it, and the cops released him.

By the time Toots Brull, the D.J., got done with the whole report, the train had cleared the crossing and me and Sam were banging on the windows, you know when you start laughing so hard that you can't stop and you get tears, and the people behind me started honking cause I didn't start going quick enough for them so I floored it over the tracks. And the last thing Toots said was that he talked to "Miss Wood" at the hospital and she told him that she'll be back on her stool at the Terminal as soon as "these crazy doctors" release her. Alright Maggie! And then KOAL played "We Will Rock You" and we just drove out to work singing—we will, we will, rock you!

GRAVES

It was just a lot of blackness. And it felt like velvet, all smooth and soft and going on forever. It was warm and I was inside of it, but it was more like clothes than a room. Everything was soft like clothes right after the dryer. It was just a feeling. Hot but not uncomfortable. And I couldn't see a foot in front of me. I couldn't even see my own skin, but I could feel it. My hairs on my skin felt like millions of pieces of warm sand, like when the air is cool but the sand is warm from the sun and you dig your feet in, only over my whole body. Sometimes sleeping is the best. I wouldn't mind going back there now, but I know I can't. Maybe when I go to sleep this morning, if I concentrate I can have the same feeling. It's probably impossible but maybe not. Because a lot of people have dreams that keep happening to them over and over and I want this one to be mine.

GRAVES

Sometimes when my alarm rings at home like today I think for a second it's the sound of the shovel horn, and that freaks me out cause it makes me think I'm at work already and I'm still in bed. 3 means back in, 1 means stop, and 2 sends you away—so that's 6 blows each time you load and a round trip from the pit to the hopper and back to the shovel takes about 25 minutes, 8 hour shift, so it's 17 or 18 trips into the pit each shift, which means like—

$$\begin{array}{r} 18 \\ \times 6 \\ \hline 108 \end{array}$$ blows a shift + 5 shifts a week so— $$\begin{array}{r} 108 \\ \times 5 \\ \hline 540 \end{array}$$ blows a week

+ each shift

3 weeks, so it's— $$\begin{array}{r} 540 \\ \times 3 \\ \hline 1620 \end{array}$$ each rotation

So if you hear that horn 540 × a week telling you what to do and where to go and when to go there—really if you're not slightly crazy it will drive you insane. I don't have any problem with that, being more than slightly. But I got to get an alarm that sounds different from the shovel horn. I got to get a clock radio so I can wake up to KOAL.

Mike's in the shovel tonight which is good because he's funny sometimes + he always drops dead center. But tonight is just one thing after another. First off my dynamics are sticking in my fave, #2003, and to be honest sticky dynamics give me the creeps. Specially when the haul road is slick like tonight. Second of all, two trips into the shift the hopper gets a head cold—all stuffed up. They said something went wrong with the secondary crusher—the one that crushes it from football to baseball size—and so the whole thing got backed up and we have to wait for operations to feed it a little dynamite, which is what everybody is doing right now. Waiting. Mike cuts on the radio, "Come on operations. I'm lonely. I'm just diddling with myself down here. Give that thing some Contac and let's get going."

Mike is great. He's about the only shovel operator that sympathizes with the haulers and isn't always yelling at us for something or looking down at us cause he's Level 9. Like when they took the tunes out of the trucks and then took the reading away too—he was the only one of them that complained. Shovel operator is too busy for reading and wasn't ever allowed to have music to begin with, so there was nothing in it for him to complain, but he did on our account. This is better than reading anyway. The problem with reading was you ended up reading the same thing over and over—because when you were being loaded, every time you got to a good spot the shovel would toot twice and send you away. It was like being in an outdoor pool on a cool day and after a long time swimming you're all tired and cold and you finally find that hot spot in the pool—that little jet where all the hot water comes in invisible—and right then your Mom tells you "It's time to go, you're going to look like a prune." That's how it was, reading. Also, you have 5 shovelfuls to take each trip to get close to your 120 tons, so that means five rumble crashes shaking the cab. So it was sort of like reading during a bombing attack. Sometimes on graves and swing I used to feel like that must of been how it was for people in Europe trying to read at night during the war, like Anne Frank.

1:47—they fixed it now. Great, they fixed it but of course they

72

messed up something else doing it. I guess the dynamite threw the laser guide out, cause now it's misdirecting everybody over the hopper bay which means we have to struggle in and out by eye cause we know they're not about to stop the coal. Not twice in the same shift they're not. What a bummer shift. What a pain to have to do this by eye at night.

It feels like the klieg lights are burning right through my safety shades. Those lights will eat your eyeballs out sure as sun if you stare at them long enough. Hey, coal = light. Major breakthrough there.

5:23—There's a pronghorn, just a silhouette of one, on the rim of the crater, staring out over the highwall of spoils. Makes my night right there. Poor happy sucker, makes me think of Bambi and relay races fast as wind.

Here comes the sun, da-da da-da. First it sort of sneaks up, it's so pink it's almost dainty. It just glints off the metal rim of the tipple. Mike cuts in on my frequency and coughs. "I'm so horny the crack of dawn better be careful around me." I believe he's right. He gives me this line about once a month, specially when we're on graves together, and every time I shoot back, "My name ain't Dawn and I'm not careful nohow." And then we leave it at that or we keep going. Tonight he goes, "I hear you been careful lately." And so I go, "That's cause there ain't nothing moving that I want to fuck." So he says, "Okay, you be on top and I won't move."

He wins tonight! So I give him the little two-points sign out my window on the way up the haul road. It's like a little routine Mike and me have and we don't say much else to each other—except business—and some people are good for that.

#2013

DAYS

I was just coming up the haul road on my last trip. Everything was just like normal. I remember clicking the load counter to 15, and logging it thinking I couldn't remember the last 15-trip shift—which was on account of the hopper thing. So really I had nothing on my mind except that and getting out of here. That's the way it always is on last shift of rotation. You can almost taste it. And the last trip up the haul road always takes forever, just cause it's the last trip. I mean, slow. Slowwwwwwww. With a full load and pedal laying metal you still can't get past 5 m.p.h. on this grade, and on the last trip up it feels like you're on a treadmill or like you're a hamster on one of those hamster wheels.

I remember being about halfway up the haul road and seeing the first day-tripper coming down, sun already up behind him. And at 7 a.m., after a long shift, sometimes the sun looks so God-damn cheery I could shoot it. And as we passed each other I looked into the other cab and see this person, this guy of course. He didn't even have his safeties on so I got a good look at him and I looked at him good, and I shot him this dumb-bunny smile I wish I could wipe off my face forever (I've tried smiling different in the mirror and it don't work) and I just shot him a little two-fingered how-do. And the guy smiled back. Sort of a pumpkin grin and his teeth woke me up. I mean, I damn near fluttered through my tired when I see this guy, why I don't know. I don't even know who he is. I've never seen him before, but it's a big mine.

So I thought—quick, Randi, cop his number—and I copped it backwards in the side-view mirror disappearing and turned the digits around in my head, #2013. Okay. So I got up to the hopper,

74

waited in line, took a dump and headed for staging as fast as I could. I mean, if you could lay rubber with one of these things that's what I wanted to do. I shimmied down my ladder at staging and clipped right on into the office. I had already figured out how I was going to find out.

So I walked up to Teena at her desk in Equipment and said real nonchalant, "You know Teena, it looked like 2013 was really pushing it into overspeed all the way down the haul road. Who's in there today?" She looks at me for a second and tilts her head, you know the way a dog does when it can't quite figure something out. So then she takes a big breath and says, "Well Randi Bruce, I never knew you cared so much about other haulers pushing the Wabcos too hard, that's mighty white of you Randi. I ought to put you up for Keller Employee of the Month."

She's got this big smile on her fat old moon face and she starts looking through the day shift schedule and when she finds 2013 her pen stops on the clipboard and she starts smiling so big I think a couple of her pimples are going to crack wide open. And then she leaned her face over the desk, like she's expecting me to do the same, like when someone is showing you they want to whisper, like it's some sort of secret game, mostly to embarrass me which is hard to do but she managed. So I took off my hard hat and leaned over her desk, and then she whispered in my ear, "That's Derek Harper. A saint and a stud if you asked me Randi, and dear concerned Employee of the Month, you did." She was giggling. Have you ever seen a big fat ugly lady giggling about true love? It's disgusting.

So I said, "Locker number, please." And she couldn't give it to me. I had to go to Personnel for that. I got to Personnel and told them through the pay window after I picked up my check, "I got to leave Derek Harper a note about services on Sunday, can you give me his locker number? Cause we belong in the same church but I don't have his phone number." Maureen didn't bat an eye. She said, "It's G-23." And I told her thanks and as I'm walking away she says behind my back, "What kind of services were you planning to offer, Randi?" And she said it loud enough for the guys waiting in line for their checks to hear and so I got the normal little comments and whistles. See, a lot of people in the office heard

I was single again—since there are not that many girls in the pit we get a lot of attention—and they got nothing to do up there but gossip. So I walked back to the Personnel window and said, "Maureen, rotate!" and flipped her the bird. All the guys cheered.

Then I wrote out a little note saying that The Charged Holes were going to have a B.Y.O.B. party over the weekend (which was a lie) and our phone number, cause I figured if he called we could get up a party quick. It was a little lie too calling us The Charged Holes, cause we haven't been a blasting team for a long time, but some people still call us that anyway—so maybe it wasn't a lie. Anyway, I wrote him this note, but of course I couldn't go into the men's locker room, so I had to wait to find a guy I knew and I could trust to go in there for me. Most of the guys I know, I don't trust. I don't trust them cause I know them. Finally Mike got his ride up from the shovel and walked in, and I asked him to stick it in G-23 and he said "Sure will" and he didn't even make any comments cause he was too tired + he's a good guy.

But so far I haven't heard anything. Ugh. It's true I was out most of the weekend being bad and so was Sam. So he might of called and the phone could of just sat there ringing in our trailer—ring ring ring ring ring. That's an awful feeling to think that.

DAYS

Still haven't heard from Derek Harper. I don't even know what shift he's on now, and I won't ask them in the office cause I'm sure they'll make a big subject out of it and I have some pride too you know. Maybe he's still on days, but probably he changed rotation. Or maybe if he's really new he's floating. I'm keeping my eyes out for him, trying not to run over anybody at the same time, even though sometimes I feel like it. And now I can't remember exactly what he looked like, except <u>good</u>. Because I hardly saw him except for his smile—so I might have walked right by him today on my way to the truck. It would be much better if he called, that way

76

I'd know. But if I could walk by him and not know, what would that mean?

Sam thinks I'm crazy. She said to me last night, "There are 10,000 men in this town looking to play with you and you have to go chase some guy who you don't know and don't see and for all you know is some hick from the sticks." She's right of course. But I told her, "Well, I'm not looking for some man to play with me." And she said, "Oh, aren't we Ms. Mature all of a sudden." We go at each other like that and it's okay cause that's how close we are. She's been calling me "Ms. Mature" the past couple days. I have to laugh.

I've tried Information—but he's not listed. Which is hardly a suprise since a lot of people share places and phones, or maybe he's so new Information doesn't have him yet. I asked Mike about it, and he told me he didn't forget—he definitely did slip it into his locker, through one of those little vents that look like fish gills. So he did get it. Anyway, I've got my eyes peeled. God, that's a horrible idea—peeling your eyes. Like if you peeled them, peeled off the skin of your eyes, what would be underneath, what kind of fruit would your eyes be? I think this waiting is jinking me out is all. It's like Tom Petty says in that song, "The way-ay-ay-ting is the hardest part." And it is. Even for Ms. Mature.

DAYS

The first thing I said to Sam this morning when I saw her in the parking lot was, "Well he may be a hick from the sticks but he definitely is not a hick with the stick. Know what I mean, Samantha?" I think she was jealous for a second there. But the fact is, nothing happened—which was the greatest. The greatest. And walking out to my truck, I told her that. She said, "Nothing happened?" I said, "I mean a lot happened, but not that." She asked me, "Well what were you doing with him all night?" She sounded irritated. I said, "Talking and sleeping." She said, "God, that is weird."

Well, he did give me a good kiss goodnight, about 10 of them actually at different times—cause we kept waking up and talking more and then going back to sleep—but I didn't tell Sam about the kisses because some things you keep to yourself. And it was hard to get back to sleep because even though we were exhausted we were excited too. So we'd get pushed over the edge to sleep after we had talked enough and then after an hour or so the feeling would wake us up again, one or the other of us, and then we'd both wake up and talk some more, and hug each other, until the tired took over again and pushed us back to sleep. And that was the way it was all night, in the corner of his room on the brown carpet on his two sleeping bags on the floor. I knew if we screwed around we'd both go to sleep for the whole night, but he didn't lead that way and I just didn't feel like being my normal jump-on-it self, cause that would have made the whole thing too normal and regular and I didn't want to feel that way about this. Because it didn't feel like that. I don't know what the reason was.

Sometimes I'd wake up, and it wasn't like I usually felt when I'd wake up in the middle of the night or even the morning someplace new—which was, where am I? and sometimes even, who in the hell is that?—cause I always knew where I was and I didn't even have to look at him to know. I'd just look at his little white plastic alarm clock on the carpet, grinding away, going "grrrrrrrr," the orange light from it being the only light in the room, except the light from the window which wasn't stopped much by the sheet he hung up across it, and I could see the boxes on the other side of the room, and all the time I knew exactly where I was. One time I woke up I felt like I was floating on a raft, cause there was nothing else in the room except the boxes, the clock, a lamp in the corner and us, and the carpet was like this dark dark water and the sleeping bags were like two little rafts tied together, just floating in the corner of a lake. I liked that.

And when we got up, he cooked me breakfast. And I came out of the shower in my t-shirt and panties and his robe, because he still hadn't seen me yet and I was being modest and there he was making scrambled eggs. So I sat down at the table on a peach crate which he used to bring out his records but now was being a chair until he got some real ones, and I watched him whip his skillet around and I thought about the day before and I thought, Girl, you are dreaming now.

What happened was I got off shift and found a note in my locker. It said, "Sorry I missed the party. See you in the lot after work?" Well, I sang about every tune I knew in the shower, trying to calm myself down and psych myself up. I think I went through about a whole bar of soap. I remember I spent a lot of time thinking, Bra vs. no bra? I can't remember the last time I thought that over a guy. Anyway, I finally just walked out there (no bra) and saw him sitting on the back of a white pickup—well, mostly it was mud color. I recognized him right away, but it's true he was looking right at the door. He had sandy hair and greenish eyes and he was shorter than I thought, kind of stocky, but not tubby or anything.

And he said, "Hey" and I said, "Hey" and I was pretty nervous, but not uncomfy—more like butterflies nervous and not math-test nervous. And he said he was sorry he didn't get to the party but that he had to go home to get the rest of his stuff to bring out and his truck broke down on the way there—it's this real beater!—and it took two days to fix and he had a lot of stuff to do when he got back so that's why it took so long for him to respond but thanks for the invite. I mean, it was like he was being polite about it. I didn't dare tell him there wasn't any party.

So I lied, "I just heard you were new in town and thought maybe you'd like to meet some new people." He said, "Well that's real nice, real nice. How about I start with you?" I went, "Sounds okay—but I don't know." I was sort of teasing-joking him. Because I just walked round the passenger side and got in. He said, "Where do you want to go?" I just about died. The guy was asking me. Not wimpy or anything, just nice. So I'm thinking, This guy sure is new in town, and wondering what planet he's from, and also I have to admit, thinking what kind of Mr. Nice Guy routine is this guy running down? The one where he nice guys the pants right off of me—I've heard it a zillion times in the bars, "I'm different from these other guys. I . . . I . . . I'm SENSITIVE!" Or the one where he's charming me for a couple hours and then all of a sudden he gets real quiet while we're driving down some dirt road, and then stops, holds me at knife-point, gags me, sticks it in every hole, cuts me up and sends different parts of me C.O.D. to relatives in

3 different states. You know, like what you read in the papers. It seems crazy now to think that he was a Mr. Nice Guy, but when you're in some guy's truck and it's only been 5 minutes you've known him you just have these thoughts.

So anyway, I told him I didn't care where we went and he said, "How about Westhope Reservoir?" He said he hadn't been out there yet and people said it was nice. I could tell how new he was cause if he had been here long he would just of said "Westhope" and not "Westhope Reservoir." I couldn't believe it. I told him, "I practically grew up out there, great." We stopped at Dairy Queen and both got medium vanillas dipped on our way through town, and drove on out with them dripping all over us. The ride felt like it took about 10 minutes.

When we got out there I showed him all my favorite spots from the days of Bruce Ski Sisters—like the rock that has a perfect spot for your buns and the tree that always has the best pine cones. Stuff like that. And we walked on the beach. He told me about his family and his friends back home which is in Minot, North Dakota and he told me about coming out to work in town and that the pay was good but he missed his family and friends. We skipped stones from the beach, and I beat him 9 skips to 8. He said, "Well it figures, you got the home beach advantage!" and I patted him on his back a little, like fake-consoling him, which was the first time we touched and it gave me the after-chills. And we just walked around and sat talking at a picnic bench and fall was really coming in pretty good, the air all suprising and cold and it was dark before we knew it.

We drove back to town and had dinner, which he treated me to at the Rustler and in the middle of his steak I asked him how did he like the floor? He said—just so nice you could die—"Excuse me, Randi?" but only after he stopped chewing. So I asked him again. He said, smiling, "You're on drugs" and then looked around at the floor, very seriously, like he was going to give me a serious answer. And then you know what he said? He said, "Well, I tell you what, I think it's flat." And I said, "Oh you say the nicest thing to a girl." So then he was really confused and I went and told him all about my McMahon job and all. We had a great time—all medium-rare.

80

And we went back to his place, which is a new apartment in Homestead Village, and walked around in our socks giving each other little electric shocks off the carpet. And he gave me a back scratch, which he did <u>over</u> my shirt and not like some guys do to get you going. I was going anyway.

We tried to fall asleep early, cause we both had to get up at 5:10 for work, but it was impossible, so we just laid around on the sleeping bags telling stories until he said, "We really better Z or tomorrow'll be today before we know it." Which I thought was a real nice way of saying it right up until he gave me that kiss, at which point I wasn't thinking anymore. What I want to know is— if love is blind, why do they say love at first sight?

DAYS

Sometimes I just want to tell him everything. Right away tell him everything. But if I do that then I might tell him something he doesn't want to hear + I might run out of things to tell him too fast. It's not that I'm afraid if I tell him something he doesn't like that he wouldn't like me anymore. It's just that I don't want to take that chance so soon. Once he gets to know me better, maybe. I think he tells <u>me</u> everything is the thing and it seems from what he says that he's very deep.

But I have no way of knowing. Maybe it just <u>seems</u> like he tells me everything. I mean, unless I knew his <u>old</u> friends or ex-girlfriends who would be talking on the side, there's no way to really know. But it does seem like he's telling me everything, especially compared to all the other guys around here who tell you nothing. Which is okay with me most of the time, because all they have to say is nothing about nothing anyway and who needs to know that?

And it seems like Derek really wants to know me more than other guys have. Like Spike or really any of them. Because Spike didn't want to know a lot of things. I could tell that after a couple of weeks, so I didn't try to tell him. And then it's almost like you get to the point where you don't know about those things yourself anymore or you stop thinking about them. They don't go away really—it's just they get hard to find.

And I want to bring up a lot of stuff with Derek, but maybe I should wait until I get to know him better. But in a weird way I think I already know everything about him I need to. I almost feel guilty about it—cause there's no way he could know everything about me he needs to, cause he doesn't know half the screwy things or the family things or the things that happened back when I didn't really know what I was doing. And that's scary. It sounds like I'm complaining, which I'm not. Because I'm happier now than I've been in a long time. It's just that when you get so happy all of a sudden it makes you start thinking you better watch out, or maybe doing things to protect that, or otherwise that happy feeling will end up in the dumper and getting ground up into little pieces and gone with the wind.

DAYS

It wasn't so much this big long dream, it was more like a dreamlette. I was walking around town and I was freezing and it was snowing. Just a dusting. So I decided to walk over to Blue Skies Lounge, which is right underneath the drugstore and the day-care center on Flying Circle. It was real warm inside, so I had to take my down jacket off right away otherwise I would of started sweating. They were giving away these pills at the bar. And you put the pills into your drink and let them dissolve, like Alka-Seltzers. So I took this red pill and this green pill, cause I guess it was Christmas, and I put them in my rum-and-coke. Then Mom came in and sat at the bar. She said, "How is my little baby?" And I said, "Bottoms up" and gulped the whole drink down and I felt very good. Good and toasty. So she got the same drink and did the same things with the pills, and said, "Bottoms up" and more like sipped hers down fast. We both sat there at the bar, smoking cigarettes—but the cigarettes were like birthday candles in all those funny colors. Mom kept asking me, "So how's my baby? How's my little baby?" It was real dark and the jukebox was playing and the snow was blowing against the windows and the Miller High Life sign was all in 3-D. That's all I can remember.

SWING

Mom called me to talk about what happened with Spike. I didn't tell her about it but she found out from Betsy and from Sam. I didn't tell her because I knew she'd find out anyway, just the way Moms do. So I figured, why bother going through it with her and getting all the questions when someone else could tell her and have to answer the questions? Then by the time she talks to me about it I won't have to answer most of them + she'll be more understanding. Because Mom always starts with—It's Your Fault. That's her assumption, and then you have to fight from there to get her to see it's not. So if other people tell her about something then they can defend me, and by the time she gets to me about it, she's almost halfway on my side.

Also, I didn't tell her about it, because I thought after our talk in the garage that day about me loving Spike so much she would think I really screwed up even worse than normal. So she called me from work to sympathize and interrogate me a little. I just said, "Things are okay"—but I hardly got a word in before she started giving me all this advice. I couldn't even get a word in about Derek, and she went on for so long that I ended up not even wanting to. After all her usual wisdom—like "When I was your age I was married and pregnant" which I've heard 100 × before—she ended up saying, "Don't worry Randi, cause men are like trains." I was suprised at her. I didn't say anything. So she said, "Do you know why Randi?" So I said, "Cause there's one coming every 20 minutes. Mom I think it's the other way around." And she said real business-like, "Randi, I'm just talking demographics." What?

That's just like Mom. She hears something fancy around the

84

office, like something some executive says on the phone to some-body back at Amax headquarters in Conneticut, and then she goes and puts it into every normal conversation she can. The last one she did that with was "bottom line." For a month she was saying bottom line this and bottom line that, everything was bottom line. Like when I told her last spring about Keller breaking up The Boom-Boom Girls she'd say, "Well, what's the bottom line Randi?" Anyway I looked up demographics and it's no big deal anyway.

I love Mom alot, but sometimes she is just so aggravating. It's almost like she can't help herself. Like the way she drives drives me crazy—she won't just leave her foot on the gas steady. No way. Instead she pushes the gas pedal down and then takes her foot off it, then rams it down again and takes her foot off it, and keeps doing that. I'm used to it from my whole life, but now it really gets on my nerves. So I decided I had to ask her about it while we were driving down to Wright to meet dad for the mall ded-ication.

Real innocent and nice, I asked her, "Why do you drive that way?" She says, "What way?" and punches the pedal down again. So I ask, "Why don't you just keep your foot steady on the gas like normal people?" And she just goes, "A lot of those normal people have totalled cars you know." I go, "What?" She goes, "A lot of those normal people end up in the hospital." Then she changed her tone, like she was letting me in on a secret. She said, "Because you never know when you might need to hit the brake, and if your foot is down on the gas it takes longer to get there."

Great, so she drives around for her whole life thinking that she's going to have to hit the brakes. I said, "Well I drive for a living and you don't have to do that Mom, really." Mom shoots back, "Yeah, you drive about 10 miles per hour for a living so I don't think you're Mrs. Expert here." That made me mad. So I said, "Mom, look, it's stupid the way you drive. No one drives like you."

And so at that point Betsy of course has to chirp up from the back seat, where her and Neil have just been sitting petting each other the whole way down. Betsy says, "Well what's it to you Randi?" And then there was a bunch of silence in the car, cause all this was in front of Neil who's not a member of the family or anything—at least not yet. A little time went by, and Mom and

Betsy and Neil probably thought it was over. But then I just said, "Screws up her mileage is all."

And then no one said anything. Except Mom started going faster—like to have the last word—and Neil rolled down his window.

SWING

I think I'm in love with Derek. Really I know it but sometimes I have to pretend I'm not just to keep expectations down. Like when I'm talking to people about it. I think we both have this feeling. The kind of feeling that makes you do things—like us fixing our schedules so we're always on the same shift—even if it means losing seniority on a piece of equipment or something. It's that kind of feeling. Like the feeling that he could tell me about playing bombardment in 5th grade gym class and I wouldn't be bored about it. And I'm not just supposing all dreamy and goo-goo eyes, because he did talk about that very thing last night and I wasn't bored in the least bit. I think maybe that's what being in love means—being able to hear about bombardment.

Or maybe the feeling when I see his truck. Sometimes I see his truck and I can't even see him in it, but I know he's in it, and that makes all the difference. And I imagine what he's thinking or what tune is going through his head. Sometimes I imagine he's imagining me, and then I try to make myself look like that—like whether I'm smiling or looking serious, or whether I'm looking out into the distance real dramatically or looking right at him all romantic, or whether I'm looking soft or hard—and I check my look in the mirror to see if it fits. Sometimes I think of him thinking of me laughing and so I make myself laugh, which is a strange feeling. But how he imagines me must be different than any way I could make myself. Which is okay I suppose.

Another thing—it's getting cold now, really cold, and usually I hate it. It makes me want to hibernate. But this fall is different. Usually when you step out on that first morning when it's freezing and really blowing, the air just about cracks your face open. It really cuts you up, just the feeling—not so much the cold itself as knowing it's going to get worse and worse until about April. But this time when that happened—yesterday, getting mail—I felt like I already had my winter coat on, which I didn't. It's like I felt that my winter coat was Derek, and that all the snuggling and Eskimo kissing we were going to do was going to keep me warm even when I was cold. That makes the cold different. (He's the first guy that lets me Eskimo kiss him, which is about the one thing Mom taught me when I was little that stuck.) Anyway, I'm almost glad it's cold because the cold gives you something to come inside to. So now that everyone's bitching about it—your basic lunchroom bitching and 7/11 check-out chitchat bitching—about winter coming on and engines not turning over, it makes me feel like I'm living in a foreign country. Because I'm happy and I don't care about it and I'm even happy about it.

SWING

The weekend was so great with Derek there is no way I could write it all down. We just had the best time you could imagine. First we went up to the Big Horns because he wanted to go for trout. I said, "It's fished-out up there, that's what it said on the radio." And he just said, "The radio does not have its feet in the water. We're going to go up there and you're going to show me where to go and I am going to catch you a trout." I love the way he says it—not going to catch trout but going to catch me a trout. He's got a way of putting things.

So we drove up there on Saturday morning, real early, like not quite as early as dad made us go on Badlands trips, but that general concept of early (TOO EARLY!) and he promised me trout for lunch. He said, "I'd guarantee it for brunch but I don't like to fish under pressure." There's a nice stream on the other side of Powder River Pass, not Crazy Woman Creek which is the fished-out one, but another one I don't know the name of that's near it. We drove down a park service road and found a nice place to camp in the woods. There wasn't anybody else around. We set up his tent and then he went off to the stream and I crawled inside and slept a little more. When I got up I made sure to zip the two sleeping bags together. (Okay it was sneaky but it wasn't wrong.) And then I got wood for the fire and went down to the stream to watch him fish.

He brought a rod for me too, and showed me how to use it, because I never knew. I went fishing once or twice with dad when I was little, except nobody was allowed to say anything to him while he was fishing. We all just sat and watched. So I never learned anything about it. Mom used to sit on the bank with me and Betsy and whisper, "Your father thinks fishing is a spectator sport." I think maybe he just watched too many American Sportsmans on T.V. and he wanted to be with Curt Gowdy instead of with us.

For a long time Derek and I stood there not catching anything. It didn't matter, cause we were having a good time joking around. I asked Derek, "Can you catch any fish while we're talking so much?" And he said, "When was the last time you saw a fish with ears?" And then I told him that they don't need ears because they don't have anything to say. And then I told him that when I was little, 9 or 10 about, I went through this period when I didn't want to eat fish cause I didn't think it was good to eat anything that's so quiet for their entire lives. Derek just stood there casting and grinning. I think I amuse him. He's got this half-smile which is his true smile. It gives him a dimple on his left side and you can never see his teeth, but it's the sort of smile where it looks like he's thinking true thoughts.

Anyway, he did not catch a trout, he caught two—big ones. We named one Billy Carter, cause he was very fat, and we named the other one—well I did—Brooke Shields, cause she was very long and skinny. (Derek didn't know who she was so I had to tell him. Sometimes I think he's from another planet.) So we went back to our campsite pretty soon after that—because fishing does get boring after awhile, no matter what those old farts say down at Bobbie Sue's stretching their arms out like they caught one the size of an Oldsmobile. I was just about to say something to Derek about it, but I think he knows too and he said "Let's quit!"

So we started up the fire. We decided to eat Billy Carter for lunch, and I put Brooke Shields on ice in the cooler in the truck. I was hauling her off by the gills and said like we were on a nature show, "And so scientists Harper and Bruce decided to preserve her fragile beauty by way of Kryogenics." And Derek yelled at the top of his lungs, "THE GIRL IS WEIRD" like he was announcing that to all the wildlife we couldn't see in the forest, and the way he said it made me think what he was saying was "I LOVE YOU." I hoped so anyway.

We ate and took a hike and drove up back to the top of the pass and smelled the sage, which really smelled strong, and had a cow chip throwing contest. They run a lot of head up there on permits in the summer so there was plenty to pick from. He won, but it was close. And then we climbed the fire tower and made out at the top in the windy cold. It looked like it wanted to snow and we couldn't even see the top of Cloud Peak, which I promised him we'd climb next summer. The sound of the wind coming through all the railings and iron stairs on the fire tower is a cold sound and I was glad I was there with Derek.

Then, on the way back down to our campsite we stopped at St. Christopher's of the Big Horns which is a little wilderness chapel— just benches and trees—and we sat there just us and the squirrels and he got real quiet, like praying, and I watched him. And on the way back down to our camp we started talking about why he is religious and why I'm not, which was a little scary but it's not important enough to get in our way. Actually, I'm sort of glad he's religious (like what comes with it) and I think he's sort of glad to be with someone who's not.

We ate sandwiches we brought from home for dinner and I made samores which I could eat by the ton. (One day I'm going to devise an "All Samore Diet" and get rich selling it.) We went through about a whole bag of marshmellows and I found out one of your most important personality traits, which is that he goes for the slow-golden-brown-toasty ones and I go for the quick-burn-blister type. He rotates his about 6 inches above the flames for about forever, and I just stick mine right in.

Okay, so maybe we are not compatible! But the good thing is I can eat about 3 marshmellows for every one of his. So I didn't encourage him to try the fast-burn technique. I decided some differences are okay to keep. Then when there were about 5 left I said, "We had better finish the bag otherwise the bears might come looking for them, cause I hear they really like marshmellows." He just looked at me and fake-roared like a grizzly and gave me a huge bear hug and said, "I love you" which was the first time he said it. I was about dying.

When we turned our flashlights off it was so dark I could hardly see he was there. It's been a long time since I was in dark like that. You forget what the dark is. There was no moon and no stars. And we did it for the first time. Girls always say when they're in love, "Oh, it was like my first time" but that's not true at all. Because my first time was about as romantic as a bad geometry problem you couldn't get—and this was not in that category. It was beautiful. Not because he was so hot or anything, just because the way he was about it. It was like he was really looking at me—instead of watching himself watching me, which is the way a lot of guys are.

And then after we went to sleep it rained instead of snowed. It was probably snowing higher up but changed its mind on the way down, and we got pretty wet because the tent wasn't perfect. It could've been this big disaster but it wasn't. In the middle of the night I said, "I wish it would stop." And Derek said, "God is trying to turn us into trout." It was one of those middle-of-the-night conversations, so I'm not sure I remember it right. I said, "Maybe the government is doing it, because we ate Billy Carter." We laughed and everything was better even though we were getting wet. I mean, with somebody else, I'd be in the truck by then saying, "Let's drive home, now." So we woke up soggy. So what?

We packed up and drove down to Ten Sleep to get a big hot breakfast. He guessed almost right what Ten Sleep means when I quizzed him about it. He said, did Indians stop here and camp for ten nights? I told him about it being ten days walking or ten sleeps to the old Sioux camp on the Platte or to the one on the Yellowstone in Montana. And so he asked how I knew this and did I have any in me? I told him ⅛ but I never exactly got it straight how, except that it was on my dad's side.

Then after breakfast we drove down to Worland and up the other side of the mountains along the river and over Granite Pass.

90

We just listened to the Sunday countdown shows on the radio and took pictures all the way and took our time. We stopped in Sheridan on the way home for early dinner, which he treated me to even though we couldn't go fancy cause we weren't hardly dressed for it.

When we got home I wanted to stay with him but he dropped me at Sam's. He said he had to call home and stuff. I got a little nervous all of a sudden but then he called later at night and said how great a time he had being alone with me in the woods and that he'd pick me up in the morning for work so I stopped being nervous and haven't been since.

SWING

I think Samantha is jealous. It's not that I think she likes Derek so much—because they've met and she thinks he's fine and all but doesn't like him in that way cause they're not the same types. It's that she's jealous cause she doesn't have her own Derek. She says that's not true, but she's lying. Also because now when I'm with him so much I'm not around to drive to work with and get stoned and pig-out with and hit the bars. Because she has been going around with the same group as always and I haven't gone with—cause Spike is in that group. So they all are still hanging around. One time I came back to the trailer and they'd been partying with Dennis and Panama and Joleen, and everybody had left except Spike, and it was weird to walk in to my own house and see him there. I treat him just fine but I got nothing to say to him. Luckily he was leaving anyway. I don't tell her she can't be friends with him cause I decided I am above that, but it does piss me off a little.

The thing is, I got better things to do than hang out with them now. Sam takes it like I'm being all superior but that's not true. I can tell just by the way she drops little things on me—like she said in front of Melody in the locker room, she said, "Randi's almost a virgin again. She's going to be the only girl in history to go backwards or something." I know she said it for Melody's benefit—

to make her feel like I'm more like her—but at the same time it was a little mean to me. Just jokes like that you can take a few ways, depending what you know. The funny thing is, Samantha can have anybody she wants in Gillette not to mention the whole state—she could get any boomer just by looking at him and she could get any sugar daddy just by her being smart—but she says she still hasn't found what she's looking for. Well I don't think it's there to find is the problem, and I don't think it's fair for her to take it out on me. The thing is, I do miss her too sometimes the past few weeks. Maybe that's because—   I don't know.

SWING

I'm still not sure what to tell Derek. I think about it all the time. Because if you start to say one thing, then it leads to everything else and it starts going faster. It's like taking the first step off somewhere steep—once you take that step, you might not be able to stop. Like if you're skiing and you're an intermediate and you decide to try an expert run, well once you start you can't stop— that's just the way it is. That's why it's an expert run. I mean, there's momentum.

If something comes up though it's not like I'm going to lie about it or anything. Like when we went up to Hole-in-the-Wall the other night after work for some beers + he was going to teach me to two-step. Well, we never got to the two-stepping part cause the beer part got too good—we both had had bummer shifts and about in the middle of our 2nd pitcher we knew there was no way we were going to do any dancing. Anyway, I was talking about wearing makeup vs. not wearing makeup, like what does he think about Debbie wearing makeup when she's driving the water truck? And he said "Lipstick and coal aren't dancing partners." Which I agreed with—cause even though I wear a little gloss sometimes I do it same as Chapstick. So anyway, we were talking about this and he was looking at me real close and he asked me about my nose. Because it's got a little bump in this one spot. Nothing too bad. I mean, you have to really be looking at me to notice. Anyway, I didn't want to make something up about it so I told him the truth.

First he was angry, he was so angry at dad. He couldn't believe he would do something like that. He was swearing about it, cursing him out. So I said, "Don't dads hit their kids where you come from?" And he said, "Not their girls they don't." He reached out and felt my nose. He was angry. But then something changed. He sunk back in his chair and looked away.

So I said, "What's wrong hon?" He looked sad about something. Then he just said, "I can't believe you went on the pill when you were a sophomore." I said, "Oh Derek listen, I was different then." I didn't know what to say. He was just sitting there, like he couldn't look at me. I felt so bad. I said, "It was better than being risky." And then he went, "So how many guys was it?" Oh God. You know it's not like he didn't know I was experienced. I mean, I told him I was but not the gory details or how old I was. But looking at him I could see he was sad more than mad so I just started crying cause that's worse, much worse. I didn't feel bad about what I did or who I did, not really. I felt bad cause it was making Derek feel so bad that I wasn't always his.

All of a sudden I felt like I had skied us right off the edge of things. But when Derek saw me crying, he reached over and wiped my tears and brushed my bangs back over my forehead. Like he forgot about himself for a second when he saw how bad I felt. I'm lucky about him.

And then he asked me, "How did he find out you were on it?" I told him that he was looking in my room for pot and he found them in the dresser, and when I got home from dance class after school he gave it to me. Derek was rubbing the back of my neck, making me feel okay. He asked did Mom know about it? I told him you could hardly see it at first, but then it was hurting alot so dad said to tell the nurse at school that a book fell out of the top of my locker—I remember him exactly, stroking his mustache and saying, "Tell them it was that big science book"—but the nurse said there was nothing they could do and it would heal by itself and that was the same story I told Mom.

I told him dad wasn't trying to hurt me, just to slap me, but that

I moved in a way he didn't expect and so he sort of missed. Then Derek said, "Don't defend him." And I went, "I am not defending him I am just explaining." I would not defend dad—no way. But then when Derek started asking me more questions about it, like did I keep on the pill (which I did in secret) and he started asking me things like, "Would you tell me what is the story with Peter and Barbara?" and other questions about what else did dad do? I couldn't say any more. What was I going to say, tell him about how dad liked to use his belt whenever we did wrong things growing up, and how sometimes he'd hold the wrong end "by mistake" and we'd get it with the buckle? I just didn't want to get into it. I just wanted Derek to hold me and drive us home and make love to me, which he did. I didn't want to go on and tell him other things, like about who dad really is.

SWING

Betsy ditched Math and I met her at Macs for lunch today. One thing about Betsy is she doesn't mind ditching Math. Or ditching Chem or English or Home Ec. I kind of thought when I graduated that I would see Betsy just like before but it's not true. What happens is if you're not in school you really don't see people who are. The people that work and the people that go to school could be in different towns, and fake I.D.s only changes that a little. I mean I see her when I go home to have a dinner with Mom or on a weekend stop-by but it's less and less really—cause it's just as easy to talk to Mom on the phone and that way you don't have to make this big complicated deal out of it.

But I am a little worried about Betsy. 1) She is a senior so she thinks she doesn't need to do any work. (Okay, maybe that's true, you don't.) 2) She is stoned even more than me, or than I was when I was a senior. And I told her to watch it, and she said, "Oh, do you have a special permit cause you're two years older?" I just told her to watch it, especially with candy and ludes. Cause I know what I'm doing more than she does + I'm out here working. 3) I can't see where a part-time job working at the airport for Alamo is really going to do her much good when she graduates. She says they'll put her on full-time, and if they don't she's going to join the Army—or that she might join the Army anyway. I can't believe she would do that, but she sounds serious! 4) Neil. (Who I think is dealing.) 5) Having to live with Mom and Dad still. I think things are worse now than when I was a senior but Betsy says that's not true. She says things are fine + she pretty much only goes home at curfew to sleep and spends the rest of her time at Neil's or as much time as she can without being grounded. I told her, "That's great Betsy—going back and forth between Mr. and Mrs. America and your derelict boyfriend's." So she goes, "Listen Titface, you are not my mother so don't try to be." Well, what am I supposed to do about it?

SWING

You load 16 nuns and what do you get?
Another day older and deeper in shit.
If it wasn't for my doobies it'd be such a bore,
I owe my soul to the company store.

I write the songs that make the whole world come,
I write the songs that make your pants come undone,
I write the songs that make me money like a pig,
So I have something to put up my nose which is so big!

    T.J. in the shovel,
    Looking for trouble,
    Dumping on the double
    In this little old mine

        Bob is the boss,
        He thinks he's a hoss,
        His dick is so little
        He's got to sit down to piddle.

Gretchen in the office,
Her face makes you wretchin',
Wears pink blouses make her
Look like a pig fetus

GRAVES

I went home with Derek for Thanksgiving weekend. It was a long drive but God cooperated and the weather stayed okay—no snowstorms or below zero. I think his poor truck is ready for the truck cemetery so it was a good thing too. He's getting a new one soon. I said on the way out there that we ought to give thanks for that and I wasn't joking.

Everyone wanted me to stay at home—Mom kept saying "We need to be a family, we need to be a family now" and all that—but Derek had been wanting me to meet his family + see where he grew up and this was the only chance to do that for a long time, what with schedules. Also I didn't think having turkey at home was going to change anything. It just would of been eating turkey.

So we left right from work Wednesday night, and drove all night so we could be there for a little of the day itself. I mean, we didn't want to just blow in over the cranberry sauce. We went straight up 85 through Custer forest, and then South Heart, and then all the little shortcuts he knows through Killdeer and Zap, and up 83 past Max right into Minot. (Zap, North Dakota is one of the best sneezetowns around, even at 4:00 in the morning.)

All the way out there I was tired from work but I had my adrenalin going. So I managed to stay up and watch for deer eyes frozen in the headlights and listen to Derek's "On The Road Again" tape—which isn't so bad really—and hear him tell me all about home. He told me so many stories that by the time we got there at about 6:00 a.m. I felt I was coming back to someplace I'd already been, instead of stepping into someplace new. What probably helped too was getting there while everybody was still asleep, and us going right upstairs to his old room and going to sleep ourselves. That does make you feel at home. Actually, he slept in his brother's room—because of his parents—but he already told me that's what we'd have to do so I didn't mind. I think that's sort of cute, the way his parents pretend about that stuff.

They are good people is the thing. Okay, so they are hickish but that's just where they come from. But they know more about more stuff than a lot of the people that think they're so hot in Gillette. Mrs. Harper substitute teaches and makes these killer sweet potatoes. And Mr. Harper is a cool guy too. He explained to me why it is that planes stay up. Hunter tried to once—I remember standing under the Twin Otter wing on the tarmac and him pointing to things—but I think I was too preoccupied with him to follow it. I think Mr. Harper making sure I really understood it was part of him being proud of his job, which was a senior mechanic over at the B-52 base until they did something in Washington which closed down his division last spring. They did something like gave underground missiles more power so that changed the numbers of bombs in some treaty and so they had to retire a bunch of B-52s. And the B-52s turned out to be his.

I don't know, it's pretty complicated—I asked Derek about it and he said something like, "They mirved the Minutemen so they mothballed us" and I said, "Well they would do that, wouldn't they?" All I know is it ended up with Mr. Harper getting laid off onto his pension and he's still pretty upset about it. He said, "That's just the way things are. Some diplomat has a hooker in Moscow one night and next day goes to the table goofy and we're out of business."

So Mr. Harper didn't have much to be super thankful about, but he sat there explaining things to me and being nice anyway. Derek says his dad might go in with his uncle at his uncle's farm near White Earth. It would be a big change but it would get him out of the house. He's overqualified for everything but B-52s around town, and the drive to White Earth isn't bad—just straight out Route 2, which is the way we went home. His uncle has more land in wheat out there than he knows what to do with, so he could use the help. But it depends on the prices too.

That's what Derek tried after he got laid off from the base, he tried farm work. Since he was only working at the base part-time, finishing his civil engineering degree, it wasn't any big deal to leave it. It wasn't his whole life like it was with his dad. Anyway on Friday me and Derek and his little sisters Judy and Julie drove up to where he worked on some family friend's farm last spring, up in Maxbass. But there wasn't enough work it turned out, and it was practically the Canadian border and he was bored stiff. Driving back to Minot he said, "Don't let anybody fool you—farming's about as exciting as watching concrete dry." Well, I know what a thrill that is.

So when it didn't pan out with those family friends, he called up some of his own friends who had summer jobs in towns around there, like in Grano and Russell. But there was nothing available. That's just the way it is up there. You can drive 400 miles and see a whole lot more geese migrating than jobs. They got bumper stickers saying "Will The Last Person Leaving North Dakota Please Turn Out The Lights." That's how bad things are. So Derek went home and just sat around trying to figure out what to do.

He had his degree and it wasn't like he didn't have any skills, and he already had time on a lot of pieces of equipment from at the base. Driving back home on Saturday—cause we had to make graveyard on Saturday night—I asked him about the day he decided to come to Gillette. Because I wanted to see if I could figure out what day it was and what I was doing. Like was I doing anything to influence our fates? (I was blasting coal or hauling coal, for sure, but I mean what else?)

Derek didn't remember the day, but he remembered exactly what he was doing. He said he was sitting at home, it was in the middle of the week and Julie and Judy were watching soap operas and him and his brother and them were all playing Monopoly. He told me he could hear his dad snoring over his newspaper in the den and Mom cooking dinner in the kitchen. It was pot roast, cause he said when they had pot roast the house smelled of it for a week, like his Mom was basting the walls or something. Anyway, he was losing at Monopoly real bad, cause his two sisters are cheats. He says they are always exchanging money under the board—so every time he looked up there was another hotel on the oranges or the yellows. He wasn't being so vigilant about it cause he was halfway through a six-pack. And he was giving his little brother Jimmy sips on the side and so eventually Jimmy who's about 13 lost interest in the Monopoly and fell asleep in the sun coming in the window, right on the carpet with their dog Skippy, who's a border collie and likes to lie in the sun and have those dreams where his little legs start twitching and his nose starts sweating, those kind of dreams.

And so they were all just hanging around there on the floor of the den, and in addition to murdering him in Monopoly his sisters started teasing him about Rachel, who broke up with him after senior prom, and they were saying that the girls he went out with since then were real dogs. They started doing little fake-growling sounds to imitate these girls calling him on the phone. But I guess after awhile they didn't stop, so Derek started teasing them back about their stupid boyfriends—I mean, they are about 10 and 12 so I'm sure their boyfriends are stupid—and their sleepover parties and Judy's training bra which he called a "Band-Aid." So all of a sudden Judy got supermad and turned over the Monopoly board— so you know she must of been really pissed cause she was winning big—and she ran into her room. So Derek and Julie just sat there looking at each other—like one of those moments where you try to see in the other person's face if they want to keep playing before you say one way or another and maybe make an idiot out of yourself—and so they were sitting there and they couldn't decide whether they were going to keep playing or quit, and the way Derek said it to me was, "And you know all of a sudden I felt like I was about 10 years old and I had to get out of there!"

4 days later he had everything in his pickup and drove out to Gillette. When he told me, he was sort of defensive about it. He said, "It wasn't exactly the most daring thing to do or anything, but it made sense." He had a friend out here—everybody that comes has a friend out here—that he knew from engineering school and was working at Buckskin. So he put in his application there and at other mines and waited. He had almost no money cause he refused to take any from his dad, so all he had was what he brought out, which was about $325, and what his Mom had hidden in the lunch she packed him for the drive out, which was $60. He said

he would of returned it to her if he hadn't been so long gone by the time he found it.

And so for the first couple of months Derek was here he was camped in the tent city behind the Husky truck stop and when it got too muddy back there he slept in the bed of his pickup with a tarp over it in the Husky lot, which was $2.50 a day + $1 for the shower. And he roofed houses up in Grandview Hills for this rich Vietnam veteran developer guy whose big goal it was to put in the golf course. Also, he did some grunt work for Grussing Water & Oil Service and a few other things to make the ends meet.

When we were just about back to town on the innerstate, he told me he used to lie on his back at night down at the Husky, and listen to all the trucks go by up on I-90, and he would think about whether they were going all the way west to Seattle or all the way east to Boston, and he would think about getting up and walking over the fence and up the embankment and hitching one way or another, to one coast or another, just leaving everything but his duffel and his tent down in his pickup. Like walking away from everything that led him up to being stuck in the mud in Gillette, and starting over someplace else, as someone else. When he told me that my heart got so sad. Just the thought of him leaving, and me not seeing him ever, and us being with different people, and no Thanksgivings like the one we just had.

GRAVES

Sometimes I think about going blind or deaf. I think about which one would be better. If I went deaf, like if someone hit me hard enough right on my ear, if that happened how would everything change? I think about people coming to the hospital with flowers and them having to write me messages on note pads and us crying about it. I don't think it would be completely quiet either. I think there would be a sound, like a hum, a quiet hum, like you were a clock or there was a clock inside you. Can you still talk if you can't hear yourself? Maybe then it all comes out as nonsense.

But there would be good things too. I wouldn't have to hear all the construction noises or the alarm in the morning or the horns at work. I'd have this special truck at work rigged all special, so the signals from the shovel for back-in, stop, and pull-away would be little lights flashing on my dashboard, and the company would get people to write articles about me, how I was triumphing over everything. There would be other advantages, like not having to talk to my parents on the phone or not having to hear Gene Shalit being vomitricious first thing in the morning on the Today show. Mostly I think I would miss rock & roll. Driving around town seeing everybody singing in their cars would be just about the worst.

Now that's deaf, but being blind I think would be much worse. First off, how would you get blind? It seems like it would take something worse than being hit—like some incredible accident or some chemical or a slow disease that they always make movies about young athletes getting. So even how it would happen would probably leave you a lot worse off.

But the good things would be you couldn't work in the mines and if they set you up with good disability pay (like if it was from a blasting accident at work) maybe you wouldn't have to work at all. Also, you wouldn't have to see all the ugly things there are— like how bad I look in the morning or my dumb moon face in the mirror, or gross and disgusting people around town or the Aya-tollah guy on the news. I think being blind would make some things better, like some drugs and sex sometimes you'd feel deeper, cause that's what you try for anyway when you close your eyes. Also, being blind you would get a lot of attention. That would be nice. But I think it's the sort of nice that would make me start crying and gets old pretty quick. Another thing is maybe I would judge people by more important things than how they looked. But then again maybe what they smelled like would start to be a lot more important, and I'd be prejudiced about the bad-smelling ones just like I am now about the ugly ones.

I don't know why I think about it. I guess it's the same thing as when you're in school, arguing about freezing vs. burning. God, we spent whole lunch periods fighting about whether it'd be better to freeze to death or burn to death in the cafeteria. I was always a freezer, cause it seemed logical—you'd just stop feeling things—instead of things getting more and more painful until you went into shock and died, like if you burned.

GRAVES

For some reason Derek had to leave town for a few days. He got a phone call and had to leave. When he got off the phone he was real preoccupied, running around getting his things together which he threw into the back of his pickup and just took off. He didn't even give me a kiss goodbye but for some reason I didn't ask for one which is not like me. And then when he left it was dark out. And the doorbell was ringing all of a sudden—but I didn't want to get the door cause I just wanted to go to sleep and I didn't care who it was. I shouted, "Who is it?" and they didn't answer. Then I knew I was in danger. It had something to do with Derek leaving. There were these men. I didn't dare turn on any lights because they might be watching me from somewhere. I'm sure they had guns. So I decided I would jump from the bedroom window and try to sneak away real quiet. There was nothing I could grab from the window, like a drainpipe, so when I heard them start knocking the door down I just jumped out into the backyard and did a tumble-roll on the lawn, which is practically a waterskiing move, and my shoulder hurt but I was okay. I wanted to hide in a basement, but not many houses have basements in the neighborhood, and when I climbed over the back fence I could see lights coming on in our house one room after the other. So I walked a couple of streets away and was cold, cause I was only in my Dr. Denton's and it was freezing out, and I finally saw the townhouses. I went in and went down the stairs to the laundry room and turned on the light, which was on a little timer, like an egg timer, it just grinds away until time's up then the lights click off, and I turned it on for about a minute or two so I could find a good place to hide. I found a place right behind the washers where the electrical meters were. And I just scrunched myself down there, right up against the washing machines. I tried to make myself as little as possible so no one would see me. The timer clicked off and the lights turned off, and I was just trying to blend in with the machines so if they came in they wouldn't see me even if they looked. I was getting ready to hide all night and wondering what my chances were of not being found by them, and right then Derek woke me up, cause I was making noises I guess. I guess I fell asleep on the couch and had sweated right through my shirt, cause the sun on me was getting magnified by the windows. At first I thought Derek was them, and I yelled cause I thought it was over for me, that this was the end, and then I didn't know what he was doing there, but then I woke up more and I was glad it was him and I knew he was him, not them.

GRAVES

Today the first thing I thought about when I woke up was, What is dust? And also how does it get where it gets? Cause I was looking through the legs of the chair by the sofa right into the kitchen, and there at the baseboard was this little pile of dust. And I cleaned-up yesterday.

So I decided to check out what it's made of. I picked up the dust bunny and there were carpet fibers + tiny pieces of paper + some of it was actually hair—which was weird, cause you wouldn't think there was so much hair coming out of people all the time. But the thing that got me was, most of it was just stuff that didn't look like anything else—except dust.

Maybe dust is just dust. Like one of those things you can't compare cause they are only like themselves—like water and air and chocolate, stuff like that. I remember once when Mom asked dad, "How's your hamburger?" She was always asking us things like that, not only when she cooked but even when we went out.

Anyway, dad just said, "Tastes like hamburger." Betsy and me thought it was the funniest thing.

So then we'd always say that to Mom. Like if we'd be out and she asked Betsy, "How's your coke?" Betsy would just say "Tastes like coke." Or if she asked me at the D.Q., "How's your ice cream?" I'd say "Tastes like ice cream." And if dad was with us he'd just smile. Finally this one time Mom made steak, which was a special treat, and she asked "How's the steak?" just like a general question, to no one in particular. Well, Betsy and dad and me—I swear this is true—said at exactly the same time, "Tastes like steak!" Mom just said "Jesus kids!" and got up and started doing the pots, leaving her steak getting cold on her plate, and dad whispered that we shouldn't do it anymore. But if you think about it, it makes sense to say that about some things.

And I think dust is just one of those things—that's why people see it every day and don't think about it. The other part of it— figuring out how it gets where it is—is easier. It probably has something to do with the way the air patterns go, like what you see in the insulation commercials on T.V. with the wind coming in under the doors and right through the windows even when they're closed. So it gets blown around by the currents right into the perfectly dead spot.

GRAVES

I think maybe the thing to do is to move in with Derek. He hasn't exactly asked, but I don't know what he's waiting for. The way to do it I think is to do it like I've been doing it anyway—moving over there a sock at a time. It's just the way it works out with us spending more and more time together. I'm not scheming. Because if I go to work from there or I come home with him and don't want to come all the way out to the trailer, I have to have stuff over there. So it's true I have been moving stuff over there. I've got one drawer of his dresser full of my things and he hasn't even noticed. Or if he's noticed, he hasn't said anything about it. But why wouldn't he say something? I'd kind of like him to say something. Maybe if I keep adding socks, like a pair a week, he'll realize I'm practically moving in on my own and he'll have to say something to at least make it partly his idea.

I talked to Sam about it even though she's not in much of a mood lately. She's been pulling a lot of overtime, just for the bucks, so she's been speeding and crashing and about the only time I've seen her is when she's crashed. We're not exactly getting along all peachy or anything. I'm still paying my share of trailer rent even though I'm not there so much, and it seems like all we talk about is the bills and the boys, all the great boys she takes home and can't stand. I still love Sam a lot. I get scared for her sometimes, because sometimes I think something weird is going to happen to her like happened to Annie—like she's going to get sick real bad or get in over her head with a bunch of guys and not be able to get out. She thinks she's so tough is the thing.

Anyway we all went out to dinner at Wendy's before work, her and me and Derek. Because I thought it would be good just us 3, cause I'm tired of feeling like a schitzo—between her place and his place, and her and him. It was friendly and all but she doesn't give him the benefit of the doubt about things, which is just like her not giving me the benefit of the doubt and it pretty much burns my ass. Like he was telling us about his engine dying after work yesterday, and needing a jump in the lot, and how he fixed the problem with new sparks, and Sam just said, "What makes you think it's not going to die again?" It's more the way she says things, not what she says.

And then at another point Derek was telling us about some friends from high school and what they're doing—one's still in Minot getting unemployment and one moved to Fargo. Okay, so it wasn't so interesting. But Sam cuts him off and says it reminds her of a joke. She goes, "Yeah, there are 3 guys on a desert island. One is from Colorado, one is from Wyoming and one is from North Dakota, and they're friends but they've been trapped there for a month. Finally a bottle washes up on the shore and a genie jumps out. And the genie says, You have 3 wishes! So they get all excited. The first guy, the one from Wyoming, says, I wish I was back home with my wife and my little girls. And POOF! he's gone. And then the second guy, the guy from Colorado, says, I wish I was back with my girlfriend skiing in the mountains, and POOF! he's gone too. So then the last guy, the guy from North Dakota, just shakes his head and says, I sure wish my two buddies would come back!"

Okay it's pretty funny but not right when Derek was talking about his friends it's not. He took it good though. He laughed hard. I was the one that was mad. Anyway, after dinner we were driving to work—me and Sam in Sam's car and Derek was driving himself right in front of us—and I did ask Sam about moving in with him, like whether I should bring it up or keep doing what I was doing. And Sam just goes, "What makes you think Derek is the kind of man you can move in with one pair of panties at a time? What makes you think he's that dense?"

GRAVES

As clear as I can remember it, this is what happened. I was playing "8 Ball Deluxe" over in the Fun Center at the Holidome. Deluxe is the best machine over there. You can put your hips into it and it won't tilt. For a while I had the 2nd best score on it, when I was working over there at Cafe Kauai. Anyway, I was playing it and the game was not ending. Betsy was there with me. She was sitting on the glass but she was close enough to the edge so that I could see all the action. For some reason the game didn't stop. Every time I screwed up another ball would pop out, like it was permanently stuck on BONUS. I was playing good enough to get extra balls but not that many. And then I put a ball in play and it just stayed in play. It's true I was making good shots but one time it was heading right for the hole and it swerved into the bumper without me pushing. Maybe Betsy moved her weight. So I kept playing this ball and it felt like I was playing it for an hour. I was getting tired of it but I couldn't just walk away. My score went over 999,999 and so it went back to 0 and started again. I couldn't just walk away from that and have everybody see such a low score.

And then Betsy got off the glass, cause she wanted to get a Milky Way from the machine, and when she got off she left a little steam mark on the glass, like condensation from different temperatures. And I didn't know why until I looked at her over at the candy machine and could see she was naked. Only her body looked different than it is—she had turned into a real Amazon. I knew she was doing weights with Neil but not enough to look like that. She was Betsy, but she didn't look like Betsy. The thing is—nobody else in the Fun Center cared about her standing there like that, and I didn't know if it was because they just were concentrating on their games or they were too young to care about it or maybe I was being old-fashioned and it was no big deal. Also all of a sudden it seemed really loud in there, the pinball and video-game noises. And when I was looking at Betsy I stopped playing, but the flippers kept going on their own and kept the ball in play and then I can't remember what happened after that.

GRAVES

Mom invited me to lunch and then drops this bomb on me. That's the way she does things now and it's almost like she likes it. Bitch bitch bitch. Not that she doesn't have the right. God, it sucks. I guess there were lots of little things happening all the time, but—the first time I knew about it was this one time when he was pushing her hard and she got a scissors out of the drawer in the kitchen and then they both came to their senses and stopped it. And after that time they went to see a counselor, and Mom told me the man said, "All personal relationships have elements of abuse in them," something like that. So she got up and said, "Well, you two gentlemen sit here and talk about it" and walked right out of there. And that was the end of that I guess. Mom said dad was pissed afterwards because she was the one that dragged him there to begin with.

But today she said it happened again, much worse. She didn't say anything about it until today. But I knew something was wrong, as usual. What it was was dad had said he wasn't seeing Shari-the-bitch anymore and he was living at home like regular, but then Mom found out later that he was still seeing her. I guess they were having dinner after work one time and Mom heard about it from someone who saw. So dad said they were just having dinner, that it was all innocent. But Mom said she was sick of him "living in and ordering out for love." So he starts making fun of her, saying something like "Oh Barbara, is that something fancy you heard in one of your country songs?" Mom told him to go ahead and tease her, she was going to fight from now on and not be so nice about it. And then I guess they sort of made up after that and Mom told me that they made love, which is the first time she ever actually told me that.

But then the next day she decided to start with her new policy, so she went over to Shari's house in the morning before work and started swearing at her when she opened the door. I guess she was just swearing at her right on the doorstep and Shari tried to close the door, but Mom got her shoulder in there and kept it open and called her a slut and tried to slap Shari but hit her wrist when Shari put her hand up. And Mom said she could feel her ring hit right on Shari's wrist bone, and how much that must of hurt, which she was happy about, and Mom could hear Shari try to spit at her but she was already halfway down the walk to the driveway.

So after that, Shari called dad at work and told him about it and that she wasn't coming in. And dad didn't go home that night. Mom is sure he stayed at Shari's. And then the next morning he went home before work and got Mom in the kitchen and held her arm behind her back, and he broke the light bulb, which is a fluorescent light, swinging his belt around at her, and it sort of exploded. Then he pushed her head down on the counter and it made one of her teeth that had a lot of fillings in it go loose and she said it was like an electric feeling in her mouth, like being shocked when your hand is wet, only in her mouth. And I guess he held her head down on the counter for a while and made her promise not to touch Shari again or ever even talk to her, and that he and her were just having dinner is all, that's all, and now she went and fucked things up again by blowing it all out of proportion. I asked

Mom what she was thinking about when he had her head down and she said "What the Formica tasted like." That's about the weirdest. I think sometimes she's losing it.

Then dad told her he wanted out and he left for work and left her there. And Mom told me she went into the bathroom and looked at herself in the mirror and started pinching the skin on her forehead until it was bleeding and she was hating her hair cause the curls got all unpermed by winter. And then she said she just sat in the kitchen and thought about not going in to work, and about how that made her feel guilty, because the company did treat her good and she was proud working for it cause it was helping everyone progress, and here she was going the wrong way and acting like a baby and how she was feeling guilty about it, but that it seemed to her that a lot of things were going the wrong way. Like Betsy and me were all grown and she never sees us, like we never ski anymore, like Westhope's going to be lower than ever they say cause of water demands being up. Like town is so green with dope it makes her sick. Just one complaint after another.

But after thinking all these bad things she said she remembered reading in a magazine that this lady shrink said when things go bad and you're at your lowest, that you should do something for yourself, indulge yourself in something you like—to get back on track. So Mom said she went into the freezer and got a family-pak of Aunt Jemima blueberry waffles and had 4 of them and then just toasted up another 4 and ate them and then figured there were only 4 left, so she finished them. And she said she actually felt much better after eating the whole package, which I can't believe anyone could. And then she got herself together a little bit in the bathroom and drank a shot for her tooth until she could get to the dentist later in the day and then went right in to work.

DAYS

Sometimes in the morning going to work when there's so much traffic because of shift change and the graveyard people are getting off and they're beat and the day people are driving to work and not even up yet, sometimes I look into the other cars and the eyes of the people look like fish eyes, all cold and gray. Like at the Gurley crossing after a train has passed or at the intersection of 59 and 14-16, people are just staring straight ahead driving and their eyes almost make them look like sharks. And when people are moving their heads back and forth just a little to music you can't hear, it's almost like the way sharks swim, the way their heads move from side to side, which I've seen a bunch of times in "Jaws" and Jacques Cousteau. They said something once on Jacques Cousteau that I always remembered, cause I did a Bio report on sharks senior year and I used it for a source. They said that the male shark bites the fin of the female shark during mating and that the female shark has skin twice as thick as the male shark. But the thing is— they don't know if her skin is twice as thick because he bites it in mating or if he bites it in mating because it's twice as thick. I always remembered that.

DAYS

Sometimes inside me is this thing. I don't have an exact thing to call it but I already said stuff about it. It's here today. It's like something you don't invite into your house but there it is in bed with you in the morning when you wake up, and there it is in your shower and here it comes sitting down to coffee. When it's around it's good to get high in the morning before work, because then even though the thing stays around, like in my truck, it's more me looking at it from the outside instead of it coming up my throat from the inside. Sometimes when I complain about it Sam says "You have the blues is all." She says it like she has no sympathy— either cause she never had it and thinks it's wimpy to have it or because she has it about all the time so why bother complaining, I can't figure out which.

But I think having the blues or having the blahs is different than from what I got. I think I got something a lot less regular than that. Sometimes I'm convinced that secretly there is this cancer growing in me, like a tumor which is pressing against a tiny little spot in my brain and giving me that indented feeling. Maybe it came from Grandma Hattie or Grandpa Al, maybe from gold particles that he breathed in the Homestake mine or the cyanide filtering tanks. I heard that it could show up two generations later, like it skipped Mom (cause even despite everything she is healthy as a horse). Or maybe it came from taking the wrong sniff of blasting chemicals or something someone gave me for free in a bar. I don't know. It's hard to know.

How you going to ever know? Betsy would say it's just me being paranoid, and it's true I don't have anything scientific about it cause it's not the kind of thing I'm going to bring up to the doctor. It's just a feeling. And that doesn't make it wrong. It's just only I don't have a name for it.

DAYS

Finally went two-stepping with Derek over at the Antler. We both were drinking blackjacks and we kept trying to dance them off. So we'd drink and dance and drink and dance, but I think we started drinking more than we were dancing, cause we were getting tired, and we both ended up completely faced. We should of kept dancing was the problem. Even though I bitch to Derek about rancher snobs—cause it's true a lot of them do think you ain't squat unless you're born with cow shit on your boots—it was fun to dance like them, dance with them for a night.

Derek dances western real good but it makes me feel like a tractor sometimes. It's so mechanical and simple you can't express yourself much. One time I bumped into him and I said, "I'm sorry" and he said, "No it's okay, you got padding." I know he was saying he likes it, but it made me feel fat. I know I'm not fat but sometimes I feel it. I went on this water diet for 4 days after Spike, and Sam said, "Why are you trying to get rid of your curves? Why don't you get rid of your blue eyes at the same time?" But that's easy for her to say. I mean, between 1 and 10, I'm about a 7, maybe on better days 7.5, but when people like Sam and Annie are around it makes you feel like a 3. Especially Annie.

She showed up with some of her friends while we were dancing. They were just sitting at the bar teasing people and Annie was talking with Krysten who's everybody's best bartender—she's the one who made up the thing about N.A.M. So I introduced Derek to Annie and they got along good. Annie was telling him about laying ribbon rail and about painting the window of Free Bird Records all psychedelic, which is what she's doing now. It's safe to introduce someone to Annie now that she's off the market. She's living with some crazy guy over in Sagebrush Hills and she was just waiting for him to show up with all the swing shifters. Her looks are going downhill a little bit. Sam says it's because of the guy. It's true being with one guy can do that to you, but there are other things about it that outweigh the disadvantages, to me at least.

Anyway we partied until the swingers started coming in and it got too crowded and too late and then we went home. Except we went to my house for a change cause Sam took one of her weeks this week and was home in Butte. Also, the trailer is closer than his place and we were both skunk drunk and Derek can't afford a D.W.I. cause he already has a speeding on account of being late for work a couple weeks ago. Driving over there I was telling Derek about all the spots I know the cops like to hide, like behind the FURNITURE sign on 59 and behind the bushes on Roundup, and I told him to go real slow in those spots but he said, "If you go too slow then they know you're drunk and they'll stop you for going under the limit." So he didn't slow down and I got mad at him. I said I didn't think there was such a thing as minimum limits and he said there was and I said, "Well I haven't heard of anybody being arrested for going too slow." Then I stopped caring about the limits until I got the spins and I had to ask him PLEASE! to slow down and he did. He said "Well, now that's a legitimate reason" or something like that. We saw a cop but he didn't stop us. Sometimes they're so busy looking at their radar gun read-out that they don't even notice if you're going completely straight. That can work in your favor.

Since Sam is gone she lets me sleep in her bed so we didn't have to sleep out on the couch. The only weird thing about it is it smells like someone else. Except that's better than waking up needing to be put in traction, which is what both of us on the couch would do. I remember Derek standing there in his Jockeys and his high-tops and I couldn't figure out how he got his pants off and he fell into bed and started mauling the sheets saying, "I've always wanted to make love in Samantha's bed"—like he was joking—and I just said, "Just don't call out her name when you're about to come, okay?" We laughed and went at it a little. Well, a lot.

The thing is, sex is more like love with Derek and I swear when we spend the night together lust wakes me up in the morning. I could set my alarm by it. It's such soft coming and going with Derek, but not wimpy either, just so silky and pretty I feel like trying everything, which is not so bad a thing as long as you don't include perversions. Then again, like they say in the oil patch—one man's perversion is another man's lunch.

And another thing is, I used to never be able to figure out why people say "Are you sleeping with so-and-so?" Because sleeping is hardly what they're interested in and if sleeping was all you were doing they wouldn't even ask. But with Derek it's true sleeping is a part of it—like a real nice part of it—so it makes sense to say "I'm sleeping with him." Because sleeping with Derek is really sleeping. Usually sleeping meant leaving when it was over—except with Spike when it meant waking up tired and bummed.

Though I got to say today I did wake up pretty tired. We were both zombieized in the morning. You know how when you wake up hung over and the light is coming through the crack in the drapes so it's hitting you right in the face and you wish you were Stevie Wonder. And of course it snowed last night—so I'm sitting there trying to make breakfast and the glare out the windows is like little knives stabbing me behind my eyes. I made us Pop-Tarts and coffee and we split one bowl of Cheerios, cause I forgot to go shopping, and let's just say it wasn't doing the job. So I asked Derek if he wanted a jump-start, which is what Sam and me always call it, and he said "What do you mean?" So I went into Sam's room and found a gram she left in her hiding spot and brought it back in and showed him. And he said he didn't think it was a good thing, but he did a little of it just following what I did, probably only because I did it, and it did make him feel better. Because I asked him a couple times driving to work and he said "I feel great Randi"—except the last time he was starting to be sarcastic about it so I shut up. I feel kind of guilty about it is the thing.

DAYS

God, it was the suckiest Christmas. Mom and dad acted like strangers most of the time and when they weren't acting like strangers they acted like enemies. And Derek was bummed because it was the first Christmas ever he didn't spend with his family. My family's not much of a replacement I guess. And Betsy was bummed because Neil didn't hardly get her anything, except blank tapes at the last minute which he didn't even wrap. So it was really good that we had a concert to go to afterwards.

We went to Rapid to see Rod Stewart and it was the best show—including him doing "Santa Claus Is Coming To Town" in these candy-cane red-striped undies. It was a scream! He did "Do Ya Think I'm Sexy?" and "Hot Legs" which everybody knew he would do, but also older ones like "You Wear It Well" and "Maggie May." Those are the ones I remember from growing up, listening to on the radio turned way down in my room, coming in all wavy and fuzzy and trying to get all the words right so I didn't make a fool of myself when I sung them at school. God, he is such a hunk! We had the best seats, cause one of Betsy's friends works at Ticketron and Betsy paid her to buy them for us the split second the computer put them on sale. We were 11 rows from the stage.

The coolest part was when he had everyone sing that line from "You Wear It Well"—he did it so that the band stopped playing right then and all you heard was 10,000 people sing "Madame Onassis got <u>nothing</u> on you!" Seriously cool. But I am so hoarse today from singing along with him the whole show. If I was singing regular I wouldn't be, cause I know how to sing, but he has the kind of voice where you don't want to just sing along in your own voice—you want to make your voice sound like his voice, cause his voice is so sexy. But it's so scratchy that it about kills your throat to do that all night. I don't know how he does it himself. I read where in People it said smoking actually helps.

It was just Derek and me and Betsy and it was like Betsy had a little mini-crush on him so it was fun to share him for the night + it was fun for Derek to walk around with The One And Only Bruce Ski Sisters in either arm dressed to kill at his first-ever Rapid concert. He got some funny looks—jealous looks—from some scroty guys with their ugly girlfriends and we all liked that cause it's like being on stage. I could do that every night. I know that it's only rock & roll but I like it like it YES I DO!

DAYS

THAT BASTARD! GOD DAMN HIM! Okay maybe it's true that she is hard to get along with, everybody knows that, but that's hardly an excuse. It makes me wonder how much happened that I never even knew about—because I was too little to know or too stupid to know. What makes me sick is that I'm not really suprised. If somebody asked me was I suprised I would have to tell them "No." But I sit there, and I see her lying there in the emergency room, and it's just so FUCKED! I feel like screaming but I got no one to scream to right now.

What happened was this orderly from the hospital called at about 7:00 yesterday night and said that everything was okay and not to panic and don't worry about anything but that Mom was over at the hospital and she wanted to see me. And I said, "What's wrong?" and he said she just had an accident and she was in the emergency room but it wasn't really an emergency. I said, "What happened?" and he said he couldn't tell me but it wasn't bad and that I could take my time getting over there—not to rush and have an accident because she is doing fine. I can't believe what people say sometimes.

So I went over there and I didn't stop at any stop signs—like I'm supposed to listen to this orderly asshole—and I got there in about 3 minutes. And I went to the emergency room and they wouldn't let me in for a second and I started hollering so they let me in. Mom was behind a blue curtain over in the corner. She was the only one in the room. It's good it wasn't Friday or Saturday night, cause then she would of had to probably wait for a long time to get treated on account of all the bar fights and accidents. She was just lying on her stomach up on a table and she had her pants and her shoes still on, but her shirt and her bra was off and her head was facing the other way. There was this yellow dishrag-type thing on her back. It looked like it was covering something up.

So I walked around to the side where her face was and I could see she was crying and stuff was coming out of her nose and she had a little tiny bruise on her cheek but she really smiled when she saw me. I felt like crying but I didn't cry cause I figured the reason she wanted me there was to be strong, that's why she called me there, that's what she needed. So I didn't cry and I said, "This wasn't an accident was it?" and she just shut her eyes. She knew I knew.

So I wanted to know what the hell happened but she just said, "Not now, I'll tell you." So I waited there with her and she reached out her hand to hold mine and I sat there with her for awhile. She sort of went to sleep from the medication they must of given her, and I kept holding her hand. Then the nurse came by and whispered that the doctor had decided to keep her in the hospital to keep treating the wounds and keep infections away. I asked the nurse what happened and the nurse goes, "She says she fell down into a cactus, but—well I'm sure that's what happened." So they rolled her out of emergency and up a floor to a room, and she was pretty much sleeping the whole way there. Then they woke her up and put a hospital gown on her and took her shoes and socks and pants off and she lied down on her bed on her stomach.

And then she told me about it. She was sort of out of it so I don't know if it's the right story, but what she said happened was she went over to see him at the McMahon office at the end of the day, cause he had called her about something. She kept saying a couple of times, "So there was no one there cause the secretaries had gone, the secretaries had gone." Anyway, they started fighting about his hours or something, and she just told him to look at the picture on his desk—it's this picture of the 4 of us taken out at Westhope a bunch of summers ago—and she said, "All I'm doing is trying to save it. All I'm doing is trying to keep that picture together." And so dad is just sitting behind his desk and takes the picture and throws it against the wall and the glass breaks.

So when that happened Mom just lost it, and she turned over his In-Out basket and all his papers went on the floor and she started to go, but he caught her before she went out the door and they fought for a second and she tried to throw his paperweight at him but she missed and so he caught her again and held her by the chin, so that she couldn't scream and she couldn't bite him and he kept holding her like that and backed her into the corner of his office and pushed her down right onto one of his cactuses. Mom said, "It was the teddy-bear cactus, that one with the big head I bought him for his birthday a couple of years ago." Mom always loved that one—she was always worried about whether he was watering it right.

She's not very sure about what happened next except that when she got up her peach blouse was all bloody and dad was sitting behind his desk, like waiting to see what was going to happen, and she just walked out of there. She said it was like she was in shock. So she got into the car, but when her back hit the seat she almost died. So she tried to crank the seat back with the lever, cause our Accord doesn't have automatic seats, and it was stuck. So she had to practically lean on the steering wheel all the way across town.

She finally got to the hospital and walked in the main entrance not the emergency one, and told me she told the girl at the desk, "I've had an accident and I can't seem to get all the thorns out."

It just seems like everything gets worse for Mom. I told her not to talk anymore about it, and that I'd tell Betsy. She just said, "Stay away from Peter." It sounded so weird the way she said it, because she didn't call him dad, and she always called him dad to us. Maybe it was because of her being out of it on account of the medication or just the pain. I didn't see any reason to keep away from him, cause I wanted to scream at him, but I didn't want to fight about it with Mom so I said, "Yeah, don't worry"—like I'd be crazy to go near him. And then she held my hand again and fell asleep again. And while she was sleeping I started crying cause she couldn't see me and I kept holding her hand and for a long time I stayed there with her, just like that.

DAYS

I told Derek about it. I had to explain why Mom is in the hospital. Except I told him it was an accident cause I didn't want to get into the whole thing about Peter. Derek trusts me I think, but he's no fool and I think he's suspicious about it. We were having dinner when I told him and he said, "How did she fall into the cactus?" I said, "She was drinking + she was upset at Peter." He goes, "What was she so upset about?" I said, "His hours or something." He said, "How could she have been drinking if she just left work?" I was getting scared about all his questions, so I blew up at him to make him stop. I just went, "Look, don't cross-examine me, okay? What difference is it to you? I'm telling you what she told me. Can we just change the subject?"

I got up to rinse the dishes which I thought would help. And while I was rinsing I said real calm, "I think she went to Ranchers Bar for a drink or two on her way over there," to show him I wasn't avoiding his questions or hiding anything. But Derek went and said, "I just don't see how a teddy-bear cactus minding its own business could put anyone in the hospital. I just don't see it." He said it in a friendly way, like to close the whole subject, so I was relieved about it. And I just said, "I know, it's weird."

And then when we were lying in bed Derek said, "What does Peter say about it?" I said, "I don't know. He had to go down to Salt Lake for business. He was upset about it though." The fact is they weren't letting Peter into her hospital room, cause the doctor told him he wasn't allowed to visit. Mom must of told her doctor. And Mom told Peter that he had to be moved out by the time she came home, which was supposed to be in a few days. It's a white lie what I told Derek, cause I will tell him everything eventually. It's not a black lie.

I had to roll away from him when I told him though. I couldn't look at him. And we just went to sleep like that. I think it's the first time we didn't make love since that first night camping in the Big Horns. That sort of jinked me out this morning when I thought about it, so I tried to stop thinking about it. I mean, by the time I woke up Derek was already in the shower, so it wasn't like I could do anything about it. It's no big deal. It's just today doesn't feel much like New Year's Eve. It feels like I'm on automatic pilot. Like I forgot to start tallying trips on the load counter when work started, so now I got to make up the right number. I think I'm on 14 by what time it is. I don't know, I'm not even watching what I'm doing, I'm just doing it. It feels good to call dad Peter though. I think that's what I'm going to do from now on.

DAYS

This is the biggest and best suprise. You are not going to believe this one. I've just been telling everybody which I know is immature but it makes me believe it myself + the last time I couldn't tell anybody and look at the way that turned out + I think if I tell everybody I know then it makes it even more impossible for it not to happen, which I don't have to worry about really because it's definitely happening and there's no way it's not. Here's what happened—

I was at Derek's yesterday for New Year's, we just drove straight over there from work. I was still a little hung from parties and so I wanted to go over there and crash, and he wanted to go watch the end of the Cotton Bowl and the Rose Bowl and just have a few hours alone. Because later we were going to Joleen's new boyfriend's for an Orange Bowl pizza party. We all were in a pool at work and Derek said we had good numbers, so including time-and-a-half for New Year's Eve and double-time for yesterday he figured we were going to clean up. I wasn't in a very good mood though. Except on the way home it looked like we were going to be boxed in by a coal train, and Derek was swearing about missing the whole 3rd quarter, but instead of underpassing he beat it to the crossing which cheered me up some. Derek's got very good hunches about the trains.

Anyway we went home and he turned on the game and started doing some woodworking, just whittling, and I made us popcorn and then I went into the bedroom to catch some Zzzs. I didn't really want to go to the party so much, but I figured if I didn't sleep through it it would be more fun. And Joleen and I already planned to make comments about what big butts (and other things) all the black players have, just to get the guys going. So I went to go nap out.

And then about 6:00 I got up and took a shower. And while I was in the shower Derek came in the bathroom and I could see him through the frosty shower glass, which made him look like a ghost, just a blob the color of his clothes, and I could hear his razor buzzing. And then I could hear him singing "Saturday" by Elton John. You know how it goes, "Saturday, Saturday, Saturday—Saturday, Saturday, Saturday—Saturday, Saturday, Saturday night's all right!" That's what he was singing. And then I could hear his razor stop, and I turned off the shower, and I could hear him open his razor and blow all the zillions of tiny pieces of beard down the drain and rinse the sink out.

And I was drying my hair in the shower—and the reason I'm going into it so much is to try to figure out why what happened happened—I was drying my hair and Derek said right out of the blue, "Do you know Randi that your body is a temple?" And I said from inside the shower, "About time you noticed." And then he goes on and says, "No, I'm serious. It's a temple on the inside and a temple on the outside, and I'm the only member of the religion and nobody else can join." I said, "Are you kidding or what?" and I slid the shower door open and came out dripping with serious nibbies in the cold draft from the window which the Reynolds Wrap don't hardly stop.

And he took my towel and wrapped it around me and pressed his chest to my back and leaned over and rested his chin on my shoulder. And then he said, "And there's absolutely positively no prostelytizing allowed Randi, you got that?" I nodded an "Of course" and I could feel his cheek go up in a half-smile. That's his real smile, his half-smile. If you don't know him it may look like a frown cause his mouth is closed and his lips go down but he is grinning and you can tell that by his eyes cause his eyes are grinning. He towelled me off and I started to put on my face and when he went to work on his woodworking and to watch the game I yelled after him, "Does that mean when you go down on me it counts for going to church?" I could hear him laughing all the way over the T.V.

So I got dressed and went down to watch the end of the Rose Bowl with him. We were rooting for the team in crimson-and-gold and against the team in red-and-gray, which was fine with me, but after the red team scored again we had to root against the crimson team kicking a field goal because if they did we wouldn't win that part of the pool just by the numbers we had. It was getting complicated and Derek was explaining it to me and the phone rang which got me off the hook. Ha! Anyway, I said "Happy Fucking 1980!" which I decided was fine phone manners for the season, and it turned out to be Mom.

I remember my wet hair was making the phone all ringy and I squeaked it back with my comb. Mom sounded drunk but she couldn't be cause she was still in the hospital. It was just that she was depressed + probably the drugs. I had told her that I was going to go see her after work and I hadn't stopped by and she was hurt about that. So I explained about being tired from last night and all. And she didn't even ask me about my New Year's, she just went on about how bad it was over there, and how she keeps calling Peter to check on when he's going to be out of the house and how he keeps saying she's not giving him enough time, what does she expect on such short notice?

Derek knew it was Mom just by the way I was talking to her. And she just kept going on about it, and I'm going "Uh-huh . . . uh-huh . . . uh-huh," you know like the way you do when you don't want to be listening but you don't want the other person to know that. After awhile I took the phone away from my ear a little bit so that I could still hear her talking over the game, but not each and every word she was saying cause she just kept talking and talking—she was saying stuff about the "accident" and it made me think of my nose after he found my pills in my dresser and I felt my nose.

So Mom kept complaining and complaining and I was putting in an "Uh-huh" or two every once in awhile to not be rude, and what happened was all of a sudden her voice was like background music and for some reason I turned to Derek and put my hand over the speaker part of the phone, real tight, and looked at Derek whittling at the table, whittling something down, and he looked up at me, like to ask me "What?" and just like that I said, "Hey lover, let's get hitched" and just like that he winked at me and went "Yeah."

I can't believe I did that. I got off pretty quick with Mom—I told her I was cooking lasagna. And then me and Derek just sat there looking at each other and smiling, and then hugging each other, and I think he couldn't believe I did that either and that he said yes. Cause I wasn't scheming it or nothing. It just came out. God we were so happy sitting there. It felt like the feeling the first time I met him, that feeling of lying there with him, only better cause I knew him now. And then we got ourselves together pretty fast—I kept hollering at him to hurry up, saying, "You don't want to miss the kickoff do you?"—because I couldn't wait to get to the party and shoot off my big mouth. You blame me?

SWING

Went X-countrying with Derek out by the Tower and wrote this,
which I'm putting in here, which I know sucks—cause it's the first
one I've done since Junior English—but like Mom always says, it's
the thought.

ANGELS & DEVILS

The cold wind blows me
But inside I am warm,
The coal blasts shake me
But inside there's no storm.

The grasslands are covered
In a violent swirl of snow,
But inside flowers bloom
As if they didn't know.

Devil's Tower is standing
Dark against the sky,
But the way I'm feeling inside
Makes angels wonder why?

The radio still rocks me
With the same old tunes,
But inside I hear love songs
Sweet as summer moons.

The trains still stop me
At the Gurley crossing,

But inside it feels like
It's my life I'm finally bossing.

Devil's Tower is still standing
Dark against the sky,
But the way I'm feeling inside
Makes angels wonder why?

SWING

We were getting married right in the middle of Derek's street.
There were little orange cones put down to keep cars from coming
down the block but they came down anyway. Each time a car came
everyone had to stand to the side and let it pass. It was like when
kids play football in the street and they have to stop whenever a
car comes. But this was my wedding. I was so upset. And the cake
was right down on the street between us and all the guests. So
when the cars came down the block they would have to swerve
around it, and sometimes their wheels squealed cause they didn't
see it until the last moment. And then the ceremony would go on
like nothing happened. Another thing was that I was wearing
shorts. I was all in white, of course, but it was like a tennis outfit
instead of a real dress. I felt so stupid! I felt like people would
think I was disrespecting the whole thing but that wasn't the case
at all. I just couldn't figure out why I was in shorts. And they
weren't even clean. The music playing was just an acoustic guitar,
but the wind was blowing so you could hardly hear it except when
it was blowing in your direction. So while we were waiting for the
music to end, Derek said, "Where's Peter and Barbara?" I said, "I
think they had raquetball time for now, and they couldn't switch."
I mean, that seemed okay to me, like it was no big deal. And then
in the middle of the ceremony, right before the "I do" part, when
we were both kneeling and the pavement was hurting my knees,
another car came over the four little cones. Except this one was a
big black 4×4 pickup with big yellow mud-flaps. And everyone

went to the side of the road to let it pass. And Derek and I got off our knees and he went to his side of the road and I went to my side of the road, and watched. And instead of going around the cake, the driver decided that even though he was going slow—it seemed like slow-motion—that he would drive right over the cake. I couldn't see who the driver was cause the windows had that privacy tint glass on them. And he just drove right over the cake, all five layers. And when all the guests saw that the cake was okay and that the little statue thing of the bride and groom wasn't even knocked off—cause I guess the guy had enough clearance—everyone started whooping and hollering and applauding. Everyone was so happy. It was absolutely great. And then it was over.

SWING

Mom drove her car home from the hospital after they let her out at noon, and I was already home waiting when she showed up. But she didn't come in right away so I went through the kitchen to the garage and there she was—cleaning the driver's seat with spit and this napkin. She looked up at me like I suprised her. She just said, "There's some blood on the seat, but it's so dark blue you can hardly see it." She said it like she was apologizing.

Then she dropped the napkin in the plastic bag they gave her for her dirty clothes—which I guess were the clothes she came in with—and stood up and gave me this huge hug. Sometimes Mom hugs you so hard you can't breathe, and it was one of those, but I didn't say anything under the circumstances. I was afraid to hug her back too hard cause I thought it might hurt her. So I gave her 3 little squeezes with my hand on her shoulder, but that just made her hug me harder cause I hadn't given her the "3 little squeezes" for a long, long time. It was always her favorite thing that she taught us—each squeeze stands for a word and it spells out "I Love You." It's been a Bruce family tradition since I can remember. It really made her happy that I did that, so she gave me squeezes back except she started multiplying instead of adding them—which is just the way she is—so I felt like a tube of toothpaste by the time she was done. I said, "Mom, how about lunch?" so I could breathe again not cause I was so hungry.

As soon as we walked into the kitchen I felt like something had changed. I can't say what exactly, but something changed. I mean, I wanted to tell her right then about Derek and me getting married, but she was talking a blue streak and I didn't want to interrupt + I thought maybe she won't be so thrilled to hear it right now. That was different, to think something like that. Because Mom usually wants to know every tidbit even before you've lived it. So even though I was bursting inside I held it back.

Mom went on about the doctors who were all so great and the nurses who were all so bitchy and I made us grilled cheese sandwiches. She asked to make them, but I wanted to. I would of felt guilty sitting there with her just back from the hospital making lunch. She said, "I want to feel useful." I said, "Mom don't be silly." Then she said, "Let me make a salad." I said, "Let's not argue, okay?" So she backed down and sat at the table and talked and talked.

She told me about different kinds of medicine. She told me about her roommate, who was this Wright woman who shot herself accidentally in the kneecap and who they medi-choppered in. She told me she had a heart-to-heart with Betsy about Neil, and Betsy promised she would stop seeing him if he kept dealing. Then we ate.

And she asked me, did I see dad? I told her "No," which is the truth, only I didn't tell her I tried to see him but he'd already gone out of town on business. She said, "You'd better stay away from that man" like it was <u>me</u> that needed protecting and that got me pissed, but I blew it <u>off</u>. Now what I think is, maybe she doesn't want me to see him cause there's more to this incident than what she told me. Maybe it's <u>her</u> she's protecting.

Anyway, after lunch we walked around the house and she got angry cause hardly any of his stuff was gone. The only thing it turns out he took was a few clothes. Everything else was there like he'd rolled out of bed in the morning and left for work in a hurry. Mom said she told him to take <u>all</u> his clothes, his fishing and hunting stuff, his guns, some of his tools which we didn't need + his antique saddle, cause no one sat in it anyway except me sometimes when I used to watch T.V. Then she went into the bathroom and shouted back, "He left his God-damn electric razor! What is he, growing a beard?" I told her "I doubt it—but maybe. Maybe he forgot it." What I was thinking though is that he left it on purpose, and that if Mom was expecting to see his tail lights in her rear view mirror anytime soon she was seriously mistaken. I couldn't tell her that though. You can't tell her things like that.

I was expecting her to go around throwing all his stuff into bags or suitcases or the garbage best of all, but she left everything right where it was and walked into the kitchen with me following her, and said, "I shouldn't, because of my medication, but I need a drink. I'm sorry Randi but I do." So we had the last two beers he left, no point throwing them out either. She asked me was it okay me drinking before work, and I shot back, "Well I only go about 10 miles per hour" and we laughed, which was good. I thought things would get better then and I could change the subject and tell her about me and Derek.

Mom decided to do laundry. I remember one time she told me, "No matter how bad you feel, doing laundry makes it better." I guess this was one of those times she was relying on the theory. Mom does wash with a vengeance. She's like the Mario Andretti of laundry, just the way she is about it, folding and all. Anyway we got a bunch of stuff together and went down to the basement. And one of the baskets had a bunch of his clothes in it, and she threw those in with her stuff. I went, "Mom!" And she just said, "Well it's too much trouble separating it out is all." I couldn't believe it. I didn't know what to say except "God, Mom" and other dumb things like that. It got really uneasy and quiet down there, except for the water filling up the machine. Neither of us was saying anything.

So I said it. I just came out and said it. I don't know why I should of felt bad about saying it, cause if anything it should make her feel better about everything. I guess just with her coming back and the house being empty, and starting to feel sorry for her in a funny way, I was holding off—but I just let it go. She was putting the detergent in, so I was looking at her back and I didn't have to look her in the eye and that helped.

When she heard me, she just turned around and her mouth was wide open. Open like she was astonished. Then she said, "When did he ask you?" I told her New Year's, only I asked him. Then she started crying and crying and hugging me and hugging me. I thought she was crying cause she was so happy—which she <u>was,</u> which she kept saying she was—but I mean she just kept crying. She cried all the way through to spin-dry of the second load. And even when she was asking me questions and being excited about it, her voice had those Mom-tears in it. I didn't know what to tell her. She just kept crying.

She was still crying folding the whites, and I told her if she kept it up we'd have to dry them again. I was just trying to make a joke, but she looked at me serious—her angry look when her eyes go small and stare through you. She went, "You'll know when you're a mother, so don't you laugh at me." I told her I was just trying to make her <u>feel</u> better, and then I gave her 3 squeezes again. We were walking up the stairs and she said, like a delayed effect, "Randi, nothing has ever made me feel better in my entire life." And that made me feel so warm inside I started pooling up.

Then she sat me down at the kitchen table and let me cry for a while. She asked if she could brush my hair. I said, "Yeah, that would be great." She went and got a brush and we just sat there at the table with her brushing my hair. It was nice. It was strange it was so nice. I think the last time I let her do that I was 14. It always made me feel good. And she did that for the longest time, until I was almost going to be late for work—cause I had Derek's truck and I had to pick him up.

I asked her if she was going to be okay, and she said of course and that Betsy had promised to come home right after school, which was soon. I was just about out the door when she covered her mouth, like she had just thought of something. I said, "What?" And she just went, "Grandpa and Grandma" and her eyes went glassy again. And I knew how she must of felt cause I thought about them right after it happened, and thought about how great it would be to be able to tell them. It's true that's a sad thing to think, them not knowing. And it must be worse for Mom not having them around to tell, because when I walked out I could see she was really crying big-time again.

SWING

I finally saw Peter. I was trying to get him for about a week on the phone over at McMahon, which is impossible to do because he's always on-site or out of town. I figured he was staying with Shari-the-bitch, but I didn't want to call him over there. Anyway, I finally got him at the office yesterday morning and told him I had to see him. He said, "What about?"—all innocent. I told him I'd tell him when I saw him. He said he could see me if I came by Hole-in-the-Wall after work, he was going to see Wild Horses—which is his favorite band. Of course I knew it was Men's Night too. They have a tacky lingerie show, models and all. Figures.

So I went right from work and got there around midnight. It took a long time to find him cause it's the biggest nightclub in the state. Wild Horses was playing "Cowboy Joe" and guys were buying samples of stuff that the models had on. The sign by the bar said "Buy The Woman In Your Life A Great Gift." It should of said "Buy The Woman Who's Not Supposed To Be In Your Life A Horny Gift." I think some of the guys were trying to buy the models and not just the samples.

Turns out Peter was in the hallway to the head, making business deals with people. He acted glad to see me though. We went back to his table, which was right under the big wagon wheel, and a bunch of guys from McMahon were there + guys from Prarie Dodge, cause he owns a little piece of that now, is how he explained it to me. He told me that they'd be leaving as soon as the band stopped and we'd be alone. So we listened to Wild Horses awhile— they're okay, sort of kick-ass country with a little rock & roll thrown in so that they go over with the boomers. Dad was chain-smoking Camels. Christmas Day he said his New Year's resolution was quitting, but he was back nailing in his coffin. He wasn't too drunk though.

We had tequila shots and then the band stopped and all his buddies left. I had waited too long to pussy-foot so I just went, "What happened with Mom?" He looked at me funny, like he was trying to figure out what I meant, and then he goes, "Well, we had an argument is all, a bad one. But she's still so angry about it I thought it might be better if I moved out for a while until she simmers down." I cut him off. "Listen, how did she end up in the hospital?" He looked at me for a long time, not saying anything.

Then he goes, "She was throwing things in my office. You know how she gets. And she threw something and slipped and fell into that cactus, the teddy-bear one with the big head sticking up. I don't know why I have to tell you this cause you've obviously talked to your mother about it." I told him that was true. But he didn't know what Mom told me. So he goes on, just to round off all the corners you know, he goes "Hey, if one of us had to have that accident I wish it had been me. It's real unfortunate, cause she's holding it against me and we're not together right now because that's the way your mother feels." I sat there and let him dig himself deeper and deeper. I wasn't going to tell him what I know about it. I'm not scared of him. It's just I like having something over him.

And I didn't go there to get his story which I knew would be a horseshit story. I went cause I wanted to tell him about me and Derek. I know Mom said not to get near him but I'm not scared of him and I wanted to see his face when I told him. Because I know he thinks I could never get a good man, or at least keep one. He thinks I'm too loose. And he always made it seem like Spike split cause of my ways or something—instead of Spike just turning into an asshole. He was a big fan of Spike's. I remember him saying one time, "Well I know it stinks, but Spike must have his reasons." After he said that, I decided I wasn't ever going to say anything to him about boys. But of course this was different. It was going to be like paying him back for what he always thought before, like saying "TAKE THAT, Mr. Prick."

So I let him go on about him sending flowers to the hospital and then let him drop Mom from the conversation. He relaxed alot because that's what he thought I needed to see him about. We had shots and I said, "Guess what?" I love doing that, because when people try to answer it tells you everything they're thinking instead of telling them what you're thinking.

He said, "Did you get a raise?" I said, "In a way." He guessed, "You back with The Boom-Boom Girls?" I told him no. He

131

guessed, "You got a new boyfriend?" I said, "The reverse of that."
So he said, "You and Sam finally dating." I said, "Very funny." He
thought he was very funny though. He thinks he's everything.

I knew he wasn't going to get close. So I started getting ready
to go. I put my coat on and my hat and got my car keys out, jingling
them around. And he was like, "Hey Randi Candy, aren't you
going to tell me? Come on, it's not fair to tease your dad so bad."
So I figured I'd give him a clue. I stuck my car key ring holder
onto my ring finger and put out my hand, real obvious like girls
do when they're showing off. So he goes, "You got a new car—
fantastic." Can you believe that?

But I didn't say nothing. I just stood up and zipped my coat and
shook my head like I was feeling sorry for him. And he was going,
"What? What?" And then I kind of started laughing at him—only
he didn't know why—and I shook my head and looked him right
in the eye and said, "Me and Derek are getting married, we're
getting fucking married." And I just turned around to walk out of
there, and I heard him go, "Hey! Hey!" But I kept walking, and
before I got to the door I turned around and saw him standing
there at the table, like his feet were welded to the floor, and I
blew him a kiss goodbye and split. It was great to see him swinging
in the breeze like that. It felt great driving all the way home to
Derek's and it still feels great tonight. Swinging in the God-damn
fucking winter breeze, Peter Peter Crow Eater.

DAYS

I'm too high these days to write anything about anything, or that's the way it seems. So I've been laying off. I mean high-on-life high and not uncontrolled substances. Like today, waiting on my truck. Usually I'd be in a pisspoor mood, cause I hate day shift in the middle of winter—it uses up all the light you've got the whole God-damn day—but today waiting I found myself smiling at people I don't ever smile at—some guys I don't like for reasons and some cause they're just, just jerk workers I never liked the looks of. And yesterday I caught myself saying "Take care, now" to the drive-up teller. It's pretty weird!

It's true work is still boring and all, but it's like I'm so busy thinking in my head that I don't really have time to put anything down. Not thinking so much as just daydreaming. Daydreaming and swingdreaming and gravedreaming. I'm spacing out about all the time I'm awake now, which is kind of funny. But I'm not having night dreams. Derek says I'm still having them only I'm not remembering them. He says you're always having them—but I don't know. I think maybe everything in life is going good enough that I don't need dreams right now. Anyway, I've been laying off doing this for awhile and I thought I should put down why—so if I ever look back at it I'll know.

GRAVES

God, it was the best! I'm glad we had a day to recover cause we
needed it. The people that were there were Jimmy Mac and his
new girl Sue, Mark Rowland, The Big O, Kevvy, Joleen, Sam, T.J.,
Mike, Toots Brull, Stormin' Norman, Nan and Kathryn, Scotty
Pippin, Judy Ruhman and brother Jim, Jose Alomar, Betsy and
Neil, Ralph The Jew, Tim Boerwinkle, Melody on a bet she
wouldn't show, the whole old gang with Spike, Sasha, Glenn
Holmquist, Siobhan, Sarah, Shari Ludwig, Annie Hall Lewis, Panama Red with his Frisbee dog Marley, Pete, Reggie, Jay and those
guys from Reggie's Roustabout, Walter and Michael, Billy, Wayne
Long, a whole lot of crashers I didn't know, Frank, Cucumber,
Patrick, Pistol, + of course Brubach and Kevin who threw it, who
are mostly friends of Derek from work.

They were saying they wanted to throw a combination Engagement Party and Housewarming but I didn't think they were going
to pull it off cause the invitations went out late. They were xeroxed
sheets saying BRUTUS ERECTUS & COALIGULA INVITE YOU TO THE
FIRST EVER MID-WINTER RAWHIDE VILLAGE TOGA PARTY
CELEBRATING THE ENGAGEMENT OF DIRTY DEREK & RANDI
CANDY PLUS THE OPENING OF THE NEW PLAYBOY MANSION
WEST AT 23 RAWHIDE DRIVE, 9 P.M./SAT. There was a picture Bru
drew of "Brutus Erectus" lying on his back drinking Jack and
wearing a toga like a tent with his own tent-pole poking it up, and
grapes being dropped into his mouth. Then there was a little map
showing how to get out to Rawhide Drive and find the house,
because it's in a brand-new subdivision way north of town and
they're about the first ones in there. And at the bottom there was

a little cartoon character guy saying, "Frostbit balls? Frozen boobs? No problem with our roaring fireplace and carpeted pleasure dens." Those guys are a riot. They are really creative.

Their house is this great house, $78,000, which they bought together. And right when you walked in, there was a sign that they took from the lobby of the Buffalo. Bru said they were just borrowing it but Kevin said it was "liberated" by a rail-crew friend of theirs and was their property now and was going to stay hanging in the entrance. It says—

CHECK OUT TIME 11:00 A.M.
LEAVE KEY AT DESK

NO REFUNDS
NO DOGS OR PETS
NO COOKING IN ROOMS
NO GUNS IN ROOMS
WE RESERVE THE RIGHT TO REFUSE SERVICE TO ANYONE!!

So that put everyone in the right mood. There was tons of food and tons of booze, a big bowl full of doobies and some people brought crank and ludes and their own stuff. Kevin's bedroom had a sign saying ORGY ROOM cause he just got his waterbed with mirrors. It was incredible and a lot of fun, and everyone was dancing in the living room cause they just got their stereo, Yamaha 1040 receiver and Bose speakers and it was shaking. I remember dancing to "What A Fool Believes" and "Don't Stop 'Til You Get Enough" and "Ride Like The Wind" and then when people got more zoned out they put on Foreigner and Dire Straits and Zeppelin. I mean they had the music programmed perfect.

And everybody looked incredible in their togas. Some had funny things on like purple sheets or their little brother's Star Wars sheets, things like that. And Panama Red had made a little toga for Marley, who's this beautiful black Lab who usually goes around in a red bandanna. And everybody was doing funny things, like fat old Boerwinkle did this joke with his belly button where he jiggled it around like the Pillsbury Doughboy with his hands and

135

said, "What's that?" No one knew. So he goes, "A naked woman running the high hurdles."

People were giving each other backscratches and in the Orgy Room they were playing strip poker, only with a scissors—so when you lost a hand, the dealer got to cut off part of your toga. Of course Sam was in there, not that she wasn't showing enough anyway. And she came out of there at about 1:30 and all she had on was one of those cut-off football mesh jerseys that you can sort of see through and what was left of her toga pinned like a diaper around her waist. She probably wanted to lose her hands, just so she could get the attention. I didn't see her much cause there were so many people there—and me and Derek were like the guests of honor—but I saw she was hanging out with the old group of Spike's in the kitchen, and I saw them dancing to REO Speedwagon, which was weird.

But it was the best party I've ever been to, cause people just kept going and it stayed fun all the way up until the end, which most of them don't. I mean, at 2:30 you see guys dancing around and arm-wrestling and going for the girls they want and you know they have to be up at 4:30 to get out to their rigs on time—so you know they'll get an hour of sleep maybe or maybe they'll just crank up, fuck sleep, and go straight on out to the patch—and it's a blast, cause you know there aren't so many places around with people like that.

Everybody was really happy about me and Derek and said what a great couple we are. I think it lasted until about 4:00. I remember Bru and Jimmy Mac and Joleen standing in the snow chanting "TO-GA, TO-GA, TO-GA" and we left right after that. I think everybody that was there at the end pretty much ended up in their underwear.

GRAVES

I can't believe Sam. We're driving out here tonight, which was the first time I came in with her for a long time—cause we've been missing each other since she went away and I was spending so much time at Derek's—and we stopped at Denny's to get something to eat, which is what we agreed to do at home. But once we sit down and look at the menu—which she's seen like 1000 X before—she decides they don't have anything she wants and so she wants to go to Long John Silver's instead. But of course it's all the way on the other side of town and the wrong direction from work. So I told her, "There a zillion things on the menu you can get here + we're already running late." She goes, "We'll eat in the car."

So Sam's driving us over there, and I'm thinking about why is it that the person who drives feels like they can make all the decisions, just cause they're driving? And also how much I hate Long John Silver's fish cause if it doesn't make you burp all night it makes you fart, and you got to keep the windows in the Wabcos closed against the cold if you're hauling, and you just feel disgusting 8 hours later climbing down from the truck, just the way it sticks in your stomach. But I didn't say anything cause I was in a good mood.

So then we're waiting at the drive-up window behind about 6 cars and it's taking forever. So Sam says, "They really shouldn't be allowed to call it fast food sometimes." And I say, "They really shouldn't be allowed to call it <u>food</u>, ever." She just blew smoke rings into the rear-view mirror and then looked at me and goes, "What is your <u>problem</u>?" I told her, I didn't have a problem, what was hers? Of course she didn't answer me, she just turned up KOAL, which had on "Against The Wind." And when I started singing with it, cause it's about my favorite song, she changed the station to KGIL—and she doesn't even like country music. Right in the middle of me singing. She was trying to get me pissed, so I just went "Jesus" and looked the other way.

After waiting about 15 minutes for our order, it finally came and she made a big point about her treating me. She starts driving to the back of the lot to park so we can eat without her having to drive for a minute and I said, "It was your turn to pay anyway." So she goes, "Boy, you're on the rag tonight." My stomach was starting to feel bad and I hadn't even eaten anything yet. I think it was just the smell.

We ate for awhile, sitting there in the car by the dumpster, listening to the radio. She said something about the toga party, which was about the last time I saw her, except from my truck at work. I told her the guys liked that midriff football jersey she had on. She just said it was her brother's but it was too long for her so she cut it off and just stuck it in her purse and brought it to the party in case her toga started coming apart or slipping off, just to be safe. Yeah, right. Then she started talking about assholes at work.

I said, "I saw you dancing with Spike." She goes, "So what?" I go, "Well I just saw you is all." And then she goes, "Randi it was a party. Dancing illegal now or what?" I told her of course not and don't insult my intelligence, cause I was just wondering about it. She was eating deep-fried shrimp and drinking her Tab and blowing smoke out the window, like she was going to make me keep wondering for a while more.

Finally she says, "I've danced with Spike lots of times and you've seen me." I said, "That was different, cause we were going out then." She goes, "Well since then too." And after that I don't know what I said. I think I said, "Congratulations" and she said, "What's that supposed to mean?"

We finished eating, except I hardly ate. And then Sam stuffed all our stuff back into the take-out bag and rolled down her window and threw it into the dumpster. I went "Two points" and gave her the little sign. She smiled and slid over on the seat and put her arm around my shoulders for a second and said, "Look, we've been best friends for 3 years, okay? We were just dancing, okay, so don't have a baby about it."

And I felt better. But then after we drove out of the lot, through town and out towards work, all of sudden she says, "But just cause we're friends for so long don't mean you own me you know." Just out of the blue. Like is that supposed to be her little polite way of telling me to mind my own business? God. And the thing is that I don't care what she does with Spike or what she doesn't do. She can dance with him or whatever. I don't care. I got more important things to think about. Better things.

Except the way she was about it is what pisses me off. It makes me feel like just not going back to the trailer with her, this morning or never. And that's a bummer feeling. Because even though I haven't been staying there much, I wanted to spend more time over there until I got married. I don't really want to move in with Derek full-time now. Because it would be so unromantic right before the wedding + I figured that now would be the last time Sam and me would get to be together like that, which I was thinking good things about. But now I don't know—

Sometimes I think love and hate are just two sides of the same nickel.

GRAVES

1) Blood tests
2) Invitations
3) Cambria Room *** date
4) Napkins color
5) Cake—Choc or Van
6) Band (Up Your Alley?)
7) Party
8) Afterparty
9) Betsy dress
10) Sam dress
11) Room for night (part of deal?)
12) Mom photo person
13) 2 superstitious
14) Don't get fat
15) Derek's family—places to stay
16) Judge Thomas vs. priest
17) Mom dress for me (altering)
18)
19)
20)
ETC. Stuff)

GRAVES

I had this talk with the Harpers tonight. Derek was out bowling for the Keller team and I called them in Minot. I had to find out about arrangements. They can't afford motel rooms for the whole family over the wedding so they asked me if maybe they could stay with my family, or I could find other places for uncles and aunts and grandparents and kids and all. They said if worse came to worse they could get motel rooms. They were nice about it, they weren't making demands or anything. I really didn't want to have to figure all of that out though. I know I should of just said, "Of course you can stay with my parents." That's what they were expecting.

But that would be so <u>crazy</u>. Because I don't know what the deal is going to be with Mom by then. It goes from completely one thing to completely another about every other week. And if Mr. and Mrs. Harper stay with them for the whole weekend—I know they will see something and the situation is going to come out. Or if Mom is alone again by then then they'll know something's wrong right to begin with + I <u>know</u> Mom, and she will tell them her life story by the end of the first night they're there. I know she will tell them more than they want to hear. So by Sunday they're going to be looking at Derek and thinking, What is he getting himself into? Which isn't fair either, but people are that way about families.

So I told them that I wasn't sure about it, because my parents are going to have family coming in—which isn't true. But I told them I'd work on it. I felt like saying, "Yeah, if I can keep my dad from attacking my Mom with a chainsaw while you're staying over there I'm sure you'll have a great time." Instead I told them that if it didn't work out at home then maybe what they could do is stay in Derek's and my new house if we've bought it by then and it's ready. Because we just started looking serious, but we've already narrowed it down to 3 houses, and 2 of them would be ready by then. That's what the contractors say. It wouldn't be too homey to stay in a practically empty house, but even if we don't have beds yet there's carpet + sleeping bags. I also told them that the Holidome is giving us special rates for all the out-of-town people coming in, since the reception is there, so even if worse came to worse it wouldn't be so bad.

Mrs. Harper said, "We're sorry to be asking, cause I know your family is paying for the whole thing, but times out here are—" and I cut her off, "Listen, don't worry, okay, we'll work it out." I felt bad for them. It's funny too cause I'm 19 and I could afford to spend a lot of nights in motels if I wanted to, and then these adult people who I think are really great, they can't. That jinks me out.

And then we started talking about the wedding and all. They sounded real happy about it, like they have ever since Derek first told them. I said it was hard to believe that when I met them Thanksgiving it was only 3 months ago, cause it feels like about 3 years so much has happened. Then Mr. Harper said, "I remember Derek telling us that weekend that he was thinking of marrying you. That's why he wanted to bring you home so much." And I said it was all great and we hung up.

But as soon as I hung up I thought, Hey, if he was thinking of marrying me way back then how come I didn't know about it? And for so long it was like he was resisting me moving in with him—and not out of being old-fashioned I don't think. It made me insecure for a second to think about it but now I'm okay. I mean, if that's what he was thinking why didn't <u>he</u> propose to <u>me</u>?

I mean, I'm the one who <u>did it</u>. It makes me feel like calling up the Harpers and telling them, "Hey, Derek ain't marrying me, I'm marrying <u>him</u>." And telling them how it came about. But I suppose it doesn't make any difference whether he's marrying me or I'm marrying him. It's the same thing isn't it, no matter who's marrying who?

GRAVES

Tonight I'm singing every song I know to keep from going lonely. All graves are lonely more or less, no matter what mood you're in. That's when having music meant the most. It's the darkness. Days and swing you could get by without it. Light helps that way

+ there are more things going around in the mine to look at then, like blasting and engineers and you can practically see faces. But not at night. All there is is coal and night and the coal is the color of the night. So if it weren't for headlights and kliegs and safeties it would just be blackness.

Sometimes on graves I wish all the power would go out. All the lights—even including our headlights and the aircraft warning lights on the tipple and the strobes, the lasers, the arrows, the ramp guides + the auxiliary generators would go down too so there'd be no emergency kick-on. Everyone would have to sit exactly where they were—halfway up the haul road, deep in the pit, wherever—have to sit right there, and no one from the company could do anything about it. Zillions of bucks of equipment sitting still, all invisible. It would get quieter than ever before. And it would stay that way right up until dawn broke. That's when work should start anyway. I mean, how did it become that people started working all night? Everybody acts like it's the most normal thing in the world but really it's screwy if you think about it. I wonder who had the idea about it first, how it came up? All I know is there must have been a lot of money involved to think of that.

3 hours later—lights are still on. I don't think I'm going to get any wishes tonight. But I did see a sign—something happened that could of been because of what I was thinking about. One of the headlights on one of the Lectra Hauls, blew out, so now every time it circles at the hopper it looks like it's winking at me. I wonder if it did that cause I was thinking what I was thinking about. That would be strange.

About the only good thing is seeing Derek's truck. He's in Wabco #2022. It used to be that we'd pass each other on the haul road—each trip going up, each trip going down—so like 40 × a shift we would wave to each other and blow kisses, stuff like that. There's no point trying to shout cause everything's too loud. One shift about a month and a half ago, we were on swing, he was coming down the haul road and he mooned me. I swear. He must of got up on his seat for a second and kept steering with two hands and then dropped trou and shot it out the side window. I was hysterical, and then all of a sudden I freaked cause I wasn't sure it was him, so I caught the truck number and it was him—which was a relief. So while I was up at the hopper I had to figure out what to do back.

Well by the time I headed back down into the pit I had my jacket off and my shirt unbuttoned and my flashlight rigged up with wire on my side mirror so it was shining into the cab. And I headed down, counting the trucks to make sure it was his—even before I could see his number—and then kneeled up on the seat and turned to the window and opened my shirt and flashed him. Man his mouth was wide open!! When you're hauling, you live for doing little things like that.

But the thing is, the haul road is changed now because of where we're mining. There's no more two-way section right now. It's all a big loop. We follow each other down and up, all the way, around and round. So unless I'm right behind him or he's behind me, we can't hardly ever see each other all shift. He's 3 trucks ahead of me tonight so I can see him being loaded when I'm coming down into the pit. It's better than nothing.

Whenever I see his truck I wonder what he's thinking. Or sometimes even when I don't see it. Is it possible to miss someone even though he's only about 400 yards away from you? Because I do. And I'm glad that dawn is starting to come earlier and earlier now, cause that's a nice feeling—it gets warmer and you see the sun sooner. Only sometimes it actually makes it harder, because as soon as it gets light out you expect that work will be over any second—like it is in the middle of winter—but now you realize that just cause it's light doesn't mean it's time. So you look at your watch and see how much time there is to go and that's depressing.

So to keep from being all depressed sometimes I think about seeing him the second we get off. Like what he'll say about shift, what he'll look like, anything really. Like tonight I'm thinking about what kind of kiss to give him, a big wet one or a little teasing one or just a hug. It's fun to think about it cause whatever it is it can change the whole way we drive home.

DAYS

"Hers is like a torn pocket in a raccoon coat." That's the words I keep remembering from my dream last night. We were having a nighttime cookout on the beach out at Westhope. There were a bunch of people around, a bunch of different fires. People were doing hot dogs and burgers and the moon was out really big. It was reflecting off the water. I don't know why everyone was eating so late. Anyway, I was turning the hamburgers so that they would be even, and Derek was pointing the flashlight on them so that I could see, cause at night it's hard to tell whether something is rare or getting burned. So I kept flipping them and tried to keep my face out of the smoke, but the wind kept shifting. There was a whole bunch of people who were having a party next to our party and they kept singing radio songs. Then one of the guys from that party came over to our fire and asked Derek for our squirt bottle to keep his flames down. I didn't see him cause it was so dark + all the smoke. But I recognized his voice from somewhere. Derek gave him our squirt bottle. But he stayed standing there, and him and Derek started laughing. I was concentrating on the burgers so I didn't know what about. Then I heard the guy say to him, "Hers is like a torn pocket in a raccoon coat." And Derek just said "Shit, yeah!" or something like that. Then they both laughed like guys do. And right after that, the guy went back to his friends and Derek just shined his light and I didn't say anything for the longest time because I was really jinked out about what the guy said. I didn't want to ask Derek who he was talking about. I was scared it might be me and I was panicked that Derek would think that way about mine, and I just remember it being really hard to think about that and cook the burgers at the same time. Because I want to be pretty all over is the thing. I heard that phrase before, once out in the oil patch. Terry used it about some lady he met at the Rusty Nail and the guys all laughed. And I even thought for a second maybe that's how some guys liked them. But that's not the way it seemed from how he said it. And also it's a whole nother thing if you hear it in a dream that was all romantic right up until then. I don't even know if we ate after that.

DAYS

I finally got Derek to play raquetball. He'd been promising for a long time but I pinned him down to a time yesterday after work and got him on the court. He's a good athlete but I'm just as good an athlete as him + he's never played before so I whipped him pretty good. He caught on fast and by the last game he was pushing me. When I beat him, 15–12, he said, "Next time your ass is mine." I told him that was already the case so he had better think of a different trophy.

I almost was going to let him beat me one game. Not because of his ego or anything but just because I knew I was going to ask him for something after we played, and I didn't want it to be like "Well, I just whipped you and now I'm asking for favors." I hate people that do that. But I didn't let him beat me 1) cause I'm a bad faker 2) cause it's dishonest and 3) I can't stand to lose, no matter what.

We drove back to his place afterwards and took our shower there cause we wanted to take it together. It's true you can do a lot of stuff in Gillette with nobody caring at all but that's one thing Gillette ain't ready for, at least not at the town courts. In the shower he got back at me for losing and it was my pleasure. That's much better than letting him win a game anyway. I love it with the soap and the hot water and all the sliding around. The only thing was I almost broke his stick off when I slipped this one time. That would have been a major disaster. That would have annulled the wedding right there. I told him not to worry though cause if I ever broke it I'd make sure to give it a proper burial—a little head stone, flowers every month and the rest. He said, "Just make sure you pick out a casket big enough not to embarrass me, okay?"

Anyway, we ordered in pizza and I brought up my question. I said, "Do you think I could move the rest of my stuff over here from Sam's?" He said, "How come?" I mean, I could see what he was saying cause I was sleeping at his place every night anyway— or every day depending on shifts—so why bother moving everything over there when we're going to move into a house in a few weeks if everything went like we planned? I told him, "Me and Sam aren't getting along super right now." He says, "How come?" He's so rational sometimes it almost makes me mad. It doesn't, but it does.

The thing is, I didn't want to say anything about me and her fighting about her and Spike. That would give him the wrong idea about everything and it's not even the problem really. The problem is just her attitude about me sucks. I told Derek, "I don't know if it's cause I'm getting married or what, but she's on the warpath over there about all the time." Derek said, "Amazon Sam on the warpath must not be a whole lot of fun." I said, "It's not."

He said it was no problem for me to bring the rest of my stuff over there. It's really just clothes, a couple kitchen things that are from home anyway, and my car having to share his apartment space. But he said I had to promise one thing about it, and that is not to let on to his parents and relatives that we are "living together." Fact is we been living together since January. But they don't really know it. Because they know I'm over there when he's on the phone, and sometimes when they call I've picked up. His parents know he's no virgin or anything. I guess they just like to make believe.

Derek asked me, "Maybe it would be good if you didn't pick up the phone so much if we think it's going to be my family, just so it's not so obvious." I don't think having a few more clothes over there makes things any more obvious—cause how would they even know that?—but it's not a hard thing to do, so I said fine. He said his grandparents would all have coronaries if they knew we were "living in sin." I told him, "You make it sound like I got a loaded gun pointed at their hearts." He looked frustrated at me,

146

so I told him not to worry, since I'd be spending a lot of time with Mom at home before the wedding anyway. I'd probably be too busy to be around much.

I didn't even want to go into the fact that I didn't really want to move every little thing over there right now—since it's more fun to think of us starting fresh together after the wedding. We've been together for at least part of every day or every night since the day we met, so it's not like I expect it to be anything new, but it's like things being on another level—being in a new house, being married, owning our own place.

The pepperoni pizza came, extra cheese for Derek and half onions for me, and we got the house pictures out. It's down to 3. What's hard is that they're so much alike—same amount of front yard and back yard, garages on the right side, normal split-levels, two bedrooms, and about the same price. One is $61,000 and one is $64 and one is $66 and Ranchers Bank is going to finance no matter which one we pick. Two of them are brownish and one is sort of green. The cheap one is on Cascade just north of the Cut-Across, and the other two are on Frontier and on Arrowhead in Mountain View subdivision. We can't figure out why they call it that—cause you can hardly see a bump from there—but the houses are pretty nice.

I think Derek likes the one on Cascade best and I like the one on Arrowhead best, partly cause the backyard faces the right way for the sun. We're both pretty much in the middle on the Frontier one. Whatever we do, we have to decide in a couple days or we might lose all of them.

DAYS

1) We decided on the Arrowhead house (YEA!), the greenish one, and we're supposed to close on it on my birthday, which is 4 days before the wedding and which I practically forgot about. (I already told Derek not to make a big deal out of it, like no fancy dinner and no cake—cause I got to fit into Mom's dress.) So it

turns out we'll be able to put some of the Harpers up at the house. It's finished except for some clean-up and details which they promised they'd do. It's really a great house—well it's not now but it will be.

2) Get beds.

3) New mud-flaps for Derek's pickup.

4) Iron out dress for Betsy. She's maid-of-honor now cause Sam got so mad at me. When I told Sam I was taking the rest of my stuff we had this fight, and Sam said, "Just cause you're getting married don't mean you have to desert me," and I told her I wasn't doing that, and she said I was kissing her off and I said, "No way, it's the reverse." So she said, "Well I don't even care so do what you want" and I told her if she didn't care then maybe she shouldn't be my maid-of-honor. She said, "It doesn't really matter cause I'll be there one way or the other" and so I told her since that's how she felt about it then I was making Betsy maid-of-honor, and she said, "Go ahead, Randolph" and I don't know if we're going to make up so fast after this one like we usually do cause it feels different. Mom says Betsy should of been maid-of-honor to begin with.

5) Mrs. Harper—okay on hymn.

6) Yellow or blue writing on cake?

7) Mom's dress—cleaners + Mom wedding dress pick up.

8)

DAYS

I don't know whether I'm going to use Mrs. Randi Harper or Ms. Randi Harper. I agree with the Ms. part of it but I think Mrs. still sounds better. I'm sorry about losing Bruce but I'm not really losing it since it'll be my middle name. The only thing I don't get is when they call you by the husband's whole name, like Mrs. Derek Harper. That's stupid. Cause why would any woman be named Derek? But I've seen that in the newspaper and on T.V.—like Mr. and

Mrs. Johnny Carson. Her name ain't Johnny. I think it's Rich Bitch actually.

So all I'm losing is Alexander, which is only my middle name cause it was my Mom's name. It's not much to lose. The only thing I liked about Alexander was the time when our friends called Betsy and me RAB & BAB—cause Betsy's middle name was Alice after Mom's grandma—and that was fun for awhile. We called ourselves by that too, like in code, until freshman year Jim Ruhman heard about it and started spreading around that RAB stood for Really Awesome Boobs, and I didn't like it even if it was a compliment + being true. I don't know how he found out about the names, cause it was just girlfriends that called us RAB & BAB, but he did and after that we stopped.

I was remembering that cause I was with Betsy yesterday, picking out shoes for her dress. She didn't want to get shoes, but Mom was making her. So of course Betsy waited till the last minute and calls up and says, "You got to do this with me cause I don't want to get yelled at if I get the wrong ones." I told her I didn't care about her shoes, but she pleaded.

Then she said, "Randi you know it's not too late for me to tell Derek a few little items about you that I bet he doesn't know." She was being so sly. She just knows how to do all those little-sister things. So I met her in town at Cinderella's after work.

I think we looked at every cream-colored shoe in the state of Wyoming and they were all super ugly. When she was trying on this extra vomitricious pair, she asked me was I going to keep my name? I told her I hadn't really thought about doing that, but why? And she just went, "Cause you're the same person even after you get married." She has a strange mind sometimes.

So I said, "Well if you're worried about having his name—like it's such a bad thing to have—then why even bother getting married?" And she said, "Yeah, exactly." She was trying to pick a fight or maybe she was just trying to see if I was freaking out about getting married (NO WAY!) or maybe both.

It took me a minute to figure out what to say back. I said, "So Mrs. Ms. Magazine"—cause I know she reads it all the time— "what are you going to do when you marry Neil?" She goes, "First I'm not going to marry him cause why should I marry him if I can just live with him. And second, if I did marry him I would keep being Betsy Bruce cause I like it. Also, I think Booth is a scroty name + whenever I said it everybody would think I had a tooth knocked out or I was shitfaced or something." We both cracked up and started saying "Betsy Booth" in all these retardo voices. And then we started laughing at everything, like this old crab-apple lady going back and forth getting inventory.

We ended up deciding Betsy could wear her Alamo Rent-a-Car shoes, and we bought some cream-colored polish for them. Mom won't know anyway. It's just a white lie. The lady working at the store wasn't exactly thrilled about it though. We left about 15 boxes all spread around with the tissue hanging out. You should of seen the way she rang up the polish.

Then Betsy took me out to fancy dinner at the Village Smithy with the shoe money Mom gave her. We talked about her and Neil and her and work and Mom and all my Derek plans. And when we got the check there was still about $20 left over from the shoe money. She just looked at me. She didn't have to say anything. I knew how she was going to spend the rest of the money and I told her so. It was great being her partner-in-crime again.

DAYS

I could of predicted that Mom and Peter would be back together by now. I knew she would take him back sooner or later. There's nothing me or Betsy could do about it. We talked to her. Betsy said, "It's almost like she wants dad to be mean to her." She was really being down on Mom. I told her I didn't think that was true. And I told her the thing about not judging someone unless you're in their moccasins.

But I told Mom it would be stupid to do it if all it was was putting on appearances for the wedding. The wedding doesn't matter enough to do that. I mean, the ceremony. It would be better if they weren't together but were being decent about it, instead of being together in a lying way. I was over there last night and I told that to Mom. She got ticked at me. She said, "We're together because it's right for your Mom and your dad to be together. The wedding is just a coincidence." I told her that if that's the way it was then it was good. But I had to tell her that if they were going to be together, in front of the Harpers and all my friends and stuff, then I hoped there wasn't going to be any problems. She acted peeved, like she thought I had an attitude on, like it wasn't my place to say that to her. She said, "We're your parents. Why would you think we'd make any problems for you on your wedding?" I didn't want to answer that.

Then she told me how it was going to be the best day of her life, which she's been telling me for a month, and how excited dad was. Things were really good between them partly on account of the time they spent apart is how she explained it. She said he was turning over a new leaf. I told her, "I hope so." But I hadn't hardly said 10 words to him for the last two months so I didn't know if she was dreaming or what.

Then Peter came home from work and he was so nice to me it was almost ridiculous. He was being on his best behavior. He was asking me questions about things he hadn't even asked about in like a year. He was giving me advice about the house—but in an unbossy way, and he was being smart about things. Mom made us Sloppy Joes for dinner and we even had it in the dining room. We all just sat there, going over stuff about the little rehearsal and who was staying where and whether any of the adults could come to the afterparty—which the answer to that was "No" of course. But it was like being in the twilight zone or something, because everything for a second was just so nice and regular. I think maybe weddings do that.

DAYS

We got the beds yesterday. T.J. said we could get the best deals if we went over to the Sunset parking lot. Lincoln Furniture has a semi-tractor trailer full of stuff, mostly couches and beds and lamps, that they bring up from Casper every week. They park it there for a day and set some of it out in the lot and just sell right out of the truck, cash only. So we went over there to check it out.

It turned out trying out mattresses in the middle of a parking lot is a blast, with the wind and the traffic and all. Derek jumped up and we started rolling around and fake-making out, well maybe it was a little real, but the Lincoln guy sitting by the truck yelled at us about our boots. He goes, "You soil it, you buy it." We bought it anyway, and a second cheap one for the extra bedroom for people that crash.

Then we put the tarp down in the back of Derek's pickup—so they wouldn't get dirty—and hauled them up there. I can't believe his truck has lasted this long. He put off getting a new one till after the house and all, but he says that's the first thing we're going to get once we're settled. Anyway, I told him I would ride over to the house in back so I could make sure the frames don't slide around and start clanging. But really I just wanted to ride over there flopping around. It was cold but the sun was out. At the Cut-Across stoplight, I was teasing Derek in his rear-view mirror, being all sprawled out on the mattresses. So he rolls down his window and leans out and half-shouts, "Criticize this truck all you want, but it's got the hottest cargo bed in town." Derek!

We drove on over to Arrowhead Estates, which is what we've been calling the house for a goof. We're making out that we're the Beverly Hillbillies, just some dirty coal miners moving into our own little mansion. Whenever we drive over there we sing the theme—"Swimming pools, movie stars, y'all come back now, ya hear!" And we hauled everything up there and into the right rooms.

There's something great about a big old empty house—well, a brand-new one—with nothing in it except beds. Mostly because there's not much to do except break them in. So we did. First ours and then the guest one. It was probably our last time sinning and it was sweet as sin. It was like eating sin sundaes—marshmellows, whipped cream, hot fudge, nuts, cherries and french vanilla. I'm probably saying that cause I'm so hungry right now. I'm starving. But I can't believe women say it actually gets better when you get older. I don't know how that could possibly be true. If that's true I'm going to be a crazy woman by the time I'm 25.

SWING

The flowers at St. John's were just too much. They were sooooo beautiful and Mom's dress too. It felt a little tight but that was probably just cause I was nervous. I know I'm not supposed to be at this kind of thing but when I walked down the aisle and saw Derek up there with that grin I was just a little damp. Peter had my arm and I didn't like the feel of it. It seems like that part of it is a really dumb tradition and I was glad when he let me go.

Mostly the ceremony was nothing but a blur. It's hard to remember exactly what happened. I was so nervous in the morning that I had to smoke a little bit, me and Betsy did, just to calm me down, but it wasn't blurry cause of that. I remember saying "I do" and right after that as a little joke under my breath like I warned Derek I was going to, I said, "You better believe it." And he blushed like he just saw his mother naked for the first time, who I remember coming rushing in the door late for the procession cause she must of got lost or maybe stuck in shift-change traffic.

And then we got the rice in the face. I've never eaten that much rice in my 20 X around the sun. And then Derek just picked me up and carried me over to the Vette he borrowed from Jimmy Mac and just dropped me into my seat, cause the top and windows were down. Derek can really orchestrate when he wants to. I turned the volume knob of the radio all the way up so when he turned it on it would really suck his socks off. And it did—it scared the shit out of him! Then Derek patched out of the parking lot over the radio and I think he embarrassed the older generation types who were standing on the curb waving at us.

For the next half hour we just drove around, killing time before the reception. What was weird was we didn't really say anything to one another—we just listened to the music and knew we were thinking the same thoughts. We raced all over town, cranked on the fact that we actually did it—who would need anything more?—and I think the one cop who made a move to stop us forgot about it as soon as he saw the JUST HITCHED sign Betsy had made for us and stuck on the trunk.

We drove out to Wyodak and watched how the strobes on the smokestack flashed right to the beat of Eddie Money, like they were synced up special for us. We drove past the old OUTER LIMITS sign and out to Lightning Speedway. We drove to Carbon Creek, which is Keller's close-in mine, and hit 95 m.p.h. on the access road, did a figure-8 around the employee checkpoint and the attendant and zig-zagged by a few guys standing in the parking lot. First they were pissed, but then they raised their arms and shouted for us when they saw our sign.

Then Derek drove over to the other side of town and up all the streets of Sagebrush Hills to the water tank, which is the highest point of town. And when we got there he reached into the glove compartment and pulled out this silver spray paint. I thought, I can't believe I married this guy cause he is really about 13 years old!! Anyway, he ran up to the tank and wrote—

ALWAYS, FOREVER + A DAY
THE COUPLE

right by where some scrote had sprayed "MY dick IS big" because it probably wasn't, but that was the only clean space left on the tank without using a ladder. Then we raced down the hills with KOAL on loud and the horn going and shot under the underpass and the innerstate and headed up to Grandview Hills which when they're done with it will be for the folks that run town. But for now it's just a few big houses and all this open space with no trees and a few mares in a prarie and streets laid out wide enough for a 747 to taxi down + they're all empty. So we circled and dragged and squealed tires and did whatever we damn well wanted listening to great Zeppelin—"Over The Hills And Far Away." It made me feel so deep in love with him that it would be impossible to ever fall out of it.

And then we went over to the Holidome for the reception, which was a kick. Everyone had a punchy good time including this guy named Flavio who showed up at the Cambria Room looking to find some work with Exxon. The guy was completely out of it—he didn't know nothing, no green card, no English hardly, hardcore M.W.C. I felt so bad for the poor old puke that I invited him in—I guess high school Spanish wasn't a total waste!—and old Flavio got wasted pretty quick on what he could understand. Nobody minded him being there, because it was that kind of day.

Sam was there, with Spike of course, and I think looking back on it what a lucky break it was he dumped me for her, except that he's pulling her away from me. Typical Gillette—lose a friend, gain a hubby. Anyway it went on for a while, all the funny toasts, and then me and Derek and all our friends kissed the parents and the whatnot goodbye, and Mom was still crying, and we tooled on over to Grady's for the afterparty, which was for the real fun.

Grady had gotten his new stereo the day before—which is the same one everyone else in town has—and we cleaned out those speakers for him and everyone got totally useless. A bunch of guys from Buckskin mine came over, and also some guys who were shooting on the Amax Nightriders skeet-shooting team. And then Joleen came over with a bunch of friends. She told me she had on her famous panties which say Serious in script across her butt—which she was wearing in honor of my wedding. She always wore them last summer when she was pitching, and you could see them through her white doubleknit softball pants. Joleen! I don't remember a whole lot else except that there was a royal wrist wrestling championship in the kitchen between my one-and-only husband and Steve from Steve's #1 Roustabout & Hotshot Service for a case of Bud. Well, we lost. But Steve can have his Bud anyway cause we were in line for bubbles and Derek got me anyway. Also, I remember everyone dancing on the carpet and us leaving.

We drove back to the Holidome for our wedding night. That must of been an interesting drive, cause I don't remember actually going there. I think we were on automatic pilot. The management gave us a big discount on the Honeymoon Suite—even below what it is if you have your reception there—because they remembered I used to work Cafe Kauai and Jesse's. We're not really going to get a honeymoon cause we don't have any vacation time for at least 4 months, and I remember thinking, I can't believe we're going to have to be at work for swing shift tomorrow. So we had to make the most of it.

I felt like a real queen in the big pink bathtub, it's heart-shaped and sunken. At least I felt that way until Derek got in and then I felt nasty. And we had 3 left-over bottles of André from the reception, which we got about halfway through and the rest we poured in the tub. Nothing too good for you, you know. One big thing though is, I discovered the circular bed was really two queen-sized beds on rollers with their edges cut off and rounded. Because when we were doing the champagne-clean and dirty deed first time as man and wife, poor happy Derek—who was in his proper place I might add—fell into the crack in the middle of the beds and right out of mine and I just laughed from here to North Dakota.

SWING

Just when you think things couldn't be more perfect, something always happens. It's like—you're finally sitting in your most comfortable chair and you're looking out your favorite window and the scene out there is just the way you like it and the feeling inside you feels just the way you always wanted, and then God sends some creep down the block who drives by your house and shoots buckshot into the window and the plate glass explodes in your face. Well, after that the view might be the same from your chair but it's hard to feel the same about it.

That's what happened yesterday after work. I'm so pissed. Derek and I had come in, and it's true we were a little hung over and sleepy and P.O.'d about working the day after instead of being in Hawaii like normal people, but mostly we felt on top of the world. Driving in I sang "Crazy Little Thing Called Love" right along with Queen on KOAL at max volume, and Derek had to say, "Please, not with a hangover." But he said it laughing, and I turned it down. We were laughing about everything. I made a joke about how we should have sized the rings bigger so we could wear them <u>over</u> our work gloves and Derek said we might as well wear signs around our necks saying, KEEP OFF—FRESHLY HITCHED. We were slappy is the thing. Slappy and happy.

And when we came in everyone gave us pats on the back and some good teasing in the lunchroom. Word travels fast + our tire squealing in the Carbon Creek lot made it official I guess. Everyone was happy for us. I kissed Derek goodbye and started walking down to my locker, but then Teena pokes her head out of the office down the hall and motions me to come. So I expected a congratulations.

But instead she tells me to come back in to the office after shift. I said, "Why?" and she said she'd tell me then, it was no emergency. And so work goes by like normal, only slower, and when I come back in she hands me a copy of the Keller Blue Book which I haven't looked at since the week I came on, and she's got a page paper-clipped. She just gives it to me and says, "There's no way around it Randi, unless you had kept it a secret." I took the book from her—it's all this little type—and started reading the page she clipped while I was walking out to the truck. And as soon as I read what she was talking about, I just threw my thermos at the truck and dented the side-panel. So we're screwed. So we're really screwed. So I'm tearing that page out and putting it in here cause I'm too pissed to say anything else about it. Shit Fuck God-Damn Fuckers.

Sec. F: Employee Relations
  (I) Non-Salaried Employees
    A) <u>Employment of Relatives</u>*
         Should a relative of a Keller Energy employee be considered for employment or for any subsequent change of jobs within the company, the following factors will be taken into consideration:
         1. Relatives shall not work for the same immediate supervisor.

2. No employee shall be related to his immediate supervisor.
3. Relatives should not be placed in positions in which one might exercise undue influence over the progress of the other.

* Relatives, in this instance, are defined as husband, father, son, stepson, brother, nephew, first cousin, father-in-law, brother-in-law, son-in-law, and females in equivalent relationships. Note: If, by marriage, you acquire a new relative with whom you work, the company will not immediately prohibit your continuing on your job, but one of you will be re-assigned at the earliest opportunity.

SWING

I am remembering a lot what Peter said to me after Spike—"Just cause things like this happen doesn't mean life is a crock." Well maybe that was true about the thing with Spike, but the company running us off the same shift—there's no way life's not a crock after that. It's like what T.J. says every time he's about to go out the door to his machine during winter. He says in his funny Boston accent, "Life's a shit sandwich, and every day you take another bite." But the thing is, he always says it smiling, sort of laughing, like he's got a secret about it. And everyone at work knows him for saying it—it's like his thing, his little superstition to say that— but I'm not hardly going to be laughing every day taking my bite.

And then I was complaining yesterday to Betsy, cause I called her on the phone to complain, and she said, "Look, even President Carter says life is unfair." Oh, like that is supposed to make a difference. Like I'm supposed to care what President Peanuthead thinks. Betsy thinks she's so up on things is the thing. It's like she thinks she's so advanced or something that she doesn't have to have feelings anymore. I can't wait until life comes up and kicks her in the butt real good. We'll see what happens to all her theories about things then.

Anyway, me and Derek went in to the office in town before work today and made a petition for waiver on the rule. But the guy said even if Duffy, our mine manager, wanted to grant it—which he probably doesn't—that Rules & Regs down at Houston H.Q. would shoot it down because there's no way we could prove "punitive effect." Punitive effect is like if you have maximum seniority which you'd lose being re-assigned or if you have like 15 kids at home and 3 of them have diseases. The guy kept saying, "The rule makes sense." I said, "That hardly helps us you know." So he goes, "It's a fair rule."

I told him what pisses us off is that we know at least one other couple that we're <u>sure</u> is married, but they never told anybody about it, so they get to keep working together and we don't. He goes, "They're not your problem." Thanks, you know. The guy is so cool about everything. He's the kind of guy who's born sitting behind a desk. Like he was born with glasses on and fat. I forgot his name.

Then I told him I didn't see why a piece of paper should have to change the whole way we're going to have to live. I said, "We were living together before, and there are at least two couples I know at the mine living together, so why don't you outlaw that too, cause it's the same thing." So the guy goes, "I'm sorry this rule is getting in your way, but it's a free country. You can leave the company anytime you want." Can you believe that? Then he gets up from his chair, like to start pushing us to the door. You know, like we've wasted enough of his time, like he's such a busy man.

Derek was right. There wasn't any point going in there anyway. Because how are you going to reason with people that think that a man driving a haul truck and his wife driving a haul truck at the same time, hundreds of yards apart from each other or even miles, not even talking to each other, that they are going to have "undue influence" over each other progressing at the company? I mean, how are you going to talk any kind of sense into people that would make up a rule like that to begin with? There's no way. Because it's not logical it's just mean.

Me and Derek talked last night about one of us trying to get on at Carbon Creek, but it turns out there's a freeze on there. And we even talked about one of us going to another company, like maybe Mom could help me get on with Amax, and Derek knows some people good at ARCO and Kerr-McGee. But the problem is that the chance of a different company having the same shift rotation with the same turnaround dates and same shift lengths as Keller does + letting a new employee get synced up in his schedule to match somebody else at another company is like the chance of Skylab falling on you. So we just have to sit and eat our sandwich. Or one of us has to quit and us be poor all of a sudden—which we can hardly afford to do now, with the house and Derek getting his new truck and improvements and all.

Sitting there talking to that guy made me feel like we had been sent to the principal's office at school for getting married or something.

SWING

I was in Sunset Market shopping because I had to get it done before the weekend. I got Life and O.J. and Pillsbury Cinnamon rolls because they're Derek's favorite, so I was over in frozen foods. And who walks down the aisle but Sam and Spike. He was pushing their shopping cart. It was funny to see him shopping. I didn't think he shopped. And they were so happy, jibber-jabbering and laughing, that they didn't even see me standing there. So I hid behind this big pile of skim milk cartons that were waiting to be shelved and listened to what they were saying. Samantha said, "When she giggles it is the sweetest thing in the world." And then Spike goes, "That's just cause she has gas." So Sam sort of fake-gets mad at him, she says, "Spike, please!" Then Spike goes, "I know, I know. I love her so much too. She means everything to me. Sometimes now I can't even imagine living without her." So then Sam jumps in, "I love her too. You know I do. I do. I really do! God, I think we both need her a lot, you know? I'm glad we can finally say this to each other." So then I thought, Jesus, they're talking about me! I was always scared I never mattered that much.

So I had this dumb smile I couldn't get rid of and I was going to jump out from behind the skim milk and suprise them, like make a big suprise. I knew it would scare them for a second and maybe they'd be a little embarrassed to think I overheard them, but mostly they'd be happy to see me. And so I came out into the aisle and they saw me and Sam goes, "Oh, hi Randi." And Spike goes, "Hey Randi Candy," like it's no big deal. They weren't embarrassed or anything. And right away I saw that in the little top part of the shopping cart, where usually you put your purse or your fragile stuff, they had a baby. A baby was riding with them in the shopping cart. I mean, it was their baby, obviously. And all that time they weren't talking about me, they were talking about their little baby girl! God. I felt like someone hit me in the stomach with a baseball bat. I couldn't say anything. I just started running out of there, and right when I went through the automatic doors I woke up. It was like a nightmare, and I was so jinked out I woke Derek up. But then when he cleared his head and got up, he started asking me about it and it was like I couldn't really tell him what it was about. And that scared me too.

SWING

When I told Sam about Derek and me getting run off the same shift, she was so nice about it. She asked if it would help any if she went and talked to Madlock, our foreman, or even to Duffy on our account, but not as if I told her to. I told her No, it wouldn't do any good but it was nice for her to think of that. I was over to the trailer to pick up a few last things and it was the first time I saw her (except at work) since the wedding. I thought she was staying far away either cause she figured I only wanted to be with Derek—since this is like our Honeymoon cause we don't have a Honeymoon—or because she was feeling guilty about going out with Spike. Not that she's ever felt guilty about anything before, but there always is a first time.

That's what she said it was, dating Spike. She said, "I'm not too comfy about it." I asked why. And she goes, "Cause of that look you shot me at the wedding + I think me not being maid-of-honor was out of revenge." First of all I told her it wasn't out of <u>my</u> revenge for her seeing Spike, but because her attitude towards <u>me</u> lately has sucked big-time, which I thought was <u>her</u> getting revenge on me for being so happy and getting married. And also because it was better for Mom, Betsy being maid-of-honor.

And as far as the look I shot her goes, I knew exactly what she was talking about. It was during the receiving line. I had seen her and Spike at the end of it trade places with people so that they wouldn't be next to each other in line when they came by us. So I shot her a look and I caught her eye. And she thought it was a "I hate you" or a "How could you?" look, but really I meant it to be "You sly fox I know what you're up to!" look. I swear that's what I meant, which is totally different. I mean, I was <u>smiling</u>— but she thought it was a sarcastic smile when it was really a I-know-you-better-than-anybody-in-the-world smile. Probably it was the champagne and me having to smile at so many people coming down the line that made her misunderstand. It was probably distorting my face. Because usually Sam and me could look at each other and know exactly what we were thinking. At least that's the way it used to be.

We talked all about it and straightened it out, which is pretty good for her, cause she isn't much for talking about things like that. I remember right when I was getting to know her when we were 16, 17, when I would ask her too many questions about things she was thinking. She'd tell me to stop cause I was making her head hurt. But now I think we'll be able to go back to being best friends, even if she is showing some pretty putrid taste in the opposite sex these days. I tell myself she's just in a phase. She's in a Spike phase. All her boys are phases + I don't think Spike is rich enough to go the distance with her. He might last a few rounds though.

Maybe she'll start to feel comfy enough about it that she could even ask my advice about things. (LEAVE HIM!) Ha! No, I mean she doesn't have all the answers she thinks she does. And I would hate to sit on the sidelines and watch him hurt her the way he hurt me. (Not that anybody's ever hurt her before, but there always is a first time for that too.) Maybe I can hang in there a little more with the old group now, even if I am a married lady. But I can't exactly see us double dating—cause Derek hates Spike just from all I've told him + his instincts, and I think there's just too much ice on the road between me and Spike for us to be in that situation without crashing.

Sam said she is going to come over this weekend to help me and Derek build our hot tub and our deck and see the house for the first time. She says, she <u>promises</u>, she will not be on Derek's case like she was before. We're putting a hot tub downstairs and a deck from the kitchen over part of the lawn. We've got to do most of it on days off cause we're too tired otherwise. I'm voting to do the hot tub first cause it's still too cold to sit out tanning, but Derek says we'll start on whichever one we can get the best wood for first.

Life at Arrowhead Estates is coming along pretty good. It's not just 333 Arrowhead anymore, it's getting to be our God-damn house, and once we do a few more things to it, like hang stuff and get a decent stereo and finish the deck and the hot tub + carpet the downstairs, it'll be our <u>home</u>. Ta-da.

So I got a lot to look forward to and I'm trying not to get too bummed about not seeing each other at work. We got good and drunk and decided that it wasn't going to be so bad. I hope it wasn't because we were faced that we decided that. But we figured it out. There are some things the company can't take away from you no matter what. But what assholes, really! If things were expanding as fast as they used to be around here we could both hire on somewhere else—cause I found out a couple mines don't outlaw married people on the same shift and at the others I could use my old name anyway cause I still have all my old I.D.s.

Anyway, today is our second-to-last shift together. Derek keeps telling me to accept it and think positive, and so I am. But some-times it feels like driving into a tunnel that you don't know how long it is or what else is in the tunnel maybe coming in your direction or even what's on the other side if you get through it.

DAYS

Derek went ahead to graves and they moved me back to days. So when I go on to swing he'll be on days, and when I go ahead to graves he'll be behind me on swing. I guess every 3 weeks we'll have to re-arrange ourselves. Madlock said he put me on days so I could train on some new equipment, the grader or the dozer, which are a level or two up. It's like he's showing what a good guy he can be, cause he knows the rules screwed us so bad. I guess he's throwing me a bone.

But for now they have me hauling spoils instead of coal, which is a step back. Which figures! I'd rather haul coal than dirt any day. Dirt keeps you too busy. The trucks are about half the size so you have to make more trips + they're not hardly half as nice. Also, all the time you're hauling, you know that every piece of earth you move is going to be moved right back when they're done mining that section and it goes into reclamation. At least with coal you know it goes somewhere and does something for someone—you know you're turning on someone's T.V. or running their dish-washer or keeping them warm in the winter. With dirt you're just stripping it off and moving it from one place to another to keep the environmental types off the company's back. I know that every-thing makes everything else possible—you know, that all the pieces add up to the finished product—but I'm talking about satisfaction here. And hauling coal is a hell of a lot more satisfying than hauling earth.

I missed Derek so much on the drive in today. I hadn't even thought of it when this all came down—that the hour to work and the hour from work is two more hours a day we can't be together.

I mean, when we worked together <u>that</u> was the time we were really together more than when we were actually working. I don't think I ever minded before being at one of the most far-out mines. In a lot of ways, I always liked having all the space between work and town. But that 50 miles felt about like 500 today, even with KOAL cranked.

DAYS

It's so strange seeing Derek for 3 minutes between shifts. It's about enough time to kiss hello and goodbye, which isn't even what it could be since there's not much privacy around here and Derek is a lot more sensitive about P.D.A. than me. But it's not enough time to say anything, especially with one of us wasted coming off graves and one of us still half-asleep starting days. I suppose we'll get used to it. If you can get used to stripping coal you can get used to anything.

This isn't so bad though with him on graves. I sleep when he's working and he sleeps when I'm working. We still have the whole day—from 4:15 when I get home until he has to go at 9:45—well it's the best part of the day, dinner and all.

Like yesterday when I came home, he was just waking up and I jumped into bed with him still wearing my work clothes—because I was so psyched to get home I didn't change or shower at work. That was the best. He was groggy and I really suprised him. His uncle gave us a Polaroid for our wedding and I decided it was the right time to start using it. I kept my hard hat on for a goof which looks hysterical. He took one of me only wearing my work boots and my hat and another one like that with me doing a headstand on the bed. It was pretty good. (I don't think it's really being exhibitionist if it's just for <u>us</u>—it's just a question of where to hide the pictures. Cause it is <u>serious</u> blackmail material!!)

One good thing about me coming home off days with him Z'ing is I'll be able to catch him pretty defenseless. Mmmmm. I think I'm going to have to watch getting speeding tickets on the way home while I'm making up stories in my mind about what I'm going to do to him when I get there.

So anyway after he took a bunch of pictures, he put another thing of film in the Polaroid and told me to follow him. I said, "Where do you expect me to go like this?"—cause I was just standing there in my boots and my hat. He said, "We're going for a drive" and pushed me down the stairs to the garage while I was going "Oh no we're not! No we're not." I mean, he was stark naked too. And he held me there by the door to the garage. I could feel his chest on my back and his fur on my butt, and then he reached around me and turned on the garage light and opened the door and there was our new truck. I couldn't believe it. He had picked it up in the morning before he went to sleep. I didn't think it was going to be in for two weeks.

God—is it sexy! It's an '80 Ford Bronco short-box 4×4, all midnight blue and silver with silver mud-flaps and yellow booster lights on the roll bar + a great cab and cassette deck and a real powerful engine even though Derek's going to modify it to make it even better. It was a killer suprise! And it put me in such a mood, cause he started taking pictures of me and the truck and my refections in the windows and the side panels cause it was all waxed perfect, there wasn't a fingerprint on it. But I said it wasn't fair doing it only one way, so I grabbed it away from him and started taking his picture, like especially with the chrome making all these funny angles and distortions. I took one where it made his dick look like a boomerang. We laughed so hard when we saw that come out.

Then he put down the lift-gate and helped me up into the back. It's so high off the ground you can't believe it. I mean, you have to grab the steering wheel to pull yourself up into the cab. Anyway, we balanced the camera on the roll bar and tried to take our picture using the timer, standing there freezing our peculiars off in the cargo bed. But the problem was, one of our heads kept getting chopped off even though we tried to squeeze together. Luckily after 4 tries the film ran out, so then Derek just held me up against the back window and then we really squeezed together—for about a half-hour—which we were a lot more successful at than pictures. It was really cold but it was really hot, so I didn't mind.

DAYS

I had my choice between front-end loader and dozer and of course I picked dozer. They're going to train me on a small Cat and if I do okay I move up to the D-9. And maybe once I can do a wheelie on the Cat they'll promote me even higher. Any earthmoving job is pretty good actually. The only bad thing is I have to come in early when I start training. Madlock says, "Training ain't working." Okay, he's got a point. They pay you something for it too, so it's not the money. It's the hours. I got to come in at 1:00 instead of 3:00. And then I'll still be hauling spoils my regular shift. I started complaining about it over the phone to Mom and she goes, "If you give a dance you got to pay the band." I told her it sure was a funny dance they were giving down there.

It'll be good to get out of the trucks though. I'm not sorry I got bumped up from blasting when I did, but at this point I'm tired of hauling. Blasting you get to run around, be outside when it's nice out, talk to people. Last spring we all wore our IT'S A BLAST! t-shirts all the time. That seems like years ago. And now sometimes I see Sam out in the pit on top of the coal, feeding holes with Buck and Waymon and Melody, and I miss it. She's wearing her FOR THE BUCKS shirt today. Anything to get people to read her chest! You get a lot of attention anyway when you're blasting, as if she doesn't get enough to begin with.

Because now Sam is the real celebrity around here on account of what happened the other day. They were blasting in Section 7 and when they went back into the pit they found this little rabbit that had been hurt by the blast. It wasn't moving or anything, it was in shock. But it was still breathing. Everybody's telling it different, but supposedly Sam goes up to the thing with Waymon and Waymon wants to take it up to the office and maybe get it help. But Sam says that the thing is going to die anyway by the way it's breathing—and even if it didn't die it would be stone-cold deaf from the blast and screwed-up from the shock and what's the point having a screwed-up deaf rabbit hopping around the pit starving or getting run over? So Sam says "The human thing to do is put it out of its misery." So Waymon says "I don't know." But Sam got her hands on it first, and just choked it to death right there. I guess it didn't put up a fight, it was almost dead like she says.

But then she took the thing and ran over to the drill truck and when she came back it was spray-painted fluorescent orange and she was holding it over her head. She goes, "Hey we got a new football!" Because sometimes people play in the pit with a day-glo football if operations are stopped up, since a regular one is too hard to see against all the black. And so then Sam starts throwing it around. I guess Waymon wouldn't catch it, but Buck did and some others, and they played for awhile. I guess they got rid of it eventually. So now the thing is, everybody is calling her "Son of Sam" like for that sick killer guy, and the thing is to call people from our mine "Rabbit Chokers." I'm sure pretty soon there'll be a t-shirt about it too.

DAYS

Feels like we spent almost the whole weekend in the hot tub, in and out of it. (When we make a little bar down there and get a second set of speakers for tunes there won't be any reason ever to leave home—except to go to work to make more dead presidents to keep us living at home to begin with.) Betsy came over with Neil to hot-tub with us + help on the deck. Maybe Neil is dealing but he is damn good with a plane and a saw. It's not even beyond the realm of possibility that I could get to like him if I absolutely positively had to—but I wouldn't tell anybody if I did, cause everybody knows I hate him.

It was the first really warm weather so Betsy and I worked in our swimsuit tops and tried to see who would get burned first. We always used to do that every year on the first really hot sunny day, but we missed last spring for the first time. I forgot why. One time I fell asleep out behind the trailer, when we were living in Spotted Horse, and Betsy came out and dropped an ice cube right down my top. I remember when I came inside I was ketchup-colored, and we took turns making thumb imprints on me. But the next day you couldn't touch me or I'd scream. I won that year for sure. This year Betsy won—even though Neil voted for me and Derek voted for Betsy, which figures—but Betsy won on account of her having a harder time sitting in the hot tub water for the first time after coming in. That's a good indicator. Fact is neither of us got very burned.

Neil brought two candygrams over and that definitely made the deck work go faster. Cause lumber work is sort of skanky work if you don't come to it natural, and I don't. Derek got very speeded up though, which was really funny. I didn't want to laugh at him, but I smiled alot behind his back to Betsy. When me and Betsy came in to hot-tub they still had about 20 boards to do, and if you heard both of them hammering out there they sounded like a machine. They were into it.

So me and Betsy tubbed-out and she gave me all the gossip about home. She says Mom and dad are really getting along good. But the way she said it didn't make her seem very happy about it. So I said, "What's wrong with them getting along, isn't it allowed or something?" And she goes, "It's too peachy. You can't believe it it's so peachy." But that's Betsy's attitude about things—she's always looking at the worst side. It's like she's Little Ms. Cynical or something.

And then out of the blue she goes, "You know when I look in the mirror sometimes I think I'm going to be Mom, and that scares me more than anything else." Something like that. And I didn't know if it was just coke-talk or the water was getting to her or what, so I told her to run it by me again. And she just said, "Sometimes in the mirror I say, God, I'm going to be exactly like Mom and that's exactly what I don't want to be." I asked her to explain herself, cause I didn't know what she was talking about, but she wasn't in a mood to say anything more about it. And then she started giggling.

I think maybe it's weird for her, me getting married and her graduating and having to decide what to do after school and whether to live with Neil all in such a short amount of time, + throw in having such schitzo parents. Also, I think she's pissed about them giving me the Accord for my wedding present, but she's not saying anything about it cause she knows it would be sour grapes. Because she was supposed to be in line for it. They told her that a long time ago. But that was before my car turned into such a beater. And she can get a ride to Alamo easy—Neil will drive her to the airport anytime—but I need a good car for the drive to work + just being an adult. So when dad got Mom the new car when he moved back in, it made sense for me to end up with the Accord and not Betsy. Also I know I'm prejudiced about it, but getting married I think is a little bit more of an occasion than graduating high school. Sooner or later I know she'll bitch to me about it but not when she's nose-candied and hot-tubbed out she won't.

Anyway, we talked about other stuff too (like her and Neil) and then the guys finished outside and they were stamping around the kitchen for awhile, drinking beers and laughing. We could hear them above our heads. I could hear Neil saying, "Do you think that will work?" And Derek goes, "Shit yeah!" And Neil says, "You might break it." So we're trying to figure out what these guys are going to break. Like that's just what me and Derek need—to break something already. Then after a while we could hear them laughing more and Derek yelled down, "Honey, I got Brooke Shields up here naked and she is one nasty, slimy woman." Me and Betsy are going, "What?" They just were laughing. And then we heard the blender go on—we got a Robot Coupe La Machine blender for our wedding from his parents—which reminds me I haven't written any of my "Thank yous" yet. God, I'm so behind people will never give us anything again.

Anyway, after we heard the La Machine it stopped, and then about 10 minutes later they came walking down the stairs in their swimsuits. Neil was carrying this tray with four big tumbler glasses, like he was some hot-shot snooty waiter at the Quality Inn restaurant, and Derek makes this big announcement, like he was the maitre-d. He goes, "Ladies and gentlemen, fresh from the Trout-O-Matic, we present you with the speciality of the house, The Brooke Shields Shake!!" You have never seen or smelled anything that gross in your entire life.

Last night, I put those glasses in the dishwasher all by themselves and put it on Heavy Scrub.

DAYS

Last night I found out that the name of the girl group is The Charged Holes, because we were going into the Rusty Nail to play and I saw our name on the sign out by the road. That was the first time I knew it. I also found out that Sam's stage name is "Son of Sam," because of the rabbit choking thing she did at work. And this time it was much more like a punk band. Everybody was angry and wearing black lipstick and black eye shadow. We were knocking over things back in the dressing room and spraying our names on the walls, all the stuff you read about real bands doing. We just felt like it. Because we were backstage with nothing to do, waiting on our drummer—who was Annie. But Annie wasn't showing up. So we kept waiting. I had to call her at her crazy boyfriend's to get her off her butt and down there. I asked Sam to call but she wouldn't. I was afraid to call cause I thought maybe she had overdosed and wouldn't answer. I think I thought if that happened I would have to talk to the newspaper and to KOAL and tell them about it, because I was the manager. But when I called, her boyfriend said she was long gone and should of been there by now. So we waited longer. But she still didn't show up. So everyone decided I had to fill in and play the drums. I didn't know how to play them, but I knew all the tunes by heart, so I was pretty scared but not panicked. I probably would of been panicked if I didn't know the tunes + if I wasn't a good dancer, since it seemed like playing drums was like dancing, only sitting down. We were about two hours late and people were getting angry at the club—so I didn't have any time to practice. Raven came over and put more makeup on me and made my hair fall over my eyes so I would look wilder. And Sam came over and ripped the arms of my t-shirt and cut some holes in it with a knife so it would look more punk and show more + she told me to take off my jeans and just play in my panties and my work boots. The rest of them were wearing these little black miniskirts. I told her "I don't know" and she said that I shouldn't worry cause I was way back on the drums and the drums covered most of me up, but if the audience saw me walk on like that then that's what they would be thinking of and <u>trying</u> to see, so that if I screwed-up playing they wouldn't notice so much. They wouldn't be listening so much to me screwing-up the drums as imagining me playing in underwear and boots. She said if I didn't do it then she would have to cut off my jeans with her knife to make them short-shorts. Otherwise I wouldn't blend in with what everybody else was wearing and we wouldn't look like a group. She said something like, "You can't let people know that someone's missing and we're fucked-up." Well, the jeans I was wearing were a favorite pair so I couldn't let her cut them off. And I did get her point. So I did what she said. And then we all got ready and were standing in this cement hallway waiting to be announced. I was hitting my drumsticks against the wall to warm up + I thought it looked good if anybody was watching. I could hear them announcing future dates out in the club. So we were going to be on any second. And then Sam came over and slung her bass around behind her and hugged me and told me that my stage name was going to be "Puss 'n' Boots." We both laughed and it made me less nervous. But then she kissed me, on the mouth and real different. I woke up right then and it was the middle of the night and I was by myself, which took me a second to figure out why. Then I tried to get back to sleep so I could keep the dream going and go on with the band and see how things turned out. But I couldn't. And when I finally fell asleep it didn't come back. And so after all that I didn't even find out if I could play.

SWING

The tech manual for the D-6 and D-9 is about the size of the phone book. I can't believe they expect me to know all that. There's a test but everybody that's done it says it's no sweat, the written part. The field part is the tough part. The thing is, I never tested too good. Like in school, I always tested below how I was supposed to do, accounting for my brains.

Derek's going to help me with it. He could walk right into an earthmoving job, he's a lot more qualified than me. He's got experience on a bunch of different pieces of equipment from Minot, but I've got the seniority at Split Branch and like Derek always says right before he tweaks me on one of my tits, "You're a girl." Derek thinks white men are going to be a declining species if things keep going the way they are. He always says, "Next war, we'll wear the aprons and you all can take the guns." Derek thinks Madlock has a crush on me is why I'm getting the chance. I told him, "Thanks for your confidence, buddy."

Okay maybe I am a slow learner, but I do learn. I didn't do too bad yesterday. Yesterday was backwards and forwards and lowering the blade. When I told that to Derek he said it reminded him of this famous coach Vince Lombardo or something, who got real fed-up with his guys and told them he was going back to basics, and so he held up a ball and said, "Gentlemen, this is a football." Well, you got to start somewhere is the thing. Today was more complicated. And I'm sure tomorrow will be more complicated than that.

SWING

Mom is pissed at me. I hate it when she gets pissed cause you can't get pissed back at her cause she's <u>Mom</u> + you think she's going to go drive over a cliff or something she gets so upset if <u>you</u> get upset at her. The reason is because she thinks I'm going to miss Betsy's graduation this week on purpose. I mean, why would I do that? The truth is that I can't find anyone to switch shifts with because this is a brand-new rotation for me and also this week a lot of people are switching out of swing for softball try-outs. But try to get Mom to get that.

She goes, "Your little sister was there for <u>your</u> graduation and she has been there for you at everything and you should be there for her at this one little thing, is that so much to expect?" Like she's going on and on on the phone—about how hard Betsy worked to be a good student and how let down she'll be if I'm not there— and I'm about ready to start playing my fake-violin for Derek, who was sitting on the couch hearing my end of it.

The truth is Betsy could care less, cause I asked her. If her graduation is anything like mine she won't even know who the hell is there—or if she knows she won't care. It's just the whole class totally wasted sitting on the dumb stage sneaking joints and flasks of Jack, listening to some guy who's going out-of-state to college (who nobody knows) give the big class speech. When principal Grote did his deal for the parents, he kind of kept turning around and looking at us—cause he probably smelled all the smoke. The best thing was when he was talking about how The Class of '78 had boomed right along with the whole town and was going to keep on booming all throughout our lives, right then Tim Boerwinkle let out this huge fart. Even some of the teachers cracked up. And then Joleen almost fell down getting her little envelope. They didn't have our diplomas. The people that made them in Laramie sent us the ones for Rock Springs instead and no one discovered it till it was too late. So I hardly think Betsy is going to know if I'm there. She probably won't hardly know that <u>she's</u> there.

174

But I can't exactly say that to Mom. So she's all out of whack about it. She said, "How is it you can go to your softball try-outs one night and you can't go to your little sister's graduation another night the same week, how is that?" She thinks I'm putting softball over Betsy even though I explained it to her about 20 × that I'm not. I explained that the company gives us a chance to switch out for softball cause it's for the company team. It's regulated. So if you want to do it you can do it. But Keller Coal don't happen to feel the same way about Betsy's graduation—as good a kid as she is. Mom goes, "Don't you get smart with me young lady." She's said that to me since I was about 5. I'm sick of her saying that.

One of these times I'm going to say back, "Don't worry about it, cause how could I be smart with you for my mother?" One of these times, maybe.

SWING

Try-outs were a blast. They weren't so much try-outs as everybody who's put their name down for it goes and registers and figures out which team you want to be on, and when you can play your games and all, and you work-out a little. Gillette is pretty into softball. The paper said National Geographic said we got more teams per person than any other city in the country. They did a story on the boom and Mayor Hewson was in there saying people should pay more attention to our bats and not our bars, and said the thing about having so many teams. He's just trying to change our sucky reputation.

The new complex over by the fairgrounds is still full of mud, but it's supposed to be done by when the season starts. 12 fields with lights! There's a hot dog stand where all the paths come together and a little monument for the people in town who got it built, which everybody knows was just cause of coal tax bucks. There's a bronze plaque saying—

GILLETTE
WORK HARD, PLAY HARD

A bunch of us decided that the motto of our team this year is going to be PLAY HARD, PLAY HARD. Like fuck work.

This year there's going to be a girls' hardball league too, but it's too much work hitting such a little ball. So I'm playing in the girls' "C" league. Derek said if I wanted we could play together on one of the co-ed teams but I told him the Mixed league is real wimpy. It's the wimpy guys that are in it, so it ends up being the wimpy girls who they're playing with. The good girls play in the girls' league. They don't want to play with the guys. The only girls who want to play with the guys are the spazzes who want sympathy and the ugly ones who can't get laid on a bet. If you're halfway decent, it's easier to pick up a guy playing in a hot-shit girls' game anyway, cause the guys always come over to watch. Derek didn't know any of this cause he didn't play last summer. Neither did I but I've been here long enough to know.

It was a good idea, us playing together, but I don't think the games would of been any fun for either of us. This way I get to play with Sam, Lucy, Cindy Lou, Teena who's so fat it's hysterical when she runs but she can hit the ball a mile, and Melody, who's our star pitcher. Melody could pitch her way into a lot of beds but she's not like that. She's real serious about it. We wanted to call ourselves The Keller Coal Karens, just to tick off our foreman. Cause Madlock used to work for Kerr-McGee and he's always spreading around what a wuss Karen Silkwood was, but Betsy read about her and said that's not true. Anyway, we knew they wouldn't let us call ourselves The Karens—cause the company pays for the uniforms and registration and all—so we're going to be The Keller Coal Kittens, at least officially. We'll probably get a lot of good pussy jokes when we cream other teams.

It was great to see Derek at try-outs. We both had on our HIS and HERS hats that they gave us at our engagement party. Only I wear his HIS hat and he wears my HERS hat just in case someone don't know, which I think is cute. Seeing him there made me realize I haven't seen him in daylight except on days off since I went over to swing shift. Cause now he's on days. So I never see him when it's light out. He leaves by 5:45 and I'm still sleeping. I don't get home till after 12 so he's already in bed. But the good thing about this rotation is we get to sleep together every night. That's nice.

It's so nice. Sometimes it's so nice I think there's no way it could be this nice for the rest of my life. It's funny to think that—because it makes you more scared about things the hotter they get, like they can't last. I don't know why not though. The idea of only sleeping with this one person for the whole rest of my life I never really thought about, because things that way were always so good. But now when they're good sometimes I think about it. Like what would I do if anything happened to him, or what would I do if things stopped being so good after being good for so long. What would you do then? I guess I'm just thinking about it cause for this shift the only place I ever get to see Derek is in bed. I suppose if there can only be one place there are worse ones than that.

SWING

Sam says Spike bought a house on Frontier. Not the one we looked at but the one next to it. I asked her why would a single guy want a whole big house to himself and she goes, "Equity." So I go, "Oh, aren't we getting pretty sophisticated about the finances these days?" She knew what I was hinting about. She didn't say nothing about it though. I give her a couple of weeks more at the trailer, tops. Spike got a promotion at Antelope Exploration is why.

Great, so I'll be able to walk over there and borrow milk from them. Because they are always together in the bars, from what I see and people say. The other night I had such a bummer shift that I went over to the '20s for a drink on the way home + I wanted to see Burn Rubber, cause I knew them from when I worked at Jesse's and they played there. Anyway, Sam was over there with Spike and some guys from his crew. They were drinking to him being promoted.

So I got Sam to the side and said, "It's pretty cozy, just Spike's boys and you." She goes, "Well, their girlfriends would of been here but they must be out screwing their best friends." I said, "That's not what I meant."

So then she got all defensive. She called me "Randiiiii." That's what she does when she's really pissed—she just grits her teeth and hisses out the end of my name. She goes, "Randiiiii, why don't you just cool-out about it. You know, it ain't a heavy-duty romance, it's just a romance." I went, "Fine, fine. It don't make any difference what it is." She goes, "Right." And I go, "I was just pointing it out is all." She said, "Let's get drunk" and so we did.

Then later when Burn Rubber was playing "Hot Blooded" I went over to Spike, cause it used to be one of our favorite songs. Well, one of his favorite songs—he used to work-out to it. And I congratulated him on making district head of Antelope. He asked how married life was treating me and I said, "So fine it should be illegal." We made a bunch of smalltalk. I guess that's what you do when you're going to be around someone, like it or not. And then I pointed over to Sam on the dance floor. She was dancing sort of with one of his guys but mostly by herself. The guy must of asked her and she didn't want to be rude cause it was Spike's friend. She was drinking a Tom Collins with a straw and dancing. So I pointed to her and said, "I really hope you appreciate what you've got there." Spike didn't look at me. He just said, "I do." And then he said, walking away, "And I don't need you to tell me either."

S.O.S.—Same Old Spike. I just went home. I was drunk but I was careful. I've gotten very good at avoiding the cops.

GRAVES

Last days off Derek and me did a lot of 4-wheeling out where they're going to build the golf course. He had the Bronc on two wheels a couple of times. I started calling him Derek Knievel and then I started telling him to slow down. I wasn't worried about us. I was worried about the truck. It's just Derek's got so much confidence about things, about himself and all, that he doesn't even ever think about doing the wrong thing. And that could be 4-wheeling or work or anything.

Like he entered the KOAL slogan contest and he's <u>sure</u> he's going to win. Because half the time he calls up the station to answer Trivia Contest questions he gets the right answer. We keep getting free breakfasts at Kountry Kitchen on account of that. We give half of the coupons away. After about the 9th breakfast, it stops being fun just because it's free.

Anyway, KOAL's slogan is so old and lame that enough people complained for them to make up a contest to find a new one. I mean, "KOAL-FM, Powder River Power 98" sucks. Everybody's sick of hearing it on the air and seeing it on bumper stickers. So Derek entered two slogans—one's technically from me and one's from him, since you can only enter one apiece. Mine is "98.5-FM, We're <u>Almost</u> Normal." And his is "KOAL-FM, Rock You Can Dig." Either one would sound great right after Paul Harvey goes "Good Day!" In fact, Derek's already counting on the $1000 prize money for a fancy waterbed and other stuff we need. He says the only way we'll lose is if the station thinks it'll look bad if he wins, since he's already famous for winning the Trivia Contest a bunch of times. Well, not famous, but they say your name on the air so some people who don't know him know his name, like when he gets introduced. He says he should of had friends enter for us. That way he'd be sure to get a fair shake. But I said that that way nobody would know you won. He goes, "Yeah, but we'd have the waterbed and I wouldn't care." See, that's what I mean about him being so confident.

GRAVES

I've decided that this is totally the worst combination of shifts ever devised by human beings, even though if they were human beings they wouldn't have devised it. They must be computers. Or very surface people. Maybe only very surface people make up the rules for the surface mining division.

I was complaining about it to Betsy—she's living over at Neil's by the way—and I told her, "Not even rats have to live like this." And Betsy just sits there and cracks her gum at me over the phone and goes, "Well, how many rat couples make 58 grand between them?" Very funny.

The problem now is that when I'm on graves and Derek is on swing, we never see each other. He sleeps while I work. I sleep while he's up. I'm up when he works. I told him I'm going to work on staying up when I come home in the morning. That way I can be with him until he goes to work in the afternoon, and then I can sleep in the evening before graves. It sort of goes against the natural way of things, but it's about the only way to see each other. I mean, I end up wanting breakfast at 10 at night and dinner in the morning. Or maybe I could split a few hours and sleep 3 after work and 3 before work. Derek's better at splitting sleep than I am. He says people did that at the air base all the time, cause the Air Force has such crazy schedules for people who need to stay on alert. All I know is I need about 6 good hours otherwise I go on the warpath at the littlest thing.

I have to be happy with it is all. Cause things are going to tighten up here sooner or later—I mean, no place keeps booming forever—

and really we're lucky to have such good jobs and be making beaucoup bucks. That's what I keep saying to myself. So for now we just have to be happy with little things, like even the couple minutes we see each other at shift change. I bring him little snacks if I'm coming on and he's coming off, like an apple or a Suzy Q. Or I leave a cold beer for him in the truck or he leaves me one in the Honda. Or I tease him if I can—just a little—so he's waiting for me to come home. He doesn't like that so much cause he's always afraid people are watching.

Last time though I wouldn't stop when he wanted me to and he got real angry at me. He took me by the arm and walked me down the corridor to the men's room—since all the office people were gone—and I thought he was going to take me in there to yell at me or something worse. But instead he took me into a stall and put his tongue in my ear and undid my overalls and we bumped uglies in a hurry. It was a super quicky but I was still late getting to my truck, and I got yelled at. I'm glad it was night, because I'm sure I had the F.F. look big-time. The thing is, I can't expect things like that to happen every day—even though I want them to.

We put in for a week off at the end of this rotation and we should get it—at least a few days of it anyway, over the 4th. We're mostly probably going to hang around home together, work on things, but I promised to take Derek climbing Cloud Peak last fall and this should be a good time to do it if he's up for it. I hope he is. Until then we'll just see each other when we see each other. It's okay, really. I'm studying up for my dozer test + there's softball + there's sitting out tanning + at least it's summer.

GRAVES

I think I'm getting pretty strange. Because yesterday morning I had another real strange one. I was locked in a bathroom and this guy said through the door, "The black-footed ferrets are littler than you, but that doesn't mean they aren't happier." I didn't know what the hell he was talking about. I mean, I know about the ferrets—

about the Wilderness Service trying to save them and make them make babies, and everybody from around the state writing in names to name them, to name the babies. Because all that stuff has been in the Daily Call. But I didn't know why this guy was saying this or why I was locked in and I didn't really care. Also he was saying stuff like, "Don't Panic!" and "Stay Calm Mrs. Harper." But I wasn't hardly panicked, I was just sitting on the counter of the sinks, combing my hair in the mirror, combing it back. And it was making me feel great, making my head feel all warm and my heart. But then this Wilderness guy started talking to me through the vent, he said something like there was a blond-footed ferret in the bathroom with me and they had to surround the place before they could open the door so that it wouldn't escape when it ran out. They couldn't let it escape, because it was endangered and it was for the breeding program. And so I said something like, "It's a black-footed ferret, right?" And that's when he said, "Just cause they're littler than you doesn't mean they aren't happier" and I could hear them working on the door and then it ended.

GRAVES

A lot of things are happening pretty fast and I want to put them down but I'm too wasted to say anything about them now. Exhausted wasted, not wasted wasted.

1) We won our first two games. 12–3 over Clovis Point Cougars and 9–7 over Amax Nightriders. 5 RBIs for Randi Candy!! Emily Mann hit a home run in the last inning to beat Amax and fat Teena even made a catch in right field.

2) I'm dozer training with Cliff Pondexter and all of a sudden he's treating it like we're competing or something. He won't give me a break.

3) I am so far behind on my tech manual. I swear when I open it up it's just like a lude. I got to get some crank from Neil to cram with for the test.

4)   Sam is practically living with Spike over on Frontier. I see her car there all the time driving home from work.

5)   Joleen's brother got shot working at the Pick 'N' Pay at 4 a.m. two nights ago. The dumb scrote that shot him got all of $27 cause they had just changed the register. It was just a flesh wound in his arm. But he could of been killed. That place is so bad. Everybody calls it the Stop 'N' Rob. Better not now in front of Jogi.

6)   I told Kevvy she should quit Quikker Likker cause of what happened to Jogi's brother. Anyplace with a drive-up is too risky cause whoever is robbing you is already in their car to get away. I got to call Mom for Kevvy cause she knows who the guy is who runs Kwik Mart, and it's a lot safer than the booze bins + it's not open 24 hours.

7)   My period is real, real, real, real late. Maybe it's just stress or something. God, I hope I don't have a little touch of pregnancy.

GRAVES

Tonight before work I went over to Spike's to see Sam cause I saw her car and not his in the driveway. Annie was over there with her and so was this little black cat that Annie brought over. I asked her was she going to keep it, and she said "Why not?" I can't believe her sometimes.

What pisses me off is I told her that me and Derek were going to get a cat right after our break and we wanted a jet-black one. And so I come over there a week later and she has a little black kitten named Darth Vader. She said it was just a coincidence. I said, "Right"—real sarcastic. And then Annie said she found it wandering around the old part of town and the only reason she brought it over is cause her boyfriend is allergic. So all of a sudden Sam is Miss Humane Society over there, taking in strays. With her and Spike living there, Mountain View is going to turn into a regular Mr. Rogers' Neighborhood. I can see that already.

But things got better as soon as I was driving in to work. Because about 20 minutes out of town on 59, I heard on KOAL that the new slogan is "KOAL-FM, Rock You Can Dig." I can't believe it! Well, I can believe it is the thing. That's my fucking husband for you!! And I speeded all the way to work so I could do something special about it at shift change. But Derek was real late coming off and I had to tell him through the fence. He was happy, but not as excited as me. I kissed him a whole bunch through the chainlink and that was kind of fun, and he said we'd go shopping early afternoon for a super fancy waterbed. And then I told him about Sam and her already having a black cat and the name. He said, "Who gives a shit?" I said, "Well I think it's tacky—after me telling her we were getting one." And Derek goes, "Don't worry about it, we'll just call ours Skywalker." See, that's why I love my husband!!!

GRAVES

I fucking flunked. Madlock just told me. They don't tell it to you that way, of course. They tell you, "We can't advance you." But it means the same thing. I can't believe it. I asked Madlock which part of it did I screw up? He said the written part was okay, but my field test had "significant flaws." Flaws! I asked him what kind of frigging flaws—this was just right up at staging before coming out here—and he goes, "I think you know what I'm talking about."

Well I didn't know what in the hell he was talking about. Unless it was this one time where my angle of attack was too high and I caught the blade edge and ended up on one tread for awhile—but it was hardly like I was about to flip the thing. He said they didn't like that move but that wasn't the deciding factor. I said, "What the hell was the deciding factor Mr. Madlock?" He said, "Look Randi, you know I like you. If I could advance you I would. But the fact is you didn't show you could get out of the D-6 close to what it's capable of. We can't have you out there working spoils at 50% of machine capability." He said I'd have a miserable time out there if I wasn't any better than that + I'd slow up the whole overburden chain.

What can I say? He said in 6 months I can take another stab at it. Some people just pick it up faster than others and that I shouldn't get down on myself about it. I said okay. And then I asked him, would he please get me re-assigned to hauling coal after my little vacation cause I'm sick of hauling spoils. He said he thinks he could work something out. I figured it was the right time to ask.

Man, I am so glad to be getting out of here after tonight. It's just, I thought I'd be leaving knowing that right after vacation I was coming back to a brand-new earthmoving job and higher pay— so it feels different now. But at least it's a break. We both need a break real bad.

DAYS

Vacation was great even though it was only 5 days. A lot of great things happened. And even though it's a major drag being back at least they switched me from dirt to coal. I'm glad Madlock likes me. If he didn't he'd probably have me breaking rocks with a pickax or hauling coal out of the pit on my back after I screwed up so bad on the test. That looks bad on him too—cause now they've got to train somebody else all over again.

Anyway, first we did a lot of the stuff we needed to do. Just things around the house. We sanded down the deck and Derek finished building the wet bar downstairs. The next day we took our bed over to Neil's. Neil and Betsy are buying it from us almost for the same we paid for it. Neil was sleeping on the floor but Betsy didn't go for that. Not full-time she didn't. So she got him to buy our bed.

Then we got our waterbed delivered and we installed it. It's incredible. It's a 4-poster one with a top that has all this curvy wood and mirrors. It's mahogany stained. It took about all our prize money but Derek said that's okay cause this'll be about the only thing we own all the way—without the bank owning it first. Also they ignored the tax at the store cause we paid cash. It's a dreamy bed. It's sexy even if you're just laying there by yourself. And with Derek there, forget it! I've got to learn getting on it gentler though, so I don't make small craft warnings for 10 minutes. Derek was fake-barfing a few times, from being seasick.

The next day we picked out Skywalker. T.J. had a litter and whichever ones friends didn't pick out, he was going to take to the park during the 4th of July concert and let them go out into the crowd and whoever they ended up with could just take them home. I'm glad we got her before he let her go like that. She is so cool. Her eyes are sort of blue-green. I think they look like the color of Derek's eyes, which was the first reason I picked her. Derek said he hoped her eyes were better than his cause he's willing to pay for cat food but not for glasses. Actually I think Skywalker would look good with little glasses on.

The first night at home she slept with us. We talked about getting her fixed, cause we don't want to deal with all that. And all the time we were talking about it I was thinking about me maybe being pregnant myself. I hadn't said anything to Derek about it and I didn't want to. And talking about Skywalker I was thinking that maybe I should get myself fixed, so I don't have to deal with all that either. I was getting pretty nervous about it. Luckily, the next day when we drove out into the Big Horns, I got my period as soon as we started climbing Cloud Peak. Got it with a vengeance. But I was so happy about it I didn't care.

We made the top by about 3 in the afternoon and it was so beautiful. 13,165 easy feet. It's more of a walk than a climb. We looked out, holding each other and kissing. You can see the curve of the earth when you're that high. And the sky isn't so big all of a sudden cause you're in it. When you're on the ground in Wyoming the sky is always so big—it's too big. Because you can put about anything up there and believe it. Any stupid thought or dream. But when you're up in the mountains, the sky is about the right size.

Derek had us build a little monument out of rocks. And he had us get real still standing over it and he said prayers for people, his family and stuff. And I closed my eyes and listened. And then he nailed my tush with a snowball and so we had a happy fight on and off all the way down. Once I tripped him and he fell bad, he was sliding, and for a second I thought, Oh no, I just killed my husband! But he stopped himself falling and was okay. I mean, my heart was stuck in my throat for a second. He wasn't mad or anything, but he did get kind of quiet on me the rest of the way down.

That night we camped out at Crazy Woman Campgrounds. It was crowded, being the 4th, but the weather was so sweet nobody cared. And we hiked around the next day and Derek fished a little and I sat out on a rock tanning and reading. Whenever I'd get hot I'd just stick my feet in the water. I hollered over a couple times to see if he landed anything and he'd say "Interesting nibbles is all." He got a lot of interesting nibbles. But there was too much competition to catch anything and we drove back before dark. It was great coming home to Skywalker instead of a big old empty house. She missed us. We probably shouldn't have left her so soon, but that's the nice thing about her being a cat and not a dog. She can keep herself happy if she's got enough to eat. Cats are lucky that way. Everybody should be that lucky.

Anyway, that's about it for our big vacation. We just hung around Sunday—Derek watched baseball and whittled and I slept and hot-tubbed my sore muscles away and gossiped on the phone. We went to the movies Sunday night. I forgot what it was called already. Betsy left a message in our mailbox for me to call her right away, which was weird, but they were out when I tried. Maybe they broke the bed already and want their money back.

Coming in to work after such a good time was pretty depressing. But when I got here everybody was laughing and screaming in the lunchroom. It really woke me up. I said "What's up guys?" And they told me. I guess this guy up at the Davis mine in Montana, he shot out the power lines going into it just so he could stop the coal and wouldn't have to work swing on the 4th. The guy just couldn't stand to miss the party! He hit a couple of relays in a tower and knocked Davis down for two days. Word is that the sheriff saw him out on a ridge over the dirt road to Otter Creek and shot him in the leg from behind with this big tranquilizer gun, using a sight and all, just like they do to bag and tag a bear. Unbefuckinglievable! Then everybody in the vending room started talking about how nobody at Split Branch has nads big enough to pull something like that. But then Buck said, "Except Son of Sam!" and everybody broke-up. Anyway, that's life back at The Branch.

DAYS

I got this letter from Mom. I could never get in touch with Betsy and now I know why she wanted me to. I don't know what to say about it. I just keep reading it over and over. So I'm putting it in here.

Dear Randi,

I don't know what to say to you, I'm so ashamed. I'm sure Betsy told you the story or at least how she saw it. Since all the doors were locked when she got home she was sure I was trying to intentionally—you know. But that's not true Randi. Don't think that. When your father left I was still on the floor of the kitchen, because he had had me down on my back and was hurting me.

I don't want to shock you Randi, but I want you to know just what kind of man your father is. He did some things to me physically, but mentally—he just broke me. And after he left, I called Amax and told them I wouldn't be in until after noon. And really all I remember after that is getting into my new car in the garage, and that it was cold. I remember it was so cold I was shaking.

The next thing I remember was being in my bedroom, and the paramedics and Betsy wiping the throw-up away. They told me that I had tried to do it, but I said "No" cause I never wanted it to be over. That is the truth dear. Then they took me in to the emergency room and ran tests and all the rest.

When Peter found out from Betsy he came over, but the doctors wouldn't let him see me. Betsy said that when the doctors said they were going to commit me, Peter said "Good." One less thing for his conscious, not that he has one. Anyway, I'm sorry I didn't call, but I didn't want to spoil your break with Derek. I know you two hardly ever get time off together and never got to get away after the wedding. It wouldn't have helped anything to call you, but I know it must have been a shock when you got home. I hope you and Betsy are helping each other. She's still so young and she's your only sister Randi, so watch out for her, O.K.? I don't want all this to make her more dependent on things.

You know dear when they flew me down here, I thought about how much time has gone by how fast. Remember when I used to walk the nut cases out to the Cessna back when I was on with Westwind and we were flying them down to Evanston regular? I remember how Hunter always wanted to have handcuffs on them, just in case. And now there I was, walking out to my plane and I saw Amax's pilot (you should see what a beauty our new Lear is!) waving to me from his cockpit. I was so embarrassed I could have just died, even though he probably didn't know why I was out there on the tarmac. And Betsy was standing there at the counter inside, in that Alamo uniform that is three times too big for her. I could see her through the window and me in the reflection and I thought—what a bunch we three girls are! It made me laugh, because I was done crying after so much.

Things are all right down here. I'm in a detox unit too so they're working on a couple of things at the same time, and I think I can lick my problems. I'm going to be stronger from now on baby, just you wait and see!!

Betsy said your father promises to have all his things out of the house by the time I get back, at the end of the month, and she told me he told her he should be transferred to Rapid City by then anyway. He knows I'm filing papers on him— first things first—right when I get back. Randi, I can't stop you from seeing your father. Just be careful he doesn't twist things around like he likes to.

Give Derek a big hug for me, and tell him I can barely wait to be a Grandma. (I know he's got it in him Randi, you could always pick them.) The doctors say I can't make any calls right now, but I can accept them on Sunday. I think I'll be O.K. to talk to, if you want. Big HUGS & SPLASHES!!!

Love,
Mom

P.S. I met a lady here whose daughter is about your age and just started in a community college program. She says it's real good, that it's not at all what she thought college would be like. What do you think?

P.P.S. There's a lot of food in the fridge at home. You should go over there and eat it before it goes bad.

DAYS

Betsy says Mom was trying to do it. Which really scares me. And also it scares me because of the times I've thought about it. Maybe it's not so unnatural. Maybe everybody does. Only if Betsy hadn't shown up maybe Mom really would of. She was just going over there to do her and Neil's wash. That's the luckiest thing or maybe we wouldn't have a Mom left. I asked her about 100 X to explain what happened—how she found her and was she awake and stuff—but Betsy just says, "I don't want to talk about it. I don't want to talk about it." She was like a broken record. So I stopped asking. It got so she was saying it all like one word— "Idontwannatalkaboutit."

Maybe someday, sometime, she'll tell me more about it. Because I'm trying to look out for her like Mom said in the letter. I'm trying to take what Mom said pretty seriously right now. I read Betsy the letter—except the part about her—and she said it was a good sign that Mom was talking about Peter leaving town and her coming home, cause the doctors told Betsy it was a good sign for Mom to be future oriented. That it's a danger sign if she's not.

The only thing that got me mad was Betsy said when Mom was at the airport that she wanted to pretend like Mom wasn't there. And another thing too was when I got to the part about Mom saying she thinks she can lick her problems, Betsy said, "Her problem is she's been licking her problem for as long as she's been married to it." I told her, "Don't be such a wise-ass just once?" It made me feel like Mom, telling her that.

Derek has been really good about it. I showed him the letter and stuff. He prayed for her last night. He said he's going to include her in all his regular prayers from now on. He's so good about things like that. It makes me feel guilty sometimes. Being back at work I really miss him so much. It's worse than before, because during the break I was with him all the time, like we used to be, and without thinking I got all used to it again, and now—BAM!— back to being ships in the night. At least on this rotation we got the evenings together. And I get to cheer him up in the parking lot with big kisses when he's coming off graves. This morning he said, "I'm the one who should be cheering you up." And I said, "Cheering you up does cheer me up." I think that's the reason love is one of those equations where you get more than the sum of the parts.

We had softball yesterday night. My game started after his, and I saw him fly out to right field twice with men on base so I decided I had to do extra good to hold up the Harper family honor out there. I got two doubles and made a throw to Mullinhead to nail someone at third + I drove Sam home with the tying run, which was especially great cause Derek came over to watch and he was there for that. Then he told me through the dugout fence he was going to go over to the Pronghorn for beers with some of his team. I told him I'd catch a ride home with Sam. I wanted to have some time to myself with her.

We ended up losing in extra-innings. Our first loss. I was so pissed, cause the umpire really screwed us. Sandy Lewis came over and said, "We had to lose sometimes Randi." But that's what I don't agree with! I always think when you're 5–0 that it can be a perfect season. If everybody does what they are supposed to do then it's not impossible for you to never lose. For a season at least.

Sam and me hung out after the game. We walked up the hill and sat by the pump jack looking out over town and the fields. I thought, When they found oil right here there must not hardly have been a town, much less playing fields. Sam said, "They'd drill a well at second base if they could." And then we sat there talking about nothing much. She said she moved in with Spike, which I knew already from scoping out his driveway. I told her I was happy for her as long as she was happy, but to watch out for herself just a little. She didn't say anything sarcastic back which was nice for a change. I asked her how work was going. She said okay except there's all this politics now with the blasting teams. I told her I sort of missed the days of The Charged Holes. She said she did too.

And then I told her about Mom. Only I just said she went in for alcohol, into a detox unit. Sam said, "I didn't ever think her drinking was that bad. It didn't seem she drank more than anybody else." I told her, "I guess it got worse lately." And then Sam looked at me and I couldn't look at her all of a sudden, and she gave me this huge hug. I can't believe it, but I cried on her shoulder and she let me. Because I didn't cry to Derek about it.

She asked me had I seen dad and I told her I just talked to him on the phone and he said he and Mom had "permanent differences" so it looked like they were going to go their own ways. I told her I didn't want to see dad. And she didn't tell me it was wrong for me not to want to see him. She told me how Mom was going to get better and that she was a strong lady and didn't I remember the thing about all the Bruces having the anti-wimp chromosome? I had to laugh.

And then Sam gave me our little secret finger shake which we made up when we were working Jesse's. (It was like a little code—where you could say whether you scored the night before or whether you were going to score that night just by how you hooked pinkies.) So when she did that, I decided we needed a new one. So I decided to teach her the 3 squeezes because I was really thinking about Mom. I held her hand and I did it, and asked her did she know what it meant? She thought for a second and did it right back to me and went, "I-love-you." I was so happy she guessed it. It means we're still on the same wavelength. She did it like she already knew it. And then we walked down to the parking lot and she drove me home.

Except when we were driving home I thought that maybe someone in my family had already taught it to her, when she was living with us. She was like part of the family then. I didn't want to think that was why she knew though. So I didn't ask her about it. I just told her thanks for being my best ever friend when she dropped me off, and gave her 3 more squeezes and told her I'd see her at work, which I do right now, out there in the pit running on top of a mountain of coal.

DAYS

Days off I went to Rapid with Betsy and had the tubal ligation. It's about the first thing I did that she's approved of in a long time. Because Betsy doesn't want kids either. She thinks if you want kids you should adopt them—cause there are so many of them around that nobody wants. I know I don't want kids. I never wanted kids. I told Derek that pretty soon after we started going out. I never held that back. And I guess it seemed like, why was I waiting around to do something about it and hassling with birth control and all?

I really didn't like the idea that I was pregnant when I thought I was. It was scaring me. And afterwards I told Derek about it. So we got to talking serious about it again. We talked about it before a bunch of times, about not having a family. He's more got two minds about it than me—he says we could do it, but then again it's okay not doing it. If he was dead set on having kids, maybe it would be different, but he's not. He says he doesn't have super-strong feelings about it.

And this way, if I died or something—he could go and have a family with someone else. If his new wife wanted one enough to make him want one, he could have all that. And this way, we don't ever have to worry about birth control again—cause I feel real sucky on the pill, even though it was always worth it cause everything else is a shot in the dark or a pain in the ass. And I definitely do not like the idea of me being pregnant or having to have abortions. And if ever we both decided that we changed our minds 1) I could have the operation reversed, because they say you can do that, even though it costs a lot or 2) we could adopt kids, maybe after they were grown a little, because I do agree with Betsy—like why have more when they're so many around needing parents to begin with? But I don't think I'll change my mind.

I just don't like babies. Why is it you're supposed to like babies? Because a lot of my high school friends are having babies with their boyfriends now and I just can't imagine it. To me they seem like babies. But that's just to me. And how are you supposed to get anyplace being tied down by a kid? Because it makes working really difficult and money doesn't hardly go as far—I mean, to get anyplace you've got to be gone working so much in the first place that why bother having the kid at all? Why not just have a cocker spaniel?

Jimmy Mac just had a baby with that Sue girl he's living with over in Powder River trailer park. And I saw him in town walking around with it, totally grunged out from the oil patch, wearing his Ted Nugent t-shirt, carrying it around under his arm like a twelve-pack. It's pretty ridiculous when you see it. Because you look at that baby and you just know how totally screwed-up it's going to be—having to listen to heavy metal at max volume all the time and being taken out with all Jimmy's stoned friends shooting rattle-snakes. I mean, if I had a kid here it'd probably end up just like I was—smoking pot 4 × a day and going to bed with anybody.

So Betsy called in sick to work and we drove out to Rapid. Derek would of taken me—he wanted to—but he had other things to do and I told him it would be better if I went with Betsy, to talk about things and just because. Most guys don't understand it when you say you want to do something just because, but Derek is pretty good at it.

I'm glad I went with Betsy. Because on the way there I drove and she got high and she told me something really heavy. She told me that one time Mom told her that I wasn't a very regular baby. She said Mom said I didn't like to be touched like other babies. I didn't like to be held. So maybe this whole thing started back then—I didn't like being a baby so now I don't like babies. Maybe something like that.

I guess it doesn't really matter what the reason is though. It's just the feeling that makes you do things. The reason is just what justifies it to everybody else. But I'm not worried about justifying it to anybody. First of all nobody is going to know about it, since it's a private thing. And second, the only person you should have to justify something to is yourself. Which is something I have already done, a bunch of times. Because this definitely makes me feel more free.

DAYS

I talked to Mom Sunday. I was expecting her to sound like she did when she was in the hospital after the cactus thing—all down and whiny—but she sounded good, really good. It really sounded like she has got her life back in shape, at least in her head it does. Maybe she needed things to get bad enough that she could finally turn the corner and not want to ever come back looking around the same corner. I hope so. She says the place down there isn't so bad, and that she's met a lot of really nice people, much nicer than all the people moving to Gillette. I was going to say, "That's probably cause they're all used to being faced all the time" but I didn't say that, of course.

Mom asked me had I seen Peter and I said, "No." Then she asked me was I going to and I said, "Maybe." Because I might. Just for my own reasons. And she got a little bit upset about that only because

FUCK

HOME

Well, I'm not working but not cause I don't want to. Greg Kite, who is a total asshole and who is the worst shovel operator out there—sometimes I swear he couldn't hit Wyoming if he fell out of bed—Greg Kite drops a whole rock on the edge of the bed and that sucker just shot through the base of the belly right up into the cab and knocked my whole neck out of whack. See, between haulers they're supposed to work on breaking up the coal with the shovel bucket, but I doubt Kite even did that he's so lazy—because it felt like one piece was about 20 tons right on the left edge of the bed.

It hurt so much all I could do was curse. And it was only his second drop, so I had to sit there and take 3 more drops which were probably dead center but each time the impact was killing me. Then he gave me the haul-away signal. Great. So I tried driving out—because I didn't want to have to leave the truck there and hold up production until they found a spare driver. Not that I was scared of stopping the coal for 20 minutes—but it would be shitty for the other haulers, just standing still, waiting in line. But when I tried driving, even before I got to the haul road I had to stop. Every time I moved my neck the pain just shot right behind my eyes and up in my shoulders. So I put a non-emergency distress call on the radio, and waited.

7 minutes later they were down in the pit talking to me on the radio. How was I going to get down from the cab was the problem. If I couldn't climb down they would have had to get a crane down there and rig up a sling for an emergency evac. I didn't want that—because then if I was okay in a day or two I'd catch some unbe-

lievable grief from the company. Also, everybody would be watching the thing, and if you need an emergency evac and you're anything less than dead, people don't have too much sympathy. So I told them I'd try to climb down on my own. I climb up and down that ladder every God-damn day, but I was scared all of a sudden. Cause what if I fell? Cause it's about 15 feet to the ground. They said they'd have some guys down there to spot me.

I was okay getting out of the cab even though it hurt like hell and it took me a long time to slide out. And I was okay on the first couple rungs of the ladder. But after that, I couldn't move— because I couldn't get my arms above my shoulders to hold on as I was climbing down. My body just froze-up on me. I was stuck there, holding on and trying not to cry. Not cause it was humiliating but because it hurt.

So two guys climbed up with a bivouac bag—like the kind they use mountain climbing—and each of them only had one foot and one arm on the ladder and they helped me the rest of the way down to the ground. Those guys must be strong. They were great. I could walk okay, but they helped me over to their pickup and laid me down in back and I rode on up to the office. I was just lying on my back looking up at the sky. I never realized how bumpy the haul road is. You don't notice it driving the Wabcos or the Lectra Hauls. But every little bump was killing me + it was embarrassing to think that the haulers coming down could see me coming up lying on my back in this dorky pickup.

Finally, after what seemed like forever, we got up to staging and I walked into the office under my own power. They gave me a little exam and I gave them an account of it, which they wrote up. One of the rescue guys asked who was in the shovel? I told him, and he said, "Kite sucks, doesn't he?" See, he knows. But then Madlock came in.

He was concerned about me, but then once he knew I was okay he got real different. I told him what happened. He said something like this wasn't the company's fault cause if I was sitting braced properly not even a neutron bomb dropped back there could give me whiplash. But he told me not to worry about my disability pay—they wouldn't monkey with that, even though it was my fault. I said, "That's mighty white of you Mr. Madlock." He said, "If you

can wise-off to me at a time like this, I figure you're going to live."
I fake-smiled at him and told him, "I'll live." Then he said he'd
find someone to drive me back to town in my car and told me to
go get x-rays done and be examined, and to call him as soon as I
knew what was what. Then the rescue guys gave me some painkillers for the ride back, and I waited.

In about 45 minutes Madlock came back and walked me out to
the car. He said not to worry about it being my fault—he told me
he only said that cause <u>his</u> boss, Duffy, who's the real boss of the
whole mine, was in the next room maybe overhearing, and how
the guy is a real hardliner about accidents like this. He said he
didn't care even if it was my fault.

I laid down on the back seat, which isn't really big enough in
the Accord but it was better than sitting. They got Cindy Lou to
drive me back. Then Madlock gave me his home number and told
me to call if I needed to. He was being so nice. He said, "Hurry
back Randi Harper, because we sure miss you around here when
you're scarce." That's the nicest thing any boss ever said to me.
And I rode back looking up at the sky and the lightning and
listening to the rain and the road and the tunes Cindy Lou was
picking on the radio, and wondering, Why is it you got to be flat
on your back before somebody ever says something like that to
you?

HOME

I'm lying on the deck and it's 10:30 in the morning and the sun is
beaming down and I got a little buzz on from the painkillers and
I'm still in my p.j.'s and Derek is sleeping off graves in the bedroom
probably dreaming about me I hope. I decided things could be
worse than this. At least I get to see my husband again.

The x-rays were negative, so it's not like anything is broken even
though it feels that way sometimes. They did say that my vertebras
were a little out of whack, but that if I was pretty immobile for a
while it should heal by itself. Derek asked them if maybe I should

be in traction—I guess his dad was in traction once—but they said they didn't think that was necessary, that it would be better for me to be at home as long as I stayed inactive. Like what do they think I'm going to do—start shooting baskets on the driveway hoop? In the meantime I've got to wear one of those dorky wraps around my neck, so I look like a mummy or something. The doctor said it's a day-to-day thing and don't get impatient. He said this stupid saying, "Good patients don't get impatient." I said I'll be a good patient as long as my painkillers don't run out.

I called Madlock yesterday and told him it was day-to-day and he said "Fine, no problem." I know from their view though they're not happy about it, 1—cause they have to use up another floater full-time on my shift and 2—because it stops the string at 58 Safe Days without lost time from an on-the-job injury. All the mines compete for safest. So we had to change our sign out by the entrance from 58 SAFE DAYS back down to 1, then 2, then 3. That looks bad, cause it makes everybody think, what happened? And you don't want to be the one to break the string.

Maybe now at least they'll change the slogan on the board. That could be the silver lining. It's supposed to change once a month—employees submit little sayings to put up there about safety—but the current one has been up there for about 3 months and everybody's sick of it. You have to see it every day driving into work. Even at night it's lit up. It's not like I wanted to memorize it. It's just like it's burned into my eyeballs from seeing it so many times—

LET'S ALL PRACTICE SAFETY IT'S NOT
BAD A COMPLETE FATHER IS BETTER
THAN HALF A DAD   C. UNDERWOOD

That's about the worst one that's ever been up there. Nobody even knows who C. Underwood is. He's probably some nerdy guy who drives the water truck or cleans out coal bins. All I know about him is that he's a real poet, Mr. C. Underwood. That probably looked real good Tuesday with 1 SAFE DAYS above it.

I think I hear Derek getting up. I promised to make him breakfast last night, and I want to do it. Even if I have to do it in slow-motion.

HOME

This guy always comes on, same time every day, and says "Hi, I'm not a doctor, but I play one on T.V." Then he tells you about some study doctors did and why they prefer this cold medicine he's selling. Well, I know who the guy is—he's Dr. Cliff Warner from "All My Children." Everybody knows that. But these people who make commercials must think everybody out here is so stupid that just since the guy is a soap doctor we should believe what he says about colds. I mean, why would we do that?

And if they take into account the people who know him from the show—which they are obviously doing—then there's even less reason. Because everybody who knows him knows Dr. Cliff Warner is the father of a bastard child + he's a hothead and a wimp who is never happy. And even though it's true he's never fucked up big-time in micro-surgery, he has lost his share of patients. So he's not even a perfect doctor. I don't know why we should take his word for anything. Even if Palmer wasn't messing in their business all the time, him and Nina would never be happy—cause they're just not smart enough to know how. Like when Nina left him to be on another soap everybody knew when she came back they would get together again and be miserable all over.

So I sit here and take my painkillers and watch all afternoon, and the guy comes on about an hour after he's gotten slapped for chasing a nurse at Pine Valley Hospital, he comes on and does his little "I'm not a doctor . . ." dance and they actually think we're going to buy that. The people that make these are really out of touch with your N.A.W.—Normal American Woman. These people that make these commercials should get into their cars and drive across the country on I-90 and get off at the Gillette exit and come on over to my house and I'll be glad to fill them in on what the deal is. Not that anybody asked me, but I play one in real life.

HOME

I had this dream about a soft porcupine. He was furry and his fur was soft and so nice. And long, like on a collie or a retriever. And he was nuzzling me and I was nuzzling him. So nice. I'm pretty sure it was a him. The thing was, he had quills but the quills were fur instead of sharp. The porcupine was in my house and we were watching T.V. together and drinking. I was drinking tequila shots and I was pouring shots for him and feeding them to him little by little, holding him in one arm and offering it up real gentle with the other. We were having a great time. Even though I knew he couldn't understand the T.V., he was curious about it. He was watching. But after a while, I thought we should do something he could enjoy more. So we went for a walk. It was nighttime and it was real quiet and cool out. There was no one around in the neighborhood—it was like everybody was at work—so we could walk over everybody's yards and across the streets without looking and then we went over someone's fence into their backyard and went up the stairs to their pool. It was one of those above-ground pools, metal and plastic, like people have out here just for summertime. And we went up to the edge and I just put my feet in. Then the porcupine saw that and he just put his little feet in too. I don't know how he could sit up like a regular person and do that but he could—he didn't fall over. The air was pretty cold and the water was steamy, superwarm like the hot springs in Thermopolis. And so we took off all our clothes—well, I did. He didn't have any of course. And we just walked over to the little blue slide they had there, and walked up the steps. At the top of the slide, I put the porcupine in front of me and I wrapped my legs around him, like the way you do when you're going double on a sled, and put my arms around him, and held him back against me. I was holding him tight. From the top of the slide it looked like we were much higher up than it looked from the pool. And the porcupine looked back at me—like asking "Is this okay?"—you know the way a puppy does the first time he has to come down the stairs, up there hesitating. And I said, "Sure! Here we go! Hold on!" And then we whizzed down that slide. We kept going and going. It was great. And then we hit the hot water and we were both underwater and I lost him, he fell out of my arms like the split second we hit the water. And I couldn't open my eyes cause the water was too hot so I was reaching around for him, reaching around for his fur—cause I didn't know if he could even swim, I hadn't even thought about that—and so I was reaching all around holding my breath and holding it longer, and right when I had to come up for air I woke up.

HOME

Dr. Atkins said that he could see a little progress even though I don't feel it. He said maybe things were more complicated cause there might have been something wrong with my back for a lot of years without me knowing it—and this just triggered it off. He felt around and hit some spots that really hurt, even though I wasn't moving. So he did some tests because he said that worried him. He said I was very strong but my spine kept locking. He said he was going to change my treatment.

So now I'm not wearing the collar except to sleep in. And I've got an appointment tomorrow with a physical therapist at the clinic, and we're going to try some exercises instead of being immobile. I said, "Does this mean it's not day-to-day anymore?" He didn't say anything at first. That's always bad, when they don't say anything back right away—when they sit there writing that impossible-to-read writing in your file while they think of how to answer. Then he goes, "Let's just say that it might be week-to-week in your case."

He said I should see progress pretty soon. And if after a week of physical therapy we don't see progress, he said he might send me down to Casper to get me Cat-Scanned. It's a machine they put you in that's more 3-D than x-rays, but we don't have one in town. He said don't worry about it though, and I said, "No problem, it sounds cool." Then he changed my painkillers to Darvon and gave me muscle relaxers for when it tightens up. I think Darvon sounds like a planet where outer-space people come from. I can just see a U.F.O. landing on Devil's Tower and these little roboty guys come out, with these little computer voices, saying, "We come from Darvon. We are here to relieve your pain. Do not be afraid of us. Repeat, do not be afraid of us. Let us help you earthlings."

I told Derek my idea and he said I'd been watching too many "Lost In Space" re-runs. It's probably true, but so what if I have?

HOME

Randi dear,

It was so good talking to you last week. You are still my girl! I'm so sorry about your injury. Please do whatever the doctors say, that's the first thing we have to do to get better. The second thing I've found is to pray. I know you have your own ideas about things, but do mind what they tell you. Please don't go off rock climbing or 4-wheeling until you have a perfectly clean bill of health. I'm sure Derek's keeping a close eye on you.

Last night after one of our bull sessions, I took a walk around the facility. It was very peaceful out. And I thought of you and Betsy looking up at the stars. Both you girls are even brighter than stars to me. I miss you both so very much.

It was so quiet that I had a thought, that possibly your injury (since it's not serious) was just a way the Lord used to let you slow down for a little bit. Dear, so much has happened for you—good things, good things—since you got out of school that maybe this is His way of telling you that no matter how high you are riding in life you can come crashing down with just the simple dropping of a stone if you haven't found Him. Your jobs and your accomplishments and your possessions and your house are wonderful things, but they are not the only things in life. And I've found out that marriage cannot be the only thing either. I found that out the hard way. I put everything into your father, and had all my little hopes and dreams in him, while I was ignoring so many other things. For instance, the spiritual side of me. I hope you understand what I am talking about.

Betsy told me that your father is transferring to Boulder and not Rapid City. Also that he's going to own his own Dodge dealership down there. Randi, I'm trying to be Christian about this but I wish for all our sakes he was going even further away. He can always come back to visit. One thing we know is he can afford air fare no matter how far away he is. That man could make a dollar falling out of bed. His mistake was in thinking that that was at all important. When I get back to town I want to sit down with you and tell you some things about your father that you probably don't know. Don't worry about it though. Just we'll have a talk.

Betsy told me that Derek won a radio contest and you got a new waterbed and a kitten. She said the kitten is beautiful. It made me think how one of these days both of you will have your own litters and you'll know God by him bringing you the gift of life. Thanks for looking out for Betsy while I'm down here. Sometimes when I think of her living with that good-for-nothing Neil I can't restrain myself, but I am trying to. I'm learning that some things are out of my hands. No matter what I want. I know Neil is not your favorite character either, so you understand.

Betsy told me you girls had a nice long day together going to Rapid City clothes shopping. I hope you found things you liked. And was your concert good? It's so nice that you can be together like that.

Anyway, it's time for me to go to another session. I can hardly wait to see you and come home. It won't be long now. Tell my #1 son hi for me and give him a kiss.

Bear Hugs and Splashes!

Love,
Mom

I got this today. I think Mom is flipping out down there or something. What's all this junk about the Lord and this praying business? Mom wouldn't know the Lord if she bumped into him coming out of the Paramount Theater on Gillette Avenue! I thought it was a state place she was at anyway, not a religious place. Maybe they have religious guys that come there. Those guys like to get people when they're down for the count—that's part of their methods. But I thought Mom had about as much chance of being a heavy-duty Christian as turning into a radical environmentalist. They all want to convert you is the thing. I just sure hope she doesn't go off the deep end about it though.

First off I got to talk to Betsy about what she told her about our "shopping trip" and our "concert." Why did she even have to tell her we went to Rapid? I know she probably was just trying to prove to Mom that we were spending a lot of time together. But still. I got to make sure Betsy knows how to keep her trap shut. I used to have to bribe her. It makes me think, What do I got around here she'd like that Neil don't already have? Sam always says, "Never trust a teenager with a secret." No, I'm sure she'll be cool about it. I'm sure.

I don't want to have to write Mom back. I think I'll wait till next weekend and call her. Because if I write her I should tell her I saw dad, and if I do that it will rile her up, and that could hardly do her any good. If I talk to her I won't be able to lie about it—but at least I can tell her it was no big deal and that he didn't get me on his side or anything. Not that he isn't trying to.

He gave me and Derek the ski boat as a delayed wedding present, because he's getting a new one when he gets to Boulder. I asked him if the boat wasn't half Mom's, and he said, "I bought the boat." Then later he said, "What's your Mom going to do with it anyhow?" He had a point. But then again I'm not exactly in serious water-skiing shape myself.

And when I told him about my injury, he was being very sympathetic about it. He gave me the name of a chiropractor he knows. He said a lot of those regular doctors were full of crap when it came to backs. He said he would even pay for the appointments if Keller doesn't cover chiropractors. See now, he's being an all-around regular Mr. Nice Guy these days. Now that he's leaving.

It's just for his ego, cause he has such a big ego. Like he told us what a great job we were doing on the house, how good we made the deck and stuff. He wants us to think that he's such a great guy and that it's all Mom's fault, so he can leave town being a hero. But me and Betsy weren't born yesterday when it comes to dad.

I asked him was Shari moving with him to Boulder? We were out on our deck, he was sitting and I was lying down cause it's more comfortable for me that way now. I could tell he didn't want to answer while Derek was out there—maybe because he thinks he can bullshit me but not Derek cause Derek is a man. So he said, "I don't know" a couple of times. Like he doesn't know. He probably knows every time she flushes the toilet. So when Derek went inside for beers I asked him again and he said, "I think Shari will be moving out there because McMahon has re-assigned her there as well."

I said, "Come off it, dad! She's not moving out there because of the company, she's moving out with you because of your company." He looked away from me, and kept looking away. I said, "What is it? What's wrong?" Then when he looked back at me his eyes were full of tears. I've never seen him like that. He really looked pathetic. I said, "What is it?" He just goes, "I love her, Randi. I love that girl."

I couldn't believe he told me that. It really gave me the chills. He said he still loved Mom but in a different way now and did I understand? He was really crying. Maybe it was all an act, but I don't think so. Then Derek came out with the beers and saw him crying, and stopped by the glass door, and said, "Uh, am I in the middle of something here?"

So dad said, "No, no, you're at the end of it" and got right up to go, like he was in a big rush all of a sudden. He said he didn't want his beer, sorry for the trouble. He told Derek how much he liked him and then walking to his truck he told me, "I don't even have to say what I think of you Randi, cause I think you know in your heart." I had a lot of questions for him but I forgot to ask them right then. Just about him and Mom mostly.

He said we should get together, me and Betsy and him, and have a big dinner at the Rustler before he leaves. He's leaving next week. He said he'd call to set it up, but I bet he won't. He just said that so he could get away. He was holding back the tears. I could see his eyes were all glassy when he drove away.

HOME

I had physical therapy today, which was the second time. I don't know about it. I don't know about doing something intentionally that hurts so much. It's one thing to get a rock dropped on you by suprise and it's another thing to go into an office 3 × a week and say, "Okay, hurt me."

I keep thinking, "No pain, no gain. No pain, no gain." That's what our gym teacher used to yell at us doing windsprints and Indian weaves. That's what Derek said at the bank when we signed our mortgage. I don't know though—I think muscle therapy is different than windsprints or mortgages. It hurts a lot more.

The one good thing about it is the woman who does it, Eva Magnusson. She is very considerate and I can tell it makes her feel bad when she hurts me. Last time I got this spasm in my shoulder and she massaged it out real nice. She's from Minnesota and her family comes from Sweden. Almost everybody in her family are doctors, she told me. I ask her stuff while I'm laying there, just so I don't think about how much it hurts. Except today she told me to be quiet so she could concentrate better on "listening to my body" and I could concentrate better on "letting things go." She's very serious about it. Her hands are really strong + I would kill to have her hair.

She gave me all these exercises to do at home, 5 × a day. She wrote them down so I wouldn't "conveniently forget them." She's got a funny way of putting things. I got to admit I didn't do them too much between the first and second time and she said she could tell. I said, "How can you tell?" She goes, "You maybe could fool me but your body can't."

She said she would know if I've been slacking off. She stepped back from the table and came around where I could see her and said if I didn't want to get better then I was in the wrong place and she wouldn't waste her time on me. The way she said it was cold and scary, like I had hurt her. I said, "No, that's why I'm here, to get better." So she goes, "Okay then, so that's why also you do your exercises at home."

But it's so hard to do something that hurts so much when you are alone and there is nobody to force you. At least once or twice a day I think I should get Derek to watch me do them and not cut me any slack, to make up for the other times when I probably let things slide. I know, I know—I'm only hurting myself when I cut corners. But I'm only hurting myself anyway. Hey—either way I'm only hurting myself. That's what sucks about it.

HOME

Mack and I have been spending a lot of time together for the first time since I was little. I haven't said anything about Mack until now but he's been around. Peter gave Mack to me when I was 5, and for a long time I was closer to him than anyone else. And then Tar Steps came along and sort of took his place, because I could do more with Tar Steps since Tar Steps was alive and Mack was stuffed.

So I put Mack way up in the closet, where I couldn't get him without a ladder. The ladder was always in the tool shed and I was too lazy. I finally got him out when we moved to town and he came along with us. But like I said before, when Betsy caught me pretending Tar Steps was my horse Blue Jean—by then I had already decided I wasn't going to pretend about anything. There were other animals too. I had a stuffed polar bear and a Bambi and a fox, but Mack was the only one with a name and that I slept with.

So he stayed in my room at the house and I left him there when I moved in with Samantha. If I had my own room with Sam I might have brought him, but sleeping on the couch in the living room there was just too much traffic. The last thing you want to do is have to explain a stuffed bear to a bunch of people—especially guys partying and acting like animals. He would have gotten messed around with and trashed is the thing.

But it's funny, when I moved in with Derek and I was at home getting some things I just picked Mack up and threw him in the plastic bag along with everything else I was bringing over there. I guess it was like wanting to have something from my life before. Derek didn't make fun of me when I said he had to sleep in the bedroom with us and he didn't make fun of Mack. Well, not too much fun. He's teased me some. He liked throwing Mack off the walls, but for fun—not vicious.

Then when I had to sleep alone because of shifts, I kept Mack in bed with me. Derek would come home and jump in and we'd start going at it and Derek would run Mack over my skin which always felt good. One time Derek joked about us having a 3-way and if the cops ever knew there was an animal involved they'd come over here and bust us for bestiality! That was funny. I remember because that was the night he told me about how a bunch of his friends in 9th grade used to go around screwing cows while they slept, cause sometimes they sleep standing up. They had a little stool to stand on and just did it. He said he didn't do it, which I was relieved about. He said he just watched—which is gross enough if you really think about it.

Anyway, I think you get to a point like I said before when you decide you're not going to pretend about things anymore, but then maybe when you're older, you can decide that pretending about things is okay again. The reason I say this is because sometimes in the afternoons now, being home alone and just doing my stretches and stuff and watching the tube, I bring Mack out to the living room and sit him down on the sofa with me. When I have to lay down on my stomach sometimes I put him on my back, like I'm a squaw and he's a papoose. And when I have to lay on my back I put him up on my chest and he just lies there nuzzling. I let him watch the shows with me and I talk to him about the shows. Sometimes I have long conversations with him.

You'd think they were all one-way, but I make up all the things Mack would say back to me. Mack is very reliable and very funny and he has gotten very smart in his old age. He's very precocious like young teenagers are supposed to be, which is what he is. If someone came in and heard us talking they would probably think I was crazy. But the fact is I just love sitting there with him, imagining things, and I love going to sleep with him curled up in my arms. Sometimes I love it so much it makes me cry.

HOME

I am so tired of not working. You just get feeling useless is all. Fat and bored too. I get up, I do my exercises, I eat breakfast, I go to therapy, I come home, I eat lunch, I tube-out, I eat, I hot-tub, I eat, I take my Darvon, I take my disability check to the bank, I nap-out, I do exercises, I bitch on the phone to whoever I can get, I eat dinner, I go watch Derek play softball, I drink with the boys, I come home, I do my exercises, I eat ice cream, I eat my husband, I call it a day, ta-da. No, seriously—even messing around with Derek isn't so fun right now on account of my back, but it's about the only thing I have to look forward to in the whole day. So it's even worse if we miss each other or if he's not in the mood or something. I AM GETTING TIRED OF THIS!!!

People say, "Well at least it's summer, you don't have to be cooped up in the house." But see that just makes it worse, cause in winter no one can do anything. But now everybody is running around doing things and I got to creep around at 3 miles per hour like I'm a cripple. It would be better if it were winter. You wait all year for summer and now it's just—

Like I went to see us play yesterday night. I was half hoping that The Karens wouldn't do so well without me, but we are winning big-time this season. I sat in the dugout and got to be the honorary manager for the night. Stormin' Norman is our manager and he didn't mind. (Big fucking deal, huh!) Someone had stolen the bases—people will steal anything here—so we had to use extra mitts as bases. So then Joleen said, "Let's use Randi for second base." And everybody laughed. And I did too, even though it hurt to laugh. Because it feels so weird to go in a few weeks from hitting clean-up to being a Helen Keller joke. So right then I decided I was going to make my big comeback pretty soon.

I told everybody I was going to come off the disabled list next week and be back at work and back in left field. It may be a little optimistic, but like Eva says, "You have to think positive." I've got to stop thinking negative. Okay, so I'm making a mid-summer resolution here—I'm going back to work next week. I'm calling Madlock to tell him, so I'll <u>have</u> to be better by then, no matter what.

HOME

I wonder if it is only my imagination or is Derek spending more time away from home these days? Maybe it's just because I'm home so much that it seems that way. Because sometimes it even seems I see him less now than when I was working. I'm not complaining, I'm just pointing it out. It's not like I wouldn't want him to be playing in the league or going out after the games with his guys, or just going out after work, but sometimes it seems like it's all the time. Maybe it's just part of how things change getting married. Things get regular like that.

I can't complain about him playing hard because he has been working hard and he deserves it. He's had a lot of overtime at work, cause they have him back to being a floater since a lot of people are taking summer vacations and he can fill in on a bunch of different jobs. He's been grading and scraping, and that tires him out more than hauling because you have to concentrate so hard. I guess this week he's blasting. Which is fine. I mean, it's fine.

But what pisses me off about it was I didn't even find out he was blasting from him. I had to find out from Sam, which jinked me out a little. I went over to Spike's house yesterday afternoon to see Sam, cause she gets home around 4 and Spike doesn't get home till after 8 since he's punching holes about 100 miles away and doing 12-hour shifts while the weather's good. It was good to see her without everybody else on the team being around, but sometimes seeing her in that house is—I don't know. The floor plan is exactly, exactly the same as our house, just turned around in a different direction. The yard is the same and the fence and the appliances. One time when I was over there I went into the fridge to get something I wanted and it wasn't there, because for a second I had thought I was in our house. That was scary. Sort of twilight zone—Ooo Eeee Ooo. Maybe it was just the Darvon making me foggy cause Sam had made us screwdrivers.

Anyway, yesterday we made margaritas and sat around the backyard talking about work and tanning. They don't have a deck, but Spike is building this funny tool shed back there. So I asked Sam why is he making it out of concrete blocks? And she goes, "Spike says that Jimmy Carter is such a weak sister about the hostages that Iran is going to nuke us, or get the Russians to do it for them. So it's like a tool shed that can also be a bomb shelter." Can you believe that? I laid down in the other direction so Sam wouldn't see me trying not to laugh, but all I could think about for awhile was one of the Ayatollah's bombs landing right on Spike's head.

Anyway, Sam said work is really going great. Production is up cause we made a bunch of spot market sales, and our new contract with Seattle Steam & Electric just kicked in so everybody's got the pedal laying metal. Sam said we owe them coal until 2005. That seems like such a long time to owe anybody anything. I said, "I wonder if we'll be around then?" And Sam goes, "I hope not." And then we started laughing about being old fogies working at the mine, like, "Hold on a second deary, let me help you up into your truck" and Sam walking back and forth between blast holes with a cane, hobbling around up there, with a hair net on. And then she said, "Yeah, and Derek would have a little chin strap on his hard hat so it wouldn't blow off during a blast and everyone see that he's bald."

Then Sam said, "Did he tell you about that?" And I go, "About what?" And she goes, "About how his hat blew off yesterday right when we blasted, cause the wind must of got it, but it looked like it blew off from the explosion. It was a riot. Even Melody cracked up." I said, "Oh yeah, yeah he told me." Because I didn't want her to know he didn't. I laid there thinking—I can't believe I didn't even know he was blasting this week, much less with my oldest best friend. So I said, "He says you guys have been real busy." And she just said, "Yeah, we've been kicking ass."

I thought right then that maybe I'll ask Derek if he could get switched back to earthmoving or hauling. It's not like I don't trust him. Because I do. It's just that I'd feel better about it—I don't know why. One thing about hauling, you're always by yourself.

After that we had more margaritas and brought the radio out and listened to KOAL. When the slogan came on after Genesis I told her how it was Derek's, and she said, "You've told me about 12 × Randi." And I said, "Well I might have to tell you 12 × more!" Then I showed her my exercises because it was time to do them, and it was a good time to do them because they hardly hurt as much with a good buzz on. Except the neck rolls. The neck rolls always hurt. And I got a spasm, like a cramp, and it was killing me and Sam rubbed it out for me, right there laying on the grass. She probably wouldn't have done that unless she was buzzed too.

She asked about Mom and I talked about her for a second because I didn't want to really. I told her dad left yesterday and she said she knew cause he called to say bye to Spike and her. Mr. Nice Guy strikes again. Well, that figures though—cause Sam was always his favorite and he thought Spike was like a little him. I told her Mom is coming home next week, but not to get freaked if she saw her and she started shooting off about Jesus. Sam said, "What happened, did she turn into a Jesus person down there or something?" I said, "I think it's just a stage." Sam said, "God, I hope so." And we laughed.

Then we went in and she went upstairs to change out of her suit. She told me to come up and see the bedroom, because Annie painted these wild designs on the walls. But the first thing I saw when I got up there is they had almost exactly the same waterbed as we do. I said, "God, you've got our bed!" She goes from the shower, "Huh?" I said the model they had was real close to the one we got with our prize money. She said, "Oh." I shouldn't be pissed about it, cause everybody under 40 in Gillette which is almost everybody in Gillette has a waterbed + they're not that many really good models to choose from. I'm sure it wasn't intentional.

I laid down on it cause my head was hurting. I checked my tan lines in the mirror and floated around and the pillows smelled like Spike which was about the weirdest. And then she came out of the bathroom dripping wet and it was the first time I saw her like that since we used to skinny dip in the Holidome pool real late after hours—after we had got done screwing around with the bands. She's gotten rid of all of her baby fat, which makes me feel even more fat. She's gotten a lot more attractive. She put on her shirt and her favorite short-shorts and I felt a funny thing watching her, I think cause I was buzzed. She didn't put on any panties so I said, "What, you're not wearing underwear these days?" She said, "Nope. Easy access." Very funny. Then she said, "Let's go over to yours."

I walked out of there thinking about the pair she had that I borrowed once back at the trailer—they said "Make Me Late For Breakfast" on them. So then we walked over the two blocks to my house. She didn't even put her shoes on. And when we got there Derek was in the garage working on the Bronc. Derek looked at his watch and said, "Did you do your exercises?" I said yep. He said, "Good" and went right back to working. But then Sam shouted "Hey" from the driveway and he came out from under the hood. He really looked like he needed a break. Because engines are frustrating.

So we sat out on the front lawn which was the first time we ever did that. They talked about something that happened at work, and I talked about how it's T minus 3 days before I come back. The wind was coming up and I was getting cold in my suit, so I went in for pants. I asked Sam if she wanted my windbreaker because I could tell she was cold too and so could Derek from the way he was staring. But she said, "No, I'm fine. I got to go home anyway cause I just saw the Trans Am cross Choctaw, and we're supposed to be going out for dinner." But she didn't leave for like 15 minutes. We sat there talking about people at work and stuff. She was wearing her white t-shirt that says "I Think You Mistake Me For Someone Who Gives A Damn." But the thing is, I know damn well she does.

GRAVES

I come back thinking I'm going to be this big hero for making such
a fast recovery, and what do they do but demote me to water truck.
I didn't know anything about it till I got to work. So I go up to
Madlock and say, "There's a mistake, because the assignment board
has me on water truck." And he says, "Let's just take it easy, Randi."
I say, "I am taking it easy, what's the problem here?" And he goes,
"Let's just see how you do on water truck and how you're feeling
before we put you back in a position where you might get hurt
again." I said, "Why didn't you tell me you were demoting me?"
And he says, "It's not a demotion, it's just a temporary bump-
down." I said, "Well, why didn't you tell me this when I called you
to tell you I was coming back?" And he goes, "Because I thought
it might slow down your miraculous recovery."

He was trying to be funny, but I wasn't laughing. Everybody
knows driving water truck is a turkey job. I mean, I know somebody has got to do it—cause you got to keep the dust down on
the haul roads—but now why does it have to be me all of a sudden?
Because they don't think I can handle the heavy stuff is why. All
because Kite dropped a rock on me which wasn't my fault. And
they make it sound like it's all for my benefit. Screw them. The
thing is, I was all psyched about coming back and I end up getting
insulted. Really, it ain't bad hauling coal but it's hell working for
the people.

GRAVES

I met Mom at the Sport Shop for breakfast. Betsy and me used to call it International House of Ammo & Pancakes. We always used to go there for breakfast on Sundays with Mom and dad, and we'd make up stories about the stuffed animals and the heads on the walls. The booth under the moose head was our all-time favorite. He was Bullwinkle and I was Natasha. I was thinking about all those times because I was waiting for Mom—as usual. I guess that's one thing about her they didn't change down there.

She was late cause she got stuck at the Gurley crossing, but when she showed up she was in a good mood—cause she underpassed and won—and wearing a dopey smile, which I figured was cause of J.C. or cause of a guy. So first she starts telling me about Don, of Don's Radiators—"Best Place In Town To Take A Leak" is what the gimme caps say. Don's got this big black beard and he's read every Louis L'Amour book, twice she says, and he's from Alabama but moved up here 4 years ago to get away from "that element." I go, "What element?" She goes, "He's prejudiced about coloreds, but that's his background. He really is a good person." I asked her, "Is this guy your boyfriend already? I mean, you just got home." She goes, "No. We're just friends right now. But he is a nice man."

Then she invited me out to Lightning Speedway Friday night to sit in the pits with her. Don's Radiators races a '76 Mustang stock body, and they're putting on an air foil for Friday, and Don made Mom an official part of the crew. I told her maybe if I had enough time before work I'd come over there. But I won't. Watching loud cars go around and around a dirt track is so stupid. I guess it's okay if you're driving them, but if you're watching it's like watching paint dry.

Then Mom asked me did I ever see how big the radiators are on the Lectra Hauls Amax runs. I said, "No, why?" She says, "You should go down to Don's and take a look!" And then she says, "You should of seen how boiled he got yesterday when some salesman came over to the shop trying to sell these computer pictures of deer and elk for $49 each. He just shooed the guy away. He's quite a guy." And then she goes, "You should get to know King, his German shepherd. He's quite a dog." And also she informed me I should spend more time with my little sister, because she's quite a sister, and she's threatening again to go off into the Army. And I should do this and do that and blah-blah-blah.

So Mom's on about her 4th cup of coffee and her 10th Salem, and I could tell she was really getting in the mood for something. So she asks me would it be okay if we had that talk now about "my father." I said, "I don't care." So she takes this big breath and looks down at her waffles, and lights another cigarette. She goes, "Okay. Okay. Well, I wouldn't say anything about this, which is why I didn't for all these years, because I thought it would be wrong to bring it up. But the doctors down there convinced me that that's not good. That's the wrong attitude really and it makes other problems."

She just kept talking around in circles. I said, "What are you trying to say?" So finally she goes, "I'm not sure—I'm not sure that Peter is your real father. Actually, I don't think he is. But he might be. Because I got pregnant with you after meeting him but I hadn't exactly gotten my previous boyfriend out of my system by then. So I didn't know, and I just told Peter it was his, and I thought you were too, except then—your cheekbones. And this other boy was part-Cheyenne. So then when Betsy came and was different, the whole thing became a big question again. And Peter said he didn't care. He always said he didn't care because he loved you so much and you were really his anyway. But maybe he took some of it out on me, the not really knowing part, or maybe on you a little bit."

I didn't know what to say to her. I didn't know if I should pretend I didn't know about what she was talking about. Because if I told her what I knew, maybe she would be mad at me for never having said anything about it to her and making her keep this big secret all these years that she didn't have to keep. The fact is that Betsy told me the whole story one time driving to school sophomore year.

See Betsy is a real snoop. And she had found these letters from the old boyfriend guy in Mom's closet when we were living in the trailer in Spotted Horse. And Betsy could never keep a secret. She would always tease you with a little piece of info and offer the whole truth for a free doobie and in those days doobies grew like fungus in my glove compartment. So I knew about the whole thing. And I told Mom.

I said, "I've been knowing that for about the last 5 years. I even tell some people I'm ⅛ Cheyenne." Mom goes, "You're kidding?" I said, "No, I'm Randi." I love saying that. She goes, "I don't believe it." I said, "You can ask Betsy." She looked like someone hit her in the stomach with a 40-ounce bat. But then in a second she looked better, like relieved. She said, all concerned, "Well hasn't it been bad for you all these years, knowing all this?"

I said, "No, the opposite. Because especially when dad turned into such a shithead it was always better thinking that he probably wasn't really my dad anyway. Like thinking that he was more foreign from me." Mom said she understood what I meant, and went, "You are really a very mature young lady, do you know that?" I think I blushed "Yeah."

Then she asked me did I want to know about the old boyfriend guy, and I said, "Not right now. Maybe someday." But I don't really want to know. I mean, what's the point? The letters said he had a family and everything up in Edmonton. So it would be like teasing to know anything more, and + it would be way too complicated for anything to ever work out.

She said she was glad it was out in the open now. And that she had thought a lot about it when she was down at the Shrink 'N' Dry. (That's what I call her hospital, but not to her I don't.) She said she never dreamed it would all work out so easy—she thought I would hate her for the rest of my life. I told her, I couldn't do that. I would never do that. And that's true.

So then she said that she really wanted to share something else with me. Something she'd been thinking about almost the whole month she was gone and every day since she's been back. So I'm thinking, Uh-oh, what now? She said she was going to be Born Again and how much it would mean to her if I would do it with her. She said how guilty she felt for not raising us Christian, and how it's not too late, it's never too late to get that in your life, and how she wants so much for me to raise my family Christian when I have one. I nipped that little topic in the bud best I could. Yikes. (I mean what was I going to say—"Uh, Mom, it don't matter what you want cause there's not going to be any family"? Because if I said that she'd probably end up finishing her waffles with scotch and soda.)

She's got the whole Born Again thing already planned. There are these classes at the church and they're going to do a whole bunch of people at once, out at Westhope in a few weeks. I told her I'd think about it. I didn't want to hurt her feelings. I asked if she asked Betsy, and she said, "Betsy cracked up laughing. I think Betsy is going to stay 14 her whole life." I said, "She's 18." Mom goes, "I mean she acts 14."

So then she told me about why it would be such a good thing and how she has a whole new outlook. And while she went on and on about things I started looking at the big bear in the glass case behind her, and thinking in private it would be fun to run off into the woods with him, and it was making me almost start giggling. But I was keeping a straight face and listening to her go on, and nodding, and trying not to look at his funny yellow teeth. But I was thinking, He ain't so bad-looking that a little flossing and a little brushing wouldn't solve. He's probably better-looking than Don of Don's Radiators.

GRAVES

We were supposed to go dancing at Roaring '20s to celebrate my comeback, but Derek's on swing so we couldn't. He says to make up for it next turnaround we're going to take a road trip, drive around the Black Hills, and stay out there one night. I can't wait for that. We haven't been away since climbing Cloud Peak and it seems like summer is almost over, maybe cause I missed a lot of it. It's good to get away.

We had this fight. Well, not a fight—not like the fights I used to have with Spike and a lot of guys right before I dumped them or we split. It was more like a disagreement. I told him about Mom and her being on this big Jesus trip and her wanting me to do the Born Again thing with her. I told him I might do it because it will really make her happy, and he says, "That's a bullshit reason." Just like that he comes out and says that. I know he's really run down from work and all, but he didn't have to say it like that.

I said, "It's as good a reason as any reason." He said, "No, it's not. There's only one reason to do that and that's if you believe it—everything else is bullshit." Like he's this big official Christian or something. So I said, "Well, whether I believe it or not, it will really be a good thing for Mom, so who cares?" He goes, "Then let her do it alone." So I go, "Well, maybe if I did it, then after I did it I'd believe in it." He said, "You're just jerking yourself off if you think that." I said, "Thanks a lot." Then we didn't talk to each other for a whole hour.

I know what he means, but he doesn't have to be such a hard-ass about it. You know, she's my Mom—so I think I should be allowed to do what I think is the right thing without him being Mr. Critic about it. So I went into "one of my moods." That's what everybody that knows me calls it. I guess I'm moody sometimes. But then he was getting ready to go to work so I really tried to come out of it. Because I didn't want him going to work pissed. Especially not on this rotation where we hardly ever see each other—except if I'm splitting sleep, which I'm not. So I tried to seduce him a little, but he didn't have enough time before work cause he had to get there early + he was still a little hung over from the night before with his buddies. Anyway, my teasing him was enough to get him to make up to me and apologize for being such a hard-ass. Which made me feel good.

So then I thought I'd tell him more about Mom. And that turned out to be a huge mistake. I told him that she is really playing up this family thing, about her being a grandmother one day and how gorgeous our kids will be, she's saying stuff like this about every other time I talk to her, just dropping little hints. So Derek said, "Why haven't you told her what you did?" I said, "Hey, what we did." He goes, "Okay, okay, but why haven't you told her?"

I tried to tell him that this would be the wrong time, really the wrong time. She would be so angry at me and it would hurt her so much that I don't know what she'd do. Derek said it would hurt her even more later if I kept it from her now. But I just said, "Not now. Now would really screw things up." And he got all pissed at me again for disagreeing with him.

I said, "Look, I think I know my Mom better than you do, okay Derek?" I tried to say his name real sweet, so he could still hear how much I loved him. But he just said back, "Well I think I know what's right better than you do, okay Randi?" And he said my name real sarcastic. And he left the house all mad—I could hear him gun the engine of the Bronc when he left.

Which was exactly what I didn't want to happen. That's the only reason I brought up the thing about Mom wanting to be a grandma and all to begin with—to get him back on my side about something after we had fought about me getting dunked. But it backfired real bad. We need to go away is all. I can't wait.

GRAVES

I had the weirdest dream about the Last Chance Summertime Bash truck standoff. It's this thing where during Crazy Days, KOAL buys a pickup truck and to win it you have to keep one hand on it for longer than anybody else. And you only get a 5-minute break each hour and you can't lean on it and if you take your hand off of it for even a second, like to scratch your nose or get something out of your eye, you're out. It starts with like 25 contestants but it gets down to the real serious people after about 48 hours. Last year, this girl Suzy got disqualified for leaning after 69-and-a-half hours, and she just started crying, and then it was just two guys for the last 12 hours. After the 75th hour the paper said the judges from KOAL weren't even letting them stretch their legs or bend, cause they had to eliminate one of them. It was going too long.

Finally, one of the guys made a mistake trying to put a glove on and the other guy won the pickup.

Anyway, in this dream I had Spike was one of the last two guys. And the other one was Timberjack Joe—who's this old guy everyone knows that lives in the mountains most of the year and hunts with a bow and arrow. He's the only white man who's ever been in this big-time Shoshoni ceremony and he leads the Heritage Day parade every year on his horse with his pet fox and his dog and his skins. And I've been thinking about him ever since I had that meal with Mom at the Sport Shop, because that was the first place I ever saw him when I was a kid. They give him meals there for free, cause a lot of the animals they have up are his kills. And I remember the first time I saw him, sitting there with this huge white beard and this bear-claw necklace. Mom told me about how he was the last mountain man. I remember he was eating his meal with his gloves on. I never forgot how he was wearing his gloves. And then a few years ago the paper did this big story on him cause he was in a movie with Robert Redford, and it had all his sayings in there—like his favorite dish is a stewed girl—and they asked him what was his favorite bar and he said, "Once you've had a few, does it matter?" and all this other stuff. He has like 15 kids from 7 different wives or something. So whenever he comes down from the Big Horns, word gets around that he's in town. He's like a celebrity. And what's funny is that he would be about the last guy in the world that would stand there for 3 days being in the truck standoff. He would hardly care about having a new truck. He has this famous old green truck from 1959 or something that everybody knows is his when they see it parked in town.

But in the dream he was standing there with Spike and they were the last two guys in the standoff. And I was trying to get Spike's attention, so I could distract him, and get him to take his hand off the truck. Because I wanted Timberjack Joe to win. But Spike wouldn't look at me. And all of his pit crew was feeding him and massaging his legs and telling him not to pay any attention to anything except his right hand. So I was trying to think of something I could do that would make him lose, but I couldn't think of anything. And then all of a sudden Timberjack Joe said, "Well, it was fun while it lasted" and just took his hand off the truck, and started walking away. He didn't even stay for his consolation prize or talk to anybody. And he didn't give a reason why he took his hand off it—cause it was on purpose that he did it. He just walked away and kept on walking. And Spike was shaking his fist in the air, like it was such a big deal he won, and I was really pissed and woke up.

DAYS

Last night we were both so tired in Spearfish that I wanted us to check into a motel, call in sick and make it a 3-day weekend. Cause we deserve it if anybody does! But Derek didn't think it was a good idea. Well, sure, he's got a whole day to sleep before graves— I'm the only one that's really got to suffer. I wish I could hide the water truck behind a spoils highwall and catch a few Zzz's. That's a good way to get fired. That happened once to some guy. But it's true when it's raining there's not much to do driving water truck. You got plenty of deadtime. So this'll have to keep me from falling out—

We had a crazy time. We did about a million things and we laughed at about a million things. We left Saturday morning first thing, after a little jump-start which I got from Neil the day before. We drove out straight to Custer, with the tunes cranked in the Bronc. Derek wanted to stop at Western Woodcarvings, because he whittles stuff, but I told him it was too dorky + I was starving so we went right to Custer for breakfast. I had blueberry pancakes, bacon, eggs and everything and we planned the whole two days on the placemat map—which was basically we were going to make a big circle. We figured out how we were going to see all the good Black Hills stuff and never have to double back.

The first stop was Bedrock City, which Derek was teasing me about all the way out because I told him it was my lifetime goal to go there. We got wired in the Bronc driving over after breakfast, which I think was a plot by Derek so we wouldn't spend too long there. The first thing you see is this huge Dino sitting on a hill. I screamed "Yabbadabbadoo!" right in Derek's ear, and he said, "Do that again and I'm going home with Wilma!" We were in this great mood.

We paid our rip-off admission, we got postcards at the curio and got them postmarked at the Bedrock post office. Then we walked down Dinosaur Avenue and went in the Water Buffalo Lodge, and saw where Betty and Wilma were having their nails filed down in the beauty shop, and looked in the jail. Then we decided we were going to set fire to Mr. Slate's house on account of him being such a bad boss, but we didn't. We listened to the tunes at K-ROCK and then went in the theater where they show famous episodes. They were showing the one where Ann Margarock plays this singer who comes to town, which I saw about 20 × when I was little. And we were doing more candy because it was dark in the theater and no one else was in there since it was in the morning, and I thought I was going to have a heart attack because right in the middle I turned around and standing right there was FRED FUCKING FLINTSTONE!

He scared the shit out of me. And Derek too! Derek was so freaked he dropped our stuff right under the bench, and we lost some of it. Like what did he think—Fred Flintstone was going to make a citizen's arrest and haul us down to the Bedrock jail? Fred sat down next to me and put his arm around me and started talking about how much he hopes Pebbles is as beautiful as me when she grows up. So I kissed his huge head, trying to make Derek jealous. Then Fred said, "It's too early for this shit" and took off his head. And then he just hung out with us in the theater for a while.

He turned out to be a cool guy. He was this football jock at Custer High and this was the only summer job he could get where he didn't need a car. We asked him if he liked being Fred and he said it's okay when he's driving around in Fred's car, but standing there in his hot costume getting his picture taken with a zillion bratty kids was a major drag. We felt real bad for him—cause his day was just starting and it was going to be super hot—so we offered him some candy and he did some with us. It was a riot, seeing that. He said he and Barney always sneak joints behind Mt. Rockmore on their lunch break, so Derek told him that if they ever get caught just to say it's all part of being a Stoned Age Family. The guy said he's heard that one before, lots of times—which wiped the smile off of Derek's face pretty fast. You can't think of everything the first time is what I told him.

We hung out there for a while, staying cool and watching another episode with Fred. He told us about how this one time he got caught screwing his girlfriend in Barney Rubble's house, but it was after work hours so the manager looked the other way. And he told us that last week a tiny little dog started humping his leg over at the campgrounds—cause his head is so big he didn't see it by his feet. That was the highlight of Bedrock City, sitting there in the dark with Fred. By the time we had Orange Crushes at the Drive-In, the place was full of screaming kids. So we didn't stay for Brontoburgers or Dino Dogs or those ribs that tip your car over, we just split.

Derek wanted to stop and see the Crazy Horse Carving, but I told him the guy worked for 30 years and barely made a dent in that mountain—it's a real rip-off. So we just drove up Needles Highway right to Rushmore. We took the helicopter ride, which was big bucks but it was worth it. Besides, we both had seen it from the ground lots of times. I remember I used to tell Mom "Not Mt. Rushmore again!" and she'd say "Stop whining." Because we went there about every summer. This was great though, this was the best way to see it. We practically flew right up George Washington's nose. Had something for it, too.

And by doing the chopper we got half-price coupons for Parade of Presidents Wax Museum. We decided it was so cheap we couldn't afford not to go. I love it when ads say that. Parade of Presidents was so bad that it was good bad and not bad bad. Derek's favorite was Franklin Pierce and mine was Millard Fillmore. I can't believe they elected people with those names. Then we had Brazier burgers at the Dairy Queen—Betsy and me always used to call them "brassiere burgers"—and we discussed how much we learned over cones, like how Thomas Jefferson was the guy who brought ice cream to America. Thank you, Tom.

After lunch, we drove up towards Rapid. We stopped at the Reptile Gardens for about 10 minutes and skipped the Black Hills Cosmos, because their sign said "The Only Black Hills Gravity

Mystery That Is Family Approved." We would of gone if they didn't have that sign. I mean, we only go to X-rated gravity mysteries. And we are anti-family besides.

But we did stop at Bear Country U.S.A., which was the best. This one bear got up on the hood of the Bronco and started slobbering all over the windshield. So Derek turned on the cleaning fluid thing and got the guy right in the nose, which really scared him. It was funny, but it was mean. So I told Derek to stop it, which he didn't do until the bear started biting off one of our windshield wipers. The buffalo were good too, except it was bumper-to-bumper and we had a Winnebago in front of us so it was hard to see all of them. Derek faked like he was taking his gun down off the rack and said, "We can have meat all winter if I nail one of these guys." I said, "Our oven's not big enough to cook a whole buffalo." We were really getting slappy.

Then we got to Rapid and stopped at the Dinosaur Park where they have these great fake-dinosaurs looking out over the city. We were up there when the sun was setting. The good motels were filled, so we had to stay at the Prince motel, which was slummy, but we went over to the Holiday bar later cause we heard on the radio they were having a tan-line contest. And Derek kept wanting me to go up and enter, because the prize was a trip to Disney World. But I told him I wasn't going to go up there cause I didn't have a bathing suit + I knew it was going to turn into a wet t-shirt contest eventually and it did of course. Derek said I could of won that too. It's true I have a better tan than a lot of the ones who were up there, not to mention my "major assets"— which is what Derek calls them. But I didn't go up there. We got drunk and laughed at them instead. I think he was daring me only because he knew I wouldn't do it.

We slept in late on Sunday and went to see the dogs at noon. We lost about $20 betting on "Gone With The Wind" who looked like there was no way he could lose. We decided he would of run faster if he was chasing Darth Vader instead of Waldo, the track's rabbit. So we quit after we lost and drove up to Sturgis to see the Biker Rally, cause Derek really likes bikes even though we can't afford one now. He used to fix them one summer in Minot. God, you've never seen that many motorcycles in one place in your life

+ that many guys with scrungy beards and leather jackets and fat girlfriends. It must be something about riding on the back of a hog that makes your thighs turn to cellulite. We hung around with these Hell's Angels guys and then with this gang of businessmen-type bikers who were all rich guys with Jap touring bikes.

It was getting late so then we drove to Lead, because I was going to try to show him where Mom grew up. But I couldn't find where Grandma and Grandpa lived. We drove around and around, up and down the hills. Derek was getting tired of it, and said, "See, your memory turns to shit when you're stoned. Are you my wife, by the way?" But it's a confusing old town and I hadn't been there in a million years. It's not cause I was high. I just couldn't find it is all. So we went out of our way, so big deal!

But it meant Derek really had to speed to get to this big suprise he was promising me. The whole week before he was saying he had a big suprise for me Sunday night. And I kept trying to figure out what it might be, from the turns he was making, but I couldn't. He wouldn't even give me the littlest hint. So when we pulled into Spearfish, and he started following the signs to the Black Hills Passion Play, I just about died. I couldn't believe he was taking me to that! I mean, I grew up seeing J.C. staring out of all the purple billboards for it wherever we drove on driving trips, but I never thought I'd actually go to it.

We were following all these Airstreams up this long hill to the parking lot and I told him, "You have the nerve to say Bedrock City is dorky and then you take me to this." He just smiled. He knew I knew his alterior motive—he was taking me so that I'd know more about what the whole thing was about in case I really did decide to get myself dunked with Mom. Which was okay I guess, but what I didn't like about it was—it was like he was doing it to prove a point. So I told Derek that if I really had to see this thing, I would—but no way could I do it straight. So I got crooked again in the truck. But he didn't want to. He just stood outside looking at his watch, like telling me to hurry up getting high so we could go in.

The place was so huge, we had to sit about a mile away from the stage. And there were about 2,000 ladies around us with blue hair and little white sweaters and binoculars. It was 3 hours long but it felt like 10. And then in a way it felt like no time at all. My favorite thing was watching the lightning in the hills. I was rooting for a storm, since the program said if it stormed before they finished The Last Supper then they stopped the performance and you got a rain check. My second favorite thing was when the sheep all ran through the town, right on cue. I whispered to Derek, "South Dakota, where men are men and sheep are nervous." And he pretended like he didn't want to smile, but I could see him trying not to. So I said, "Oh, don't even think about laughing! Uh-oh, do I see a little crack there?" And so he did crack a smile, and that made me start really giggling and these old ladies in front of us turned around and looked like they were about to crucify fucking <u>me</u>.

Some of the special effects were good but I've got to admit it was pretty boring. I hope it wasn't that boring when all the stuff really happened. I was trying hard not to laugh it was so boring. By the end of it I gave up rooting for the rain and started rooting for the Romans, which really burned Derek's butt. He told me he didn't know he had married the anti-christ. I said, "Too late now, you better just lay back and enjoy it."

The best thing is we got these 3-D postcards of J.C. in the curio at intermission and looked at them whenever we got too bored. I don't think Derek was so bored actually, even though he knew the story much better than me. He was just quiet, especially at the end. He was super quiet.

It ended at 11:something and I was tired and horny (okay, I admit it, religious stuff always makes me think about it) so I thought it would be fun to spend the night in Spearfish and have me call in sick, but Derek said we should go home. Even though it was my turn to drive, he said he'd drive back. I guess he didn't think I was in the best driving shape. Especially since he's convinced I'm going to wreck the Bronc one day anyway. He always says I'm going to hit a police car head-on right in the middle of town.

So he had to drive all the way back. We had a little candy left, and that about got him to Sundance and past Devil's Tower, and I tried talking to him to stay awake but I guess he wasn't feeling talkative, so I put the radio on but I fell asleep anyway. And I didn't wake up till I heard our garage door going up and we were in our driveway.

It was a good road trip. I mean, it was a blast. It was crazy and good. But I don't know. I mean, it was good—but it's just I have this funny feeling sometimes now and sometimes it scares me a little bit, just a tiny little bit.

DAYS

My back sort of hurts but I don't want to say anything about it. Because Madlock promised me he'd switch me off water truck and back to coal next shift. I asked for blasting, but that's not in the cards. It might hook Derek and me up on the same shift sometimes, if someone has to cover. Which is illegal of course.

It didn't hurt really last weekend, but maybe I slept funny coming back from Spearfish cause I've felt stiff since then, especially waking up. And my neck is making all these crinkly noises when I move it. Like the gears in there are grinding. But if I tell Madlock, he'll keep me on water truck. Water truck makes me feel like I'm driving with training wheels on.

There isn't much going on. Watering the roads and wishing something other than dust would grow out of them. Driving around in circles. Daydreaming about people. I dream a lot. I don't know that it's such a good thing. When I was really drunk Saturday night at the Holiday, I told Derek about wanting to be with Sam—like I was making it sort of a joke—and he said it was okay as long as he could watch, which was like his joke. But I think it might be true. And I'm afraid he'd want that so he could watch her, which wouldn't be very funny. I think I dream a lot is the thing. I know I do. I think it's bad.

I think you daydream to keep yourself from falling asleep. Because it's just the boringest routine sometimes. That's why Derek signed up for the mine rescue competition—to give himself something else to do at work. (Every mine has a team, and they give them a whole set of problems, and they get timed and judged making simulated rescues. You don't win anything except bragging rights, but teams from Canada and New Mexico are even coming this year because miners like to brag.) I would of signed up but I'm not feeling too sparky right now. I don't feel like biting off anything new to chew.

DAYS

Crazy Days was as crazy as usually. We really sucked big-time in the Bed Race. We sucked worse than usual even. We finished 8th which was almost dead last. Last year we did a lot better but this year we had a different strategy—we decided to put fat Teena in the sleeping position. We figured since the course is mostly downhill, she would increase our momentum more lying on the bed than pushing it. But what happened was our right front wheel caught a sewer drain crossing 4th and Gillette, and I guess the extra weight just made the wheel break right off. So 3 of us had to hold up that corner the rest of the way. We wanted to make Teena get off but that would of disqualified us—you can't change sleepers in the middle of the race. So we practically had to drag the thing over the finish line and everybody was hooting at us. Because we'd been talking like we were going to win it this year, on account of our studly softball record.

The only girls team that finished below us was Tomorrow's Image Beauty Salon—they wiped-out bad at the bottom of the hill and their sleeper went flying onto the sidewalk. Semler Welding won for the 3rd straight time of course. They have all the best technology, which everybody knows the guy welders do, + the girls who work there are real mooses. Last year their bed was like a 4-poster tank, but this year they changed to a streamlined one with wings and a little plate for the point-man to stand on like a musher driving huskies. Sam said that the only reason they're so serious about the Bed Race is that since nobody ever wants to take them to bed, they got to carry theirs around with them, offering. But that's just sour grapes because they kicked our butts.

Let's see, what else—Betsy was on the kidnapping team, where they go out onto the innerstate and kidnap tourists by the Gillette exit and get them to spend the weekend in town and give them motel rooms and food and rental cars for free, which is why Betsy was doing it for Alamo.

Annie entered the Last Chance truck standoff for her crazy boyfriend but Sam said she lasted about 5 hours is all. I saw the beginning of it over at the fairgrounds and it didn't look like she was going to last 5 minutes. Sam says how much she loves that guy, but I don't think she loves him _that_ much. Derek was going to enter the watermelon eating but he chickened out when he saw the other guys signing up. I mean, they looked like guys who lift locomotives from track to track in the B.N. yards. We should of entered Teena under Derek's name.

He did enter the cow chip throwing—but he didn't place. Then all the guys running for mayor and sheriff and all had their own division—the politics division—on account of them being the best bullshit artists of all. The crowd liked that the best. Then the women's division went, and Derek was trying to get me to enter. But I begged off cause I didn't want to throw my back out. He said, "The way you sling bullshit, you're sure to win." I went, "Ha-ha." Sometimes Derek thinks he's funny now when he's not funny. Mostly little comments like that. I don't know how to describe it.

Anyway, the best thing over Crazy Days was the "Craziest Thing You'd Do In Public" contest which KGIL was doing. KGIL is the wimp station, it's all country-and-western, so they are trying to do stuff to get people to listen—like giving away $1,000 to whoever does the craziest thing in public. Sam said she was going to do a striptease all the way down from her work overalls, boots, hard hat and Halloween mask that makes her look like a guy, all the way down to her little fake-leopard bikini, all while reading the federal mine blasting code regulations. But she never showed up, because it turned out Spike stopped her from doing it.

So Joleen was the only person I knew in it. She wore a bathing suit and smeared peanut butter all over herself and then swam around in a bathtub full of marshmellows. Which she got 3rd place for—a bunch of dork gift certificates. 2nd place was these 3 guys who dressed up like the Supremes and painted their faces black and sang this song they made up called "Stop! In The Name of Coal" to the music of "Stop! In The Name of Love." Those guys were a riot, they should of won. But the judges gave it to this girl who had all her beautiful long blond hair shaved off while she was singing "Do Ya Think I'm Sexy?" She sure wasn't by the end of it—unless you are an android and like stark bald women—but she was rich enough. I sure hope she has a boyfriend.

SWING

I think I'm going to get myself dunked. I know Derek says it's for
the wrong reason, but can't you ever do something just for no
reason? Isn't that allowed? The thing is, I went to two of those
classes at the church and they said if you don't do it you will go
to Hell. No matter what. No matter what else you do or what else
you think for the rest of your life. And I know that I've done a
lot of things and thought a lot of things that I could go to Hell
for, and I sure don't want to do that. I'm not saying that I believe
what they are saying about it, but if you have as bad a record as I
do, why take the chance? I mean, just in case they happen to be
right.

I asked Sam if she would do it with me and she just looked at
me and said, "You're on drugs." I knew she wouldn't do it. I said,
"Just do it for me, okay, you don't have to tell anyone." She said
I was crazy. I know I can't expect her to do it for me like I'm doing
it for Mom, but it would of been nice if she did. I didn't bother
asking Betsy. Betsy is Ms. Above It All.

The thing is, I've been thinking that my luck has not been so
perfect lately, and sometimes you have to do something big to
change your luck. I'm not saying I'm superstitious. Only maybe
that getting myself dunked might put the right spin back on my
serve—that sort of thing. Because I'm in "one of my moods" at
work all the time now and the pain in my neck keeps hanging
around and maybe this will make that go away too. They don't like
it if you don't ever smile at work, and if I never smile they will
never advance me to a better position, and maybe this will change
my attitude about things and make me smile more. Not because

I'll be trying to smile more, but because just naturally it'll happen—
since I'll be smiling more inside, since it will make my spirit saved.

SWING

It's good to be back hauling coal. I never thought I'd say that. It helps that Mike is the shovel, because he's so good. And I am being careful careful careful careful. I'm not giving Madlock any excuses to demote me again. I'm being such a good doobie, sitting braced perfect for the drops like they tell you to be, even though no one really does that. So—

> Let's all practice safety
> It's not bad,
> A complete wimp is better than
> Half a fag.
>
> Let's all practice safety
> It's not so wimpy,
> A complete hooker is better than
> Half a pimpy.
>
> Let's all drive real slow
> Because we're stoned,
> A complete daddy is better if
> You're being boned.
>
> Let's screw around and mess
> Up your truck,
> Cause Madlock is a dickface
> Who doesn't give a fuck.
>
> She offered her honor,
> He honored her offer,
> And all night long it was
> Honor, offer, honor, offer!

SWING

I know I wanted to do it for Mom, but the whole thing turned into such a pain in the ass. First we had to take this dorky school bus out to Westhope. They wouldn't let us drive, even though there were only 11 of us, which I don't know why. I'm sure there would have been enough cars. So it took a long time to get there. The guy was going about 35 miles per hour and stopping every time he crossed the tracks and opening his door even on this one track where everybody <u>knows</u> they don't run trains anymore.

Then on the beach we each had to give little speeches about who we were and why we had chosen this path and everything. Luckily I came right after Mom so I could say I wanted to do it for all the same reasons + not going to Hell. And then of course they picked the windy side of the reservoir to do it on. I don't think the minister guy has a direct line in to God or anything, because we sure had shitty weather. Some September days can be perfect out there, nicer than in the middle of summer, but this was hardly one of them. It was hardly a day you'd pick to go swimming.

And then when they dunked you, you had to stand there in your sopping wet clothes. You couldn't go change into your other clothes until he was done with everybody. And the towels they had were like hand towels, not beach towels, so you could hardly get dry. And the thing is, I think when he pushed me down into the water he did something funny to my back, because it hurt right then and it got stiff on me right away as soon as I got out of the water, standing there with my teeth chattering. And it still hurts, like it did back when I injured it but different now—more all around.

I'm not saying I wish I didn't do it. It's just that it turned out to be real different than I thought it was going to be. Everybody was singing all these Jesus songs on the bus on the way back to town, and they were trying to make me sing along with them. I was about dying.

SWING

I felt like shit today when I woke up. I shouldn't of come in, but they would of busted my butt about it. It just hurts all over. I wish I had enough room to lie down in the cab. I need to stand up and stretch all the time. Stretching hurts too, but sitting is about the most uncomfortable. Sitting is the worst. It's like there's the spring of a clock all wound up in my back and I can't unwind it and I can't do anything to make the alarm go off so it'll be better. And sometimes now it goes down my legs like pins and needles and it makes my butt feel like I'm sitting on a stove or something. I am really getting freaked out about this because it's not going away, it's like it's coming. I can't write anything more because it hurts my shoulder too much—

SWING

It's getting real cold, specially when the sun lays down. I'm all frozen up in here and crinkly. I just don't think I can do this anymore. Because if I keep taking more stuff so it doesn't hurt so much then I'll end up going too slow or going too fast or getting in an accident or falling asleep or something. And if I don't take anything then it just makes me want to scream. It makes me want to cry.

I don't know what to do. I can't get fired. But if they think I'm wimping—I don't know. I want to go home right now but I don't know—

HOME

I couldn't get out of bed this morning. Derek asked me before he left if I was okay and going to be coming in and I said "Yeah," but I wasn't even up then. Once I got up, I realized I couldn't get up. It's all frozen, like in a big knot, like it feels like the knots you see growing out of tree trunks look. Then also once I moved around I got the pins and needles again down my legs. I kept trying to stretch it out in bed but I couldn't get anything untight. Then for awhile it was better to lay on the floor. Now the sofa feels best.

I finally called the office and told them I wasn't coming in. I told Madlock what was wrong and he goes, "When did you hurt yourself again?" I said, "I didn't hurt myself again." He said, "Well you're hurt again, aren't you? And you were hauling coal." I told him that nothing happened to me this time hauling. I told him it was all from the original whiplash.

He goes, "I find that hard to believe." So I go, "Why?" He goes, "Because you were fine for weeks, you were doing fine driving water truck." I said, "I was fine but it never totally went away, it always felt a little different. I guess it just never healed over completely and now I'm back to where I was." I didn't want to tell him it's worse than before.

He said in order for my benefits not to get cut I had to bring them a note from my doctor proving what I say. I said, "Do I have to pin it to my shirt?" Because that's what it felt like—like having to bring a doctor's note to school which Mom used to safety pin to my shirt so I wouldn't lose it on the way. He said, "I don't want to hear your sarcasm Randi." I told him that maybe I couldn't bring it in if I felt too bad to come all the way out there. He said

I could give it to Derek to bring in. I go, "Don't you have laws about that too?" He goes, "You're skating on thin ice, honey."

He is so two-faced, Madlock. He was so nice about it the first time, and now it's like he's on my back about everything. I know what policy is, but it's the way he said everything—like I was a criminal or something for being hurt, like how I have to prove I'm not. I thought it was supposed to be you're innocent before you're guilty in this country.

I called Dr. Atkins' office and he's on vacation. Great. So they referred me to another office, but they can't see me for 3 days. They asked me if it was an emergency and I told them "No" and as soon as I hung up the phone I realized that was stupid. But I didn't want to lie. I mean, they asked if I had pain and I said yeah, lots of it, and they asked if I had anything for it and I told them a few left-over Darvons from before + alcohol. The lady said that was fine but don't mix them. So I have to wait. Yuck. Fuck a Duck.

HOME

I was reading where it said that unless you love yourself that you can't love anybody else. Where do they come up with this stuff? They make it sound like math. And if you really think about it, it seems the problem around here isn't that nobody loves themselves so they can't love anybody else, but the other way around. It seems like people love themselves so much that they don't got any love left over for anybody else.

If you want to be mathological about it, that makes more sense anyway. Because people who are so busy loving themselves don't got time to love a lover or a best friend. Now the guy that doesn't love himself—it wouldn't seem like that should exclude him from loving somebody else. I mean, maybe that's <u>why</u> he's got to love somebody else—because he doesn't have everything he's looking for right in himself. Actually, that makes more sense. Because loving somebody else makes you feel more love about yourself—cause of what you're doing with that person and what you're creating there. So really they got things reversed. Otherwise you wouldn't see bumper stickers saying "Have You Hugged Your Kids Today?" but instead they would say "Have You Hugged Yourself Today?" I mean, who would want to see that?

I'm not saying you should hate yourself or anything. But if people followed the golden rule instead of all this loving yourself crap everybody would be a lot better off. The golden rule doesn't have much of a chance though, cause if you follow it here you're just a stupid fool. The way it goes in Gillette is—Do unto others before they can do unto you. Screw them over before they screw you over. Fuck them before they fuck you. Do them before they undo you. I think sometimes if it keeps going like this there's going to be a war.

HOME

I was sitting in the pit, belly-dump backed in snug. That's a good position and a good feeling. And T.J. Christopher swung to load me. But the sound was different when he dropped his first shovelful, less rumbly and more wet, like pants ripping. And then I smelled something funny. On the second load I noticed it started smelling real bad. I checked my mirror. T.J. was singing inside the shovel, lip-syncing something to KOAL. I guess we were allowed to have radios again in the trucks. But the smell got worse on the 3rd and 4th loads. So I shut my window and turned on the electric fresh air intake—it had a little "Sanitized For Your Protection" strip across it like at Super 8 motels which I tore off. And then I tried to get Madlock on the two-way to tell him something is wrong, but he was out with the blasters. T.J. gave me two toots goodbye and I started up the haul road and I could practically taste the smell coming through the air vents. I almost puked but I kept sniffing somehow. So I'm going by Tim Frisell in the scraper and as I go by he gives me the old P.U. sign—with his thumb and index finger holding his nose shut. Only he's laughing. And then I see Buck checking cable up on the spoils highwall and he looks down at me and cuts onto my channel and goes, "Randi do you read me? Jesus fucking Christ Randi how long you been wearing the same underwear?" And then he laughed and all the other men came on my channel and started laughing and it was like I could tell each one's laugh by the color it was. I started panicking—like maybe the smell is actually coming from the cab. Like maybe it's me! But I Arrided my arms in the morning and I had new clothes on. So I didn't think it was me. Then the smell of the truck came and met me when I turned the corner and all of a sudden I knew what it was. Shit! And all the guys were laughing at me. "Randi's got a load of shit, there's nothing she can do about it," they were shouting sort of like a song. And then Madlock pulled a banjo-type thing out of his truck and he was playing it over the radio. I finally make it up to the hopper, where there was a whole row of clean-smelling trucks and all the drivers were guys I had been with and they were smiling at me with noseplugs on. I kept whiffing it and eventually I figured out it was cow shit T.J. dumped and not people shit. Like the company went into the fertilizer business and not just energy—like we're mining the shit. And when I thought that, on top of the tipple was old Mr. Graham, whose ranch the mine used to be. He was raising his cowboy hat and yelling, "That's my shit, that's my shit." Then he goes, "You killed my cattle and ran them off, but you can't avoid this, Randi Bruce, you cow!" So I yelled back something like, "Bullshit, Graham! You sold your God-damn land, nobody made you do it. And + we can burn this shit just as good as coal." Something like that. And after I yelled that, I aimed the laser box in the cab out the window and shot Graham down, and he fell from the tipple like a sack of oats and when he hit the ground he went right into the coal, just disappeared. And then all the men in the clean-smelling trucks leapt from their trucks onto the snow and didn't break their legs—like they should of if they jumped off them from the cab—but they started dancing and singing a song about Mr. Graham and me, with Madlock playing along. They were all looking up at me and cheering me on, cause I was their hero for hauling it. So I put that sucker in gear and rumbled up to the hopper and dumped it. There was all kinds of yelling and clapping. And after I dumped my load I drove out of the mine and all the way to town in my Wabco with a police escort and cars carrying WIDE LOAD signs and red flags and I went straight to the Rustler, and I sat down and waited to order. And all the other people eating there except me and dad were cows, sitting in these special booths to fit them. They were talking just like you and me and ordering salads and it was nothing out of the ordinary. They were all regular cattle, not even the special hormones kind. And all of a sudden I saw one at the table next to mine eating Rocky Mountain Oysters. Only they're not the kind cowboys and dogs eat after a roundup—they're the kind I usually eat myself in the privacy of my own home for a late late night snack or maybe breakfast in bed. So I try to order some, only I can't get the attention of the waitress and when I was trying to get her attention I woke up, because my leg was getting a little wet before I knew what the hell was happening and could stop it, which the whole thing was about the weirdest and I probably shouldn't even say anything more about it. Except that it's still freaking me out.

HOME

Dr. Bonnell says I got disk problems and a pinched nerve which is what's causing the sciatica thing. He said I might have had an injury a long time ago that's only coming out now—which is sort of what Dr. Atkins said it might be. They were looking at the same chart is the thing. But Dr. Bonnell said no way should I of gone back to work so fast or gotten active so fast. He says that's what made it worse to begin with. He said, "Right now you only have to remember 3 things—rest, rest and more rest." If I try to do too much I'll only make it worse—like even if I just turn in a funny way or get caught by suprise.

So I have to wear the neck collar again full-time. He gave me an even bigger one than I had before. I'm really Mrs. Mummy now. I asked him could I have sex with my husband, and he said, "Only if you do it like two porcupines. Be very careful." The thing is, he said I could hurt it worse without knowing it right away if something else was making me feel too good physically or the medication was covering up the pain—sort of cancelling out the messages my back was sending telling me to stop. So he wants to be a lot more conservative with painkiller medication than Atkins was the first time. He said, "You seem like one tough lady. I think it's better if you handle it than if we mask it." That made me feel real good, him thinking that. Of course it's easy for him to say— I'm the one that's got to do it.

He wrote the note for Madlock, and Derek brought it out there. He said he made it a strong opinion—he said stuff about "significant trauma" and "vertebrae compaction" so that the company would know it was serious. He sympathized alot with me. I asked him could I go back to the physical therapist and he said in my case it might not help but if I wanted to I could. I told him I did. He said he'd talk to Eva and tell her how slow to go. I got my first session in 2 days, so at least I got something to look forward to other than doctor appointments.

Meanwhile Mom is giving me advice by the pound about what doctors to go to and what routines to follow. She always thinks she knows best + she's still saying about how all this is a message from the Lord. I go, "Is it the same one he sent me last time or is this a new one?" I went over there after Dr. Bonnell and she made me dinner. She goes, "You just didn't get the message the last time." I go, "Why doesn't he just send me a Mailgram?" Don choked on his Coke—he really thought that was funny—so Mom had to smile to show him she wasn't taking herself too serious. It was official Come-Home-And-Meet-Don-Night at 1038 Oak Ridge Drive. Except Betsy didn't show up.

Actually I think Don is not as much of a redneck as Mom made him into. He laughs a lot which is a good thing—cause anybody with Mom had better laugh a lot or they're in for a very long life. He's not real talky or anything. Like when I asked him about his business, he didn't say much, just "It's alright I guess." So Mom said, "You should be super proud of your business, Don." Then she looks at me and goes, like it's this inside secret, "Don's Ra-diators is a real cash cow." So Don leans back in his chair and goes, "Moooooooo." It was great.

Then when we started talking about Betsy, I asked her how did she feel now about Betsy living with Neil? And she said, "Well, after the mess I made in my life I can't very well dictate to my daughters." I couldn't believe that she said something like that. It's so against the way she is. But now I've got it figured that she's got an alterior motive for saying that.

I think she wants Don to move in with her. And she knows if she jumps down Betsy's throat for living in sin and all that we'll call her a hypocrite if she does it herself. That must be the reason. I think she's making her moves on Don. She was making eyes at him over there. And she couldn't get married now even if she wanted to, cause it will take awhile for the divorce to go through. But there's nothing against her living with him, cause it all happened after Peter left town. Actually, after Peter, Don is not the worst guy in the world. I was going to say to her, "Don't you think it's a little quick for all this?" but I watched my attitude and shut up.

HOME

I saw Eva. What she did this time was more like massage, not so heavy-duty. It actually felt good, which was the first thing that has in so long. She said she had wondered how I was doing back at work and had thought about me, which is hard to believe. I mean, she has about 80 patients between the clinic, the hospital and private people. She has this table at home. It's cheaper but benefits don't cover it if she does it there. She says it's not any different than what she's doing to me now at the clinic. She lives in a town-house over in Sagebrush Hills. I wonder what it looks like. That's a pretty nice development over there, if you don't have a family.

I laid there with my head in the donut and told her about what's been going on—how screwed up the people are at work and my road trip with Derek and stuff I did Crazy Days. It's nice to lay there with my eyes closed and everything all black. She said she was in the Bed Race on the nurse team from the hospital but I didn't see her there. We don't know any of the same people I guess. She was asking me about growing up in town and how it changed and being married. She's never been married—even though she's 27. She said I seemed sort of young to be married, which was funny. I mean, I never thought about that before. I told her I was real happy about it even though I was young.

She gave me this back brace Dr. Bonnell ordered for me. She said it was optional. Putting it on and taking it off is what sort of hurts. It doesn't hurt so much when it's on—except it makes me itch. She showed me how to put it on. I'm supposed to see how it feels over this week. It's more protection than anything + it makes my posture right. Eva has this perfect posture, which I never used to notice things like that. She has posture like one of those really special horses they use for shows—the ones that step high and keep their heads up straight and have their manes braided. I'm not saying she looks like a horse though. No way.

HOME

I went 4-wheeling with Derek which really turned out to be a big mistake. I wanted to do it because I wanted to be with him and still be able to do things. I mean—just because I've got this back thing doesn't mean I should be treated like an invalid. A lot of people have bad backs. President Kennedy had a bad back and he went sailing and played football and stuff not to mention being up for being President. So.

But when Derek came home from work to go out there he was real hyper. It was like he was speeding or something. I didn't even want to ask him about it—because he says I have this double standard where I say it's okay for me to take anything I want, but not okay for him, since I handle it better and it's just more my personality. I don't think I think that, but maybe I do. Anyway, he was really going. And driving over to Grandview Hills to 4-wheel, he asked me about Mom and did I tell her yet?

And I told him "No" and he got all out of whack. I told him I didn't want to tell her on the phone and when I was over there the other night for dinner it was hardly the right time, because

Don was there. He goes, "I'm sure you could of found a few minutes to be alone with her." So I said, "I just wasn't thinking about it." And that's true—I wasn't.

So he told me I <u>should</u> of been thinking about it and that he didn't have any trouble telling <u>his</u> parents. I told him that was different. And he starts going, "Why is that different? Why is it different? Tell me why that's different?" and we almost had an accident with this cattle truck at Cut-Across and Stampede cause Derek wasn't paying good attention. I told him for one thing it was different cause <u>all</u> he told them was that we weren't planning a family, and I just thought it was different is all. He goes, "Just tell me why?" So I go, "Well for one thing, I'm the one that had to do it, not you."

He started laughing and saying, "Oh, you <u>had</u> to, huh? You had to? I don't believe this, I really don't. You <u>didn't have</u> to do anything." I said, "I thought that's what <u>we</u> decided." And then he calmed down a little and agreed with <u>me</u>. He said we did decide it, but it wasn't like I <u>had</u> to do anything and if anything it was much more me than <u>him</u> that wanted to do it. So I go, "Much more?" And he said, "You know what I mean." And we talked about it more and he said what we did was still okay by him, even though he still has two minds about it. And everything was okay until I told him to just not worry about the telling Mom part of it—that I'd tell her, but it's not like it's going to change anything and there's no big rush.

So then he said, "I don't believe you are ever going to tell her." I said, "Does that mean you are calling me a liar?" And he just let my question hang out there in the air—which is about the worst answer you can give. I told him, "Thanks a lot for trusting me." He didn't say anything back.

So then finally we were getting about near where they're making the golf course, which is where we go off-road, and he slowed down and said much nicer, "Look, you're just going to break your Mom's heart if you don't tell her soon. She says all these little things to me about kids every time I talk to her on the phone, what do you want me to say?" I said, "Just keep your trap shut about it, okay?" which I shouldn't of said like that—I know it, I know it—but I was still so mad at him. So he said, "Well I might have to tell her myself." I said, "You can't do that." And he goes, "It's a free country." And I said, "What would you know about it?"

And then he gunned the Bronc and we went off onto the hills. And he was so charged up—either cause he was pissed or cause he was cranked—that he was going so fast over the ridges that every time we came down it about killed my back. I had my brace on and my collar on and everything, I was sitting right and I was telling him to just take it easy—but he was taking chances. I swear, it was almost like he was doing it to punish me or something. Then this one time we went over a rise and really got pounded coming down, and I said he had to go slower otherwise I couldn't keep going. So he goes, "If you have to go so slow why even bother doing it? You were the one that wanted to do this." I told him, "Well I was wrong."

So he starts driving home, just ridiculously slow and being all silent, and then he says, "I told you you shouldn't do this." Like he turns the whole thing into my fault. The thing is, I probably would of been fine if he had just taken it easier. So now my back is even more fucked up and the pins and needles are like chainsaws and daggers. I know what Bonnell said about painkillers but I had to take a triple dose. Also Derek didn't even touch me once we got home.

HOME

I think now is the first time I've ever been broke. I used to always dream about having a broken arm or a broken leg. Everybody in school would wonder why I wasn't there and then when I came back everybody would sign my cast and carry stuff for me. The whole thing was super appealing. Especially if I did it being a hero like sliding into home with the winning run or on a jump in waterski trials. Except for that very first minute when you got hurt and it really hurt, I always thought the whole thing would be pretty romantic. But in real life it doesn't feel that way at all.

It feels much more just like rotating knives. And then some-times, sometimes it feels like I'm almost dead. That's the better feeling—which is what's scary. I can just hear Betsy telling me how I'm being so over-dramatic. I can just hear her saying, "You'll get better Randi, just don't have a cow about it!" I know it's true. I know I shouldn't be afraid—because it's just me. But what's weird is sometimes now it feels like I'm this foreign country and I don't even talk the language anymore. I know it seems impossible but it's true.

Maybe it's sort of like I'm under construction. Everything wouldn't be so bad if that's the case. Maybe I'm like that sign they put up out at the airport when the boom started—

PLEASE . . . EXCUSE OUR DUST as we expand for the FUTURE

But then everybody got sick of that sign because it was up for so long, so they put up another one—AFTER THE TURMOIL ALL OVER THE PLACE YOU'LL LIKE THE LOOK OF OUR NEW FACE. Betsy had to look at it every day because it was opposite the Alamo counter. She used to make a joke out of it. One time I called her at work and she answered the phone, "After-the-turmoil-all-over-the-place-you'll-like-the-look-of-our-new-face-hello-Alamo-this-is-Betsy-can-I-help-you?" I think she was stoned.

What I'm saying is that if those signs are true—like if everything is such a mess right now but that's only because something better is under construction—then really all this bullshit that's happening to me really isn't so bad. That's what I think when I'm trying to be positive. It's just like what those signs say on the bank—"A Temporary Inconvenience for a Permanent Improvement." But I feel that way about 10% of the time and the rest of the time I feel like I said, rotating knives or this kind of dull hell.

The thing is, I just want to do the things that normal people do. A lot of the time now I end up thinking, What would a normal person do in my situation? But then I think a normal person would never have gotten themselves into my situation. Not at all. A normal person would have found a way out before falling down so bad. Normal people just keep drinking or keep falling asleep just when the truth is coming out or they run away from the whole thing. Really I shouldn't be so hard on normal people. It's just I'm jealous of them right now.

Because everybody else goes on with their lives when you stop. I mean, stuff for me stopped so fast it was like I was one of those cars with the dummies strapped inside that you always see on T.V. crashing into concrete walls to test safety things. Or like, when there's a crash, and everybody else slows down for a second to stare, and then they go on doing whatever they were doing.

I guess everybody has to put themselves first to get by. Which is fine when everything is going super for each person, but when someone crashes, then it's not so fine. I guess that's all I'm doing now by complaining—putting myself first just like they are. If it wasn't me I'd probably drive right by me too. For one thing, the brain I got left is about as smart as one of those dummies in those cars + I'm about as much fun to be around. Derek doesn't even want to fuck me anymore. That was always something at least.

Time to go.

HOME

I was at home and my back was hurting. So I was sitting in the hot tub. I was getting tired from all the hot but I couldn't get out of the tub, maybe because I was too tired to actually get out, even though I needed to. You know how sometimes things work like that—like being too tired to go to sleep. Anyway, I was getting mad at myself. Because I knew I should get out after being in so long. I couldn't feel any of my muscles. Everything felt like flesh. Then I reached back and turned on the radio without even wiping my hand dry because I just didn't care anymore—but it didn't electrocute me. KOAL was playing this old-timey music, two-stepping music and Charley Pride instead of normal, and all that jangly country stuff was rattling my brain. It made my brain feel like rusty iron so I shut it off. Then I turned on my Walkman and put on my headphones and listened to Elton John sing "Rocket Man." I was singing real loud cause no one was home. "And I think it's gonna be a long long time—And I think it's gonna be a long long time oh no no no." Then all the lights dimmed down real low without me even doing anything. Then a bunch of stuff I can't remember happened. Then the next thing was the doorbell rang. And it rang again. It was like part of the music, it fit right in. And a couple of guys come in. They are some guys from the mine on other shifts, guys I've seen but I don't really know. "Hi-Bye" type guys. They had their hard hats and their work gloves on and their boots and they were carrying their lunch boxes. It was pretty dark so I couldn't see too good. There were 3 guys. And they were saying things to one another but I couldn't hear them cause I had headphones on but I didn't try to take them off either. I just saw their mouths moving. Then the guys walked up the steps to the hot tub and they all get in, little by little. They're my friends. I'm singing and it looks like they're happy to see me. After they get used to the water they slide over to my side of the tub. Then they take their hats off and put them on the edge of the tub next to their lunch boxes. And then they start kissing my hands and my elbows. They were being so gentle it was unbelievable. Then they started kissing my mouth at different times. Then I felt their hands on my legs and my boobs underwater. Their gloves felt all warm and frictiony. These guys, they were like an octopus, but not ugly like an octopus. I felt so hot from the water and from them that it felt like I had a temperature, a little bit of pounding in my forehead, but it was okay. Each guy took a turn licking the sweat off above my top lip—where my peachfuzz always holds my sweat. And then one guy goes over to his lunch box and takes out an envelope which has like his paycheck and a bank slip or some little slip of paper. And the other two guys are still touching me and biting my earlobes under the headphones and stuff while he does this. And the one guy comes back and he takes the envelope and he touches my button a little bit underwater—which felt so strong—and he puts it up into me. And then he starts kissing me again and another one goes and checks his envelope and comes back and does the same thing. It didn't hurt or anything. And then the third guy did it, except when he came back over he took a breath and went underwater and kissed all around me and sucked and pressed down on my button like a fish or something with his mouth and then he put the envelope up into me and it just went up there like it was being drawn up or it was automatic or something. I was just about dying, because it was so unbelievable. And then the guys kissed me more and real nice, not cold or anything, and got up out of the tub and walked out of the basement and out of the house all sopping wet. And I just sat there soaking and I fell asleep and then I woke up.

HOME

When I asked Dr. Bonnell if I could see a chiropractor he took it like I was making a big insult. That's not true. It's just that after 3 weeks I think I have the right to expect to be a little better and I'm still the same. And it seems like he's hardly doing anything about it except seeing me once a week and giving me instructions not to do anything. He said since I was over 18 there's nothing he could do to stop me from going but it might reverse my progress up till now. I go, "What progress, Dr. Bonnell?" He said he could see some but I just didn't feel it yet. He said, "Sometimes with these things you don't see the light until you're already out of the tunnel." He said I might just wake up some morning and the pain won't be there. He told me not to get frustrated.

But I'd rather do something about it than nothing. So I did go see the Dr. Biletnikoff guy Peter told me about. He asked me all these funny questions about what I eat and drink, like that has something to do with my back. And he put stuff on my tongue—like coffee and sugar and chocolate—and tried to pull my fingers apart, and kept changing the stuff on my tongue and pulling. He said maybe I had an allergy that was behind the whole thing. Then he felt all around on my neck and my back. He touched this one spot and goes, "Ah-ha." And he kept touching it. And he says, "I would like to crack your back. Is that okay with you?"

I didn't know what in the hell to say. Like, why is he asking me? He's the God-damn doctor. It made me think that something could go wrong with it, if it was something I had to give him approval for. And it made me think about how Dr. Bonnell said don't do anything like that. It made me think that maybe after weeks of doing just what he said that maybe, <u>maybe</u> I was just on the edge of getting better, and if Dr. Biletnikoff cracked my back it might send me all the way back to where I was—like being sent back to GO in a board game. So I told him I wasn't ready for it right then and he gave me this big speech about how he could help me and to come back the next day.

Which I did, which I did because it was really, really hurting. And he put all these different vitamins on my tongue and tried pulling my fingers apart and then he put them right on my chest, like on my breast bone, and was doing the same thing. And with some of them he couldn't hardly pull my fingers apart, and with others he could pull them apart, like no problem. But I couldn't tell if sometimes he was trying harder or not. Because that's what it felt like—like sometimes he was using his muscles and sometimes he was faking it. And I was thinking that maybe he was doing this just to see my chest, which was weird, since he was a friend of Peter's. But his assistant was standing there writing down all the results on my chart, so maybe there was something to it.

And then he asked me to turn over and he felt around until he got to the "Ah-ha" spot and he just told me to relax and let out my breath and he was going to crack it. So I did and he did it. The sound was incredible. It was like I had a snare drum in my back. And when I sat up he asked me how I felt and I did feel better. When he rotated my neck, that felt better too—just looser. So he told me to come back in two days and not eat chocolate. I paid him and he gave me these vitamins to start taking right away. But when I got home, I saw they had cow brains and DNA and pituitary glands and rice and garlic in them + they smell like shit. But I figured I paid for them, and it says on the bottle they come from Douglas, Wyoming, so how bad can they be? So I'm taking them. Because Biletnikoff was the first doctor that did anything to make me feel better. And I was real happy going to sleep, because it did feel better.

But when I woke up yesterday right away it was back to the same thing again. And when I got up for breakfast, right where the two disks are that Bonnell said were off kilter, which is right where he cracked it, the pain was real bad. It was like electric—like voltage going from being off to being on and back to off, just depending how I moved. And it didn't go away. So I was getting scared. I called Biletnikoff's office but it was his day in Buffalo. So I didn't know what to do—because I didn't want to call Bonnell and tell him, because I felt guilty and I didn't think I could lie to him about it. And if I went to him, maybe he would find out something worse.

So I called Eva at the clinic, but she was on private hours. So I called Information and got her number. And I was lucky because she was home—and she really calmed me down on the phone and told me to come over at noon. And when I got there, I told her everything that happened. Then she gave me the best massage. Mostly on my neck and my head and my face. I fell asleep right on the table and when I woke up she was making lunch for both of us. These big salads and apple juice.

She told me stuff about herself which I could finally ask her about since she didn't have to be listening to my body, and it just made me want to know more. She lives over there with a nurse from the hospital. But there's only one bedroom. I guess I was staring at the sofa—it didn't look like a fold-out and it was too short to sleep on unless you were a munchkin—because she said, "What are you looking at?" and I told her "Nothing." What was I supposed to say, tell her I was wondering where her friend slept? I mean, there were a bunch of pictures of them together. One was them dancing in this place in Jackson Hole and one was climbing Devil's Tower. She technical climbs, which I told her I always wanted to do but never learned. She said she would teach me next summer. So I said, "I can't imagine driving there much less climbing there right now." She put her hand on my neck and said, "You will get better. Trust me." Which I really do.

She had to go for afternoon hours at the clinic and I swear I wanted to ask her could I stay there for awhile, just hang out at her place for the afternoon, because it felt good being there and not being at home. It felt like I was away from things for a second. It wasn't like I was expecting her to give me massages for free or anything. It felt more like I owed her one. But I didn't say anything.

HOME

I get up and I don't have anything to do is the thing. I almost went back to Biletnikoff just to have something to do, but I didn't. I think he's a quack. Those vitamins turned my pee day-glo. But I paid for them so I'm keeping taking them + they probably can't hurt me—which is more than I can say for him.

I think I do candy just to have something to do now. But I got to cut down otherwise I'll use it up so fast since the day is so long when you're home alone all day. It's about the only thing that gives me anything to look forward to—even though it isn't hardly that good when you're not with people or at work + it's like I have to hide it from Derek. I think I miss work. Not the working part but the being out there. You ain't shit around here if you're not working.

This is starting to feel pretty stupid because all I do is bitch about everything. The way everything's going I should be using this for toilet paper instead. It wouldn't be any great loss for humanity's sake.

HOME

I met this guy who is this black guy from Detroit and we had this great time drinking at the Outlaw Inn. There weren't many people in there on account of it being in the middle of the afternoon, so it wasn't so loud that you couldn't talk the way it usually is. No one was riding the bull. I just didn't feel like eating lunch so I went over there. I was just going to have one lite beer and play the jukebox for 15 minutes, but I ended up staying there the whole afternoon because this guy was so funny that I liked listening to him talk.

I've only ever seen about 3 black guys around town. There's the fat guy that stays at the Buffalo, and Kerwin who worked with Dean as a maid at the Holidome, and there was a guy who played softball for Belle Ayr last summer. They really stick out. So when I saw this guy I was suprised cause I didn't recognize him at all. The reason turned out to be that he's only been out here for a month.

I can't blame him for talking to me because I was the one that talked to him first. What happened was I put "Tears Of A Clown" on the jukebox—which was my favorite growing up—and I could see his hat moving to it at the bar. He had this cowboy hat on, only it was sort of floppy. So I said, "You like this?" And he said, "It's my town. Yeah, it reminds me of my town." He turned around and I didn't even really realize he was black before that—because of his hat and he had his jacket up and guys come off rigs sometimes looking about that black anyway. It didn't freak me out or anything. I mean, Mom raised us to be liberals. But it was my first time talking personal to one. The only other time I talked to one was in a store in Rapid.

So he started telling me about being from Detroit and how he used to work for this big hotel there in this big new complex that nobody can find their way around, and how he quit because they wouldn't promote him. I was just standing up for about the first 10 minutes we were talking, and then I finally sat down. It was like he didn't want to ask me to sit down with him. Anybody else that would of been the first thing they did. Maybe it was on account of him trying to stay out of trouble around here. Maybe they have to be careful. I don't know.

Anyway, it turns out he's 34 and he's from this superbig family and his name is Kenny Carr. The first thing he said when he told me was, "It really sucks being a Carr from Detroit, it's a cliché it sucks so much." So right away I knew he was funny. He just had a funny way of looking at stuff and of talking—he had this kind of lisp. Not a lisp, but his voice trailed off soft whenever he'd finish saying something. I don't know if it was a defect or just his accent.

It turns out he was in Vietnam for awhile, which he kept calling his "vacation." He said he was waiting for us to get into a war with Iran so he could go there and fight for the <u>money</u>. I said, "What money?" And he goes, "War is good fucking money. You go some-place, destroy it, and build it up again." See the thing is, he's having a hard time getting a job, which he says is not because people are

256

prejudiced but because they are stupid—because he can do a lot of different things. But he thinks they don't want you to use your mind, they just want you to show up, so they're scared of him because he wants to use his mind. He said he interviewed for this construction job and the pipe welders didn't even know what they were doing. But he's paying $500 a month rent and going through his money quick. He goes, "It really runs you a nickel out here, doesn't it? Strange planet, Wyoming, fucking strange planet." I told him it's not so strange once you get used to it.

So then he ordered us drinks and we went and sat at a table. I asked why was he drinking white wine? He goes, "I don't like beer—it sucks it really sucks—I drink wine." So I told him if he wanted I would call my Mom over at Amax and see if I could get him an interview. He goes, "My recommendation is don't get into the mines, don't get into them. They take a body and use it up in 5 years." I said, "Yeah, but the money is the best." So he goes, "Okay, the money is there—you can buy a lot of junk, a car. It depends on what you want out of life." So I said, "So what do you want?" Because he was acting sort of superior. He goes, "I don't know. I've been in school half my life and a lot of things I know but what freaks me out is what I don't know. I came out here like everybody else, to find something new."

So I asked him what he found so far, after a month. He goes, "Nothing. Not enough trees and not enough niggers." I laughed, because I thought that was a funny thing for him to say, and he looked at me strange. He tilted his head and stared. Then he goes, "I been checking you all out out here. You know—the toys, the cars, the stupid pets, the kids. Oh my God I feel sorry for you. It's like a big suburb of nowhere. It's very hard to identify a real cowboy out here." I'm not sure I'm getting right exactly what he said, because he said a lot of things real fast and I was getting a little loose. Then he said all the cowboys he sees out here are really C'boys—which is what he calls them. He goes, "The urban type, the wanna-be type, the farmer type, the heavy pickup type—it's just some funky dream they're trying on."

I said, "Maybe my husband is a heavy pickup type." He pretended like he was shocked, and goes, "You're married?" I said uh-huh. Real fast he goes, "Good." I said why was it good? And he goes, "Because I have too many women." So I asked him why was that? And he goes, "Because when I talk people tend to listen, specially women. So I'm satisfied in that respect. Piece of ass is a piece of ass, business is business. Women come up to me. You have to satisfy one's needs right away, so I satisfy them." He was acting so stuck up. But I was wondering if he knew what my needs were.

I said, "Do you know what I need?" He goes, "Yeah, you need to get that funny thing from around your neck. You need to bend your back like a tree in the fucking wind. And you probably need something I don't got. What happened to you anyway?" So I told him about the whiplash, and he goes, "See what I mean about the mines." I told him, "It was fine up until then, really." He goes, "I don't know."

So I said, "Well what do you need?" He goes, "Hey, I need a job." It turns out he interviewed already for an engineering job at Mobil with 52 other people, but he didn't get it. Then he thought he could catch on with the railroad, but it hasn't happened. He said he knows engineering, marine engineering, math, climate control, management, concrete and welding, but he can't get a job. He goes down to the employment office every morning at 4:30, so he's always one of the first in line when it opens. He just looked at me and said, "Everybody said go west so I went west, and I think it's a mistake." We talked about concrete for awhile. I told him his best bet is to put his name in the fishbowl at the Terminal Bar. He said that's what a bunch of people told him, but they also said the Terminal is the one bar he better not go in. I told him that's probably true.

We drank for a while more and played more tunes on the juke-box. He only has this one tape he brought out with him—it's this jazzy tape called "Mellow Madness"—and he says he plays it like 5 × a day so he's pretty sick of it, and he was hurting to hear tunes you can't hear on KOAL. Then I told him let's go downtown and I'll put his name in the fishbowl at the Terminal. Because I told him nobody's going to mess with me on account of my mummy wrap and my backbrace + I can take care of myself anyway. He goes, "It's good that someone can take care of you."

I said, "Hey, my husband takes pretty good care of me." He

just stared at me, grinning. So I said, "Well, he used to." And so Kenny goes, "Two different things, girl." I said, "I know." So he asked me what was up and I told him that maybe Derek's not as attracted to me since I got hurt. He tilted his head at me and stroked his little goatee beard and went, "I don't know. I think that brace is pretty kinky. I seen businessmen at my old hotel pay a lot of money for that kind of thing, if you know what I mean." We both laughed real hard. I told him maybe I should move to Detroit.

Then he wrote out his name and number and when he's home on a bunch of pieces of paper, and what his skills are, and we drove over there in our cars and parked. I took them in and gave them to Chief-the-Barkeep and he put them in the bowl. And the good thing about this is—from just his name and number nobody will even know he is a black guy when they call. I don't think he sounds black exactly.

I came out and told him it was done and he thanked me real nice. So I said, "What are you doing?" He goes, "What does it look like? I'm sitting in my tank on Gillette Avenue waiting for some C'boy to come by and try to kick my ass." I said I wanted to walk off my beers, and he could come if he wanted. So he did. We walked over to the train yards and walked up the footbridge over the tracks and just stood up there for awhile.

You can see a lot of town from up there. It's just like this big chainlink cage bridge, and you can watch the coal trains go under you and the crews change. I always used to go up there when I was thinking about stuff. Sometimes after working Jesse's, I'd go up there and sit for a while before going home—nobody but me and the trains and the Big Dipper and the wind.

I showed Kenny a lot of stuff about town from up there, like where the new bank building is going to be and where you can park without getting a ticket. I told him about last year—the hobo who was riding the rails in a coal car and fell asleep or something before it went out to one of the mines. They didn't find him till 3 days later when they were dumping the coal at this power plant in Louisiana and he came sliding out onto the conveyor. Kenny said he didn't think that was a bad way to go—in your sleep under 100 tons of coal. That's sort of true.

Anyway, there was nothing to do so we walked around town for awhile. He said he goes to the library a lot. He likes it there. Then we walked to Bobbie Sue's and had pie. But I still didn't want to go home, and it was too cold to keep walking around cause I didn't have my heavy jacket and my back was getting stiff, so I convinced him to go to the early movie with me at the Paramount. It was James Bond. Getting tickets he did this weird James Bond impression to the lady selling them, like if James Bond was a black guy. There were only about 7 people in the theater. The lady looked at me funny when I went to get Twizzlers. Like, fuck her! I wasn't doing anything.

We just sat there watching the movie. I don't think there's anything wrong with that. I did hold onto him at this one superscary part. He put his arm around me cause he could see how jinked out I was. I hate that guy Jaws—the guy with the metal teeth. He gives me the big-time creeps. But it wasn't like anything happened. Kenny's a really nice guy, a funny guy. I think about him sometimes. I got his number, cause I kept one of his little slips of paper for myself. I might call him one of these days just to say hi. Or maybe I'll run into him. I think that would be okay. It wouldn't be bad.

HOME

Sam came over to tube-out with me yesterday afternoon, which was the first time I saw her in awhile. I think she thinks I'm not very much fun since I can't do anything. Sitting around watching "The Price Is Right" isn't so much fun. I admit it. Other than maybe me impressing her by how many right answers I know. You watch it every day and you just get a feeling about the prices, like Amana side-by-sides and stuff they always show. The women on the show are so dumb they don't have a clue.

Sam told me about this big weekend she had in Denver. She was wearing this outfit she bought down there. It has this leather vest and pants that match. She went dancing at all these places and stayed at the Sheraton downtown. She went down there with Jo-leen, just them. I asked her where was Spike? She said he had to go to Oklahoma City for an industry seminar or something. And then she gives me the eye—like I don't already know what she's saying. It's not like I need her to wink at me or anything.

What I think about it is, it's really unfair. She lives over there with him and gets all the benefits but she doesn't even have to be married. So if she wants to go fuck around it's like there's nothing to stop her. Other than maybe Spike finding out, which she's too smart for + she'd find a way out of it even if he did. And even if she couldn't, she could just go find somebody better than Spike anyway. That wouldn't be too hard. What gets me though is then she comes back to the house on Frontier and plays like she's Ms. Wife or something. It's unbelievable. And it's probably the same thing Betsy is doing over there with Neil, or at least what she could be if she wanted to. And Mom and Don too, even though I know that's a little different. But still it is living together and playing house and not being married.

Also it pisses me off that Sam and Joleen didn't even invite me down with them. I said, "You know it's not like I'm so busy these days." She went, "Oh, we thought you wouldn't be up for the drive, with your back and all. You can't go dancing with that thing, can you?" She was pointing at my brace. I told her, "I wouldn't of had to go dancing, I could of just hung out with you guys." Then she goes, "Sorry, sorry. I didn't even think you'd want to come. Don't make me feel guilty about it just cause we had a great time." Then she went on telling me about what they did and these guys they met who are these big Denver oil hot-shots and I didn't want to listen to it, but I did. It was making me sick though, hearing her, so I told her I wanted to go to sleep, which was a white lie.

She went off to go bowling—I guess the winter league has started. And she left Derek a schedule for the mine rescue competition coming up at Black Thunder. I didn't even know she was going to be on the team doing that. She said she's just an alternate. But she does everything with them, so she'll step in if someone gets sick + she'll have a better shot at the team next year. Sam is always scheming ahead is the thing.

I think one of these days she's going to get what's coming to her. I don't mean anything bad, I mean just like a lesson. Because if she keeps going the way she is, sooner or later something will happen. Because what I figured out is that when you do life in the fast lane, you are nearest to the lane of the people who are going in the other direction just as fast. So it's a mess when you collide, a real mess. And sooner or later you will collide. And that's what you get away from when you get married—you get shelter from all that. It's just that you've got to make sure the guy has a high insulation factor. I think Derek is a very high number, mostly because of his family + he's just got good character. But most of the other guys I know, they talk big about protecting their women but when it really gets down to it their women about end up with frostbite. I swear that's true.

I could be scared about that too. Because it's easy to be scared. Sometimes I am actually, only I sit here and tell myself not to be. Because what can you do if you get scared? Sometimes I think being married is like what you do to keep from the cold of being alone. But the thing is, what if you're together and you're still cold—even though the other one doesn't want you to be? Like for instance, there's enough snow on the ground to build a snowman— and both people want to build it—but the problem is that it's so cold that the snow doesn't pack together, it just blows away in the wind. That's a cold feeling. Mister, that's the coldest feeling, like it says in that song, that love song.

Hey, why do they call them love songs when most of them are lack-of-love songs? I think they should have separate categories for them. One is for your love songs, when you're all romantic, and one is for your lack-of-love songs—when you feel like the chain on a tire going around and around trying to get out of a ditch.

HOME

This has been about the worst day ever. I should of known it when I woke up and saw snow blowing sideways out the window when they said it was going to be rain. Not that it stuck, but still. Maybe if I had just stayed in bed things wouldn't have happened the way they did. I'm starting to get superstitious. Because what else is there to believe?

What happened was I was over at Dr. Bonnell's for my visit and he was saying that I was improving, which I feel I am, sort of. But in the middle of him examining me he got a phone call from the hospital about a patient. And I heard him say the name of the patient. I wasn't trying to snoop, I just heard him say the name. And it was Teagle, Terry's last name and it turned out it was his little brother Rick, who I know is roughnecking with him. I asked Dr. Bonnell about it and he said that last night, actually this morning, he fell from the top of a rig out near Savageton and broke his ankle and his collarbone and his legs are partially paralyzed but they think that part might be reversed. God! He could of got killed. I don't really know him and I don't keep up much with Terry but he was always so great to me, and it just sucks.

I asked Dr. Bonnell all about it but he couldn't tell me anything more than the hospital released because of things being confidential. So I went over there right after my appointment. But they weren't letting anybody in to see Rick. I guess Terry had gone home to sleep. But one of his friends said that Rick had been on for 22 straight hours right before he fell and Terry was talking about how he was going to sue Knox Oil on account of that. Like that's going to do anything.

So I was driving back home and feeling kind of guilty about my back—because here I am with this wimpy little problem and look what happened to Rick. It sort of puts things in perspective. And I was thinking about how much I just wanted to have a quiet night with Derek, you know, stay in for dinner and take a hot tub together, whatever. I was getting almost teary thinking about it, just how nice it would be. But when I got home he wasn't home from work yet, which he should of been. So I just started getting dinner all ready. I know I can't cook worth shit, but it's the thought.

Then, about an hour and a half later, he comes in and I go, "Hey where you been?" I wasn't criticizing him or nothing. And he goes, "I don't know, where have you been?" I didn't know why he was asking that. He didn't kiss me hello. I told him I've been home since the doctor, fixing dinner. He goes, "Well, maybe today you have." I didn't know what he was talking about. He was really scaring me.

Then he told me he was home late because he had a flat tire. I said, "I thought it was almost impossible for those tires to go flat." He goes, "Not if someone nails an aluminum nail into them they're not." So I asked him why anybody would do that? And he goes, "I don't know. Maybe you know." I didn't know what he was getting at—it was like he was playing this game. His face was all red and he was just standing there kicking the kitchen stool with his boot, looking away from me. I said, "Tell me what's wrong, would you?"

So he goes, "Someone left me a note in the parking lot at work, under my windshield wiper, and I guess just by coincidence my left front tire went completely flat by the time I'm halfway back on 59, and when I pulled off I see there's an aluminum nail punched in there perfect, like someone hammered it in. So it took me awhile to change the tire and then I went to the Pronghorn for a beer on the way home, or isn't that allowed?" I told him of course and I was sorry about it—that he had to fix the flat in bad weather and all, after a long day working. But I said how did he know someone nailed the nail in there, and who would want to do that?

He goes all sarcastic, "Maybe if you read the note you'll be able to tell me." And he takes out this crumbly piece of 3-hole paper from his pocket and gives it to me. The writing on it is all awkward and thick, like with a purple magic marker. It goes—

> HEY HARPER—WHAT DO YOU THINK
> YOUR LITTLE RANDI HAS BEEN DOING
> WITH ALL HER FREE TIME WHILE
> YOU'VE BEEN OUT HERE WORKING?
>   A CONCERNED FRIEND

I mean, I had no idea what that is about and I told Derek that. But he started raising his voice and punching at the wall. I kept trying to get him to calm down. The first thing I could think of was that someone was playing a practical joke on him. He goes, "I don't know anyone out there that would think that was funny." So I told him maybe there's somebody out there that doesn't like him, some asshole just pulling his hose, being a prick. He said he can't think of anybody.

I don't know. I don't know who would do that. So he kept asking me, "What have you been doing behind my back?" And I kept telling him I hadn't been doing anything behind his back! But he didn't want to believe me. He kept saying it would be much better if I fessed up, and not to think that he was going to hit me or anything. I didn't know what to think. I didn't know what to tell him. I told him maybe it was someone trying to get back at <u>me</u> for something. He says, "Like who?" I told him, "I don't know." And then he goes, "And for what?" I said, "I don't know. Something. Anything."

And I thought I had him all calmed down and that he believed it was just a joke or a stupid thing some asshole did, but then he said he didn't want dinner and he was going out. So I said, "Where are you going?" He goes, "I don't know." So I asked him, "Could I come with?" and he says "uh-uh" and walks out.

And so he just leaves me here and I'm still sitting here and he hasn't come back yet. And I don't know whether to call some of his friends to see where he is or to call Sam or maybe Eva just to talk, not that she hardly knows me. I don't know. It's too late really.

The only thing I can think of is, somebody saw me in town with Kenny that day. But I didn't see anybody at the Outlaw or the Paramount that knows me or Derek. Maybe outside the Terminal though or standing up on the footbridge. Shit! Maybe one of Spike's little shit railroad friends was at the B.N. office and saw us up there over the tracks, and then Spike told one of his buddies at Split Branch to leave the note. That would be just like Spike to do something like that. But it wasn't even like we were <u>doing</u> anything! We didn't do <u>anything</u>. Not that I could explain that to Derek. Shit.

So the only thing I can do is just sit here and look at the Goddamn note, and try to figure out if I can recognize the writing. I mean, I want to tear it into a million pieces, but maybe I should keep it, like for evidence. Like it makes a difference—

HOME

I have been wishing for things. Impossible things. For a long time I wished that I would feel better. But I stopped wishing that. It's not that I don't think that I will ever feel better—because I'm sure I will, with time and all, like everybody says. But I'm afraid even when I get better there will be this thing gnawing at my insides, like I'll never be the same person again. I mean, even though I'll get better, it's like I'll never get well.

So I stopped wishing to feel better. If I do, I do. Instead I'm wishing for things more on the line of science fiction. Not that they're make-believe, because it said on the news that they are both around the corner. The first thing is an artificial heart. There's a guy in Salt Lake that has a plastic one all figured out. Now, I figure if they took mine out and put one of those in then it wouldn't hurt so much. I know people say it is not really your heart that hurts, but I swear that is right where I feel it. Right there.

But if that doesn't work out, the second thing would be more radical. I could be frozen in one of those Kryogenic labs in California that rich people go to when they die so they can come back to life once there's a cure for whatever they died of. Only I wouldn't wait till I died—I would go right now and just have myself frozen for a few years. And then when they thawed me out, like in 1984 on my 24th birthday, everything would be different. There would be different people around. Town would be different. My back would be all better. Derek would be more like he used to be or at least there would be better guys. All the bad stuff would be numbed out of me. To test it out I could stowaway on a senior citizen bus to Rushmore—to see what being frozen alive with a bunch of dead people feels like. Ha!

I know these are ridiculous wishes. But thinking about them gets me through a lot of bad afternoons, you know. They're just to fix me in the meantime. Yeah, that's pretty true—time is mean. Time can be mean.

HOME

Thanksgiving is getting all screwed up. First we were trying to plan to go to Minot just like last year, because I miss the Harpers bad and Derek too. I haven't even seen them since the wedding. The phone is just not the same. But Derek couldn't get enough time off. Everyone tries to get time off then which is the problem. So then I thought maybe the Harpers could come here. But Derek said he won't be free enough to justify asking them to bring the whole family out all that way, that he really won't have enough time off.

So we were stuck planning it here. I mean, Peter called Betsy and invited me and Derek and her and Neil down to Boulder to show off his dealership and have Thanksgiving with him, but I think it's like a package deal—we'd have to be with Shari at the same time. Which would be about the weirdest. Betsy didn't want to go. I didn't either, but maybe I did a tiny little more than her— just because I'm curious. But it would about kill Mom if me and Betsy went down there instead of being with her.

So it's down to being here for it. And it already started out to be a problem, because Mom didn't want to invite Neil. But I told her she had to, because Neil doesn't have any family around here and why was it worth pissing Betsy off so much about one place at the table? It's not worth it. I told her Neil isn't so bad as he used to be. So I convinced her to invite him. She said the real deal was she was worried Don would be upset, because Don hasn't taken to him. I told her I didn't think it was right to have him making decisions about stuff like that. She said, "Don wouldn't dream of doing that." She said it was only her "trying to protect everybody's nice time." Someday I hope they study Mom's brain in a laboratory. I want to see the results of that.

Anyway, so that was all set. But now the time is getting all screwy, because it turns out Derek is going to be on swing shift then and he can't find anybody to flip with him. Nobody wants to work 3–11 on Thanksgiving. I mean, he needs to be done by about 1:45 in order to get to work on time. And the problem is Betsy has to be at Alamo until noon because there are flights coming in until 11:45. So Mom is all jinked out because the whole thing is going to be such a rush.

Yesterday she said to me all sarcastic on the phone, "Well, if this is going to be the way it is, I don't know why we just don't go to McDonald's." I told her Derek was still working on flipping and Betsy was still trying to get off. The problem is, I think Mom wants to make it this big thing, and show us how good everything is with her new life and with Don. And she keeps saying how I went out of town last year so this year is extra special. But on the other hand maybe it's good that me and Derek aren't over there the whole day anyway. I don't really want Mom looking at us so close right now.

When I was at Eva's today for therapy I was almost going to invite her too. Because I doubt she's going all the way back to Minnesota and I don't think Mom would mind. I was telling her all about last year—driving all night to Minot, about Derek's sisters and all, all about Mrs. Harper and Mr. Harper and the air base. It doesn't seem like it was a year ago.

And then I guess I was complaining pretty much about how the people running town now on all their stupid schedules are such assholes and all that's doing is attracting other stupid assholes here. Because I was saying how could it be such a big deal that they can't turn off the coal for one God-damn day? I said, "I guess if they did that then Gillette couldn't put 'Energy Capital of the Nation' on the doors of all the stupid police cars." I must of really been bitching about it, because Eva just said, "People expect too much out of towns" and she went off to wash her hands like she was mad at me or something. So I didn't ask her to Mom's after all.

HOME

The wind is blowing so hard today it's like it wants to make Gillette a town in Nebraska. Northwest wind is always the worst one in winter. It's the one that goes right through you—like it makes an x-ray of your bones and comes out the other side. Or if you're driving down the road in a Japmobile it can put you on the shoulder in a second or over the center line if you're not really paying attention and holding 10/2 like Driver's Ed taught. I've seen it happen.

It's making a new sound in the house which I never heard before. Sort of like a "Wooo Wooo Wooo" coming up out of the heat vents. It's not a whistle, it's more a moan. Maybe there's a vacuum somewhere. Or it could be that something's not finished right in the crawl space. It sounds like there's a hole in the furnace and the wind is whipping right in there and coming out the vents. I suppose it doesn't matter what's causing it. My back hurts too much to find out. Because if I find out what it is and it's fixable—then I'd have to fix it and I'm really not up for that.

About all I'm up for is sitting here looking out my window. Because they keep interrupting my soaps with stuff about Bonzo vs. Peanuts, so it's not even worth trying to watch them today. I'm not voting either because Bonzo is going to win Wyoming so big what's the point? Every long-hair burnout I know from construction + all the rock & roll rednecks from work are voting for him, not to mention all the rich ranchers, so what's my little vote? Maybe if it was nice weather I'd go out and make my little protest vote for Peanuthead along with Betsy. She's going to be on my case big-time if I tell her I didn't vote. I'll have to lie. I'm too lazy and it's too shitty out and Skywalker is sleeping on my foot and I wouldn't want to wake him. See, it's just I'm being considerate.

So I got the mute button on and I'm watching the fast-paced, exciting world of Arrowhead Road go by out the window. Right this second there is—

1) dirty snow blowing around
2) an old Daily Call sticking to the branch of our skinny little front yard tree, but trying to blow off it
3) McHale's beater orange Torino backing out of his driveway with real white exhaust.

Hey, that's fucking entertainment! I admit it's pretty exciting.

Of course there is the beep-beep-beep sound of construction

269

equipment backing up. God, you know no matter where there is construction in town or subdivisions you always hear that beep-beep-beep. It makes everyplace in town sound like work. Because if there's not someone doing it around the corner, which there usually is, then the wind blows it over from some other part of town. Beep-beep-beep. It's some fedreg thing—they made them put it on all heavy equipment after someone got run over by something backing up a few years ago. You know how like the news has a theme song? Beep-beep-beep is like the theme song for Gillette.

It sounds like they're working right down the street. But they're not. They're finishing streets up in Grandview Hills and it's probably just the wind blowing it all the way over. It's really blowing today.

That's why they say no women love their men as much as Wyoming women do—because if they didn't love them that much then they wouldn't stay, that all the wind and the winter would drive them away. I don't know who made that one up. I think it's an old wives' tale. I decided I'm divided about it today. About the wind. For a while I liked the sound it was making, because it was nice to have a sound. But now I think I've been listening to it for too long. And I kind of just wish the wind would shut up.

HOME

I had the scariest one ever—I was just holding on to this ledge for the longest time. And my arms were getting tired. I said, "I don't think I can hold on anymore. I think I'm going to fall." He was sitting up on the ledge, so he didn't have to hold on. He said, "Don't worry. I know you can hold on longer." He said something like that. The ledge was like a window sill, and on one side of it was a house, way way up in the air, and on the other side, the side I was hanging over, was thousands of feet of nothing with rocks at the bottom of it. My shoulders were starting to burn and it felt like the skin was coming off my hands from holding on. I said,

"Pull me up! I can't hold on any longer." He said, "How do you know that? How do you know you can't? You're always afraid to try things. Sometimes you make me sick." I couldn't believe it. If I fell I knew I'd die, I'd die as soon as I hit the rocks. I said, "God, come on, help me!" He said, "Hold on a minute, I'm watching." I was dying. I knew I was a dead girl. I was barely holding on. I was looking down and kicking my legs. And then I just pulled myself up somehow and sat on the ledge. I was crying. I had slivers in my hands from the window sill. I was trying to catch my breath. And he just got up and walked along the ledge and walked away from me. It freaks me out that he did that, even if it wasn't real.

HOME

I don't know what to say. But I have to put something down because—I don't know. It's just, the way things are going I don't know. Sometimes I think, God, maybe I'm not going to make it. Maybe I'm not. But maybe that wouldn't be such a bad thing. If I didn't.

See, Derek called. He called me from Wright at about 5:30. And he said that he had to stay down there with the rescue team on account of the weather. Because it's supposed to get worse. I asked him could he come home—since it was hardly snowing here + he has the 4 × 4 anyway if it does—but he said if it really snowed he'd be up shit creek cause there's no way he'd be able to get back to Black Thunder for Day 2 of the competition. So they are all spending the night in Wright since it's so close to Black Thunder. I mean, Wright is for the people that work there. There's only this one motel.

So I didn't think anything about it. Except just for being bummed he wasn't coming home. But then a little later I heard the weather on KOAL and it said it wasn't supposed to snow tonight anymore and that it was turning real clear and real cold. And so I thought it would be the same for Wright, since it's only 40 miles away. I thought maybe they got a wrong prediction down there or it changed real sudden. It can do that. So I called the office down at Black Thunder, to see if I could get him, but they had already gone. Then I got the number for the motel in Wright, and I called down there to tell him that the weather changed and it would be cool for him to come back to town. But the lady, the lady on phone said they hadn't checked in or anything. So I thought maybe they went out to eat dinner or drink first. There's nothing else to do in Wright.

So I kept calling down there. I wasn't calling that much but the lady started getting irritated at me. She said I should just leave her a message and if he shows up to check in she'll give it to him. But the thing is, I don't trust people like that to give messages. They forget things. So I was just calling down there, maybe once a half hour, not like every 5 minutes or anything. And finally when I called about 7:00 she said some Keller Coal people had checked in. But she didn't have his name down there.

So I asked her who had checked in and she said she couldn't give that out. I mean, why the fuck not? Because the thing is, I didn't really know who was on the team with Derek—especially last names—since I haven't been at work. So I explained all that to her but she still wouldn't tell me, so I yelled at her and hung up. Because she was being such a bitch about it. But then I thought, I thought I might as well try to get Sam down there. That was about the last thing I wanted to do, but it wasn't like I had a choice. I mean, I was hoping she wasn't there but I thought she probably was. And the last thing I wanted was for her to even think I was looking for my husband—so I decided to make it like I was just calling to ask her about going to a movie tomorrow night.

I called back and I tried to make my voice different so the desk lady wouldn't know it was me and hang up. And I put one of those handi wipes from the kitchen over the phone to make it sound like long distance. And she put me through to Sam's room. But there was no answer. And I tried a bunch more times and finally after 8:00 I called her room and someone picks up and it sounded like my fucking husband. I go, "Derek, is that you?" I knew it was him but it was like I was in a little shock, I mean my stomach. And he goes, "Yeah, what's going on?" He sounded real distant. Just his voice. I wanted to ask him what was he doing there but I was too scared to.

I told him, "Nothing, I just called to tell you they say the weather is fine, so you don't have to stay down there or anything." And he goes, "Well, it's not so bad down here either. It's pretty much stopped. But we've all checked in and eaten and all, so I might as well stay." So I go, "Why?" So he starts getting a little impatient and goes, "Because everybody's here and we're going out for beers and it's too late now to drive all the way home just to have to turn around first thing in the a.m. and come all the way back." I said it was only just after 8:00. But he said it was too late anyway because he already paid for his room. I said, "Isn't the company paying?" And he goes, "Yeah, I mean they paid already."

So I asked him who was he staying with—because they didn't have him listed at the front desk—and he said he was in a room with Mark Reiner. So I said, "So what are you doing in Sam's room?" I mean I was asking him in a funny way, not like anything heavy. I guess I was getting less scared. But he goes, "What kind of a question is that?" I said, "Nothing, it's just a question." And he goes, "Well I don't fucking like it." So I said, "Well how fucking come?" Because I didn't like the way he was talking to me. He goes, "How come? How come?"

And then he goes, he goes "How come I don't ask you about all the blowjobs you give guys out in the oil patch?" I'm like, "What?" And he says, "Yeah, Randi, why don't you tell me about that?" I said, "Because there's nothing to tell you." So he goes, "I heard different."

And then he starts telling me stuff he heard, and I can't believe it. So I asked him where did he hear that, and he says Reno Junction Bar. That's a bar down there. And I asked him from who and he said it was none of my business, and I asked him when and he said it was none of my business. Which made me think that somebody told him something today and twisted it all around and I don't even want to think about who.

So he said he was going but I said, "Don't hang up, don't." And I told him there was a tiny little bit of truth to the story, because something did happen once, but it was a long time ago—and I never told him because I didn't want him to be mad about it and maybe go start trouble with the guy, and I told him the only reason it happened was because the guy was trying to—the guy wanted to rape me. He goes, "Sure!" I told him it was fucking <u>true</u>. But then he goes, "I guess you can't teach an old dog new tricks" and he hung up. He hung up just like that. And I called back. And I called back again. I kept calling back the room, but nobody ever picked up.

Ta-da! it's later. I wanted to pass out but I couldn't—except maybe for a second. It's 1:00 or something. Because falling asleep—I want to. But if I could go to sleep I would but I can't so I won't. So big deal! Big fucking deal. I keep waking Skywalker up and he keeps back falling to sleep. Mr. Loyal Pet there—see he don't care. I wish I were a cat cause they know new tricks—Trix are for kids. But they have alot of lives is the thing. How comes it that test patterns on the TV look like bullseyes? One station is in black and white but the other color. I don't know why that is. I think I broke the clicker. Cause now it's staying on mute. I got to pee. Hold on. But the stereo works. Hold on—

We're out of vodka. It's still no sound, but I can still go around the channels. 3 is the flag and this plane, 5 still got tests and 9 got snow. Why do they call that snow? FUCK! Fred and Barney! Reruns aren't this late or early whatever it is but they're on on 11. Mr. Fucking Slate is reaming Fred about something. And then Fred is going "Willllma!" I can't hear cause of the sound but I can tell cause of his mouth being open so long. God, I got to fucking get out of hear. I'm going.

I'm going—maybe to Roaring 20s cause its Ladys Night. And who knows what the hell I'll do when I get there—maybe alot of guys will buy me alot of drinks—or who cares even—

HOME

KOAL says a bunch of people are out there taking pictures of what happened. It's unbelievable! But I don't exactly remember too much exactly. I sort of remember coming across 59 and them following me and then me jumping off and running, running real fast into the old part of town and hiding. And then I remember in this little toolshed turning my coat inside-out so it would be a different color. It's really about the weirdest. No, no—it is the weirdest. The weirdest ever. God, I'm just waiting for the paper to come out. Because what if they know? If they know, I'm <u>dead</u>. I don't know what I'd do then. Maybe they are looking for me. Oh shit. Maybe I should take off—but I can't. They could be looking for me. I could borrow a car maybe. But maybe it'll all be okay. I got to lie down. I hope Derek comes home real soon. But I hope the paper comes before that.

HOME

I put all the pictures in my scrapbook because they're too big + they'll keep better. But I cut up the articles and I'm putting them in here—

BULLDOZER RAMPAGE CLEARS ALL IN ITS PATH

By Deenah Herman, Daily Call Writer

Someone took a 47-ton bulldozer on an early morning joy ride through the streets of Gillette, and today residents are still sifting through the damage. As the police conduct their investigation, the culprit remains at large.

The $350,000, D-9 Caterpillar bulldozer, which is the property of the Keller Energy Corp., was parked in a field behind the Ramada Inn. The machine was on loan to the city to help make flood-channel improvements in conjunction with the building of the Gurley Avenue rail overpass.

It was apparently "stolen" at approximately 3 a.m., and driven down a number of east side streets—damaging cars, pickup trucks, power lines, gas mains, sidewalks, fences, parking lots and two condominium buildings.

After surveying the damage, Police Chief Billy "Tex" Perkins said, "This country ought to mothball the MX missile and deploy the S.O.B. who did this. It looks like a tornado went right through the east side. It's incredible."

Damage estimates vary. "The number people are throwing around is $3 million," said Assistant City Administrator Spencer Hayworth. But Buffalo insurance adjuster Charley Parker, who was on the scene this morning, believes that figure is inflated. "It will be in the low hundreds of thousands" he said, admitting the figure is only a rough estimate.

Keller officials said the key may have been left in the ignition of the bulldozer at the end of the work day Thursday, but that this would not be an unusual practice at such a construction site.

(More stories, photos on Back Page)

"HE TORE UP THE TOWN, BUT GOOD": RESIDENT

By Mark Rowland, Daily Call Writer

East side residents are in shock today over the devastating bulldozer rampage of last night. From their earwitness and eyewitness accounts, a sketchy story can be pieced together.

Just after 3 a.m. Julie Farmer, of 129 Brown St., heard a loud noise from the general direction of the Ramada Inn parking lot. "I thought it was a semi-truck with a bad engine starting up, so I ignored it," she said.

At the same time, Patrolman Mo Lucas of the Gillette Police Department was responding to a disorderly conduct call at the Ramada's Roaring '20s bar. "I did hear an unusual noise," he said, "but by that time, I was headed into the bar and once in there I had my hands full with a major altercation." (Patrolman

276

Lucas and two back-up teams made seven arrests stemming from the disturbance, which involved 25 people.)

Meanwhile, tracks show the operator of the bulldozer drove across the field, up the drainage ditch and out onto Gurley Avenue, heading south. He then turned west on Fairview.

"I heard this amazing crunch, like an explosion," said Steven James of 441 Fairview. "By the time I turned on the lights and put on my coat and went outside, all I could see was the back of the dozer heading down the street. And then I saw my car and heard him going over the other ones." James' new red Datsun 280-Z was totalled.

James, like a number of other area residents, said he was so shocked by what he saw that he did not call the police. A few apparently followed the bulldozer on foot as it crossed Highway 59 on its path of destruction.

It went as far east as Ramsey Street before doubling back toward Highway 59. Julie Blatt, who was working at the Quikker Likker store, saw the dozer through her drive-up window and immediately called authorities.

"He was going down Collins and he put the tooth down in back and started ripping up the street," she said. "Then I saw him turn into the Keller office parking lot and sideswipe the three pickups. He kept going and headed back across 59 toward the school."

The bulldozer crashed through a fence at Lincoln School and knocked down four telephone poles as it headed up toward the Indian Hill area. As it did so, three lightposts were bowled over.

Big Sky Court resident Stephen Mitchell said, "I could see his blade was up and his tooth was down, and that's when he must have gotten the gas main. He nailed our bushes, but he missed our car, thank God. Let me tell you, he tore up the town, but good."

By approximately 3:25 a.m., police officers were arriving on the scene. Some pursued by foot and others in their patrol cars. Patrolman Brad Sellers got closest. He attempted to board the bulldozer from the rear, but reportedly ran in the other direction when it began backing up. The canine unit released its two German shepherds, "Rocky" and "K9," but neither was able to gain access to the driver.

At this point, the 47-ton D-9 swung onto Cheyenne Circle and demolished six vehicles parked around the cul-de-sac. When it ripped into the Church Street apartment building, tenant Mimi Read was already standing outside, shivering in her pajamas. "The dozer just ripped into the corner of the building, shucked it and kept right on going," she said.

Police then attempted to shoot out the engine block of the D-9 before the culprit killed or seriously hurt someone. Patrolman Jeff Biddle fired four lead slugs from his 12-gauge shotgun. One or two apparently hit the engine, causing it to smoke.

Eyewitnesses report that after the shots were fired, the driver lowered the blade of the D-9 as it turned from Apache Drive onto Indian Hill and at that time must have bailed out. The bulldozer then crashed into the first floor of the Indian Hill Apartments, which are not yet occupied, and got stuck. City employee E. D. Darst leapt onto the bulldozer and turned it off, but the driver had already fled the scene.

POLICE, COMPANY CRITICIZED
BY RAZOR CITY RESIDENTS

By Deenah Herman, Daily Call Writer

Today some residents of Gillette's east side are boiling mad at local police and officials of the Keller Energy company.

"What were they doing leaving a D-9 Cat with a key in the ignition?" asked Ron St. Germain of 202 Apache. "It's like a loaded weapon, like a tank."

Longtime resident Sybil Thornridge, whose lawn and driveway opposite the Ramada lot were damaged, said, "I don't know who's responsible, whether it's the city or whether it's Keller. All I know is that someone is responsible."

Keller spokesman Bill Biederman, speaking this morning from company headquarters in Houston, said, "The machine was loaned to the city on a good-will basis. However much we regret the damage caused by the equipment, we bear no responsibility for the manner in which the city, or any other third party who may have illegally gained access to it, have chosen to operate it. Any discussion of company liability would be at the very best premature at this point in time."

Certain residents say they plan to sue the company for damages, no matter what it says. Bea Thompson says in addition to losing a vehicle, she suffered from "mental anguish." She said, "It was like a nightmare."

Those in the Indian Hill neighborhood put more of the blame on the police. As curious onlookers drove by the scene late this morning, many taking pictures, area residents complained about the length of time it took police to arrive at the scene and the manner in which they responded to the incident.

"They should have done something to stop him sooner, because this guy was dangerous" said one resident, who asked not to be identified. "I saw him drive over a Honda Accord, back up, and drive over it again. The guy obviously didn't have both oars in the water. But when he was backing up, the only policeman I saw was running away from the Cat!"

Police Chief Billy "Tex" Perkins indicated that a number of officers were busy with a major bar disturbance, and others called from the north side of town were delayed in getting to the scene by a slow-moving train at the Gurley crossing. He said by the end of the incident, all 29 of Gillette's officers had been called there.

He said, "We did what we could, without risking men or cruisers. Anybody who is saying we should have shot to kill doesn't understand our business."

Police Chief Perkins admits that due to a mix-up at the scene, the eight officers assigned to search for the culprit left by car instead of on foot. They were initially blocked by other cars, and were not as flexible in their pursuit as had they been on foot. But he says a thorough investigation is being conducted, based on eyewitness reports.

The driver was described as a medium-to-heavy build man, wearing dark glasses, a brown or black jacket, and a "gimme" cap. A partially shredded Amax cap was found in the path of the bulldozer, near where it stalled. Police Detective Jack Mattox stated that it is probably the hat the driver was wearing, which fell off when he bailed out of the machine.

HOME

I don't know much where to begin because so much has happened and everything has changed. I mean, nothing has changed really. It just seems like everything has changed. Maybe it's inside me is the thing.

The good thing is it's been 9 days and I don't think they have a clue. At least not from what's in the Daily Call and what they're saying on KOAL. For awhile I was really insulted about the description—the part about being "medium-to-heavy." I wanted to call up KOAL anonymously and say that ain't the case and hang up. But I decided that would be being too vain for my own good. So I'm living with the insult, which is helping me anyway. I think the only people that got a good look were right where I mowed the lights down so it was real dark + I had my neck wrap and my brace on under my coat which probably made them think I was chunky. And I was wearing my dark blue down coat that makes me look like the Pillsbury Doughboy to begin with. Because I am not medium-to-heavy. Medium maybe. And that's for being a girl.

So now I'm not even wearing my mummy wrap or my brace. For a couple days I was wearing them in the house, and just not wearing them outside—because I was sure I was going to be walking in town and have these two little ladies look at me and say, "Good gracious Maggie, it's her! Call the authorities." But now I'm not even wearing them at home—not cause I'm paranoid so much as they weren't doing anything anyway. I don't think I need them really. I threw them out. And it doesn't feel worse. It feels better actually. Maybe that's because I was just about healed anyway. Maybe I was so bummed about everything it was like I didn't feel better, even though I was pretty much better. That's what Dr. Bonnell says could be true. He says he thinks I seem a lot better—that my back seems better, which he's not sure why. Hell, I'll take it.

Not that I feel like going out and skiing down suicide runs or anything. I mean, I feel like skiing and doing everything fast, but I'm going to take it a little bit at a time. I'm going skating tomorrow with Eva and Betsy and she's trying to drag Neil's butt out there too. Neil on skates will be a trip. I just hope nobody from work sees me.

It's not like I'm not going to go back to work. I am. It's just I'm not in the biggest rush in the world. And I don't want someone from work seeing me at the rink and coming up like Snidely Whiplash going, "Oh, so you can skate figure-8's but you can't haul coal? Well, we'll fix you!" The thing is, I would really like to quit work, period. But if I did it right now the company might be too suspicious. Maybe I'm paranoid, but they're assholes. And if they know even the littlest thing, they'll figure out some way to trick me into putting my foot in my mouth. They don't have fingerprints, because I was wearing gloves. They don't have the right hat, because I never wore an Amax hat in my life—Amax hats suck the big one. But they might have something else.

So I'll go back to work pretty soon—like the day after they cut off my disability, ha!—no, pretty soon, like in a week or two weeks or something. Because I think maybe I'll feel up to it then. Not the people, but the work. But over the long haul I'm not going to stay working there, that's one thing we decided. Because we're probably not even going to be here is the thing. For a little while though it won't be bad—just to keep the bucks coming in and until everything dies down for sure. Then I'll kiss them off for good.

My big problem is keeping my trap shut. Because I want to tell everybody, but I know I can't. No way. Derek and Betsy is all. It's just that it makes me mad when I hear something which wasn't the way it really was, like on Paul Harvey. He had it on "Page 1" the other day and they got a bunch of things wrong. But the worst part about it is when people are saying great stuff about it and I can't even take any credit. Like on ABC they said whoever did it was "an extremely skilled Cat operator." I wanted to call Madlock right then and tell him to catch that little comment.

And in town, in town the silkscreen store already has these t-shirts that say across them the same thing as the bumper sticker about handguns—like it says WHEN D-9'S ARE OUTLAWED, ONLY OUTLAWS WILL HAVE D-9'S—and then it has a little picture of a bulldozer on it and it says under it, "Keep Gillette Safe." And I had this daydream that I could go there and be signing them for people that bought them, like bands do at record stores with their records. I know I can't do that—because probably nobody would believe me anyway—but it's fun to think about.

It's just—the guy who did this is like this big underground hero and none of my friends can even know! Derek says I should wear one of the t-shirts around, just so I blend in with everybody else wearing them. Derek's very smart about stuff like that. But we haven't gotten one yet. He's going to have to go get it. I know I couldn't walk in there without cracking up.

That's the hardest thing—not cracking up when people are talking about it. I have to really work hard at pretending when that happens. Like yesterday night at the Pronghorn, everybody was there watching big screen football, and Joleen was showing around all these Polaroids she took of it—mostly the crushed cars—from that morning when everybody was out taking pictures, and when they got passed to me I guess I had my dumb-bunny smile all over my face, because Sam said, "You find it amusing?"

And so I said, "Yeah, I think it's fucking amusing" and I handed the pictures away superfast. So Sam goes, "That's pretty fucking strange, considering your car got creamed so bad." I said, "Not really, since we're going to wind up with a better car anyway with the insurance money. The Accord's not worth crying about." And Joleen shouted, "Yeah, especially now that it's an Accordion!" and everybody broke up, which really got me off the hook.

But Sam goes, "Well you should talk to my friend Billy, because he's not so amused." So I said, "Sam, it's just stuff. Nobody got killed. Nobody even got a sprained ankle. The guy didn't even hurt any trees. So I don't see why it's such a big deal." Actually, Sam is in the minority about it because of her friend Billy's Pacer—

which is a shitty little car anyway. Most everybody else—at least all the people we know, I guess the younger people—think the whole thing is a riot. Like it's the best thing that's happened to town since Steven Spielberg was here making "Close Encounters" at Devil's Tower.

And I wasn't even pretending when I said it's not such a big deal. Because that's the way I feel. I feel like worse things happen every day in town that nobody makes nearly as big a deal about. People get hit over the head with bottles and shot at and punched and lots of people get hurt. Shitfaced people smash into other people and put them in the hospital all the time and nobody makes such a big deal about it. There's about a crack-up a day at the corner of 59 and 14-16 and nobody goes out taking Polaroids.

I mean, I do feel bad about causing those people so much trouble—but almost everyone has insurance and the city has insurance and we pay a lot of taxes so they just have to use some of it to fix things up. It's just a bunch of things anyway. Actually, I was glad I nailed the Accord. It's one of the only things I remember doing perfectly. It was like in slow-motion.

And I don't feel bad about the company getting bad publicity. Because they'll pay to replace someone's bushes and they'll end up getting a lot of good publicity out of it. I know they will. After I told Derek, one of the things he said was, "Didn't you feel like you were biting the hand that feeds you?" So I said, "Lots of people do that." I told him I didn't think it was such a bad thing to bite the hand. Anyway, I hardly knew it was Keller's Cat when I went out there. I just saw it and felt like driving it and there was a key. I didn't know whose it was until I saw the paper like everybody else. But I got to admit I didn't exactly go out of my way to avoid hitting those pickups in the Keller office lot. Hey, some things you just can't help.

I think Derek gets what I mean. He has been so good about it. I'll never forget when he came home that Friday from Black Thunder. He was really tired and sort of pissed because they had really messed up in the rescue competition and placed 10th. But mostly I think he was scared to come home and see me, because of what happened on the phone when he was down in Wright. I think maybe he expected to see all his clothes blowing around the front lawn when he got home. Or like he said, he thought I'd either be face-down in the hot tub or waiting for him behind the front door with a frying pan, fixing to whack him.

So he was pretty relieved to see me sleeping upstairs when he got home. I was still sleeping off the night before. It was a long night, you know. Anyway, when I woke up he was sitting at the edge of the bed, and he was smiling at me and looking sort of sheepish. I guess he was relieved. And the first words out of his mouth were "I'm sorry."

It sounded funny coming out of him. He's never had too much practice saying that. I said, "What for?" and rolled over. He knows when I roll over like that it's cause I want him to scratch my back. I don't have to say nothing. And so he said, "For everything, you know." And I said, "I know. You are a dickhead." And then I started crying a little bit.

So he was scratching my back and I said that I had something very important to tell him. And he goes, "Look, look, I said I'm sorry. Don't say you're leaving, because I know this can work out. Don't tell me that you're going to—" And I cut him off, because he was all worked-up and scared, not that I minded seeing him that way. So I said, "Would you just shut up and let me talk?" So he goes, "Look I said I was sorry and if you want to know the truth, absolutely nothing happened with Sam or ever has and it never will, it was just a really horrible coincidence and I was being an asshole about it and I never should of said what I did about what you did and—" He was talking like that guy that talks so fast in those commercials. So I said, "Would you just shut up, please? Pretty please?" So finally he did. Then I said, "And keep scratching my back."

So finally I could ask him had he heard about the bulldozer? And he goes, "Yeah, I heard about it on KOAL driving back. Unbelievable huh?" And I asked him what he thought about it. And he said, "I don't know. It's pretty amazing. I wasn't thinking too much about it because I was preoccupied about coming home." So I said, "Who do you think would do something like that?" And so he says, "I don't know. Some crazy guy with elephant balls. I don't know. Someone pretty mad."

Then I just turned over and looked at him. And I took his hand

285

and moved it down my t-shirt and held it right on my crotch, and said, "What do you feel?" So he got real nervous and goes, "Uh, I don't know. You. Warm. Uh, Lily of France undies." So I said, "No elephant balls?" And he laughs and goes, "Uh, no, I don't think so."

So I said, "Well, it was me." And he goes, "What was you?" And I said, "The pretty mad guy." And he just kept looking at me. He kept going, "What was you? What?" So I said, "The guy on the D-9, that was me." And he goes, "You're shitting me." I said, "No." He goes, "You're jerking my string." But I said I wasn't doing any of those things. He just looked at me, shaking his head and sort of smirking.

I looked him right in the eye and smiled at him, and then I flipped back over and said, "Keep scratching." And he did, and neither of us said anything for a while. So finally I said real calm and polite, like I was just stating a fact into the pillow, I said, "You don't have to believe me if you don't want to. But if you don't believe me, it's just that I'm never going to speak to you again." And after I said that he got quiet for a second and I guess in that second he must of decided to believe me. Because he just started screaming and hollering and jumping around, making huge waves on the bed until I got seasick.

And then I told him all about it. I told him everything I could remember, which wasn't all that much. Just about me getting plowed at home after he hung up on me and going to the '20s, and then getting so pissed at all the scrotes making passes at me that when I went to the head to take a pee I ended up walking right out the back door into the field behind the Ramada. And Derek kept going, "I don't believe this, I don't believe this." But I knew he did.

The weird thing is, it was almost like he was proud of me or something. I mean, he wasn't proud that I trashed so much stuff and he was real glad that nobody got killed and all, but it was like it made him look at me different. Like I was more serious or something. I mean, that I could get so upset that I would do that. It was like he was proud that everything mattered that much.

But sometimes I could tell the thing was really jinking him out. Like over the first couple of days. A couple times he looked at me and said, "Boy, I am really stuck with a weird one." And it was making me feel bad, a little bit. So finally I said, "Hey, listen, lots of guys have wives that'll cook for them, but how many have one that'll tear up the town?" He smiled his half-smile, his good one, and he hasn't said I'm weird since then. Or at least not too weird for him. And now we have this secret, which is a good thing to have.

I mean, it's not like everything is perfect or anything, because it hardly is. I'm unhappy about a real lot of stuff. Maybe it's true me and Derek have big-time problems. I don't know. I do believe him about Sam. Maybe I'm stupid to, but I do. Because I asked him all about it, about every little detail—and it did seem he was telling the truth. Okay, maybe he was tempted—cause she's a tease, a real tease—but I do believe him. And if I'm honest with myself for a second (which happens about once a month, for about exactly a second!) I got to say that I can't blame him about being tempted, cause I haven't exactly been Ms. Congeniality around here since my whiplash—not to mention Sam being Sam. So by the time I got done asking him questions about the whole thing (about 4 days later!) I was pretty satisfied he was telling me the truth. Also, just by the way he was acting towards me.

The only thing he wouldn't tell me was who told him the thing about what happened in the oil patch. He wouldn't tell me that. He kept saying, "It doesn't matter who told me and what they said wasn't the truth anyway." But I kept wanting to know. One day I kept asking and he went, "Boy, you say your Mom likes to inter-rogate—I think she could take lessons from you!" And that shut me up pretty fast, and I haven't asked him since. Cause I don't want him comparing me to Mom.

Not that I think Mom is so horrible. Okay she's pretty bad sometimes but she's not horrible. I figured it out that in between the end of Peter and the beginning of Don, Jesus was just like another boyfriend for her. And he's not the worst guy to pick. Okay, I'd rather see Peter up on the cross, because he deserves it a lot more—but J.C. has a lot to recommend him when you're going through a superweak time. And Mom was, she really was. And compared to both of those guys, Don is a real bargain. Mom's got to love somebody is the thing, and I'm glad he's around to take

287

the pressure off me and Betsy. Maybe it's not so bad loving as hard as Mom does. I guess there are a lot of worse things to do.

I'm talking like I got it all figured, but it's probably just coke-talk, cause that's what's getting me to the end of this and I wanted to get to the end of it too. Stuff still does scare me a little—only now when it does, it feels like I'm on the other side of it. Because I think Derek's a little scared too. And it's one thing to be scared all by yourself and it's another to be there in the dark with someone else. And I think a lot of the stuff isn't even about Derek so much, even though it was screwing stuff up with Derek just like it was. It's stuff about Sam and Mom and Peter and work and about every-thing else. It's hardly like I got everything straight. It's just not as crooked as it was. Maybe sometimes things are so simple it's about impossible to figure them out. I think that's true.

So we're talking about stuff, like maybe the idea that next year in spring or summer or something we'll move. I know that's pretty radical but it might not be bad. The thing is, I wouldn't mind being away from Gillette. There are too many people I've known here too long, and that have known me. And I'm real tired of it. I know what Mom will say. She'll say, "Oh, you're just escaping." That's her big thing—escaping—since she detoxed. But the thing is, maybe there are some things that are okay to escape from.

Derek says it wouldn't be such a bad thing to get out of town before all the bang is out of the boom. Because it's going to happen someday and he says it's better to leave when things are still going up than when they start sliding down into a bust. I know one thing—I really don't want to be here when all the boomers are running around without jobs and everything is rusting in the wind. It's just that we don't exactly have it figured out where to go.

I sort of like the idea of Salt Lake. Because I could be a ski instructor—since the mountains are so close in winter and the water in summer—and there's a lot of civil engineering work out there for Derek. There's some good mines too. But both of us decided that if we worked in a mine it would have to be together and that we wouldn't work underground. Strip mining is one thing, we could probably live with that. But no way will either of us work underground.

And even if that didn't work out, then we could find something

288

else. It would just be like it was before I got on at Split Branch—little jobs, low pay. We'd be scrapping but at least we'd be away from Gillette. I know there are Mormons out there, but there's rednecks here. And they're just as bad. Or maybe, maybe we could go to Boulder. It's a lot more sophisticated than here + there's good skiing and no Mormons. Okay, Peter is there, but it's a big city and I don't figure we have to see him any more than I did as soon as I moved out of home—which was hardly ever. We don't even have to tell him we're there, unless we want to. Peter could stand not knowing where I am or who I am for a while. He could put that in his pipe and smoke it for a while. He's going to get cancer anyway.

I'm not saying I know definitely that's where we're going, but we're going <u>somewhere</u>. I'm not saying like I know what's going to happen because maybe I never had less of an idea about it in my life. But that's not a bad thing, to have no idea—as long as you got someone to have no idea with. So for now I'm just imagining skiing down mountains in bright cold with the wind rushing into my mouth like something new. And for right now that's keeping me going. I don't care if it's escaping.

The reason I'm saying all this is cause I'm stopping now. It's not that I don't want to keep up, it's just that I really should hide this. Because I could get in trouble, big-time trouble, on account of a lot of the things I've said here. I think probably I'll start another one, at some other time and if I'm halfway lucky at all, in some other place. I just hope it's not from in jail with a bunch of mean-looking women staring at me.